LITTLE
GIRL
LOST

DI ROBYN CARTER
BOOK ONE

ALSO BY CAROL WYER

LITTLE GIRL LOST

DI ROBYN CARTER
BOOK ONE

CAROL WYER

bookouture

Published by Bookouture
An imprint of StoryFire Ltd.
23 Sussex Road, Ickenham, UB10 8PN
United Kingdom
www.bookouture.com

ISBN: 978-1-78681-141-7
E-book ISBN: 978-1-78681-122-6

PROLOGUE

Alice couldn't shake the ominous feeling that had plagued her all evening, no matter how hard she tried. It was going to happen again – even though he wasn't in the house. She just knew. Her anxiety made her grasp Mr Big Ears so tightly he grumbled. On the television, a cartoon bird ran off at high speed as a coyote wearing supersonic skates fell off a mountainside. Tonight she did not chuckle at the programme.

Her mother bustled into the room, looking like a princess in her long gown.

'See you in the morning, sweetie. Sleep well.'

She bent to drop a gentle kiss on her daughter's cheek then brushed a lock of hair away from the child's face. As she did so she looked into the large pale blue eyes, fringed by impossibly long dark lashes, and was hit by a wave of love. She stroked Alice's forehead and whispered, 'Night, night, sweetheart,' then drew away, leaving behind a familiar scent of lemon, bergamot and orange, which normally would have comforted the girl. Tonight, Alice was not comforted. She did not want to be left in the huge three-storey house with a fourteen-year-old goth who wore black eyeliner so thickly on her pale face that she looked like a zombie. She shrank further into the chair, one arm around her toy rabbit, Mister Big Ears.

In a small voice she whined, 'Do you have to go out?'

Her mother's mood changed instantly. 'Of course I do. Paul is up for best actor award. You know all this.' Her voice rose as it did when she was displeased. That was her mother, one moment happy and lovable, the next cold and bad tempered. 'We talked about it earlier when you were in the bath. I know things have felt different since we moved here but you'll get used to it. You'll have to get used to it. It's only been three weeks. It's going to feel odd. Now stop being difficult and make an effort. This is where we're going to live, like it or not. And Natasha may look a little bit strange but she really likes you. She's not one to show her emotions. Paul told me she likes you a lot. She's going to be your new big sister when Paul and I get married.'

Alice hated the idea of someone replacing Daddy but, no matter what, she knew it was going to happen. She had sulked and cried about it but Mummy only got cross with her and said she was behaving like a spoilt brat. The wedding was going to take place very soon. 'A whirlwind romance,' her mother had said. Alice fumed quietly. How could Daddy be so quickly forgotten? Her mother had met Paul and fallen head over heels in love with him less than a year after Daddy had been killed. Paul was obviously keen on Mummy too. He had showered her with expensive presents, including the beautiful crystal bracelet she was wearing. It had taken only three months of dating before he had invited her to move into the Farmhouse with him and his two teenagers, Natasha and Lucas.

'I don't want to leave,' she wailed when her mother told her they were moving. 'This is home. This is where you, me and Daddy lived.'

Her mother held her by the wrists and looked into her eyes.

'I know this is hard for you, but it has been dreadful for me too. I miss your father. I miss him so much but I can't carry on living alone, trying to make ends meet for us both. Paul is a good man. He's kind and will look after us both. He's very wealthy. He has a beautiful house near a lake and woods with a paddock. He even has ponies. What little girl wouldn't want to live in a big house with a huge bedroom and ride ponies?'

The truth was she didn't care where they lived as long as she and Mummy were together. Ever since she had met Paul, Mummy hadn't been so interested in her. She shooed her out of the room when Paul visited and instead of it being about what she and Mummy were going to do for the day, it became about what Mummy and Paul were going to do. She was losing Mummy day by day.

She really wanted it to be just her and Mummy and Daddy again but that was never going to happen even though she had prayed and prayed for a miracle. She got a mini miracle when Mr Big Ears began to talk to her. He spoke to her just after Paul started coming around. He didn't like Paul either. She understood the first time he spoke that somehow her daddy had worked out a way to come back and be with her. If only he could have found a way to be with Mummy. Life had been miserable without him, with Mummy crying all the time, and the flat getting dirtier and dirtier as she moped about the place. She knew Mummy liked Paul a lot. Too much. He had a nice smile and was very tall. He didn't speak to Alice as if she was a little kid, and had told her he would never try to replace her father but he would always look out for her, and if she needed anything, she was to ask. Mr Big Ears didn't believe him. Neither did she.

She looked at her mother's face, once again radiant at the prospect of going to a special film event, and she gripped Mr Big Ears tighter. He folded into her tiny frame, appearing to return the squeeze. Daddy had given her the toy rabbit and she adored him. Now, of course, since the mini miracle, he went everywhere with her. Mr Big Ears was her friend, her confidant and comfort when she was upset or had concerns. She spoke to him all the time and listened intently for her dead father's voice coming from Mr Big Ear's mouth. At the moment, he was keeping council and stared into the distance, ignoring the conversation.

Her mother walked away, collected her evening bag with the long gold chain from the granite top in the kitchen and glanced back into the snug.

'Now, you'll be a good girl for Natasha, won't you? She's in the front room watching a film if you need her.'

She nodded. 'Lucas?' she asked in a small voice.

'Lucas is in the village staying the night with his friend, Dan. Did you want him to be here too?'

She shook her head. That was the last thing she wanted. Not after the last time.

'Don't go yet, Mummy,' she shouted, panic rising in her small chest.

Her mother hesitated at the kitchen door. 'Don't be silly. You're a big girl now. You'll have to get accustomed to me leaving you from time to time. We'll be here when you wake up. Now, no more of this nonsense. Go straight up to bed when you've finished watching your cartoons and don't play up for Natasha. Show her what a good girl you can be.'

She wanted to call out again but her mother slipped through the door, leaving her curled up on the large chair, staring at the screen. She caught distant murmurings. Paul was telling Natasha to phone if she needed them. Natasha mumbled something in response. The heavy front door shut with a bang and she was left alone in the snug with only the sound of the Roadrunner beeping triumphantly as it ran away from Wile E. Coyote. How she wished she could run like that. If she could, Lucas wouldn't be able to catch her. She brushed the thoughts of Lucas away. He was not here tonight. She need not worry.

The snug was the friendliest room in the vast house. It was an extension of the kitchen filled with bouncy pale green settees that matched the decor and a large television screen that dominated one wall. She preferred to stay in here rather than the formidable sitting room with its large settees facing each other beside a huge fireplace, and china ornaments of pale women who stared into space. She did not like the wooden-floored Victorian conservatory either, with huge glass windows that made her feel like she was in a giant goldfish bowl, and she had no interest in the music room, although she had tried to play a couple of tunes on the piano once or twice.

Her mother was usually in the kitchen and Alice preferred to be near her, even if she was just in the background watching television while her mother drank wine with Paul. Natasha was fourteen and spent most of her time skulking in her room, her dark-rimmed eyes full of resentment and teenage angst. Lucas hardly frequented the snug, preferring his own room where he played loud rock music whose beat could be felt resonating throughout the house. Both of them spent most of the year at boarding schools but were currently at home for the school holidays.

She had not made up her mind about how friendly Natasha really was. Natasha rarely smiled and seemed to ignore everything going on around her, especially her and Mummy, yet just occasionally she seemed to regard them both with something of a wistful stare, much like a puppy who wants to be friends but is unsure how to instigate the relationship. However, before anyone could act upon it, the look would have vanished and Natasha would have retreated behind her white expressionless mask. She was probably not looking forward to gaining a little sister full-time.

Then there was Lucas. A chill ran through her. He had seemed nice at first. A slight boy for his age who at almost sixteen had acne-scarred skin, eyes like dark coals and a cruel way of curling his lip when examining you. He had looked her up and down when she had first arrived then cocked his head on one side and announced it would be cool to have a kid sister. She had believed he was okay then. That was before. Before the horrible evening when he had done those things to her.

The cartoon finished and she turned off the set. The Aga in the kitchen was alight and the place felt warm and cosy. The house was so different from where she and Mummy had lived before Mummy met Paul. Even though it had not been huge like this house, she had preferred the old flat with its shabbier furnishings and now she missed it. It was where she, Mummy and Daddy had lived before the accident. Clutching her rabbit, she headed to her room on the third floor away from the others. She preferred it that way. Up here she could hide from the life below and talk to Mr Big Ears.

Her bedroom had been decorated for her in shades of pink with a princess theme. It was surprisingly neat for a young girl's room but she liked order and all her toys and dolls were lined up on the shelf at the far end of the room next to the en-suite bathroom. Tall wardrobes filled the other wall and the room seemed bare apart from the bed, a dressing table on which were displayed various ceramic animals all in a neat line, and a bedside table. She tidied from her bed the pencils and colouring book she had been using earlier that evening, placing the pencils in order of size on the bedside table. She pulled down the duvet cover and tucked Mr Big Ears into bed before removing her slippers and sliding in next to him. She kept her night light on and stared at the shadows on the walls.

Darkness had always been her friend. Before that night, she had always welcomed it and snuggled down in her bed next to the rabbit, listening to his soft voice until sleep overtook her. Since that night, she had been more wary, leaving on the owl-shaped night light and often burying herself deep under the pink duvet covered with large flowers.

It wouldn't happen tonight. Lucas was out. She was safe. She hugged Mr Big Ears goodnight. He whispered that he thought Mummy had looked beautiful tonight and that one day she, Alice, would wear an identical dress to a ball and would look like a princess. She gave him an extra squeeze. She was sure he would have preferred Mummy to stay at home too.

Just as she felt the first drifts of sleep overtaking her body, a creak on the stairs startled her awake. Mr Big Ears seemed to sit upright in dismay. She shoved him towards the bottom of the bed to hide him. Blood rushed to her ears and thudded there, its drumming obliterating any further sound. Her mind raced. Someone was heading for her room. The fifth stair on the staircase to the top floor let out a little groan when it was trodden on. That had been the sound she had heard.

She had the sudden urge to go to the toilet. She could not wet the bed. She was a big girl. She would be nine years old in three months. She fought to control her bladder as she heard the door to her bedroom ease open and a voice whisper, 'I'm coming to play. Are you ready?'

Her body began to tremble. It was going to happen again. She wormed her way down the bed to hide then let out an inaudible squeak of terror as she felt the duvet being tugged away from her. She screwed her eyes up and wound herself into a tight ball. She felt cold hands pull at her shoulders. She curled up tighter.

'Come on, little sister. It's time to play our secret game. Wake up. You know you enjoy it.'

The same hands pulled at her nightdress and raised it high above her hips. She could feel the cool air on her buttocks. Tears filled her eyes as she tried to wriggle away. She received a sharp slap on her backside. 'Shush! No one can hear you.'

He grabbed at her and tugged at her legs, twisting and pulling until she was flat on her back looking up into the soulless eyes.

'That's better. Time to play nicely,' Lucas said. He stroked her face with a finger. She could smell alcohol on his breath. Sometimes Mummy smelt of drink. It usually made her more affectionate and after a night of drinking wine downstairs, she would come to check on her daughter and plant a little kiss on her head before turning in for the night. This was nothing like that. Lucas's breath smelt sour and she turned her head away. He didn't care. He leant closer towards her, eyes slightly unfocused and mumbled, 'You're so pretty. You're perfect. I'll like having such a pretty sister.'

She tried to hold her breath while he spoke. Her heart hammered against her chest. She could feel him pressing into her and she knew what he was going to do next. It would be like last time when Mummy had gone out for dinner with Paul. That time, Lucas had been forced to stop his actions because they had returned unexpectedly. He had threatened her as he left and she had not said a word about that night. Her mind had blocked most of it out and she had hoped it would not happen again but feeling his warmth on top of her thin nightdress she knew this time she was not going to be so lucky.

'You know what you have to do, don't you, or I'll tear off your rabbit's head and pull out all his stuffing and I'll make you watch while I do it. You wouldn't want to be without Rabbit, would you?' A malevolent grin spread across his face.

He had threatened the same last time he had come to her room. He was going to rip Mr Big Ears apart if she didn't play his little game with him. She couldn't lose her rabbit. It was all that remained of Daddy. She fought back tears.

Without taking his eyes off her, Lucas dropped his hand to the waistband on his tracksuit trousers. 'Ready, little sister?'

He dropped his pants and bottoms in one movement, releasing his member in front of her, and climbed on top of her again.

'Go on. Touch it.' He grabbed her wrist and forced her hand towards it. 'Hold it,' he hissed. She opened her hand and grasped it. He groaned.

'That's it. Rub it like I told you last time.'

She did as bidden.

'No. That's not right,' he suddenly exclaimed as his erection began to wither. 'You're doing it wrong!' He grabbed her by the waist and in one easy movement, rolled over onto his back, pulling her on onto his lap, clamping her there. He could feel her nakedness against his own. A smile played across his face as a new thought occurred to him.

'It won't hurt. It'll be our special bond. Our brother and sister secret,' he whispered.

A finger found its way into her, pushed deeper into her, probing and searching. Too terrified to move, she allowed another finger to enter her, stretching her further. Large tears began to form. She wanted Lucas to stop but he was lost in his world muttering incoherent words.

She squirmed and wriggled but he was too strong for her. He was hurting her. She was about to scream for him to stop then she heard Daddy's voice. He was very cross with Lucas. Lucas should not be doing this. Mr Big Ears had moved and was now beside her leg. He looked up at her earnestly. He had something urgent to tell her about her bedside table. She listened. The tears stopped, to be replaced by a rush of something else – a force so great she had little control over it. She was not going to let Lucas do this to her. Lucas was now making guttural noises of pleasure, his eyes closed. She chose her moment and when Big Ears shouted 'Ready!' she reached forward for the object, breaking contact with Lucas and distracting him. His eyes flew open and he screamed in surprise as she raised the sharpened red pencil in her hand, and jabbed it hard into his left eye.

CHAPTER ONE

Robyn Carter sat in her five-year-old silver Polo watching and waiting for the front door to open – she couldn't pass the time by reading or doing a crossword because she had to be ready to act. Her video camera lay on the passenger seat next to a discarded fruit-and-nut-bar wrapper.

Her quarry, Terence Smith, was inside number 52 Rosewood Avenue and she needed to catch him soon. Terence had made an insurance claim for a bad back, allegedly injured while lifting barrels at a pub. Something about his claim had raised suspicions at the insurance company and they had hired R&J Associates to investigate its validity.

She had been in her car since seven o'clock simply staring at the door. Much of her work involved hanging around outside houses or workplaces and could be mind-numbingly dull at times but Robyn did not mind it. She had time on her side and she had plenty of patience; her skills had been honed in the police force.

She checked her watch – a sixteenth birthday present from her parents who, at the time, had despaired at their daughter's terrible timekeeping. Simple in style with a white face and delicate golden pointers, the watch kept accurate time. It had never let her down. Thanks to it, Robyn had known exactly what time her parents had been struck and killed by a drunken lorry driver while out walking their retriever, Rufus. She had known what time Dr Mahmoud had given her the news she was expecting a child. She had even known what time she had returned to their hotel room in Marrakesh, bursting to tell her fiancé Davies who worked for Military Intelligence about the baby. He was not back from a meeting with an informant who knew the location of several militant cells, and she had waited eagerly, anticipating the look that would appear on his face when she told him. She also had known what time the phone rang when a subdued voice told her Davies had been killed in an ambush just outside the city. And she had known what time she miscarried the tiny life form inside her. All of which seemed a lifetime ago. She had changed a lot since those days. She rubbed the leather strap absent-mindedly and checked the time. It was exactly nine-thirty when the man emerged from his home.

Robyn was parked thirty yards down the road. Ross, her associate, was parked facing the opposite direction so they had the man covered should he turn right or left out of the driveway.

Robyn snatched the video camera from the seat and pressed the record button. Terence Smith was in his fifties, stocky and balding. He whistled as he headed with a confident swagger towards the driver's door of his Ford Mondeo. As he reached it, the car keys slipped from his grip, tumbling to the floor with a clatter. He bent down to collect them in one swoop before swinging open the door to the car and jumping in. 'Gotcha,' she murmured as she captured footage of him getting into the vehicle with no evidence of any back pain or restricted movement.

Robyn had been trailing the man all week and had already filmed him going to the supermarket where he had emerged with two large carrier bags of goods that he had hurled into the back of his car with little effort.

She put aside the camera. It was time to pursue Terence. She guessed he would be heading to the Mucky Duck, a down-and-out pub in the nearby village where he had a part-time job as a barman. She might even catch him out, declaring he needed to change a barrel. Sure enough, Terence's car passed hers and she started the Polo's motor, ready to follow at a safe distance.

Unlike surveillance of unfaithful husbands, gathering evidence for an insurance claim could take weeks if not months of watching the claimant for hours on end. Robyn accepted the tedium that accompanied such a case, focusing only on getting results. She was a results woman. She would catch this guy no matter how long it took to collect the evidence. She overtook a Toyota Prius driven at a snail's pace and eased in behind the Ford Mondeo. She was not concerned about being spotted. She had perfected the art of being a chameleon. Neither she nor her bland car attracted attention of any kind. Her dashboard lit up as a telephone call came through.

'Hey, Ross.'

A voice, roughened by decades of smoking growled, 'Looks like you win again. I'm going back to the office and let you deal with this.'

'No problems. I'll catch up with you later.'

'No can do. I'm going to check out Robert Brannigan tonight. His wife phoned the office earlier and said he was going out with friends but she thinks he's going to see the new mistress. Said something about telltale signs of new jeans and aftershave. It's happened before. She's highly suspicious.'

'Good luck with that. Not my favourite job.' She hated having to tell the client they were right all along and email them photographs of their loved one in compromising situations, all the while knowing it would rip them apart.

'A job's a job. You become hardened to it after a while, although looking at Robert Brannigan, I'd be very surprised if he's having an affair. He's got to be one of the ugliest guys on the planet. Who'd want to shag him?'

'Women are attracted to power. Maybe that's the reason. Think of all those ugly pop stars and politicians with stunning girlfriends.

Robert's a local councillor. Bet someone got all heated up at the prospect of him making important decisions about speed bumps and rubbish recycling and couldn't wait to jump into bed with him.'

Ross picked up on the tone in her voice and scoffed in agreement. 'That'll be it. Or some old dear wants him to get her a disabled badge so she can park closer to the shops.' He laughed at the thought. 'Okay, I'll catch you tomorrow. Hope you have a barrel of laughs at the pub.'

Ross disconnected, leaving Robyn shaking her head at the terrible pun. Ross was never one for long conversations. He was her cousin and a decade older than her at almost fifty. His face was friendly at times with heavy brows over green eyes that waggled in amusement, but generally it was unremarkable. His dark hair, flecked with the odd grey, had a life of its own, sticking up regardless of how often he combed it, making him look unkempt and vague; a look that was deceptive, disguising, as it did, a sharp brain and a keen eye.

Robyn had a great deal of respect for her cousin. He had been there for her when she returned to the UK from Morocco, a shadow of her former self. Her lover and unborn child had both been stolen from her so quickly that her mind and spirit were shattered. She needed time to heal. She took a leave of absence from the police force – a job that until then she had loved. Ross and his wife, Jeanette, had looked after her, coaxed her back to life and, ever practical, Ross had suggested she join him at his private investigation agency for a while, until she could face a future with the force again. It had been the lifeline she needed. She had begun working with Ross. The work was varied but not too tasking, the hours were dreadful, allowing her no social life whatsoever, and most of the time she didn't need to talk to anyone. In short, it was perfect for her.

She glanced in the rear-view mirror. The Prius had disappeared from sight and was undoubtedly holding up a stream of traffic.

They were approaching the Mucky Duck pub, so she dropped back, waited for Terence Smith to signal and turn into the car park, then she drove past and parked further down the road. Robyn checked her mobile, ensuring it was on record mode, waited five minutes, then grabbed her notepad and pen and headed into the pub.

Behind the bar Terence was chatting to a girl in her early twenties, heavily made-up and wearing what Robyn's mother would have described as a belt for a skirt. For one moment her thoughts drifted to her parents and her mother's effervescent laugh. Both of her parents had enjoyed life, their house filled with laughter. Her childhood had been a happy one. But she couldn't dwell on that now. She shook her head to clear it and slid up to the bar where Terence threw her a cursory glance.

'What can I get you, love?' he asked.

'Orange juice,' she replied. He nodded and turned away. She had barely flickered on his radar. He was more engrossed in the conversation about a customer who had come on to his young colleague.

'Dirty little sod. I bet he was married 'n' all,' Terence commented as he poured the orange juice.

He plonked the glass on a mat in front of Robyn. 'Two pounds fifty, love, ta,' he said, collecting the coins she had pushed forward and turning his attention to two new customers, now greeting him in loud voices.

'All right, Smithy? You still on for the match on Saturday?'

'Yeah, reckon,' replied Terence. 'It's gonna be a right ol' game. Those boys from Sandtown are reckless bastards. Reckon they'll try and mince us good 'n' proper. More likely want to give us a good kicking than play friendly footie. I've been in training though.' He shot a grin and flexed his biceps. 'Lifted thirty kilos today. I'll be ready to punch the livin' daylights out of that clever twat of a midfielder. I'll smack him on the nose if he tries anything this week. He sliced through Gazza deliberately last time and it's about time we evened with him.'

No one gave Robyn a second glance. Her phone rested on the bar and she scribbled a few lines in her book that referred to 'presentation' and 'blue sky thinking'. If anyone glanced at it they would assume she was preparing for a meeting. Although she was tall at five foot ten inches, her flat-heeled boots, worn under dark jeans and teamed with a grey hooded top, did nothing to attract attention. Her mousy-brown hair tumbled forward, hiding her face that was free of make-up, and her large dark-framed glasses hid the deep blue, searching eyes behind them. When Robyn wanted to, she could shake off any attention. It was a skill she had perfected over the years and it had served her well. Even after meeting her, no one could ever describe her appearance. She was 'average', and as far as she was concerned that was the best cover possible for a private investigator or, at times, for a detective inspector in the Staffordshire Police.

The men continued to bandy insults and talk about football while Terence Smith went out the back. Along with the photographs, Robyn had sufficient evidence from his earlier conversation along with the photographs to leave him be for now. She had already built up a pretty damning case against him. The match at the weekend should prove to be the final piece she required and once she had photographic evidence of him playing in the match, she would hand it all over to the insurance company to take the necessary measures. She downed her juice and left the bar without anyone noticing her.

Once back in the Polo, she checked the recording. Smith's voice was clear. This was useful evidence. She looked in the rear-view mirror and smiled without humour at her reflection. The plain woman with the large aquiline nose and pale face who stared back could be any age from thirty to fifty. Within seconds she had discarded the glasses, yanked off the wig and twisted her long chestnut hair into a ponytail. She put the car into first gear and puttered away. Her stomach growled loudly, reminding her she had not eaten all day. Robyn rarely listened to her stomach's complaints. She was not interested in food or drink. What she needed now was a serious endorphin rush.

* * *

The gym was empty apart from the usual gym rats always there at this time of day. Robyn wondered if they actually ever left the place. It didn't seem to matter when she arrived, whether that was six o'clock in the morning or nine at night, the same three people would be found pumping iron or racing on one of the treadmills, heads down, lost in a world of music piped into their ears. Robyn needed her fix but at least she could still drag herself away and hold down a job. These guys looked like they'd break down and cry if you told them they couldn't work out.

She dropped her towel over the front of the treadmill and performed some stretches to limber up. She'd been cooped up in the Polo too long and her neck crunched as she gently stretched it to one side and then the other.

Climbing onto the treadmill, she set off at a gentle pace. Robyn didn't hold with starting too quickly. Like everything in her life, her training was measured, slow and steady. She would increase the speed when her body was ready. She fell into a rhythmical stride, ignoring her reflection in the mirror as her ponytail bounced up and down. Although it was useful to check positions when working with weights or equipment, she didn't like watching herself run. Instead, she lazily regarded the reflections of the other people in the gym. In one corner, a woman in her forties was performing crunches while lying on a large blue stability ball. Tricia was divorced and hell-bent on attracting as much male attention as possible.

She had spent a considerable amount of the divorce settlement on liposuction and breast augmentation and had been coming to the gym every day for the last six months. She took delight in wearing the skimpiest of tops and figure-hugging Lycra shorts. She nodded at Robyn. She only ever spoke to the male members of the gym.

Robyn upped the speed on the treadmill. Unlike others, she didn't use headphones when she exercised. She preferred her senses to always be on alert.

Tricia finished her crunches and admired her reflection before heading towards the exit where she stood chatting to one of the trainers – Dean. He taught the kick-boxing classes and some of the high-impact aerobics. Robyn preferred spinning classes during which she would work out on a stationary bike to improve her stamina. It did not encourage chatter or conviviality – certainly not the way Robyn approached it, ratcheting the resistance up as high as she could on her bicycle and racing at full speed, motivated by the pumping beat of the music and the shouts of encouragement from the fitness instructor.

When she was training for one of the many triathlons she entered, she would combine spinning classes and weight training with running and would also ride for miles on her racing bike – an Italian model with a carbon frame. She wasn't going through such a high period of training at the moment and allowed herself some slack.

Robyn appreciated her body. It had seen her through some horrendous situations and in return she looked after it. Her physique was like that of a highly trained athlete – muscular, taut and ready for any eventuality.

A quiet inner voice asked her if this was what she had become, no more than a robotic machine that trained, fuelled up and worked all hours possible. She silenced the voice and pounded along the treadmill at a faster pace, wondering if she had sufficient evidence to convict Terence Smith of fraud. If she had, she would need another case, something new to distract her from the voices in her head and the pain that threatened to overwhelm her. She listened to the comforting swoosh, swoosh noise of the machine as she ran. Endorphins began to build up in her body and produce a feeling of well-being that was addictive. The moment of anxiety passed. She would control the voices and keep the pain caged. Heaven help her if ever they became unleashed.

CHAPTER TWO

Abigail Thorne wiped her daughter's face with a damp cloth and admired her handiwork. Izzy gave her a gummy smile, revealing the two bottom incisors that had been troubling her the last few weeks. The puréed apple that had been all over her dimpled cheeks had vanished.

'That's better, you little monkey,' she joked, tickling Izzy's toes. 'No more breakfast or snacks for you, young lady. Not until everyone has seen how pretty you look in your new dress.'

Two arms circled her waist and she felt warm breath as her husband Jackson pressed his lips against the nape of her neck. A frisson of pleasure rippled through her for the briefest of seconds. She tried to conjure its return but it had vanished as quickly as it had arrived.

'How's our little angel today?'

'She's great. She doesn't seem bothered any more by the second tooth and she ate all her breakfast.'

Abigail moved away reluctantly to replace the facecloth on the sink. Izzy let out a coo of excitement at seeing her father and raised her arms.

'Hello, little splodge,' he said, making her burble with glee. 'Do you want to be an aeroplane?' She gurgled some more and tried to wriggle free from the highchair.

'Whoa. Wait for Daddy,' he said, unfastening the restraining strap and releasing the child. Izzy's eyes opened wide with delight as he hoisted her above his head and spun her around, all the while making a low drone like the noise of an engine.

Abigail cautioned him. 'Don't spin her too much. She's only just finished eating.'

'She'll be fine. Takes after the old man. Constitution of an ox,' he replied, whooshing Izzy high and low, relishing the hearty chuckles that burst forth from the child's mouth. Abigail smiled at their antics and for a moment forgot why she had been feeling so low. Jackson stopped at last and held Izzy at arm's length. 'That's enough, Splodge. Don't want purée surprise in my face.' He settled the child in her playpen in the corner of the kitchen where she rolled onto her side contentedly and grabbed at a small patchwork dog, stuffing it in her mouth, all the while observing her parents with large blue eyes.

'How's my big angel, then?' Jackson asked, moving towards the coffee maker and putting a cup under the machine.

'Fine,' she replied.

'You sure? You've been a bit quiet the last few weeks,' he said, trying to keep his voice light. 'I know I've been getting in at all hours and I expect that doesn't help.'

'It's not that,' she replied. Her problems weren't down to Jackson. 'I've been a bit under the weather. Izzy has been grumbling at nights thanks to teething and I've not been getting enough sleep. And when she is awake, she's full on. Never seems to need a nap, unlike her mum. I'm just lacking energy, that's all.'

She understood the subtext of his concern. The night before, Jackson had come to bed ready for some action but she had pretended to be asleep. He had tried the usual tactics, but she had feigned sleep and lay still until he had given up, and with a sigh, rolled away to the far side of the bed. She had stayed stock-still until she heard his breathing begin to deepen and only then had she dared to move and roll onto her back, where she stared into the dark space and wondered for the umpteenth time what to do about her flagging sex drive.

Jackson should have been at work that morning. It felt strange to have him at home. They had a set routine and it unsettled her to have it disturbed. Normally, he would have left early and even if he was on a later flight, it was Abigail who rose early to attend to Izzy while he caught up on precious sleep before showering and heading off to the airport to file his flight plan and check on weather conditions.

Izzy was the focus of her attention these days. Each day was carefully planned around Izzy's needs and demands. If they went out, it required forethought to ensure Abigail left with sufficient baby wipes, nappies, fresh clothes, bottles and the usual paraphernalia that parents acquire along with their child. If they were at home, it was surprising how quickly the day passed juggling housework, shopping and caring for Izzy. Abigail adored being a mother. She had loved being pregnant and read up on what stage of development baby Izzy had reached. She bloomed during pregnancy, enjoying the ripeness of her body, the fullness of her breasts and she was filled with anticipation and love for the child she had yet to meet.

Motherhood had come naturally to her and she did not want to let her precious baby out of her sight for one minute. She was going to give her child every ounce of attention. That was part of the problem. While Abigail was so focused on being a great mother, she had given up on being a wife.

Then there was Jackson's job. He worked odd hours as a private pilot for an executive airline – BizzyAir Business Aviation – an airline he had set up himself with only one small aircraft two years before he had met Abigail. Nowadays, he operated two aircraft – a Gulfstream 550 jet that could carry up to sixteen passengers and fly for over twelve hours without a fuel stop, which was popular for transatlantic flights, and a Citation Jet III that carried up to seven passengers and could fly up to almost five hours without a fuel stop, which he used mostly for trips into Europe. He employed several pilots to take them all over the world but he still flew regularly and it was not unusual for him to get called into work at an ungodly hour to fly a jet to Amsterdam or the south of Spain where his clients could attend meetings and return home in time for an evening meal with family, or in time to join them for breakfast. His erratic hours meant they had little family life but Abigail had not minded, happy to enjoy the time he was away with her pink-cheeked daughter.

'So what shall we do today?' he said, collecting his cup from the coffee machine. 'Fancy taking Izzy to see the animals at the petting zoo?'

She felt guilty at her response. 'I'm meeting the girls for coffee this morning. I haven't seen them for ages what with Izzy being so miserable with her teeth and their busy work schedules. I didn't expect you to get a day off,' she added, spotting the flash of disappointment cross his face. He lifted the cup to his lips.

'You could cancel,' he said. 'Tell them I'm home?'

He grinned at her – a sexy smile that had always made her veins fizz with desire. Today, it did not have the desired effect. She shook her head.

'Sorry, it's too last minute to cancel. Zoe has used a day off especially. It's a lot harder for her now she works in London,' she said, knowing it was a lame excuse.

Jackson opened his mouth to speak but Izzy chose that moment to belch loudly and regurgitate some of her breakfast. Abigail sighed and started over to the playpen to collect her daughter whose chin was now covered in yellow-green goo. Jackson raised his eyebrows in apology. 'Maybe she hasn't got her daddy's constitution,' he said. 'Sorry, babe.' He reached out a hand as Abigail passed, rested it on her arm and looked into her eyes.

She halted for a moment. 'It's okay.'

'Is it?' The meaning in his question was clear.

'Of course it is. Now, I'd better get this little lady cleaned up.'

She lifted the child from the playpen complete with patchwork dog clutched firmly in her tiny fist. Izzy regarded her with innocent eyes and a look of wonder, and she cooed – a warm, bubbly sound that made Abigail smile.

'I'll clean her up,' said Jackson. 'It was my fault.'

Abigail shook her head. 'It's fine. I'll sort her out.' She left him standing against the kitchen top. He looked slightly forlorn and she hesitated, wanting to say something appropriate to make everything right again, but she couldn't. She had kept too many secrets from him and she couldn't tell him the real reason she had been anxious and so distracted. The note that had been hand-delivered through her letter box the week before had thrown her out completely. Someone knew about her past and it had unnerved her. She had used Izzy's teething problems as an excuse for her behaviour but the true reason was one she could not share with anyone, not even Jackson. And now, added to that, the mobile phone pressed into the back pocket of her jeans with its taunting message was threatening to change everything.

As she cleaned up the wriggling baby, she reflected on her life with Jackson. He had never given her any reason to doubt him. Life was as near perfect as it could be. She had everything she could ever hope for – a kind, handsome husband who doted on her and baby Izzy. He could not fake that look he got in his eyes when he gazed at their daughter curled up, tiny fist in her mouth, or the way he held Abigail in bed at night, one arm protectively around her shoulders, holding her towards his chest where she could hear his heartbeat, steady, regular and strong. The text on her mobile was no more than a stupid prank or it had been sent to the wrong person. She needed to get a grip.

That said, since she'd given birth to Izzy a few things had changed. First, the endless sleepless nights where Izzy had cried and cried and cried. Nothing Abigail or Jackson had tried pacified the baby. She took it on herself to stay up with Izzy, comforting her, rocking her, singing to her and walking up and down the nursery until she knew every inch of the room. As she became worn down through lack of sleep, she lost confidence in herself. Even though Jackson never gave her reason to doubt she was still attractive, she became convinced she was. She was far too aware of her floppy belly and sagging breasts that had never had enough milk for Izzy and now were empty and useless. Her insides felt stretched and the rip she had suffered when Izzy's head had pushed forward still seemed to be sore even though the stitches had long since dissolved.

She needed to remember who she had been before baby Izzy became the focus of their existence; she needed to make more of herself. Jackson had fallen for a vibrant woman filled with energy who loved being with people and laughing at life.

He laughed less these days. When had she lost the ability to make him laugh? She gazed at her dark-circled eyes and noticed the roots of her hair were showing. They needed some attention. She ought to have made an appointment at the hairdressers before now. Somehow, it hadn't seemed important and there was always Izzy to play with or sort out. There was no time for Abigail herself any more. Abigail had transformed into a tracksuit-wearing frump. If she didn't watch out, Jackson would definitely become fed up with his dull wife and look elsewhere. Izzy looked up with bright, focused eyes filled with wonder. Abigail's heart flipped much as it had when she had first set eyes on Jackson and sudden warmth filled her entire being. Love was such a fierce, protective emotion. In that instance, she reached a decision. The warning text was the wake-up call she needed.

She headed for the bedroom and placed the now clean Izzy on the carpet. The baby watched her, fist in mouth. Abigail hunted in her wardrobe, slipped into a pair of black fitted trousers and teamed it with a fetching Armani T-shirt that flattered her shape. Jackson had always liked her in it. She slicked on some mascara, bounced a brush with bronzer over her cheekbones and applied a deep red lipstick that harmonised with the auburn lowlights in her hair. Izzy gurgled in approval.

She extracted the phone and read the text for the last time: You are not the only one keeping secrets. Ask Jackson what his are. Surely it was a joke? The text came from a number she did not know. Her fingers hovered over the keys. She ought to reply but she didn't want to engage in conversation with a stranger. There were all sorts of weird scams these days. In the end she replied: Go and annoy someone else and deleted the offending text once and for all. She picked up Izzy who began to jiggle up and down in delight at going back downstairs to see her father.

'Come on, little Miss Mischief, let's go show Daddy how pretty we both are.'

CHAPTER THREE

Paul Matthews laced his Skechers Go Run trainers, a bargain at less than twenty-five pounds, yet rated as one of the best in a survey that claimed expensive, top-brand running shoes were rated more poorly than some cheap brands. They were, he concluded, very comfortable and didn't rub his feet, which were calloused and worn through neglect. The same article went on to say that an anonymous bidder now owned the spikes Roger Bannister wore during that record-breaking four-minute mile. They were purchased at auction at Christie's in London. The shoes sold for seven times their estimated value. He gave a wry smile and looked at his blue trainers. He'd be lucky if his fetched a few pounds in a charity shop.

His back twinged in protest as he drew his six-foot, three-inch frame up to its full height, a reminder that he ought to sit down for such actions. He was no longer a young man and although, at sixty, Paul still had the physique of a man some twenty years younger, he had recently begun to feel his age. That was in part due to his son, Lucas, but more to the guilt that weighed him down each day. He mentally cursed Lucas who had brought his problems to Paul's door and opened up the past – a past that Paul had wanted to obliterate from his memory.

He lifted his house key from inside a wooden box on the wall, easily mistaken for a piece of art. Paul was cautious. He had watched documentaries about house safety and knew some of the tricks thieves employed to find keys carelessly abandoned on console tables in entrance halls or left in door locks. And now, there was a new threat. He locked the back door and checked the handle. He needed to be even more careful now. He slipped the key into his lightweight jacket pocket, zipping it and patting it, feeling the metal for reassurance before he jogged down his garden path and into a vast field of maize, following the trodden path that skirted it, just as he did every afternoon.

A pale yellow sun in a lightly veiled sky struggled to warm the ground. A heavy shower had fallen earlier, and now the air smelled damp and humid. Paul ran on, lost in thought, oblivious to the wet leaves that slapped against his legs as he brushed past the tall plants and headed down the hillside towards the reservoir, which sparkled like a huge, grey diamond in the near distance. Paul preferred to run in the late afternoon. He was unlikely to meet any dog walkers, ramblers or twitchers, most of whom would have packed up and returned home by now, or they'd be sitting in any one of the welcoming pubs in Abbots Bromley, enjoying a well-earned pint.

He ran lightly, heels bouncing over pine-needle-strewn paths that twisted between tall trees whose canopies rose so high, little light could enter. He weaved past aged oak trees, guided by memory, ducking under boughs gnarled with time and jumping over broken branches that lay dry and twisted like dark brown bones on the floor. The organic compost aroma of rotting vegetation rose like waves around him and the freshness chilled the sweat that trickled down his neck.

En route he passed golden dock and orange foxtail plants – beautiful names for plants associated with the muddy, seasonally inundated edges of water bodies, which had chosen the reservoir woods as their habitat. Now flanked by elm, oak, birch and several sycamore trees with trunks of light grey and white, he jogged on, his breath deeper, his muscles beginning to ache with the effort of driving onwards at the same relentless pace. These grey-trunked trees were his favourites and best enjoyed in autumn.

For a while he forgot about Lucas, recalling an article he had recently come across about the Egyptian goddess Hathor, the holy cow, who sat in a sycamore at sunset and created the earth, everything living on it, and the sun.

There was no goddess in these sycamore trees, only a pair of rather agitated blackbirds who chattered angrily as he raced by, his heels crushing fallen leaves.

Autumn was Paul's favourite season. The wood took on rich colours; russets, chartreuse, and cardinal reds he wished he could capture on canvas. Then sycamore seeds, the samara or keys, would detach themselves with free-spirited abandonment and rotate to the ground like small helicopters. He wished he had spent time with Lucas and shown him such beauty. Maybe his son would have turned out differently if only Paul had invested the time. *Bad father.* You could learn so much from nature. Sycamores possess the ability to grow in the shade of their parent. *What a shame Lucas had not grown in his father's shade. Things would have been so different.*

From the corner of his eye Paul spotted a movement but didn't catch what it was. Deer often roamed in these woods and he had seen a roe deer only a couple of weeks ago, the russet brown of its rump and the flash of white of its under-tail as it fled into the dark woods.

He squinted as rays of light seeped through trees and blinded him temporarily, and then he felt the trees folding in on him, his brain not comprehending but his instinct forcing his arms forward to break the fall. He lay winded, hands grazed, a sharp pain in his right ankle. Then, grimacing, he hauled himself to an upright position, clinging onto the gnarly tree where he had fallen. A paper-thin piece of bark pulled away, crumbled and dropped its powder residue onto his bleeding fingers. He touched his face, already swollen, and traced a thick line of blood that trickled down his cheek.

His ankle protested at the weight on it. He had never fallen over before. He must be getting really old, he mused. He should take up a different activity. Then there was a crack. Someone or something was hidden in the trees, a walker, or a birdwatcher perhaps. He searched for life but saw nothing.

'Hello! Is there anyone there? Could you give me hand? I've had a fall,' he shouted. 'Please,' he shouted. There was no reply. He looked down at his cheap trainers, wondering if they were to blame for his accident, and spotted the reason he had tumbled. A piece of thick plastic rope like washing line was attached to the tree. Someone had intentionally tripped him.

He had no time to deliberate further. A figure came into view and stood by the trees.

An invisible hand gripped Paul's pulsating heart. His senses told him to run but the pain emanating from his foot meant he would manage no more than a hobble.

The figure moved closer. Shadows fell across its face, creating a grotesque mask.

Paul drew a deep breath. 'We need to talk. This is getting out of hand. We can sort it out.'

The figure moved even closer, and camouflaged against the trees it seemed like a spirit or angel floating towards him. It raised both hands, revealing what it had been hidden before.

'Too late,' the figure replied. 'You had your chance.'

Before he could react, the figure flew at him. A scream rose in his throat but did not reach his mouth. He dropped to the ground soundlessly. His final performance over.

CHAPTER FOUR

The coughing alerted Robyn to the fact Ross had arrived.

'I hate these bloody e-cigarette things,' he grumbled. 'I look such a twit smoking them. They are so uncool.'

'Unlike other cigarettes that make you look really cool especially when you hack your lungs up. And don't get me started on how they lead to potential life-threatening illnesses. Get over it. You know we only make you smoke those e-cigarettes because we care about you and you refused to go cold turkey. You'll feel much healthier once you get some of that tar out of your system.'

'I should know better than to expect any sympathy from you. You're one of those health nuts. You eat muesli for breakfast, for heaven's sake,' he said in a disgusted tone. 'You can't possibly understand what it's like for me. I've been a smoker since I was twelve. It's not easy to give up just like that.' He dragged on the e-cigarette and scowled. 'And these are really pricey.'

'I guess so and you can hardly roll your own e-ciggy, can you?'

He barked a quick laugh. That was one of the things about Ross she liked, he never stayed in a bad mood for long. He shoved the metallic object into his pocket and squatted against the corner of his desk. His blue trousers rucked up to reveal mismatched socks. Sartorial elegance wasn't his forte.

'Sorted the Terence Smith case?' he enquired, noting the paperwork next to her computer.

Robyn swivelled to face him. 'It was just a matter of time. Once he admitted to playing football, I knew I didn't need much more evidence. I've typed up the report,' she said. 'It's ready to be sent to the insurance company. Just need some photographs of him playing football at the weekend and it's all set to go. How did you get on last night?'

He scratched away an itch on his ear. 'Wasted night. I tailed Robert to the pub. Figured he was meeting his woman there but it turned out he was involved in a card game with his mates and they had a lock-in. Sat in the car in case he went onto his mistress afterwards but he didn't. He rolled out of the pub and went home like a good boy. I didn't get home till after two o'clock. Woke up Jeanette. You can imagine how that went down. She's got an important meeting this morning.'

Jeanette Cunningham was a 'vintage dolly' – a slim woman in her late thirties, usually dressed in a skirt teamed with a jacket or cardigan and with hair immaculately swept into a pompadour hairstyle. She was a complete contrast to her husband. Although she had no full-time employment, she was an active member of the local Women's Institute, sat on the board of various local charities and was highly respected within the community. It was a surprise to most people in the town that she and Ross had survived twenty years of marriage given his ridiculous working hours and lack of dress sense but anyone who knew them well understood the fierce loyalty and love that kept them glued together.

'I don't suppose Jeanette was that annoyed. It's not in her nature to get cross with you over work. More likely annoyed that you had been scoffing large bags of crisps while on watch. You did, didn't you? You really are going to have to get on board with these lifestyle changes she's implementing or you won't see sixty.'

Ross made a harrumphing noise, indicating the subject was closed.

'I'll go to the football match on Saturday and take photographs of Smith. There's a new case if you want to take it,' he said. 'I know

you are returning to Staffordshire Police imminently but it looks like
I'm stuck with Robert Brannigan for some time yet and can't get
started on it. And it's an urgent case. Trailing Robert is a dull job,
especially if he isn't having an affair at all. I'll have to follow him
around all the pubs in the area. Still, I suppose it's more interesting
than being an accountant, or a window cleaner, or a train driver…'

Robyn held up her hand to stop his meanderings. 'I've got the
idea. So what's this case? Will I have time to see it through before
I start work again for the police?'

He dropped a piece of paper onto her desk. 'Possibly not. It's a
missing husband. Lucas Matthews, aged thirty. His wife says he's
been gone almost two weeks. She's not keen to contact the police,
which seems a bit curious. I explained you are a DI who is working
temporarily with me, and after a while she said she'd talk to you first.
She doesn't want to officially report him missing until she's spoken
to you. Apparently, he often goes away but this time it's different.
He's not been in contact. Be something fresh to get your teeth into
and hopefully a darn sight more interesting than chasing around
after fraudulent insurance-claim cases. If you could at least get
started on it while I deal with Bob, then I'll take over. You've got a
few days before you return to the fold. The wife sounded desperate.'

'Okay. But you already knew I'd say that, didn't you?'

Ross gave her a sheepish grin. 'I thought it would pique your
interest.'

Robyn tilted back on her chair and levelled her gaze at her
cousin. He was clearing his throat as he did when he was about to
say something he didn't want to say. He scrubbed a hand across
his face, as if he was trying to rub some life into it.

'On another matter, Jeanette is a little concerned about you.
We both are.'

It came out in a rush, his eyebrows high apologetic arches.

'You have no need to be worried.'

'She thinks you're losing weight again and not eating properly. She's been blaming me for putting you on these long hours. You sure you're ready to return to the force?'

Robyn studied her fingernails intently before replying. 'I'm ready. It's been great doing this job with you but I need to get my teeth into more juicy cases. I need more stimulation. You understand, don't you? No offence. And I am fine. Just been training harder than usual. Helps to numb the pain.'

Ross nodded his affirmation. 'That's what I told her. I know you've been going to the gym after work. I figured out the reason. You see, I'm not a bad detective. All those years working for the Staffordshire Police have paid off. I can still sniff out trouble and can still spot all the clues, although it didn't take a great brain to work out you'd be feeling low at this time. Jeanette wants to know if you'd like to come round for dinner at the weekend. She's planning on making one of her special lasagne dishes. The one filled with artery-clogging béchamel sauce and juicy mincemeat.'

'I thought you were supposed to be eating healthily.'

'It's a treat for doing so well with my e-cigarettes. Man has to have his little treats. So will you join us?'

'Thanks. I'd love to.'

She knew Jeanette would have planned the meal deliberately. This weekend marked the anniversary of the death of Robyn and Davies's daughter. It made no difference that she had only been nine weeks and probably weighed no more than three grams. She would have resembled a very tiny human being, complete with internal organs. Robyn fought back the memory. She swung her chair back, rose in one swift movement and, grabbing her car keys, picked up the paper and said, 'Right, that's sorted. I'll get onto this case straight away. I'll call Matthews en route.'

She tossed the Smith file onto his desk, gave Ross a quick peck on the cheek, mumbled her thanks and disappeared out of the door.

Ross pulled out his e-cigarette and dragged thoughtfully on it, before opening a drawer in his desk and pulling out a packet of biscuits.

* * *

Mulwood Avenue was grand, lined with leafy mulberry trees and bordered by wide pavements. This was an upmarket neighbourhood with large residences hidden behind high brick walls and gated entrances. Robyn arrived at number thirty-three and pressed the intercom button, staring directly into the camera placed strategically above it. A buzzer sounded and the imposing gates creaked open inch by inch to reveal a characterless, modern, detached house. Somebody had attempted to give it some individuality by creating a large, stained-glass window to one side of the front door. Robyn pulled up beside the new BMW cabriolet standing on the drive and crunched over gravel to the door where she was met by frenzied barking. A woman's voice shouted, 'Just a moment. I need to put the dog in the kitchen.' This was followed by various commands to the small animal that was clearly reluctant to be dragged away.

Finally, the door opened to reveal a woman in her fifties, plump and homely, her blonde hair cut in a severe bob that only just reached her ears. Dressed in a yellow top and leggings that clung to chunky legs, she welcomed Robyn and beckoned her into the sitting room, filled with floral upholstery and far too many ornaments for Robyn's taste. The walls were covered in various paintings of wild-eyed Spanish dancers. There were fans spread out in a cabinet, and a pair of castanets. In one corner stood a guitar on a stand, a gaily coloured ribbon around it where the neck met the headstock. The dog continued to bark, hurling itself against the kitchen door with determined thuds.

'Don't mind Archie, he'll stop in a moment and I'll let him out. He's a great guard dog although sometimes too overprotective.'

Robyn handed over her business card. 'I've come about your missing husband. I understand you spoke to my partner, Ross.'

The woman ran her hand lightly through her thick hair, mustering courage to explain. 'That's right. He's missing.' She searched about for a photograph and handed it to Robyn. 'That's him,' she said, indicating the man in the photograph who was smiling but whose dark eyes, the colour of coal, were empty of emotion. 'You probably think I should contact the police and I wanted to but it's a bit delicate. Your partner told me you are a policewoman. You'll understand my predicament when I explain it to you.' She searched for words and failed. 'I don't really know where to begin.' She paused and then asked, 'Would you like a cup of tea, officer?'

Robyn didn't clarify she was actually a detective inspector. She didn't want to come across as pompous.

'Thanks. That'd be lovely. I'm here in my capacity as a private investigator today. I don't return to the force until next week. Just call me Robyn.'

Mary looked relieved and leaving Robyn to sit down, she headed in the direction of the barking. Robyn sat on a highly stuffed chair, taking in the photograph of the couple, trying to understand what it might tell her, while Matthews busied herself in the kitchen, returning not only with a pot of tea under a tea cosy but with the small white terrier that had been barking.

'Hope you don't mind Archie,' said Mary as the dog immediately headed for Robyn. Robyn greeted the animal, patted it once and then ignored it. This tactic had worked before for her. Archie snuffled around Robyn's feet for a few seconds and then lost interest, leaping up instead on the settee where he settled down and observed his mistress.

'How long have you been married?' Robyn asked as the woman poured the tea. In her experience it was good to get the person to open up, even if the answers weren't relevant. She needed to gain Mary Matthews' trust and develop a relationship with her.

Mary didn't answer immediately but pushed a delicate, floral china cup towards Robyn. She offered the sugar bowl but Robyn shook her head. The bowl was returned and silence hung as Mary wrestled with what she wanted to say. She looked directly into Robyn's eyes.

'You may have noticed I'm a little older than my husband.' She laughed, a joyless sound. 'Actually, I'm fifty and I'm twenty years older than him and for the record he's my second husband. In a fortnight, we'll have been married two years.' She broke off to consider her next words, took a sip of the warm liquid, added a lump of sugar, stirred it in thoroughly and then continued.

'I met Lucas at a school event. My nephew was playing in the orchestra. Lucas was his music teacher. After the event we got chatting and discovered we both had a love of classical music. He lent me a CD of John Williams playing a piece I particularly love, Rodrigo's 'Concierto de Aranjuez'. Surprisingly, one thing led to another. We went to a few concerts together. I asked him to teach me to play the classical guitar. I'd always wanted to learn and Lucas is an accomplished guitar player. He gave me private lessons. It's very intimate, you know, learning to play an instrument like that. You sit close to each other. You feel the other person's body heat and their hands as they guide yours on the strings.' She stopped and sighed at the memory. 'I should tell you that Lucas is not like other men. That's to say, he's a quiet man. He's not a man's man. He doesn't go down the pub or off to football matches. He isn't into sport at all. He prefers art and music. Those nights learning to play the guitar, well, I learned quite a bit about him. He hung around after the lessons and we talked and talked, and then soon enough a little more than talking. He started staying over for the odd night. I thought him charming, good company and sensitive, and to cut a long story short, I fell for him. I didn't hold back. The lessons were coming to an end and I didn't want to be without him. I asked him to marry me. Shocking, isn't it?' She laughed. 'I'm not getting any younger and I thought it was worth asking. He could only refuse me. As it happened, he said yes.'

She sipped her tea, glanced at the guitar in the corner and continued.

'My friends thought Lucas was marrying me for my money. They were all concerned on my behalf. Thought he'd marry me then race off into the sunset with my savings. I knew differently. Lucas is definitely not motivated by money. He doesn't need a rich woman. He does, however, need someone who can understand him and that's because he's what you might call "damaged". I suppose he was looking for a maternal figure rather than a lover and wife. He lost his mother when he was very young. It was tragic. The poor woman had breast cancer but she wasn't diagnosed with it until it was too late to help her. It was horribly aggressive and she died within months. It was a dreadful time for Lucas who was only eleven years old when she passed away. He was very close to his mother and he took her death badly. He was a proper mummy's boy.'

She paused, choosing her words carefully in order to paint an accurate picture of her husband. Robyn waited and sipped her tea.

'That goes some way to explaining why he didn't get on so well with his father, and after his mother's death his father became even more distant. I don't know if he had trouble grieving for his wife or being a single father or what but the upshot was Lucas was sent to boarding school. He had a rotten time at the school too. Lucas refuses to talk about those days. He has a lot of sorrow buried deep inside and I don't push him. He tells me things when he wants to.'

She stopped to look at the photograph of them. 'I saw the ache in his eyes when he talked about losing his mother. He became that little boy again, still needing and craving that love. I think that's why I fell for him. I wanted to care for him. Mend him. Help him. And in a way I filled the role that his mother had left.'

Robyn nodded to indicate she was listening intently. Mary Matthews rose from her seat, crossed the room and picked up another photograph that she handed to Robyn. It showed the couple in evening dress. They made an odd couple – her short, plain and smiling – him tall and brooding with dark looks that bordered on handsome.

'I've put on weight since that photo. It happens when you're complacent. Besides, I like baking and what can you do when there's a batch of cherry scones fresh out of the oven? Difficult to resist.' She shrugged. 'Lucas hasn't changed. He's always been lean.' She studied the photo and exhaled softly. 'He sometimes takes trips away during school holidays. He has friends from the school where he works who now live in Thailand and well, to be honest it's a destination that doesn't appeal to me. I have a fear of flying and I'd never manage on a long-haul flight even if you knocked me out for hours. So, he goes on his own.'

She lifted her cup again and balanced it on her knee. 'He arranged to go away last Monday – the twenty-fifth of July,' she added as if the date had significance. 'I had no reason to suspect he was doing anything different to normal. He packed his case, told me he loved me and set off to the airport in his car. I didn't think anything of it. I knew he was ready for a holiday. Although he's a master at masking his emotions, he's seemed low the last few weeks but refused to discuss what's been bothering him. I thought going to Thailand would help give him time to reflect and heal.'

Robyn listened without interruption.

'He didn't phone on arrival and when I rang him the mobile went to answerphone. He's lost his signal over there before so I wasn't too anxious but I had one of those niggling doubts. I don't have the phone number of the couple Lucas was staying with – the

Devlins – they're parents of one of the boys he used to teach at Blinkley Manor. I really should have asked for the number but I always talk to Lucas on his mobile or Skype him. I was going to ask Nick Pearson-Firth, that's Lucas's head of department, for it. That was until I was cleaning in Lucas's study. I was turfing out the drawers of his desk and stumbled across his passport in the bottom drawer of his desk. He couldn't possibly have flown to Thailand without it.'

She gnawed at her bottom lip for a moment.

'Discovering that passport got me fired up. I'm a patient woman. I don't mind that he keeps secrets about his past from me but I will not be lied to. I hate being lied to.' Her voice rose in indignation. 'I was furious. I had no idea what he was up to and I couldn't work out why he hadn't spoken to me about it, or why he hadn't phoned me. I tried his mobile again and again it went to answerphone, so I left another message. I left several more and by night-time I was furious with him. Then I tried to rationalise what had happened. I went through all the possibilities – maybe he had upped and left me for someone else but that made no sense. We've not had any arguments or disagreements and there have been no indications he's fed up of me or put off by me, if you know what I mean.' She blushed. Robyn caught the meaning and gave a small smile to acknowledge the fact. Mary continued, 'There would have been some signs if he had intended to leave me. Then I wondered if he had money troubles he hadn't wanted to discuss with me. I even had the crazy idea he might have got into trouble with online gambling. I'd read about a husband who was addicted to poker so I searched his computer for anything to give me a hint as to where he was or why he had gone, and that's when I knew he might be in trouble.'

She licked her lips nervously.

'His browsing history didn't help but I came across a file entitled "Sugar and Spice" and opened it.' She cast her eyes downward and shook her head. 'I wish I hadn't,' she continued more to herself than to Robyn. She drew a breath and looked back up. Robyn could see the confusion flitting across her face and knew what she was going to say. In a quiet voice Mary confirmed her suspicions, 'The file contained images of children in various poses and stages of undress. It appears my husband has yet another secret I was unaware of. Lucas has a penchant for young girls. And I mean *very* young girls.'

CHAPTER FIVE

THEN

I sit on the landing in my favourite polka dot leggings and pink top, straining to hear every word. Mr Big Ears, tucked under my arm, wears a look of concern. This is not going well at all and he seems anxious about the outcome.

Grandma Jane is in the kitchen arguing loudly with Mummy. Mummy arrived late to pick me up. Normally, she only stays for a moment and we race off to catch the train but today Grandma Jane invited Mummy inside and insisted they had a chat. Mummy did not look like she wanted a chat. Grandpa Clifford put a DVD on upstairs for me to watch while they talked. He said it was best to wait until they asked me to come back downstairs.

Grandpa doesn't have many DVDs I want to watch and I've seen the Tom and Jerry cartoons loads of times so I slip onto the landing, curious to find out what the adults are talking about. Their voices are clear even though the kitchen door is shut. Grandma Jane is speaking. She sounds concerned like she did when I fell off the swings at the park and cut my chin.

'I know you've been through a lot. We all have. Losing Josh was dreadful. It affected us all. You hardly had a chance to get over it... that unfortunate episode with Paul and his son.'

Words rise and fall and I cannot catch the drift of the conversation.

Then Mummy mutters something but I can't hear what she says. Grandma Jane speaks again. 'She's a child! She was probably frightened or half asleep or, I don't know what but you can't keep reading more into it than it was an unfortunate accident.' The voices continue until Mummy shouts, 'It ruined my relationship with Paul, a man who was going to look after me and help me live again. You can't understand that. I needed him. I had a second chance at happiness and it was snatched away before it even began. You can only think about losing Josh. You have no idea what it was like for me trying to cope all alone without him. You have each other. I had no one. Then I found Paul and then suddenly, I had no one again.'

I feel my heart begin to beat quickly. They are arguing about me. They are talking about what happened at Paul's house 'that night'. No one had believed my version of events. After Lucas screamed, Natasha had rushed upstairs. She hadn't panicked but telephoned for an ambulance and rung her father immediately. She'd got a towel and covered his eye that was bleeding and soothed him as he cried out. She pulled Lucas's trousers back on him and without a word to me escorted him downstairs, shutting me in my room. Afterwards, Paul had been furious with me and I'd never seen Mummy so cross. She shook me so hard I thought my head would fall off.

'Why did you do it?' she yelled time and time again. I tried to explain but she wouldn't listen. She was more worried about what Paul would think of me than what had really happened. She accused me of lying to cover up my actions. She said I was a malicious child. Her words hurt. They cut through me. I threw my arms around her waist, cried and begged her to listen to me but she pushed me away. Just like that. She unfurled my arms, held me at arm's length and told me to go to my room. Why didn't she believe me? I was her daughter. I needed her. Lucas convinced them he'd come home early because he had a headache. He told them he had gone upstairs to bed and heard me crying. He claimed he had only come into my room to see if I was

okay. When he did, I apparently hurled myself at him brandishing my pencil, screaming that I hated him and the whole family.

There were angry words between my mother and Paul. There were tears and tantrums and silences. Paul wouldn't even look at me after the event.

Mummy told me I was a horrible little girl who was ungrateful for what I had. She kept asking me why I had done it but each time I explained she silenced me with a look and told me not to come up with the same old lie. She told me to apologise to Paul and Lucas but I refused and that made her even angrier. Why should I? Lucas should say sorry. A day after Lucas returned home from hospital, pale-faced with a white bandage wrapped around his head and eye, looking far less menacing than he had that night, Paul asked Mummy and me to leave. He couldn't marry Mummy. He wouldn't feel comfortable having me in the house. My mother didn't speak to me for days. I hated every second of that time. If it hadn't been for Mr Big Ears, I'd have gone mad.

* * *

I sit here on the landing and hope the grown-ups aren't going to make me go through the events of that night. I don't want to ever talk about it again.

Mr Big Ears hugs me and whispers that it'll okay. Grandpa Clifford speaks, his voice calm and gravelly. It reminds me of Daddy's voice and I feel a pain in my chest that Daddy is not here any more. Mr Big Ears squeezes my hand with his soft paw.

'*Of course we can understand. That's why we're only too happy to help out and have her over whenever you want. You need to move on and start life again. Except, and I say this with great affection, we think you need some assistance. We want to help you. You can't keep struggling as you are. Alice's shoes are way too tight. She needs new ones and when was the last time she had a haircut?*'

'How dare you! How dare you look down your nose at me? Don't think I haven't noticed the little looks that pass between you and Jane when I come to drop her off here. You think I'm a rubbish mother. You've always thought that. You never made me feel welcome here. It was always, "Josh this" and "Josh that" and you never really wanted to know about me. It was like I was just someone you had to put up with. I was never good enough for your precious son, was I?'

Grandpa Clifford speaks again. 'Not at all. We just don't want to see you struggle. Alice is our granddaughter, after all. And you don't have any other family. We can loan you the money if you'd rather.'

'I may not have any other family and thanks for bringing that up,' she replies, eyes blazing, 'but I can manage perfectly well, thank you. I might not have a fancy job but pulling pints brings in money. She doesn't go without. Okay, so she doesn't wear the latest fashion or have a shedload of toys but she's fine. She gets fed and looked after.'

'That's not what we mean,' says Grandma Jane. 'We know how difficult it's been for you, struggling after the death of your parents and then losing Josh. You've had such a lot to cope with. We understand that. We're merely concerned that Alice is becoming increasingly withdrawn. She never talks about her friends. She's lost weight and she has those large, dark bags under her eyes all the time and an almost haunted look. And she's always cuddling the rabbit Josh gave her. Maybe if you could afford to move nearer to us…'

I can't hear the rest of the sentence. It would be lovely to live near Grandma and Grandpa Clifford. They are Daddy's parents and being here makes me imagine he's still alive. There are photographs of him and Mummy and me everywhere, on walls, in the sitting room and even a large framed photograph in the hall. I like visiting Granny and Grandpa. They don't hassle me. Usually they take me to the park or to the café in town and let me have a large milkshake or ice cream. Sometimes they buy me new clothes and the odd present but Mummy always gets ratty when they do that, so they don't do it as often as they used to.

Mummy and me now live in a block of flats in Nottingham. It's a small flat and much smaller than our old flat. It has a sitting room and tiny kitchen and we have to share a bedroom. We can hear the neighbours' television through the thin walls but Mummy has now got a job in a nightclub and says when we get enough money, we'll leave. I hope that will happen soon. I don't like the place and the lifts that always smell of pee.

Grandma Jane suddenly starts to cry. 'We're concerned, damn it! You shouldn't leave Alice alone at night. She's far too young. What if there's a fire or something?'

Back on the landing, I look at Mr Big Ears and squirm. Mummy will be mad at me for letting slip to my grandparents that I'm now left alone at night while she goes out to work. I didn't mean to say anything but Grandma Jane was quizzing me about all sorts of things and I wasn't thinking when I answered her. I was enjoying my strawberry smoothie and panini in the café and it just came out before I could stop it. Mummy told me it was to be our secret. I hadn't wanted a babysitter. Not after the last time. I screamed and screamed when Mummy suggested getting one for me and insisted I could look after myself. I'm happy to go to bed when Mummy goes out and I just read until it's time to go to sleep. I never want another babysitter. I have Mr Big Ears. I don't need anyone else. Mummy gave up in the end and said it was just as well because babysitters are expensive and made me promise not to tell anyone.

'It's illegal,' says Grandma Jane firmly after more muffled raised voices. 'And it's not right. She's only just turned ten years old. We could report you, you know. We could tell the authorities...'

The voices all begin shouting at the same time. It's becoming too much for me to bear. I'm to blame for whatever is happening in the kitchen. I shouldn't have blurted out the secret. I hear Mummy's voice shouting that it is none of their business what she does and how she brings up her child before Grandpa says something that makes them all lower their voices. I catch snippets of words, spoken in harsh voices.

'What do you think, Mr Big Ears?' I ask. He stares down the staircase, a forlorn look on his face, then suddenly the kitchen door is thrown open with a smack as it bounces against the wall. Mummy yells at me to hurry up because we have a train to catch. I descend obediently, reluctant to leave this house where I feel safe and loved. Mummy is standing at the bottom of the stairs, hands on hips, face unreadable but as I approach, I can feel the anger emitting from her.

Grandma Jane is crying quietly and won't look up. Grandpa Clifford has a gnarly hand around Grandma's shoulder and looks really, really sad.

'Please,' Grandpa Clifford calls as Mummy grabs my hand and marches me out of the house. 'There's no need for this. Don't go.'

Mummy ignores his pleas and stony-faced continues down the path. I twist my head to look back at my grandparents on the doorstep. Both look so very old and frail. I try to wave but I'm holding Mr Big Ears in one hand and Mummy has a tight grip on my other as she hustles me down the street.

'When will I see them again?' I ask after a while, a strange tightness in my chest.

Mummy doesn't reply but picks up the pace. Her silence says it all. I'm never going to see my grandparents again.

CHAPTER SIX

The leaden skies that had threatened all morning now opened up and fat drops of rain hurled themselves into Robyn's windscreen, making it almost impossible to see the road ahead. She navigated the car away from the sides and peered into the gloom where large puddles of water appeared from nowhere.

Mary Matthews was right to be concerned. Her husband could be involved in something bigger than he realised. Robyn needed to learn more about the friends in Thailand in case Lucas had two passports and had scarpered abroad. She had managed to contact Nick Pearson-Firth, the head of the music department where Lucas worked, and he had agreed to a meeting. Dark fields whipped past the Polo's windows. Blinkley Manor was in the middle of Derbyshire countryside away from towns and villages. She wondered idly what had made Lucas teach at a public school when he had clearly hated his own.

She drove past several attractive cottages in dark stone and a pub with a welcoming chalkboard offering special-priced meals. She pulled into its car park to call Ross. His voice was crackly.

'I hope you're having more luck than me,' he said. 'I'm getting nowhere.'

'Not sure about luck but I have a couple of leads for our elusive husband. The wife is concerned Lucas will be in trouble for having images of young girls on his computer. Certainly, if the police get hold of the computer and discover worse than I saw, then he might face charges. They were mostly photographs of girls in uniforms. Still dodgy though. Mary's convinced it's all some sort of ghastly mistake and is having difficulty in believing her husband is into that sort of thing. She even came up with the idea that he might be trying to play detective and has discovered one of his work colleagues or pupils is guilty of downloading this stuff and now has got into trouble while tracking them down. I got the number for the head of the music department at the school where Lucas works. I'm going to have a word with him now to see if he can shed any light on Lucas's whereabouts. Apparently, Lucas doesn't have many friends but he and Nick Pearson-Firth have known each other for a long time and have even travelled to Thailand together in the past.'

'Okay. Let me know if you need me to steam over and help you out. I'm dying of boredom here.'

The entrance for Blinkley Manor Preparatory School for three- to thirteen-year-old boys and girls was well concealed and had it not been for her sharp eyes spotting a small, smart, maroon sign screwed to a tree beside the turning, Robyn would have passed it. Once into the grounds, she drove on a pristine tarmac road that undulated past woods filled with oak trees. Soft green moss carpeted the floor. Some tall foxgloves stood at the woodland edge; their pink-purple heads a cheerful contrast to the deep green. The woods gave way to the school grounds, huge playing fields of immaculately mown grass, a large lake and the school itself. She whistled in appreciation. This was a far cry from the village school she had attended.

Robyn drew up to the car park in front of the school. She breathed in the air cleansed by the recent rain. The building itself was a Georgian Palladian country house with an imposing portico, cursive and round domes, chamber, pillars and a magnificent south front. A double spiral staircase led up to a rectangular balcony and a pillared entrance to the main hall. Following directions to the music department, she climbed the staircase and into the hall, once a living area in the building. The room was now filled with trophy cabinets, a large oak table and dominated by two imposing fireplaces and a glass chandelier.

A small cough diverted her attention from the gardens below. 'Might I help you?'

Robyn turned to face the plump man whose round-rimmed glasses filled his face.

'I'm looking for the music department. I have an appointment to meet Mr Pearson-Firth.'

'I'll take you. I'm headed that way myself.'

Without further conversation he opened the back door and ushered her through, down the stairs and into a tunnel that led into the main school.

'It's a devil to find the first time you come here. You'll soon get used to the layout though. All the parents do.'

He pointed out the office, gave a brief nod and left her. She wanted to correct him and explain she wasn't a potential parent but it didn't seem worth it. Instead she knocked on the door.

Nick Pearson-Firth was not what Robyn expected. He was in his early forties, slim built, about five foot ten with dark curly hair and dancing brown eyes that sparkled with vitality.

'Miss Carter?' he asked, holding out a manicured hand that gripped hers firmly. 'I'm Nick Pearson-Firth but please call me Nick. Come in.'

The office was a light airy space containing only a desk, chairs and a large piano. The walls were filled with framed certificates. He dropped back into his chair, a sense of restlessness about his body as he swivelled slightly from side to side. She sat in one of the seats opposite and gazed out beyond him onto the manicured lawns she had spotted earlier.

'So, how can I help you?' he asked, cutting straight to it.

Robyn was about to reply when the silence was punctuated by a fine soprano voice singing 'Un Bel Di Vedremo' from Puccini's *Madame Butterfly*. The notes rose and fell against the adjoining wall. Robyn was transported to Butterfly's world. It was one of the most breathtaking arias in the whole operatic repertoire with syncopated rhythms representing Butterfly's longing for her lover Pinkerton, a beautiful melody, and a high B flat at the end. A memory of watching a performance of the opera with Davies rose with the music but she forced it away. This was not the time for such indulgences.

'Is that a CD?' she asked. 'The singing,' she added.

A relaxed smile stretched across his face. 'That's my daughter, Sophia. She's practising with her mother. My wife is a singer too and an accomplished pianist. You might have heard of her – Katarina Pearson.'

Robyn nodded. Of course she had heard of Katarina Pearson, the well-known soprano who had shot to fame on a television talent show in her thirties. A tiny, frail woman, the watching public had been first amazed at the purity and strength of her voice and then reduced to tears at her rendition of 'O Mio Babbino Caro'.

'I have her album, *Greatest Arias*. I should have put two and two together,' She said. 'Of course, Pearson-Firth.'

Nick looked pleased. 'Katarina always wanted to keep her maiden and professional name and Firth on its own sounded boring, so we put them together when we got married.'

'Do you sing too?'

'I'm more of a brass man. I play trumpet and tuba but can also play piano and violin. I'm not a great singer. Sometimes I accompany my wife or Sophia. You like classical music?'

'Some. I like opera. *Madame Butterfly* is one of my favourites.'

His head bobbed up and down in agreement. 'One of the most enduring tales of unrequited love,' he murmured. 'So, what can I tell you about Lucas?' he continued, steepling his fingers.

'How well do you know him?' she asked.

'Well enough. As well as one knows one's colleagues. He's worked here for nine years – all the time I've been head of the department. He's a peripatetic tutor rather than full-time; he comes in four times a week and teaches at homes as well as at school. He doesn't hang about after lessons in the common room with any of the staff. He's an excellent musician. He always gets involved in school musical performances and is in charge of the school orchestra. The pupils like him. He has a high success rate. And there's not much else I can add other than he sent me his resignation last week and I'm now looking for a replacement for him. I've got my work cut out trying to find a substitute teacher with similar qualifications at such short notice. He really dropped me in it.'

'He's resigned?' Robyn said.

'Yes. I was as surprised as you. I thought he'd stay here for life. He's never given me reason to think he'd leave. He gets on with all the kids too. I don't know if his leaving is anything to do with his dad passing away. I have a feeling Lucas might have come into some serious money. His father was an actor – Paul Matthews. In his heyday Paul was as popular and talented as Leonardo DiCaprio or Tom Cruise and was headed for the big time. I'm not sure what happened and there were a lot of rumours circulating at the time in the press but he just gave it all up and dropped out of the scene. He became a recluse. Hid in his massive house in Staffordshire. I believe he lived off investments he'd made when he was doing well with his acting. He was heavily into fitness and ran around the reservoir near where he lived every day. A few days ago, he had a heart attack while running and died. There was a piece in the newspaper about it otherwise I wouldn't have known. Anyway, I suspect Lucas no longer needs to work. His resignation letter was very brief.'

'I understand you went with Lucas to Thailand on one of his trips,' said Robin. There it was: a flicker in his eyes. She'd been expecting it. His voice adopted an even more casual tone. 'That was a while ago. We were invited by the parents of one of the lads in his final year.'

'Is that normal?' she asked. 'For parents to invite you on holiday?'

He casually threw one leg over the other and thought for a moment before responding. 'Miss Carter, this is a private school. The pupils live here during term time and we are in loco parentis. We are like one gigantic family. It is not unusual for us to develop healthy relationships with our pupils and their parents especially when we have taught them over several years. Max Devlin was one such pupil. He was head boy and a fine music scholar. We had watched him grow from an immature boy into a confident young man and attain a music scholarship to a prestigious senior school. Although his parents lived in Thailand, they attended as many end-of-term performances as possible and came to all the major school calendar events so obviously we got to know them. When Max left the school, Jo and Stuart Devlin invited both Lucas and me to their home in Thailand on a holiday as a thank you. Katarina was too busy to come and Mary, Lucas's wife, apparently hates flying so it was just us chaps. I haven't been since though – too humid and noisy for me. I believe Lucas has been a few times as he worked with Max far more than I did. He was Max's personal tutor.'

He ran a tongue over dry lips and waited for her to question him further but she changed tack.

'Have you heard from Lucas this holiday?'

'No, but I wouldn't expect to. The staff here usually can't wait to get away from this place and we don't tend to stay in touch until the new term. We see enough of each other during term.'

'So no texts or emails?' she said. He shook his head.

'Is there any way I can get in contact with Jo and Stuart Devlin?'

He regarded her cagily. 'I can't give out confidential information like that. I'd need to see some identification.'

Robyn pulled out her Private Investigator's licence and passed it to him. 'This isn't an official inquiry yet, Nick, but it soon will be. If you could get those details to me as soon as possible it would help enormously.'

'I'll get the school secretary to contact you,' he said, lines appearing between his eyebrows. 'The information will be on the school database.'

Robyn wrote down her number. 'This is my personal number but you'll also be able to get me at Staffordshire Police headquarters next week.'

'Can I ask why you are asking about him? Is it to do with Thailand?'

'Do you think it is to do with Thailand?' She sat back and observed him. He shuffled in his seat for a moment before readopting his casual poise. 'Well, I don't think he's up to anything over there, if that's what you are suggesting.'

'I'm not suggesting anything. I'm merely trying to build up a picture of a man who has suddenly given up a job he seemed to like and left. I'm looking for any leads that might help me work out why and where he's gone.'

'So he has gone, then?' Nick said, a furrow appearing between his eyebrows. 'Look, I wasn't very close to the man. I was merely his head of department. I didn't even like him that much. He was far too reserved for my liking and never integrated with the rest of us. That time we went to Thailand. It was embarrassing. I don't like to discuss it.'

Robyn gave an encouraging nod and continued to sit back in her chair, allowing Nick plenty of space.

'We went out for a meal with the Devlins on the first night. Lucas claimed he was a bit jet-lagged and had a headache so he left early. I stayed on and went back to their house for a nightcap so I didn't return to the hotel until about one o'clock in the morning.

I was waiting for the lift when a couple came through the hotel doors, arms wrapped around each other, clearly no eyes for anyone else. She was stunning, long sleek dark hair with orange streaks. It struck me she was quite tall for a Thai girl and dressed in a short white skirt, thigh-length boots and a glittery feather boa. She also seemed very young to me. When I looked more closely I was convinced she was a *katoey* – a lady boy. Her voice was not quite the right pitch and she had an Adam's apple. That didn't surprise me as much as the man necking her. It was Lucas.'

'Did he see you?'

'Luckily, I ducked into the lift and hit the button before he made it across the foyer and spotted me. I didn't say anything to him about it but the next day, instead of going on a tour around Bangkok with the Devlins he cried off saying he felt sick and I have a feeling he spent the day with the same lady boy. It's not that I'm a prude or anything. I know these girls are exciting and different. But it was the look on his face. I can't describe it. It wasn't like the Lucas I knew at all. It was lust and cruelty mixed together – it was primeval and it changed my opinion of him.'

'Did you not say anything to him about it?'

'It was none of my business. Exotic countries can encourage odd behaviour. People feel less inhibited when they are away. Like holidaymakers who start drinking alcohol at eleven in the morning in Spain or young people who behave wildly in places like Aya Napa or Ibiza. I figured it was one of those "What happens in Thailand, stays in Thailand" moments. Lucas has never given me reason to doubt his integrity at this school, so why question what he does when he is not here?'

* * *

Robyn left the school with a nagging feeling that Lucas Matthews was someone who would be of interest to the police and that his disappearance was without doubt suspicious. She would call her boss DCI Mulholland and request that this investigation be turned into an official police one.

CHAPTER SEVEN

The coffee shop was alive with chattering voices periodically drowned out by the deafening hiss of the coffee machine. Abigail spotted her friends clustered in the corner – Zoe's bright green hair stood out. A child's highchair was propped next to her other friend Claire, who suddenly spotted her and waved. Abigail wielded the buggy in their direction and was met with squeals of delight as she unbuckled Izzy and passed her to Claire, who wore an expression of adoration and held out her arms eagerly to take the child.

'Hasn't she grown?' said Zoe from her seat, wiggling her fingers at the child. 'I can't believe it's been two months since we saw you last. Good you've come out at last. Did you get lost under an enormous pile of nappies?' She laughed. 'Seriously, it's great to see you. I know I've been a terrible friend but the new job has been so demanding and travelling up and down to London every day really takes it out of me after all those classes.'

'It's okay. I kind of lost track of time. Izzy's been grumpy with her teeth coming through and before that she had a cold so I was frightened to take her out in case it got worse. And, I'm so tired I can hardly do anything some days. I don't know where all the time has gone. I seem to drift from one day to the next and never have time for anything.'

'I told you, she needs a nanny,' said Claire, jiggling Izzy up and down. 'Then we could go out like we used to.'

'I couldn't get a nanny for her. She's so little. She needs me,' said Abigail with a horrified expression.

'Well, a babysitter then,' suggested Zoe.

Abigail felt her skin go clammy and her heart began to pound. 'No, not a babysitter. I'd prefer to look after her myself. There'll be plenty of chances to go out again when she's older and Jackson can have her for a few hours.' She shut out the memory that was trying to surface and busied herself with her buggy.

Izzy gurgled contentedly and shook a plastic ring in Zoe's direction while Claire continued to bounce the child on her knee. 'You are so lucky,' Claire murmured, smiling at the wriggling form. 'She's a poppet.'

'She has her moments,' replied Abigail with pride.

Zoe leaned forward to air-kiss her before taking her turn with Izzy. Izzy grabbed Zoe's chunky necklace and sucked on it.

'You look fabulous,' Zoe gushed. 'You're looking much less mumsy today. Love the outfit. Is it new? Where did you get it? And how's the gorgeous Jackson? Is he flying today?' Her questions came out in a rush. That was Zoe, impatient, eager and almost puppy-like with her enthusiasm. 'By the way, Rachel is getting the drinks. She insisted even though money is a bit tight for her. Wasn't that sweet of her? She's been struggling to make ends meet since the divorce and she doesn't earn a fortune. She's only part time at the dentist surgery and I certainly wouldn't want her job, peering into people's mouths and cleaning between the teeth no matter what it paid. Imagine cleaning out bits of decaying food. Yuck,' she added, wrinkling her snub nose. 'Rachel's amazing.'

Claire threw Abigail a look that said otherwise.

'That's really nice of her to buy the drinks,' Abigail agreed.

'Poor Rachel. She's really going through it at the moment,' continued Zoe, her large grey eyes full of concern. 'She was so pleased when I invited her to join us today.'

Izzy extracted the necklace, examined it closely and shoved it back in her mouth. Zoe smiled at her.

'Why exactly did you invite Rachel today?' asked Claire bluntly, simultaneously waving plastic rings at Izzy who let go of the necklace and reached out for them. 'It's not like she knows us very well. We only met her the once when you brought her to the last meet-up.'

Zoe's eyes grew large. 'My bad. I felt sorry for her. She's been struggling to make new friends. I think I'm the only person she knows in the area. She's been through a horrible time with the divorce – it's been very acrimonious – and I thought it would be okay if she came along. It'll do her good to get out. Besides, she didn't stop talking about you after the last meeting. She really liked you both. Obviously you didn't feel the same.' Claire scowled but said nothing. 'You're okay with it, aren't you, Abby?' Zoe asked.

Abigail wasn't too comfortable with the situation but she didn't want to upset Zoe. Rachel was a little weird and made her feel uneasy for some reason.

'Yes, it's fine. I'm cool with it. It's hard to make new friends.'

Claire made no further comment as the fourth member of the group arrived with a tray laden with drinks and plonked it down.

'I got you a latte, Abigail,' Rachel said. 'Hope that was okay. I got them to put some caramel syrup in it as a treat. You probably need the energy after running around looking after Izzy.'

Abigail wasn't a fan of syrup but she didn't want to appear ungrateful. 'Great. Thanks.'

'I love Izzy's dress,' said Rachel, stroking the child's soft fleshy arm. 'It's very pretty. You're very pretty,' she added, talking to Izzy who beamed a happy smile. 'There are times when I wish we'd had children. I'd have loved to,' she said, a heavy sadness in her voice. 'Still, it would have been a horrible experience to put them through. What with the whole divorce thing.' She stopped, aware she was in danger of bringing everyone down, and instead adopted a more enthusiastic tone. 'I happened to be passing a toy shop on the way here and I saw this.'

She rummaged in her large canvas bag and pulled out a rainbow-coloured teddy bear that she shook in front of Izzy who immediately held her hands out for the furry toy, burbling with pleasure. She put one of the feet in her mouth.

'It is okay, isn't it?' asked Rachel. 'You don't mind me buying her a present?'

'Of course. It was a lovely thing to do. Thank you,' replied Abigail

'She seems to like it. I still have my teddy from when I was a girl,' continued Rachel, oblivious to the looks passing between Claire and Abigail. 'You can never have too many soft toys. I have a collection of thirty now.'

'Thirty?' repeated Zoe in disbelief.

'I'm a bit soft like that. I see them in shops and they seem to be begging me to take them home.' Rachel giggled nervously. Izzy chose that moment to burp loudly and the conversation turned back to the child before moving on to catching up with each of their lives.

* * *

An hour later, the conversation was beginning to wane.

'I ought to take some more photos of Izzy,' said Claire, as the child bounced up and down. 'She's changing all the time. She's also very photogenic. I could do a mother and child shot for you.'

Abigail had first met Claire when she'd turned up at the boutique in town to take photographs of several brides and mothers in their outfits for a feature about weddings. The feature was to appear on wedding websites and the shop owner had been keen to participate and promote the shop. Abigail, who worked at the boutique, was in charge of the outfits and ensured all the models looked wonderful while Claire clicked away with her Canon, encouraging people to smile and putting them at ease. After the event, both women were exhausted and Abigail poured them champagne from the shop's special hoard. They had a laugh about the picky mothers and diva brides-to-be and a friendship was born.

Due to the nature of her occupation, Claire travelled the country taking photographs for various magazines and websites, and she had her own site filled with magnificent shots of birds. She spent hours in hides, waiting to capture a bird in flight or feeding. She had shown Abigail many of her photographs and divulged that her true ambition was to work on a television wildlife programme as a camera operator. Abigail felt Claire was often more comfortable squatting in a bunch of reeds waiting for that elusive photo opportunity than in company.

'Do you prefer photographing people or nature?' asked Rachel, twirling the long spoon that had accompanied her coffee around and around the empty glass.

'Nature. I always feel I'm taking false images of people. They fake their smiles and hide behind masks. I'd rather take photographs of wild horses galloping about a field on a winter's day, frosted clods of earth flying from their hooves and clouds of steam pouring from their nostrils and freedom in their eyes. Nature doesn't disappoint. People do,' she said.

Rachel regarded her warily. 'But you photograph lots of people. Surely they're not all like that.'

'No. Children are nearly always natural, especially babies.' She looked across at Izzy who was producing a large spit bubble. 'See? Natural,' said Claire, making Abigail and Zoe splutter.

'She took some super photographs of Abigail when she was pregnant,' offered Zoe. 'Abby looked so serene and beautiful.'

'Less so now the little monkey is out,' said Abigail, changing the subject. She didn't want Rachel to know about those intimate photographs. They were very artistic but personal and Zoe had no right to mention them.

'Really?' said Rachel, unwilling to let go of the subject. 'How lovely. I admire women that make the most of their bodies and show them off. I'd love to see the photos some time. I bet you look beautiful, Abby – maternal and composed.'

Abigail winced. The woman was already becoming too familiar. Only her good friends called her Abby. Rachel had turned her attention to Claire now. 'So, tell me, Claire, is there anyone special in your life? You haven't mentioned anyone.'

'Once upon a time but it didn't work out,' replied Claire, levelling her nonchalant gaze at Rachel. 'I'm a bit busy for relationships at the moment and I'm happy on my own. I'm not old enough to be left on the shelf yet and I want to become a successful photographer – have a career before I tie myself down. There's plenty of time for relationships.'

'You'd soon fall into one if you met a bloke like Jackson,' said Zoe. 'Abigail's husband,' she explained to Rachel. 'He's totally gorgeous.'

Abigail smiled and was about to protest.

'But, Jackson's only got eyes for Abby,' replied Claire. 'So, Zoe, what about Andy? What's happened there?' she asked.

'No. We split up last month. The relationship's been going downhill for a while. He got into all that muscle-building stuff and I sort of went off him. I preferred it when he looked less like a Neanderthal. Besides, I'm with someone else.'

'Really? Another guy from the gym?'

'No. It's early days though. I'm keeping this one quiet for the moment and seeing how it goes.'

'Good for you,' replied Rachel. 'I hope you have more luck than me.' She suddenly stood up. 'Too much coffee. I need the loo.' She squeezed past Zoe and headed for the toilets up the stairs.

'Is she for real?' said Claire.

'She's nervous, that's all,' Zoe retorted. 'Hardly surprising since you've been glaring at her almost non-stop since she sat down. What's the matter with you?'

'I don't much like her. She's a bit blunt with her questions. Like she's interviewing us or interrogating us.'

Zoe drew herself up on her seat and snapped, 'For goodness sake. She doesn't know much about you and she's trying hard. At least she's making an effort to be friendly. Honestly, Claire, sometimes you can be so frustrating. Ease up, will you? She's just a lonely woman.'

'Okay. But I'm not feeling any affection for her. She's a bit of a whiner. Don't bring her along next time.'

'Don't be such a cow. I don't see why you have a problem. It's no big deal. Rachel is a nice woman who could do with a friend or two. I thought you would understand that. You're hardly Miss Popular yourself.'

'Stop it, you two.' Abigail waved her hands at them both. 'You're upsetting Izzy.'

On cue, Izzy let out a wail of dismay, diffusing the anger that was mounting, and Claire leant across to rub her arm very gently, coaxing her to smile. A large tear fell down the child's face and plopped onto the highchair but she stopped crying when Claire handed her her car keys to play with. She jangled them in delight.

'There, there. We were just having a girlie row. It was my fault. I was being silly. Sorry, Zoe. I didn't get much sleep last night and I'm out of sorts.'

Zoe huffed but nodded tersely.

Claire lifted the baby. 'I'll take her outside for some air,' she said. Abigail agreed and watched as her friend wandered towards the door, her child smiling again.

'I'm going to get a glass of water. Flipping Claire. She can be so difficult at times. Sometimes I want to throttle her,' said Zoe, standing up. 'Back in a moment.'

Zoe went to an adjacent room where water jugs filled with cold water and ice stood in a line next to paper cups. Once she vanished from view, Abigail sat back and sighed.

Her phone buzzed. It was probably Jackson. She smiled at the thought and answered without checking the number. A mocking robotic voice spoke.

'Hello, Abigail. What a perfect little family you have. Sadly, it won't be perfect for much longer. You can't trust anyone. You think you can but you can't. So many secrets being kept. Not just you, either. Ask Jackson about his new lover. That is, if you dare. You might lose him. Poor Abigail. What would you do then?'

Abigail's heartbeat quickened but an inner anger at the cruel voice steadied her nerves. 'Who is this? What do you want?'

There was a brief pause then the sound of laughter made more menacing by the machinelike tone. 'Never mind who I am. Who are you? I am watching your every move. And, I am going to destroy your life.'

The phone went dead. Abigail flicked through the log but it was a withheld number. Her heart hammered as she anxiously ran through her options. There weren't many. She couldn't trace the call as it had come from an unknown number and there was no one she could confront. A shiver travelled through her as the message from the caller ran through her mind. *You can't trust anyone.* She stuffed the phone in her bag and tried to calm down. She couldn't let on that something was up. She needed time to think. She chewed on her lip, wondering what to do. A flustered Rachel reappeared.

'The queue for the loo was ridiculous. I was nearly bursting by the time I got in. Where is everyone? Look, I have to go. I didn't know it was so late. I'll be late for work. Sorry to rush off. Lovely to see you and Izzy. We must do this again soon,' she said. 'Can you say goodbye to the others for me?' She leant forward and air-kissed Abigail.

Abigail nodded dumbly before managing to thank her for the toy bear. Rachel dismissed her thanks with a smile and a wave and beetled off.

Zoe reappeared as soon as Rachel left. She gave a small shrug of apology.

'Got caught. Met someone I used to teach,' she said. 'Wouldn't stop talking. She's put some weight on. I guess she doesn't work out as much nowadays. You okay? You look startled.'

'No, I'm fine. Rachel surprised me by suddenly leaving.'

'Oh, she's probably got to go to work. She was on this afternoon's shift.'

'That's what she said.'

'I really like her. She's so different. She makes me laugh.' Zoe cocked her head to one side, like a sparrow searching for insects, while her eyes sparkled with merriment. Zoe was not someone who took life seriously. Abigail suddenly had the urge to leave and get away from Zoe, the café and everyone. She began picking up the plastic tubs and bottle and shoving them in her bag.

'You going too?' asked Zoe.

'Yes. I've got a headache coming on and I promised Jackson I wouldn't be long. He's off today.'

'You certainly don't want to have too many headaches with Jackson at home,' joked Zoe. Abigail forced her mouth to smile. Claire chose that moment to return. Izzy was gurgling again and drooling over the keys in her mouth.

'One happy little monkey,' said Claire, handing Izzy to her mother and removing the keys. 'Oh, please don't tell me you're leaving? I was hoping now Rachel's gone we could have more of a giggle.'

'Jackson's at home,' explained Zoe with a wink.

'I see,' replied Claire, grinning. 'Can't leave the man alone, eh? I quite understand.'

Abigail faked another smile and hustled Izzy into her buggy where she protested and began to howl. Feeling far more flustered than she wished to show, she said her goodbyes and left the café wondering what to do next, how she was going to tackle Jackson, or indeed if she ought to. The mocking voice echoed in her ears as she started the car. Who was it and how far would they really go to destroy everything she had built up?

CHAPTER EIGHT

NOW

The newspaper article not only managed to get Paul Matthews' age wrong, claiming he was fifty-nine, but has reported he suffered a heart attack while running.

I am torn between laughter and indignation. I want to email the journalist who wrote it and tell him the truth; that I am responsible for Paul's demise.

It was brilliantly executed. I strategically set up a tripwire that caused him to fall onto an upright stub of a tree with sharp branches poking out from its base. I had rather hoped one of the cruel branches, sharp as knives, would stick in his eye and splinter into his brain but that didn't happen. However, smashing a branch into his face worked a treat. I had thought about aiming for the midline of his face where I could cause the most damage and fracture his nose, which would result in laceration or dissection of the carotid arteries and fatal damage to the brainstem. However, that sort of damage is more likely to occur when the victim is in a high-speed situation, not jogging, and given that I didn't want to raise suspicions I settled for a blow to the temple. My research had paid off. He dropped like a stone.

CHAPTER NINE

'Thank you very much for your help and for getting back to me so promptly,' said Robyn politely before disconnecting the Skype call from Thailand. She relaxed against the leather chair and thoughtfully tapped her teeth with a pencil.

Ross was staring glumly at a pile of receipts. He detested paperwork and if it weren't for his wife who helped out with the books, the business would not be as lucrative as it was. Before Jeanette had become responsible for the accounts, Ross would even forget to bill clients. He hunted through his trouser pockets and unearthed a tatty receipt, unfolded it and added it to the pile. He looked up as Robyn replaced the telephone receiver. 'I don't know why Jeanette insists on me keeping every receipt. Do you think she's checking up on what I buy?'

'No. I think she's making sure you put the correct expenses through the books. If it weren't for her, the accounts would be in a right state every year. I hardly think she's checking through each one to see if you bought a Mars bar for your lunch.'

Ross closed his eyes for a second. 'I could just eat one or two of those,' he murmured. 'All that delicious caramel coating my mouth.'

'Stop torturing yourself. Think of your arteries. They don't need a coating of any description. You've already had one wake-up call. How many more do you need?'

Ross had been with the police all his life and risen to the same rank as Robyn, a detective inspector, until his heart had started playing up. Plagued by bouts of tachycardia and sweating, he had finally gone to the doctor only to be referred to a specialist. Twenty-four-hour Holter monitoring, exercise tolerance tests, clinical and echographic examinations resulted in a diagnosis of ventricular extrasystole, an erratic heartbeat which, although not life-threatening, made him rethink his lifestyle and work choices. He had moved into the field of private investigation to have less stress but still struggled with other lifestyle choices.

Ross grimaced. 'True. No joy with the Devlins, then?'

'They haven't seen Lucas Matthews in months. In fact, Lucas hasn't been in contact with them at all, which they thought strange. They've sent the usual chatty emails with the latest news about their son Max, but he didn't reply. Normally, he's keen to know how his protégé is doing. They issued an invite to come and stay and celebrate Max's birthday with them but he said he was a "little busy" this year to visit. They couldn't tell me any more than that he was a dedicated teacher who had really looked after Max. Max was picked on in his first year at school for looking and acting a little effeminate but Lucas took him under his wing and ensured he had a happy time at boarding school. His mother went on and on about how Lucas had been like an older brother to Max.'

Ross shrugged. 'Dead end.'

'If they knew about his penchant for lady boys, they certainly weren't willing to tell me.'

Ross unwrapped a piece of gum, balled the wrapper and tossed it in the direction of the bin.

'I wouldn't choose to go to Thailand myself. Don't fancy the food much.'

'I thought you liked all food,' she retorted.

'I like stuff that fills you up. I don't think lemongrass soup and noodles or whatever they serve will do that for me.'

'Might be a great diet for you. Low in calories. High in nutritious goodies. I ought to pass a few recipes to Jeanette for her to test out on you.'

'You do and I'll make you trail boring Bob for the next few nights until you start back at the station.'

'You having no luck either?'

'If Bob is having an affair then I'll be very surprised. He's so squeaky clean I half expect him to suddenly put on a dog collar and go to church.'

'Most women have good instincts. If his wife thinks he's having an affair then it's likely he is. You need to keep an eye on him. She's paying you for your time so at least you aren't wasting it.'

'I feel like I am. Last night he went to the cinema with one of his mates from the pub. Hardly bonking the night away, is he?'

Robyn chuckled. She scrolled through news items about Paul Matthews as Ross spoke, half-listening to his complaints about spending another night in his car while Bob ate popcorn. Paul Matthews had indeed been an attractive man. She could see where Lucas got his looks. Paul had enjoyed a rise in popularity in the nineties, playing the role of a doctor in a soap opera before he was snapped up by a film studio to play the lead role in a film adaptation of a bonkbuster.

'He didn't give up acting when his wife passed away,' said Robyn, speed-reading the information. 'It was four years later, in 2000. That seems odd. Why would he suddenly drop out of a lucrative career and become reclusive?'

'Drugs?'

'Possibly so. However, he jogged regularly so that suggests he looked after his health. Though I won't rule out anything at this stage.'

'Another woman?'

'Doesn't seem to have been a second Mrs Matthews. There was someone for a while. I've discovered some photographs of her from one of the national newspapers.'

She angled the screen so Ross could see. He whistled. 'Now, she's hot.'

The photograph was from an awards ceremony and showed a suave Paul Matthews in evening dress smiling broadly at the camera. Beside him stood a willowy blonde wearing an evening dress that clung to her shapely body. She radiated elegance with her hair neatly folded in a classic French plait. Her manicured red nails clutched a designer handbag and her flawless skin had been expertly made-up. On her wrist dangled an expensive bracelet made of crystals that caught the light and sparkled. Her large grey eyes were fringed with eyelashes almost impossibly long to be her own and her lips were plump, sexy with a tinge of wanton about them. It was little wonder Paul had his arm hooked through hers and looked content.

'A babe,' said Ross, still studying the photo. 'I guess she's no longer his girlfriend. Christina Forman,' he added, reading aloud the name under the picture. 'Says here she's his fiancée.'

'Paul lived alone. He wasn't married. I'll follow it up. Christina might be able to tell me something about Lucas. There's more to him than meets the eye. Nick, Lucas's head of department, mentioned the look on Lucas's face when he saw him in the hotel lobby with the lady boy. He described it as "lust and cruelty mixed – primeval". It shocked Nick. There's another side to Lucas for sure. And then there was the easy way he lied to get out of being with the Devlins. He also fibbed to his wife although I can't work out why. And there are the photographs of young girls in school uniforms on his computer and even though there was nothing pornographic about them, I'm going to have him looked into by the paedophile squad. I'm worried that this is going to prove to be more than a missing-person inquiry. Sorry, Ross, but I'm taking this case over in an official capacity.'

'I thought you weren't starting back until next week.'

'I spoke to DCI Mulholland late last night and asked her to let me start earlier and run with this. She agreed, so I'm the officer in charge as of today. I'll keep you informed though.'

* * *

She recalled her brief conversation with Louisa Mulholland, her boss, who had sounded more stressed than usual. 'I'm happy for you to return to work as soon as you can,' Louisa said. 'We could do with you back. I don't have many officers who can assist but I'll allow PC Mitz Patel to work on this as long as he stays at or close to headquarters. We will need to use him too. And you can have our newbie PC Anna Shamash, but be gentle with her; she's learning the ropes and I don't want her picking up any bad habits. We'll be short-handed if we put anyone else on this with you. Operation Goofy is taking up all our manpower at the moment.'

'That's fine. I won't need much assistance and if it's okay with you, I'll use ex-DI Ross Cunningham to help if it gets tough.'

Louisa Mulholland had no favourites but Ross had always managed to crack a smile when he had been part of the team.

'Good idea. He's a useful man to know. I trust you'll be adhering to protocols on this, DI Carter.'

'Of course.'

'Good.'

They both knew she was referring to Robyn's sudden impulses that often led her to chase off at a tangent.

'I'll play by the book, ma'am.'

* * *

'How is Louisa? She keeping all the minions in order?' Ross grinned.

Robyn thought back to when she left the force and her conversation with the chief inspector. A slight woman, she looked more like a secretary than a high-ranking policewoman. Louisa Mulholland was in her late fifties, widowed and dedicated to her job and those she worked with. Her door was always open for those who needed her. When Robyn had stumbled through to hand in her notice, Louisa had shut the door to the office. She had moved to sit next to Robyn, and when Robyn had broken down in tears she had comforted her. Finally, they had talked. Louisa had gazed at Robyn intently with friendly, olive-green eyes.

'You'll be back, Robyn,' she had said. 'You've had a dreadful time but you'll be back and I'll be the first to welcome you when you return. Do what you need to do. Grieve. Cry. Howl. Scream. Kick walls. I did all of those things when I lost my husband, Graham, but after a few months alone in the house, I realised the only important thing left was this station, the team who work tirelessly and this job. We are all here because we want a better place to live – one where there aren't so many scumbags on the streets. And this is where you belong. You believe in better too.'

Louisa was right. Robyn belonged on the force. And all the months she had cried herself to sleep, she thought of solemn-faced Louisa who believed in justice and who had never given up.

'Louisa managed to keep you in order so I'm sure she can handle anyone after that.'

'She's one of a kind. Send her my love, won't you? Some days, I wish I were back there too. It gets lonely here in this office. It's been good having you help out. Anyway, I'll stick to the mundane stuff but let me know if I can help at all with this case. You still have a private investigator's licence so you are very welcome to work out of this office whenever you want.'

She looked over at him and grinned. 'Thanks. I might just need you. I've been off duty for a year. I'm probably a bit rusty.'

'Yeah, and I'm the Queen's official corgi walker.'

Robyn scrolled through the pages about Paul Matthews and sighed.

'So, what do you know?'

'There's not much here. Paul kept his family life private. There are a couple of photographs of him and his wife, Linda, before she died. Nice-looking lady. She was a dancer – performed under her maiden name – Bridges. Look, there's one of her and probably Lucas on the beach with Paul.'

Ross scooted forward and squinted at the picture. 'Who's the little kid beside them with a bucket on their head?'

'Hang on, I'll drag down the actual article. It's from a local paper.' She read the report out:

Paul Matthews took a few hours off filming from popular drama Doctor Pippin to join his family in Scarborough. With his wife Linda Bridges, 32, and children Lucas, 10, and Natasha, 8, Paul enjoyed an afternoon sunbathing in temperatures of 26 degrees. Paul Matthews said, 'Who wants to head off to Spain when we have beautiful summer temperatures like these? Scarborough is much more fun than Benidorm. We have super beaches, delicious rock and the best donkey rides.'

Robyn halted and tapped the screen. 'Lucas has a sister. Nobody's mentioned her to me. I'll have to find out more about Natasha Matthews.'

'When did his wife pass away, again?'

'The following year, in 1996. Lucas would have been eleven then. Paul took it badly, had a mini breakdown and packed Lucas off to boarding school. Wonder if he did the same to Natasha. Bet he did. Poor buggers. They lost more than their mum. I don't know why parents do that. I couldn't bear to let any son or daughter of mine go away.'

Ross threw her an uneasy look but Robyn was focused on searching for more information about Lucas Matthews, his sister Natasha and fiancée Christina Forman.

At last she spoke. 'Nothing on Natasha Matthews. That's weird. Got some stuff on Christina Forman. Christina was definitely his fiancée. In July 2000 they were engaged but there was no wedding. I can't find any records of one taking place and in the autumn of that year, Paul Matthews turned down the biggest role of his career and dropped off the scene. The only other news items I can find are of him hiding his face as he goes jogging, or of his house. So, what happened to the fiancée? Where are you, Christina, and can you help me?' Robyn stared at the screen for a little longer before putting the name into a search engine. Then she tried social media websites: Twitter, Facebook and LinkedIn. She frowned. 'Nothing. I knew this wasn't going to be easy.'

'Robert isn't easy either. Still, I'll catch him at some stage. Sooner or later he's going to make a mistake and I'll be waiting. They all make mistakes in the end.'

Ross was right. They all made mistakes in the end and she would find Lucas.

An alarm beeped on her phone to remind her she had an appointment. This was something she couldn't put off so she shut down her computer and steeled herself. She had a little girl to visit.

CHAPTER TEN

Abigail directed her white Evoque out of the car park and into the busy town, her mind racing with possible scenarios that might unfold if she confronted Jackson. She needed to look at his face and know this was just a prank. Surely she would be able to tell if he was messing about with someone else. He had been fully hers that morning. He was waiting for her back home. Jackson wouldn't cheat on her. Someone behind blew his or her horn. She shook herself from her daze and realised she had been sitting at lights that had already turned green. She needed to get a grip or she'd have an accident.

Izzy was strapped in her baby seat in the back of the car and had nodded off, thumb in mouth, oblivious to her mother's plight. Abigail turned briefly and took in the long dark eyelashes, just like Jackson's, and the sweet, contented face of her child. A hot salty tear trickled down her face. This wasn't happening. She and Jackson were sound.

When Izzy first came home from hospital, she had needed undivided attention and Abigail had spent night after night cuddling her precious bundle in the nursery, sitting in the large chair by the cot, singing softly to her little miracle. But Jackson hadn't objected to her absence. He'd even sometimes strolled in to watch them both. He'd stood by the door and smiled at them.

Izzy hadn't settled into a routine though and instead of beginning to sleep through the night, she cried and cried, tormenting Abigail who spent hours trying to coax her to sleep. Izzy didn't settle for four months and when Abigail had returned to their bedroom she'd felt so tired; she hadn't welcomed any of his advances. She told herself there would be time later for all of that. Then Izzy began to teethe and it started over again. And more recently there had been the note that had been delivered by hand, posted through her letter box. At first, it seemed to be an innocuous white envelope, but the contents chilled Abigail to the bone. She had hidden it in her bedside drawer, too frightened to tell Jackson. To tell him would be to reveal her whole life was a lie. The note contained words cut out from a newspaper:

KEEPING SECRETS LEADS TO UNHAPPINESS AS YOU WILL SOON FIND OUT.

Added to this there was the recent call. If the individual had been telling the truth, why couldn't Jackson have talked to her first about their lacklustre love life instead of having some sordid affair? Abigail swatted at another tear and braked hard to avoid colliding with the vehicle in front that was now turning left. *Concentrate*, she told herself.

She needed to navigate the roundabouts that lay between here and Hartley Witney, where she lived. The road was as busy as always, filled with commuters and people who worked in the air industry. She and Jackson had moved here when he had started up the business. They hadn't wanted to live in busy Farnborough or some of the surrounding towns, but preferred the village feel of Hartley Witney with its village green and duck pond with a charming thatched duck house. It was only eight miles away from Farnborough.

Jackson had put a lot on the line to set up and run BizzyAir Business Aviation– a commercial airline aimed at wealthier people or businessmen who wished to fly privately. He had risked their new home, which had cost them a fortune. Luckily, it was a gamble that had paid off handsomely and now they no longer had a mortgage on their beautiful, five-bedroomed, detached house.

Her route took her past Minley and the impressive Minley Manor, a Grade II listed country manor built in the French style in 1850 by Henry Clutton. When they first arrived in the area it had belonged to and was used by the Ministry of Defence as an officer's mess and had also been used as a film location for several blockbuster movies before finally being sold by the MOD to an international investor. She reminisced about walking around the vast grounds there before it was sold and around Hawley Lake with Jackson, admiring the huge rhododendron bushes. He had joked that maybe one day they could afford to buy it but with a price tag of five million pounds at the time that didn't seem likely. They had laughed at the prospect but Jackson had assured her that one day they would be able to afford their very own Minley Manor.

That seemed a lifetime ago. She entered the village, passed the rows of shops and houses before turning off the high street. Smart houses stood behind leafy hedges and trees. She wasn't far from her house. She grappled to regain control of her emotions as she turned into her road, the sense of familiarity assisting as she drove past houses she had driven past every day for years, their neat lawns and hedges trimmed by professional gardeners while the occupants of the homes fought with other daily commuters on the drag to London and worked all hours. She was lucky she and Jackson did not have lives like that. His hours were difficult at times but he did not have to catch trains or drive for hours and come home drained. And he never brought work home with him. He always had time for Izzy and her.

Izzy stirred as if she too knew she was home, and she gave a half smile in her sleep. Abigail breathed out, feeling more relaxed.

It was going to be okay. Jackson would be there waiting. He'd be pleased she had returned early. He'd play with Izzy or maybe they could go out to the petting farm. There was plenty of time to do that. She might even make a romantic supper for them afterwards and rekindle their earlier passionate session. Her pulse quickened as she neared the house towards the end of the lane. She could see its roof. She would make this right. The text was a hoax. It had to be. She turned onto the large front drive. The large stone owl – a wedding present from friends – that stood in the middle of their front garden gave her a mocking stare and she hunched over the wheel defeated. Jackson's Maserati was not in its usual space. He had gone out. The mechanical voice played in her head again. Maybe Jackson had gone to meet his lover.

CHAPTER ELEVEN

THEN

The front door opens with a clatter that wakes me with a start and my mum tumbles into the sitting room, her hair wild, and her coat already removed to expose a tight blouse that shows off her ample bosom. She is giggling and leaning into a bear of a man who has one huge, hairy hand draped around her shoulder; the other is groping at her backside, making her titter like a teenager on her first date. I groan inwardly. I should have gone to bed earlier but I was watching a film and forgot the time. Normally, I go to bed at eight. Mum says eleven-year-olds like me need their sleep. I think that's an excuse so she can bring home men without them being put off by a kid hanging around.

She spots me curled on the sofa, brushes away his hand and extracts herself from the arm of the large goon who has accompanied her. The man's attention is now focused on me and he stares at my bare legs as I move off the sofa, ready to leave the room. His tongue flickers from his mouth and passes over his lips as he tries not to gawp too hard but I know he is looking and what he is thinking.

'You should be in bed,' says my mother, a flicker of concern in her eyes.

'Sorry, I dozed off in front of the telly. I'll go now,' I reply and sidle past the pair of them and race for my bedroom, eager to get to sleep before the noises begin. Unfortunately, this man is overenthusiastic and it is not long before I can hear loud grunts coming from the bedroom next door and my mother's fake, high-pitched squeals of delight. It is

the same most nights. A different man but the same muffled squeals and groans of pleasure. I hate it. My mother sometimes emerges the next day with bruises on her arms and dark rings under her eyes. She is no longer as beautiful as she once was and she is nervous all the time. She's started smoking and drinks too much.

I tried to tackle her about the men but she laughed in my face and said, 'How else do you think we can afford to live here? Serving drinks in some bar isn't going to pay many bills. At least this way I can afford nice clothes and a better life.'

She refused to talk about it again.

'Here' is a semi-detached house near Birmingham. It is a vast improvement on the last flat and I have my own room, which is just as well given my mother's new occupation. I can't judge her too harshly though. I have brought this on us. This is the only way we can survive. She has to take on these 'extra jobs' to pay the bills. Her penchant for designer clothes hasn't helped the situation. If she didn't waste so much money on them we might be able to afford the other bills without her degrading herself. My father thinks the same. He grumbles frequently when he hears the noises. He and I don't discuss what is going on though. I am old enough to understand the situation but Dad is unwilling to share his opinion on the matter.

The man in her room tonight sounds like an animal. I don't want to think about what they are doing. I put my head under the cover to muffle the noises and eventually I begin to doze off again only to be woken by a light rapping on my door. I pull the covers up to my chin. A streak of light falls across the front of the room and the large man is silhouetted against the doorframe. He scratches his chin and says, 'Your mum's asleep. She needn't know about it. I'll pay you. I won't hurt you. Hundred quid. All yours. You can say no if you want.'

I ponder his question. At least he has asked my permission and a hundred pounds is a huge amount of money. I whisper, 'Okay' and lower the duvet to reveal my naked frame. He ambles towards the bed and removing his trousers and underwear, slides in beside me, pulling my trembling body towards him, caressing my face and stroking my hair. He breathes in deeply and sighs then curls a lock of my hair around his fat finger. He stares at me in the gloom, lit only by the digital display of my clock.

'You're so pretty,' he murmurs. 'Really pretty. I love pretty girls.' Small sour puffs of breath hit my face as he speaks but I force myself not to recoil. I lie as still as I can, waiting for this to be over. He grunts in approval. His chest is covered in dark curly hairs that make me itch as he rubs against me, his head travelling down my body until he finds my budding breasts with his lips. He is trying to be gentle. A shiver goes through me and I shut out what is happening. I focus only on the one hundred pounds that will soon be mine. I already know what I'll spend it on.

The act is painful but mercifully quick. The deed done, he hastens from the room, unable to look me in the eye any longer. I stare at the ceiling, my mind blank. I am numb inside. From the shelf beside the bed I hear Mr Big Ears speaking in angry whispers. I do not want to listen to my father but he tells me to remember this moment and store it up. He says it will make me stronger and it will fuel my hate. I take the money that has been thrown on the bedside table and lift a jewellery box from my drawer, listening to the comforting musical tune as a ballerina in a pink tutu gracefully pirouettes, before placing the money inside.

I pad silently to the bathroom where I lock the door, and clean the sticky bloody mess from between my legs. I stare at my reflection then reach for a pair of nail scissors from the cabinet. I watch my face, devoid of expression as I systematically cut my hair until all the golden tendrils have fallen in the sink then I turn the scissors onto my flesh and stab the top of my thighs until I have to bite my lips to prevent myself from crying out.

CHAPTER TWELVE

Robyn rang the doorbell. It chimed cheerily then there was an eager shuffling behind the door before it was unlocked. A woman appeared, petite with ebony hair that cascaded to her shoulders, and dark soft eyes, wearing a red dress with a belt which emphasised her wasp-like waist, a small smile lifting the corners of her mouth.

'What a wonderful surprise. Come in. Come in.' There was a trace of an accent that belied her French roots more noticeable as she shouted, 'Amélie, *chérie*. Come and see who is here.'

She kissed Robyn on both cheeks before ushering her down the hall and into the kitchen, rich in warm Mediterranean colours more fitting of the south of France than the Midlands.

'I can't stay long. I have to track down a missing person,' said Robyn, ashamed that she felt the need to escape so soon after arriving.

'Nonsense, you can't rush off immediately. We haven't seen you in months. Amélie will be so thrilled. At least stay for a coffee.'

Robyn nodded reluctantly. 'Just a quick coffee. I have to get on the road. I'll stay longer next time.'

Brigitte was always warm and welcoming but Robyn did not feel she had the right to be part of this family any longer. It had been different when Davies was alive. Brigitte gestured for her to sit down as she spooned aromatic ground beans into the top of a pewter pot, and filled the base with water before placing it on the hob. Brigitte had not left all of her traditions behind. She always insisted on offering strong percolated coffee served in small delicate cups and accompanied by biscuits.

When Robyn began seeing Davies on an official basis he had insisted she meet his ex-wife and daughter. In spite of her concerns, there had been no tension at all between the two women and his daughter had accepted her immediately. Before long, Amélie was spending weekends with Robyn and Davies. Robyn forced back the memories. Not everyone got to have a happy ever after. Those days were short-lived and, no matter how strong an attachment she felt to the girl, she reminded herself that Amélie was not her daughter.

Robyn dropped down on one of the kitchen chairs, painted in duck-egg blue to match the distressed cupboards. Brigitte was an artist who specialised in restoring and painting furniture.

'I guess she's excited about her birthday party,' said Robyn.

'Amélie has talked non-stop about Jump Nation. It's the first "grown-up" party she's had. It only seems five minutes ago she was into unicorns and Peppa Pig, now it's all Harry Potter, *Twilight* and One Direction. It's good she loves reading. I bet she didn't hear me call her. She'll have her nose stuck in a book and be lost to the world. I'll call her again in a moment.'

The room began to fill with the aroma of quality coffee. The pot began to bubble as the coffee percolated, making small put-put-put noises. Brigitte lifted the percolator from the hob, poured the steaming brown liquid into the thimble-sized cups then placed them onto the heavy wooden table that filled the kitchen. She moved the dried-flower display gracing the centre of the table and replaced it with a tin of finger-sized French biscuits before sitting down opposite Robyn. Brigitte took a sip of her coffee, giving an imperceptible nod of approval. 'So, how are you?' she asked.

'Okay. Busy. I've returned to the police force. I'm training for a ten-kilometre race and I've got an interesting case to work on.'

'That's not what I mean,' replied Brigitte, setting down her cup and pushing the tin of biscuits towards Robyn. Robyn took one and nibbled on it before speaking again.

'I get by. I keep hoping it'll get easier.'

'It will,' said Brigitte. 'It will but alas, I don't know when. I miss Davies too but it is so much harder for you.'

Robyn was reluctant to continue the conversation but Brigitte was not one to hide her feelings. 'Have you started dating again?' she asked suddenly.

'Heavens no!' replied Robyn. 'No way. I couldn't…' she said.

'But why not? It's been over a year and you are an attractive woman. You can't want to hide yourself away forever.'

Brigitte's blunt tone unnerved Robyn and she silently cursed the French gene that allowed Brigitte to be completely at ease discussing feelings and sensitive matters and her own stiff British gene that left her uptight and unwilling to talk.

'It's not right for me,' she said. Brigitte surveyed her through clear navy eyes that seemed to search her very soul before nodding. 'Maybe you need more time. He wouldn't have wanted you to mourn him forever, you know. He was a very practical man.'

Robyn agreed with that. Davies was not a soft, mushy man. He was stoical but she couldn't imagine even looking for someone else. No one could replace him. He had been her soulmate.

The kitchen door opened and a slight girl with shining eyes and dark brown hair interrupted their conversation, her mouth widening into a smile as she saw who was in the kitchen.

'Robyn!' she exclaimed, rushing over and throwing her arms around her. Robyn felt a familiar ache. Amélie looked so much like Davies, the same nose, the same wide, gentle eyes, the same thick dark hair and the smattering of freckles sprinkled across her cheeks.

'It's been ages since you visited. Have you heard about my birthday party? Are you coming to it? We're going to Jump Nation.

The place with all the trampolines. All my friends are coming. It's going to be awesome.'

Robyn returned the smile. 'I have heard about it and it will be awesome but I can't come as I have to work. However,' she added, seeing a flash of disappointment cross the child's face, 'I've got an early birthday present for you.' She handed over a coloured gift bag she had brought in with her.

'Can I open it now?' She looked across at her mother who nodded her consent. The girl delved into the bag pulling out a parcel wrapped in silver and white. She tore open the paper and squealed in delight. 'It's a Fitbit Alta. Oh my gosh! I really wanted one of these. Toni Clarkson has one and it's wicked. It tells you how many calories you've burned and works out how far you've walked and even tells you if you've had enough sleep. I love it. I love purple too.'

The women watched as the girl put on the stylish purple band, her face glowing with excitement. 'Robyn, thank you. It's fabulous. Mum, can I wear it to my party?'

'Yes, but not on the trampoline, *ma belle*. In case it breaks.'

Amélie hugged Robyn again and kissed her on the cheek. 'I must show my friends on Snapchat,' she said. 'They'll be so envious. Back in a minute.' She scampered off, leaving behind smiles.

'Thank you for buying such a lovely present,' said Brigitte. 'She's really into healthy living even though she's so young. I'm sure she'll want to wear it all the time. It is hard to think she is eleven now. She will soon enter the dark world of teenage years and heartbreak and change.'

'She'll be fine. She has a sensible head on those young shoulders.'

A frown flitted across Brigitte's smooth forehead. 'She still misses her father but she understands he's gone forever. She has come to terms with it. Of course she has me and she has Richard,' she purred his name as only a French woman could. 'At least she knew Richard before Davies…' She hesitated, choosing words that felt appropriate. 'Before Davies was taken from us all. At school this year they had to draw a Father's Day card and she made two. One for Davies and one for Richard. We all went to the cemetery and placed the card for Davies on his grave.' Her eyes filled. 'It was emotional but I think it helped her. She has been more settled since.'

Robyn put a hand on top of Brigitte's and left it for a moment. After a moment, Brigitte murmured, 'I miss him too. He was such a good man.'

'We're going to France after my birthday for the holidays,' said Amélie, re-entering the kitchen, her Fitbit now on her arm. 'Would you like to join us? Grandma won't mind. Her house is enormous. You could meet Pipette and her kittens.'

Robyn was touched. 'I'd love to but I have to work. And talking of work, I have to rush off. I have to interview someone.'

Amélie looked disappointed. 'What a pity. I wanted to show you my iPhone. It's on charge upstairs at the moment.'

'Next time, I promise,' Robyn added, standing to leave.

'Thank you for the present. I can't wait to show Florence. She's my best friend. She's going to be so jealous when she sees it.'

Both Brigitte and Amélie accompanied her to the door. 'Send my regards to Richard, won't you?' Robyn said, once Amélie had hugged her goodbye.

'I shall, and Robyn, look after yourself. Don't be a stranger. You are always welcome here, you know.'

Robyn nodded. It was true but nevertheless she did not feel she deserved to be part of this family. Davies was gone and with him he had removed her right to be involved. Amélie had parents and grandparents who loved her. Robyn could only ever be on the periphery. As she pulled off the drive, waving at them both, she knew it would be some time before she returned. There was only so much pain she could handle.

CHAPTER THIRTEEN

Abigail carried Izzy into her bedroom. She had settled back into a slumber and had not stirred even when removed from the car seat. Abigail laid her in her cot; pausing to take in the tiny fists bunched up next to the face she loved so much, before heading for the kitchen. Toffee, her Persian cat, appeared from nowhere and, purring rhythmically, wound figure of eights around his mistress, rubbing his damp nose against her legs to welcome her. She bent to stroke the animal. 'At least you're here to greet me,' she whispered into Toffee's fur.

The kitchen looked much as it had done before she left except for a dirty mug and plate in the sink. Jackson hadn't even bothered to put them in the dishwasher in his haste to get out of the house. She felt a prickle of annoyance. Toffee became more insistent and nudged her again. She ripped open a pouch of food and squeezed it into his dish. He eagerly nosed at it, taking dainty bites. Standing up, she felt a little queasy. She steadied herself against the kitchen top and spotted a yellow Post-it stuck on the kettle that read,

Sorry Abby.
James is ill so they need me to work. Don't wait up. Probably won't get back until tomorrow morning.
X

James was one of the firm's pilots – a recent addition to the team. She recollected Jackson mentioning him only recently. She reasoned it was quite feasible James had not been well enough to fly. Had

Jackson really stood in at the last minute? She didn't have James's phone number or she might have checked to see if he really was off work. Her stomach gurgled loudly. She was definitely feeling off colour. It was probably all the anxiety of the anonymous phone call. She racked her brain to remember what Jackson might have said about the new pilot and came to the conclusion that he had kept fairly quiet about him although he had spoken regularly about his other pilots. Jackson often flew with Stu Grant and Gavin Singer, both of whom were close friends.

Gavin had been at BizzyAir since the outset and started as Jackson's first officer before becoming captain on the fights. He was married to Sarah, a lawyer, who often joked that he stuck with her and her ridiculous work schedule because he knew he could never afford to divorce her.

Stu Grant was unmarried and devoted to flying. He had dumped his job as an engineer in his thirties and put himself through flying school. He relished every opportunity to fly one of the aircraft at BizzyAir and was often in the crew room even when not on duty. A timid man who was teetotal, he rarely socialised other than to pop around to see Jackson and Abigail when invited.

Abigail meandered about the kitchen in a daze. She had no idea what to do next. She tried to call Jackson but his phone was off and she was redirected to the answering service. He always switched off when he was flying but today she wondered if he had done so for a different reason. She was trying to decide if she should phone Stu or Gavin to find out more about James when a rush of nausea sent her racing to the sink. She retched once, twice and brought up her breakfast and the latte from earlier. Her head suddenly felt hot and she began to feel disorientated. She needed to lie down. She heaved again. Her legs began to feel weak and buckled under her. She collapsed onto the floor, while waves of pain rippled through her belly making her groan.

Her mobile rang. She struggled to stand and take it from the kitchen top, hoping it was Jackson.

'Feeling off colour, Abigail?' The robotic voice taunted her as her stomach muscles spasmed.

'How do you know? Who are you?' she gasped.

'All in good time. This is only the beginning, Abigail.'

'Please. Don't do this.'

'Do what, Abigail? How can I possibly be to blame for your present condition? You've obviously picked up a bug. Pity Jackson isn't there. What a shame he's shagging his lover instead of mopping your brow!'

Another cramp doubled Abigail over in agony and the phone tumbled to the floor, trailing insane, robotic laughter behind it.

She desperately wanted Jackson to come home. She needed him. *Damn it! Where was he?* Her head swam with muddled thoughts and then a soft whisper of a child's voice saying, 'Bye, bye, Mummy' penetrated her foggy brain. She let out a weak cry of protest. An inner strength combined with the fiercest instincts drove her upstairs, inch by inch, calling, 'Izzy, I'm coming!'

She crawled into the nursery on all fours, sobbing, and saw a figure standing in the shadows. She slurred, 'Get away from her,' and launched herself at the cot with what strength she had. The figure moved towards her but Abigail's vision began to narrow as little by little it was eaten away at the edges by black dots until they joined together and she drifted out of consciousness and slumped against the cot.

* * *

She was not sure how long she had been out of it but wails from Izzy finally roused her. It took a Herculean effort to raise her body from the floor. Izzy was screaming hysterically, her face screwed up and crimson through effort.

'It's okay,' Abigail murmured, trying to ignore the awful nausea that had left her weakened. Izzy was not easily placated and writhed from side to side, clenching and unclenching her fists. She continued to scream at full volume, making Abigail's pulse quicken.

'It's okay, my baby girl. Mummy's here.' She leant into the cot and recoiled at the pungent aroma that rose to greet her. The smell made Abigail gag and she had to wait a moment before she could lean in again. Izzy continued to howl. Abigail finally lifted her, her face wrinkling in disgust. Izzy had made a horrible mess that had filled her nappy. Her dress and the bed sheets were covered in runny excrement. Abigail fought back the urge to be sick again. Her baby needed her. She rubbed the child's back and made soothing noises then carried Izzy to the bathroom where she cleaned her, then changed her clothes and held her, even though she felt drained. The screams abated and then the sobs subsided as Izzy calmed down.

Abigail stumbled back to the nursery and sat in the chair beside the cot, like she had done on many a night. As her child drifted off to sleep, she sat trembling, recalling the whispered voice she had heard and the person she had thought was in the nursery. There had been no one. She reasoned that both had been figments of her turmoiled imagination that left her disorientated and frightened. This bug, or whatever had taken hold of her, was to blame. She figured that the mind was capable of playing tricks, especially when the body was shutting down. And it was true to say she was overprotective when it came to Izzy. She might have dreamt up the scenario – a product of a fevered mind. Or, she was beginning to unravel. The phone call and note had shaken her. Her marriage might be in jeopardy, and someone was spying on her. Her stalker was real and had somehow known she was ill. What was this person capable of? She ought to confide in Jackson. But now, she was no longer sure she could trust him. This could be some plan dreamed up by him and a lover to send her mad. Her confused mind could find no answers, and plagued her with wild ideas until she too dozed off. The sound of a ringtone penetrated her jumbled dreams in which a ghastly clown face loomed over her, laughing like the person on her phone. It was her mobile again. She had unconsciously picked it up and now it was in her pocket. She looked at the number and gave a relieved sigh.

'Hey! Hope I'm not disturbing your hot date with Jackson,' said Claire. 'I wanted to let you know you left Izzy's new teddy bear behind and I have it here. Don't want Rachel to think you didn't like it.'

Abigail fought back the sob of relief. 'Claire. Jackson had to go out on a job. I can't get hold of him. Claire, I need you. Can you come around?'

'Sure. You okay? You sound awful.'

'No, I've picked up a horrendous stomach bug and keep being sick. Izzy's sick too.'

'Izzy! Oh my gosh! You poor things. I'll come straight over. Don't worry. I'll be there in a jiffy.'

Abigail laid back – her energy spent. Claire would help her. She'd look after Izzy while Abigail rested. She felt so weak. Another rush of nausea hit her and she heaved but there was nothing left in her stomach. A hazy thought hit her as she slumped on the floor next to the playpen: she could trust Claire. Wherever Jackson was, he wasn't with her friend.

CHAPTER FOURTEEN

Wisps of cirrus cloud, painted by nature's artistic hand, stretched across a deep blue sky as Robyn travelled towards the Farmhouse, Paul Matthews' home. An elderly lady, Geraldine Marsh, who cleaned for Paul Matthews, was looking after the house. Robyn had succeeded in tracking down a phone number for her and had arranged to speak to her at the house.

The navigation system in her car could not locate the area she needed but Geraldine had given her explicit instructions of how to get there. Her directions consisted of navigating via various pubs and shops but they were accurate and Robyn soon passed through the quaint village of Abbots Bromley towards Uttoxeter, before turning down a lane that led onto an uneven track and finally to the Farmhouse. The house was isolated, one side shrouded by woods and the other overlooking fields and the large reservoir in the valley. Paul Matthews had indeed enjoyed solitude. There were no neighbours for some distance.

An old-fashioned 'sit up and beg' bicycle with a front basket was propped up against the wall. Given there was no car to be seen, Robyn guessed it was Geraldine's mode of transport. She must be fit to climb the hill to the house on it. Robyn lifted the heavy iron knocker and let it drop with a loud clatter against the door of the house. Within seconds, a large woman with a round, healthy face and florid complexion brought about by a map of broken veins on her cheeks, opened the door and introduced herself as Geraldine

Marsh. She could have been any age from sixty to eighty, with steely grey hair arranged in an old-fashioned bun, and sharp hazel eyes that looked Robyn up and down before allowing her to enter. Robyn showed her warrant card, which the woman examined thoroughly before pointing towards a door down the hall.

'Best off in the kitchen,' Geraldine said. 'It's the friendliest room. I don't much care for the huge reception rooms in this house. They're utilitarian. Mr Matthews never used them. Waste of space, if you ask me. I prefer cosy sitting rooms or kitchens. They're far more intimate. Who wants to sit in massive conservatories shouting across the room at each other?'

The kitchen was a mismatch of modern amenities including a coffee machine that would not look out of place in a coffee shop. There was a large American fridge with ice-making facilities and a control panel that would confuse a computer programmer, along with an Aga stove that she doubted had been used in years, and an ancient rocking chair, handles worn shiny through use, tucked away in one corner of the room.

The place smacked of confusion. It was no longer the house it had once been. The large island in the centre of the room must have been used as a family breakfast table but now the granite top was covered with magazines, laid neatly in several piles. No one ate here any more. Off the room was a smaller room – a snug. It boasted a fireplace but a dark screen had been placed across it, suggesting it was no longer lit on cold evenings. A black leather chair faced a unit containing a television and a DVD player. Beside it lay a small pile of DVDs. Robyn glanced at the titles. They were all nature documentaries. A bookcase filling the other wall housed more DVDs – a few comedies, action films and documentaries – and a large number of books, mostly hardbacks, arranged according to size. Paul Matthews was an avid reader of autobiographies and non-fiction. The room was clinical in its layout and lacked a feminine touch. There was nothing personal in the place – no ornaments, photographs, cushions or flowers. The plush curtains and thick carpet clashed in colour and pattern. Paul Matthews may have had money but he did not have any sense of interior design.

Geraldine Marsh offered her a stool to sit on and drew up another, letting out a sigh as she sank onto it. She peered at Robyn in a disapproving manner. 'Mr Matthews lived here alone. I don't know what more I can really tell you.'

Robyn adopted an appreciative expression. She had come across protective types before. Geraldine Marsh clearly thought highly of her employer. She looked around the room as if hoping he might reappear.

'I'm grateful for your time. As I explained on the phone, I'm searching for Paul's son, Lucas. He's gone missing and we're anxious to find out if he is okay. I was hoping you could give me some insight into the family that might help me locate him. I was rather hoping Lucas might have visited here in recent weeks.'

Geraldine wrinkled her nose as if a bad smell had permeated her nostrils. 'He came back recently. Surprised me, it did. It was a few weeks ago. I came in as usual and there he was, bold as brass, sitting in that chair.' She pointed to the rocking chair. 'I didn't recognise him at first but he still had that callous look he always had, and the glass eye, of course. Mr Matthews asked me to leave them alone to talk but he didn't look thrilled at Lucas being here. I didn't eavesdrop but Mr Matthews seemed quite agitated and I heard raised voices a few times. After Lucas left, Mr Matthews thumped about the place. He knocked the books off the bookcase, and broke a teacup by slamming it on the surface. He wasn't himself at all. Lucas had really annoyed him. I haven't seen him since. You'd think he be up here now, especially after what happened to his father. A fine man, Mr Matthews.' She extracted a handkerchief from her apron pocket and sniffed into it, eyes bleary with tears.

Robyn softened her tone. 'I am sorry. It must have been such a shock.'

Geraldine dabbed at the tears, grappling with her emotions. 'It was,' she said simply.

Robyn allowed the woman some time to control her feelings then asked gently, 'You mentioned Lucas had a glass eye, do you know anything about that? Did he have an accident?'

Geraldine snorted. 'Let me tell you about Lucas. He was a cocky young teenager when I first met him. I wasn't working here then but I lived in the village. It's a nice village. I've been there all my life. A lot of us have. We look out for each other. You don't get that in many places nowadays. No one knows their neighbours, do they? I love being able to cycle to the shops or go to the pub and have an orange juice or a bottle of stout with my friends; we're a close bunch although there are more outsiders now who have come in over recent years. They aren't as friendly.'

Robyn let the woman chat. Patience would pay off and Geraldine was beginning to relax. She wagged her finger as she spoke as if it would somehow help explain.

'Me and my husband Alf lived right beside the village green near the pub, the Goat, and used to go in there most nights. One evening, we discovered Mr Matthews had bought the Farmhouse. You can't keep something like that secret in our village. Well, he was a star, wasn't he? I watched all his films and never missed an episode of *Doctor Pippin*. I was so excited.

'Truth be told, it wasn't as exciting as we imagined. We hoped he would come into Abbots Bromley, send his children to the local school there and get involved with events, maybe even come to the annual Horn Dance festival we put on, but no, he kept himself to himself. He never once came into the place. We didn't see him or his children to start with. Interest fizzled out and he became "the actor who lived on the hill". Poor man.'

She pulled a white cotton handkerchief from her pocket and rubbed at her nose.

'I learned why we never saw him. It was such a sad story. I can see him now, his face all serious, telling me how much he had messed up his life. He had acted on impulse and bought the Farmhouse without even visiting it. He knows... he knew,' she corrected herself, 'that I'd never gossip about him. He told me he couldn't cope with the memories of his wife Linda in every room of his old house. She was a beautiful woman. Used to be a dancer before she married him. She got cancer and died. Neither of them expected it, and she went so suddenly it really shook him. For some time after she passed away, he spent his days wandering about the house, imagining he could hear her, or would drive to town and think he had spotted her. One day, he chased after a woman who looked just like Linda only to discover it wasn't, of course. The woman was quite abusive, even when he explained. Not everyone is sympathetic or kind,' she added, her lips curling at the thought. 'It messed with his mind and in the end he had to get away. He saw an advert for the Farmhouse in one of the glossy magazines and put in an offer. Just like that. That's how he ended up here.

'Anyhow, I am digressing. You asked about Lucas. After Mr Matthews moved here, he began having difficulties with his son. He couldn't keep him under control. Lucas was rude, surly, aggressive even. Mr Matthews made the decision to send him to boarding school so the boy could have some consistency in his life. Paul felt he had failed his son. At the time Paul was still working and trying to combine his career with looking after the children. It was all too much for him on top of the death of his wife. He believed Lucas would be better off away in a stable environment with other boys. It cost a fortune to keep Lucas there and all he learnt was how to answer back and get up to mischief. During school holidays he'd come into the village and sit in the bus shelter drinking alcohol and smoking and generally being rude to people. He used to hang about with a couple of other ne'er-do-wells from the village – Charlie Finder and Richie Turnbull. They left the village years ago. Charlie's in prison now, I hear. Anyway, they made the locals nervous. Then a few others from another village joined the boys in the bus shelter and it got out of hand. Some nights they'd play music loudly and others they'd fight. Our house overlooked the bus shelter and one evening, Alf and me noticed a car – a black BMW – pull up, and a chap wound down the window and handed out packets of something to the kids. We were sure it was drugs. Lucas seemed to be the ringleader. He strolled up to the car, leant in, took the packet, stuck his finger in and licked it, then handed the man some money. We rang the police but there was no evidence and Lucas denied it and so did the other boys.

'I wished we hadn't reported it. For a few weeks afterwards they congregated on the path right outside our front window and stared in at us. They did nothing but stare but it was awful. Alf went out to tell them to clear off but one of the lads laughed, spat at him and called him "an old git". Lucas didn't say anything but I had the feeling he was behind the harassment. Charlie Finder said they weren't doing anything wrong and we could call the police if we wanted. We didn't, of course. We didn't want any more trouble. I told Alf to ignore them and that's what we did. They stopped soon after.

'The next school holidays Lucas didn't come into the village. I think the boys started going into Uttoxeter or Burton-upon-Trent to cause mischief instead. Then I heard that Lucas had had an accident and was in hospital. Mr Matthews sent him on to a private hospital in London and paid for a top surgeon to treat him but they couldn't save his eye. Mr Matthews never spoke about it but there was talk in the village that Lucas had been out of his head on drugs and managed to stab himself with a sharp implement when his father was out for the night.'

'Lucas wasn't here when you started working for Mr Matthews?'

Geraldine shook her head. 'He had left home for good by then. I think the rift between him and his father had grown too big for them both and between you and me, I think Mr Matthews suffered a breakdown. The house was in a terrible mess when I arrived. There was plenty of evidence that he drank heavily too. I feel bad telling you all this,' she said, 'but if it helps you find his son then I suppose it's okay to tell you – what with you being a police officer.'

Robyn gave her a small smile of encouragement. The woman took a long breath before continuing, 'He stopped drinking suddenly. He became one of those health-conscious people overnight. I left him on Friday night sitting in that chair,' she pointed to the black leather chair, 'in jeans and an old tatty jumper, slumped in front of the television with a bottle of whisky by his side and came in Monday morning to find him dressed in a tracksuit and trainers, about to jog around the woods.

'He said, "Morning, Geraldine. I've turned over a new leaf. I'm not going to mope about any longer. I've chucked out the last of the whisky." And he never touched a drop again to my knowledge. After that, he spent a lot of time in the garden or by the reservoir birdwatching, or jogging. There are some wonderful routes around the reservoir. He used to take the path from the back of the house through the woods and then join a path that ran right around the edge. It's so peaceful there too.' She paused, her eyes filling up with tears.

Robyn waited for a moment then changing the subject asked, 'Have you seen Lucas in the village or in the area at all in recent weeks, apart from the day he was here?'

'No.' She looked around the house with red-rimmed eyes. Robyn could see that Geraldine had lost more than an employer. Looking after Paul Matthews had been her *raison d'être* and soon there would be a hole in her life that she could not fill. Robyn felt sorry for the woman.

'Did you know Lucas's sister too?'

Geraldine pulled a face. 'Natasha? She was a strange creature. People in the village said she was a vampire, what with her white face and black clothes. She came to the village once, to the store, but I believe that was the only time. She was a very peculiar girl. She was sent to boarding school at the same time as Lucas. It was an all-girls school, as I recall, in the south somewhere. She left home as soon as she'd completed her exams and hasn't been seen since. She's never contacted her father. What a family, eh?'

Robyn pursed her lips and blew quietly. She wasn't making much headway. 'Is there anything at all you can tell me about Lucas that might help me? Is there a mobile phone or laptop that Paul might have used to contact him?' she asked.

Geraldine shook her head. 'He didn't have a mobile phone. Didn't much care for them. There is a laptop but it's not in its usual place. He had been using it more than normal the last few days before the accident. I haven't seen it since.'

The doorbell rang, interrupting their conversation. 'Excuse me a minute,' said Geraldine, leaving Robyn alone in the kitchen. Robyn glanced at the pile of magazines in front of her. They were stacked in piles but one was open wide at pages featuring a photographic competition. There were some excellent entries of birds from puffins to common garden birds, but the winning shot was of a magnificent marsh eagle with wings forming a shallow V as it flew above a body of water, a small sparrow clutched in its talons. Paul Matthews was obviously into his birdwatching. Below the photograph was a small picture of the winner, a plain-faced woman in glasses, Miss Zoe Cooper, from Farnborough. Robyn looked around the room again. She wanted to get her hands on Paul's laptop but she couldn't see it anywhere. She could ask for a warrant and search for it but that would take time. A rustling alerted her to the return of the housekeeper.

'That was the farmer. He wanted to know if he should cut the hedges. According to Mr Matthews' wishes, the house is up for sale and all proceeds go to charity but I'm to stay on and look after it until it is sold. He left me a lovely settlement. Enough to pay off the mortgage on my house and have a nice holiday.' She pulled a handkerchief from her sleeve and dabbed at moist eyes. 'He was such a kind man. He deserved better.'

'So the house hasn't been left to his children?'

'No. And why should it? I blame them. Those children of his, they are the ones who really broke his heart.'

'And you don't know where his laptop is?'

'I'm sorry I can't help. He leaves it here.' She gestured towards the island. And, I never move anything. I leave it just as he wants... wanted it. I remember he was using it the day before the accident because he asked me if I knew anything about Hampshire. He was planning on a few days away in Farnborough. "Going to look up someone," that's what he said. I was speechless: after all, he wasn't one for company. I told him I've not even been to London, let alone Hampshire. We laughed at that. And he told me I should go and watch a show in London. He said I'd like *Chicago*. Maybe I should go. In his memory. As a sort of tribute,' she added, looking down at her damp handkerchief. 'Sorry, but I don't know what happened to the laptop. If I find it, should I let you know?'

'Yes please. It would be most helpful.'

Robyn left shortly afterwards. There was no more to be gleaned from the woman. She had begun to get a picture of the Matthews family. Even though Geraldine Marsh had not been able to give her much information about Lucas, Robyn felt she was onto something. Maybe Paul Matthews had been making arrangements to meet Lucas in Farnborough in Hampshire.

She took the route that Paul Matthews had followed the day he died. It led down to a road, over a gate and into the woods in front of the reservoir. According to a sign, she was now on the Blue Route and she breathed in the heady scent of pine and crunched over carpets of dead leaves fallen from the mix of broadleaf and coniferous woodland including English oak, sycamore, maple, birch and larch. A persistent loud tapping alerted her to a woodpecker searching for grubs and in the distance she could make out the occasional cry of a pheasant. It was pleasantly fresh in the woods. She could understand why Paul Matthews had chosen to live here, away from everyday madness. At the far end of the route, she came across a feeder-station and hide hidden among the trees. Several tits had settled on the nut feeders there. No doubt Paul had spent a few hours here watching the birds.

She joined the Yellow Route at a stone trough and cut through a wildflower meadow where a few cornflowers, daisies and poppies raised their heads above the wild grasses which swayed in a light breeze, before entering Stansley Wood, where she followed an undulating path that rose above the reservoir. Soon she came across a small posy of wild flowers in a jam jar beside a tree. She wondered if Geraldine Marsh had put them there. It no doubt marked where Paul Matthews had tumbled and died. He had at least died in a beautiful spot. After paying her respects, she continued along the route and passed the 'petrified pond' where the scenery changed dramatically. She marvelled at the view of the magnificent reservoir, its water a deep inky blue. Several swans swam by the edge, bobbing occasionally for food before gliding across the water, making no ripples. There were wading birds searching in the shallower waters. She didn't know much about birds but there were plenty here including many Canadian geese. A buzzard soared above her head. She couldn't help but feel she was missing something back at the house. Something wasn't sitting right. But she couldn't put her finger on it.

CHAPTER FIFTEEN

THEN

I knew as soon as I entered the playground that it was going to be a difficult day. I could see them, waiting by the school entrance, watching my every move like vultures waiting to descend on a human carcass.

Becky Stone is the ringleader. I call her Beaky because she's always sticking her nose in other people's business. Beaky has hated me from the first day I was introduced to the class. Mrs France, all smiles and pretend matronly concern, ushered me into the room of twenty-five pupils, their cold stares doing nothing to make me want to like them. I glowered back.

'Try and make her feel welcome. Becky, maybe you could show her around the school at breaktime?'

Beaky marched about the school, pointing out where everything was then left me. 'I don't want to be your friend,' she hissed as she headed back to her cronies. 'We all know what sort of person you are.'

I was mystified. They couldn't possibly know what sort of person I was. I barely knew what sort of person I was. I did however know I would never want to be friends with any of those snooty cows. I was used to my own company. I would be fine without them.

Today, something was different. Beaky was standing by the entrance with a fat grin on her stupid, freckled, goody-two-shoe face. Her groupies copied her stance and all stared at me. They hissed as I walked by. I felt my hands tighten. I could wrap them around Becky Stone's neck and strangle her before they could pull me off her.

Throughout the day I sense a tension. It's as if Beaky wants to challenge me, goad me, but I am too clever for her and I sit away from her in lessons and disappear into the fields behind the school during lunchtime. But in the afternoon we have art and I am partnered with her, of all people. She sits next to me with her arms folded and a sullen look on her spoilt face.

The class has been given the task of making a poster for the annual best-kept-village competition. It is supposed to encourage everyone who lives in the village to keep it tidy until judges decide which out of the many villages that enter will win. I don't care which village wins. We've only been living in this place eight weeks and already I loathe it. I preferred the suburbs of Birmingham. We lived near the shops and I could move about without anyone noticing me. Here in this village, everyone notices an eleven-year-old girl out on her own. I have had to be stealthy and hide in the shadows. I wish we could leave. My mother, on the other hand, loves it. She thinks we are finally getting out of the financial pit we have been in. We're renting a bungalow on an estate. It belongs to my mum's new boss. He comes around a few nights a week, sometimes bringing several of his male friends with him. I am sent outside to roam the streets while Mum serves them drinks and looks after them. She doesn't want me in the house while they are there. I'm not entirely sure what she means by 'looking after them' but I have a fairly good idea.

'Do I have to?' Beaky whines when Mrs France makes her move her desk.

'You have to work together on this project. It won't hurt you to be apart from Maisie Johnson and Eve Hubbert for once.'

Beaky pulls a face behind the teacher's back and screws around to look at her friends who have already become too involved with the project to pay any attention to her. She shrugs and pulls out a large fluffy pink pencil case stuffed with coloured crayons and pens, then spots my avaricious glances and says, 'Don't even think about it. They're my pens.

You use your own. I don't want to catch your germs. You'll contaminate them.' She glances at my paltry collection that I have amassed. Mum never has enough money to buy me nice pencils so I only have a few I have come across dropped or left behind in various classes. I really shall have to steal some. Beaky scowls at me and announces, 'I have the best pens so I'm doing the writing.'

She leans across the paper and begins to draw large bubble-writing using various shades of purple, pink and orange. Her elbows fill most of the paper, making it impossible to work. Every time I try to work on my area she leans further forward, tongue out in concentration, and hogs the large sheet of paper. I sharpen my pencil to a fine point. If she doesn't move soon... Mrs France appears.

'That's very good, Becky,' she gushes, her piggy eyes taking in the gaudy colours. She'd have said anything Beaky did was very good. She's teacher's pet. Beaky smirks in an irritating 'Yes, I know it is' way and I grip my pencil tighter.

'Jody, what are you supposed to be doing?' I almost forget to answer. Jody is the latest name I have been given. Jody Farmer. What a stupid name. Mum insisted we changed them again when we came to the village so she is Samantha and I am Jody. She thought the names sounded 'wholesome'. What a joke. Neither of us fit that description.

'Dustbins,' I reply. 'Becky is just finishing here so I can draw dustbins.' Mrs France moves off, satisfied with my response. Beaky huffs but moves over. I ignore her and set to drawing rows of dustbins all in grey. It is therapeutic drawing bin after bin all in neat rows, all identical. Suddenly I feel a sharp elbow in my ribs. Beaky hisses at me to move over and give her space to finish the wording. I protest but Beaky states that because she has the best pencils and pens, there is no point in anyone else doing the artwork. I sit back in irritation. There is no way the stupid girl is going to let me contribute to the poster. Mrs France passes by again.

'Have you given up?' she asks. 'No, miss,' I reply. 'I'm waiting for Becky to finish so I can get back into my bin corner.'

Maisie, sitting behind us both, sniggers and mumbles something about it being the best place for me. Mrs France pretends she hasn't heard and moves away. Beaky sticks out her tongue at me. Maisie and Eve are now tittering behind me. I feel the curtain of red beginning to descend again. How I loathe all the stupid girls in the class with their silly bright bobbles in their hair and their high-pitched whiny voices.

Most of all I hate Beaky who is sneaky and cruel and spreads rumours about other classmates to her friends. Her mother is the local gossip who works in the post office and Beaky will be exactly like her when she's older – hard-faced and mean. I hate Beaky's mum almost as much as I hate Beaky. She accused me of stealing sellotape from the Post Office. I told her if I were going to steal something it wouldn't be a roll of useless sellotape. She made me stand in the back room and called the local community officer to search me. Of course, I didn't have any sellotape on me. Luckily I didn't have the Yorkie bar I had stolen either. I dropped it as soon as I realised she was onto me.

I glare at Beaky and hiss, 'You wait until after class.'

Instead of looking afraid she grins at me and squirms around to speak to Maisie. 'You're right,' she whispers. 'Jody should live in a bin. Did you hear about last night?'

My heart hammers. She couldn't possibly know. Not unless that mother of hers had seen what happened. I drop my head. Beaky is mean but surely she wouldn't share this latest information. Her mother would never have told her. Then she looks at me, sneering as she does, and I can tell that she knows.

'Jody spent the night on her doorstep by the bins. She got locked out by her mum.'

The girls make oohing noises, eyes wide open. Beaky's eyes glitter. She's been dying to share the next bit of information and I cringe inwardly and curse my mother.

'*But that's not all.*' *She lowers a voice in a conspiratorial whisper.* '*Her mum was discovered asleep in the playground by the swings. She was dead drunk with her knickers around her ankles.*'

There are gasps and looks of horror. This information is going to be spread around the school like wildfire and I shall be the butt of jokes again. I'm angry at whoever it was that spotted my mum and spread the news so quickly. I'm angry at Beaky for telling everyone but mostly I am angry with my mum. A rush of sadness overcomes me and I hear my father's voice telling me to ignore them. I lower my head. I won't let them see me defeated.

The class falls silent as Mrs France appears near our tables. As juicy as this latest titbit of knowledge is, they know better than to annoy the teacher by talking when they should be working.

I fume quietly, letting Beaky cover the entire poster with bright-coloured writing. I am reluctant to admit it is very eye-catching. Finally the lesson draws to an end. Our poster is chosen as the winner.

'*Well done, Becky and Jody,*' *says Mrs France holding up the poster. The class politely applauds and Beaky looks smugger than I've ever seen her. The bell rings to signal the end of the lesson and she files out with her stupid friends who congratulate her on a fabulous poster and go with her to watch it being pinned up for all to see. Thanks to all the attention she has forgotten to pick up her precious pencil case. No one spots me as I slide it into my bag and head off. English is the last lesson of the day and we are free to go home. I don't want to go back to the bungalow. I'm not sure whether my mother will be entertaining men or not. I head to the river where I sit on the bank and watch a pair of ducks bob for food.*

After a while, I pull out the pencil case and snap each pencil in half before weighing the entire case down with small stones and throwing it as far as I can into the water. I wish I could weigh Beaky Stone down with something and throw her into the river. My father, who I hear all the time now, whispers, 'Along with your mother.'

CHAPTER SIXTEEN

'Abby, Abby?' Claire spoke softly.

Abigail looked up from the chair. There was a taste of stale vomit in her mouth and her eyes felt like they had sand in them.

'Abby, are you okay?' Claire's face was white with anxiety. 'Come on, let me help you up. You need to get cleaned up.'

Abby blinked several times and then looked down at her expensive T-shirt now splattered with yellow and brown stains. It stank. 'Claire, I don't feel too good.'

'Come on, hun. Let's get you cleaned up and into bed. You'll be fine. You've got one of those twenty-four-hour bugs. Zoe had it a while ago. It's been doing the rounds. Up you get.' She held out a strong arm and helped Abigail up from the chair.

'Izzy,' she said, her mind racing with possibilities.

'Is fast asleep. Poor little mite. I don't think she got it as bad as you. She's out for the count though. Don't worry. She'll be fine. I'll make sure she gets plenty of fluids when she wakes up. Now, get undressed and get into the bath. I've put some of the bath oil I came across in the cupboard. Hope that was okay.'

Abigail acquiesced mutely.

* * *

It was several hours later when Abigail awoke once more. Her stomach felt calmer although she still felt disorientated and weak. She eased herself to the edge of the bed and gingerly stood, swaying slightly. The digital clock revealed it was 3.25 in the morning. She had been ill for over twelve hours. She needed to see how Izzy was.

The door to the nursery was ajar and glancing in she spotted Claire, fully dressed, slumped in the chair, with Izzy asleep in her arms. Claire's glasses were propped on the table next to her. Somehow she looked younger, more vulnerable without them. Abigail felt a surge of affection for her friend who had looked after them in their hour of need. Abigail moved away, and headed downstairs for a drink.

Claire had cleaned the sink and it smelt of lemons. As Abigail stood against it, sipping a glass of water, her mobile rang and she answered quickly, not wanting it to wake anyone. 'Why are you doing this?' she hissed into the phone.

'Feeling better?' answered the mechanical voice.

'Leave me alone or I'll get the police onto you.'

The voice gave a snort of laughter. 'I hardly think so.'

'I have evidence,' she said in a low voice. 'I have the note you sent me. The one you constructed from newspaper cuttings.'

'You could have set that up yourself. You don't have a postmarked envelope,' said the voice. 'You have a nice house, Abigail. I like the furnishings. They're very luxurious. No cheap furniture there. What a shame you'll lose it all. I'll contact you again soon. I'll leave you with the thought that while you've been sick, Jackson's been having a whale of a time.'

The phone went dead.

Abigail shivered. The person had been in her house. She climbed the stairs quietly. There was no sound from the nursery. She tiptoed into her own room and opened the bedside drawer. She knew it was gone before she looked inside. Her knickers that were normally laid neatly in lines now lay haphazardly in the drawer. She would throw them away and replace them. She ought to change the locks but how would she explain that to Jackson without telling him everything? And she couldn't do that. She would change the burglar alarm code and hope that would keep any further intruders at bay. She could always tell Jackson she felt it was prudent to change the code from time to time. Her heart sank as she acknowledged that someone had removed the note. It was no longer at the bottom of the drawer. Bile filled her mouth and she ran to the toilet.

Claire called through the door. 'You okay?'

Abigail emerged from the bathroom, wiping her face with a damp flannel.

'Better now.'

Claire yawned and stretched. 'I'll make you some tea.'

'No, you've done enough. Why not nip to the spare room and get some sleep?'

Claire peered at her myopically. 'If you're feeling better, I'd rather head off home. I have an early start tomorrow.'

'You sure? It's awfully late.'

'Yes. I'll need to get my camera and equipment ready. Izzy's fine. I gave her some water earlier. She's fast asleep. I put her in her cot.' Claire stared at a large photograph of Jackson and Abigail. They were wearing beanie hats and gloves and both laughing. 'I rang Jackson to let him know you were both sick,' said Claire in a low voice, 'but his phone went to the messaging service.'

'He turns his mobile off when he's flying,' explained Abigail.

'Surely he's reached his destination by now? Doesn't he stay in contact when he's away?'

'Depends what time of the night it is,' Abigail replied, feeling less confident than she sounded. Ordinarily, if Jackson were out overnight, he would telephone to chat to her if it wasn't too late when he landed, or at least send a text to tell her he loved her. It niggled her that he hadn't contacted her this time.

She forced a smile. 'He'll be back tomorrow morning and me and Izzy will both feel much better. Thanks to you,' she added.

'It's a good thing I decided to phone you about the teddy bear. Blast! I left it in my flat.'

'Don't worry. Izzy has loads of toys. She isn't going to miss the teddy. I'll pick it up from you when we next meet up.'

'Or before. Why not come around this week for coffee at my place? I haven't got a lot of work on until I do the shoot in Scotland and it would be great to have you over.'

'Okay. That would be lovely. It seems ages since you and I had time together.'

Abigail watched her friend leave then returned to the kitchen. She was no longer tired but still felt muzzy and confused.

Toffee uncurled from one of the kitchen chairs and gave a plaintive meow. She bent to pick him up, feeling his glossy fur across her face. He purred in contentment as she stroked his soft head, butting her when she stopped and gazing at her with trusting, amber eyes. Abigail was not at such ease. The nausea had departed, only to be replaced with a sense of impending doom.

CHAPTER SEVENTEEN

It was a warm, muggy night and Robyn was struggling to sleep. Her semi-conscious slumber was filled with troubled dreams that made her fling out arms and legs and groan quietly.

In the latest nightmare, she was wandering around the centre of Marrakesh, the Jemaa el-Fnaa. During the day it was the place of thousands of people, motorbikes, yellow taxis and horses crossing the medina from west to east and south to north. At night, it transformed into a melting pot of noises, smells and activity, as Gnaoua musicians, actors, snake charmers, storytellers, dancers, fortune readers and henna tattoo artists all jostled for space, and aromas of exotic spices and cooked food from the food and drink stands assaulted the senses.

In her dream, it appeared to be evening and she was headed to one of the streets behind the square that led into the medina, a labyrinth of market stalls, scents and colours. She knew she should not go into the area alone but an invisible thread had pulled her in that direction and ignoring the advice that rang in her ears, she strode purposefully towards the tiny streets. Davies had told her to wait for him at the hotel. It was not safe for her to navigate the souk alone, especially at night. He had warned her of danger there. Military intelligence sources had discovered a sect hidden within the city that was planning to plant bombs in the area. He was working with the authorities to apprehend the group who also intended targeting the UK. In spite of that knowledge she walked onwards. She put a hand on her stomach and felt a burst of pride and love for the child that was inside her. She couldn't wait to share the news with Davies. He was in the souk. She would find him and tell him, and together they would celebrate.

It was chilly in the streets behind the lively square and just as if someone had turned off a switch, she could suddenly no longer hear the musicians parping their trumpets or sense the lively buzz. The silence was eerie and within seconds the street fell into complete darkness. Shadows emerged from buildings and figures filled the narrow street. She cried out for Davies but there was no one other than the stony-faced Arabs who wagged their fingers at her for stupidly entering the medina. One man, much taller than the others and dressed in a long grey djellaba, a rifle slung across his chest, approached her. He towered above her, feet planted to block her route. She suddenly felt fear not just for herself but also for her child as she searched his face. The man resembled Peter Cross, Davies's superior. But the man in her dream was hostile, so unlike the Peter Cross they had met and dined with, and as he spoke, the face that looked so like Peter's melted away to reveal another under it, one whose mouth was a cruel slit and who bared his teeth, brown and cracked.

'You should not have entered the souk,' he snarled in Arabic. 'You were told not to. Now you must pay the price.' In one fluid movement his gun slid into his hands, he gripped it, turned and fired into the distance further up the street. The noise of the explosion rang in her ears for a few moments. The men melted into the street. Her eyes searched in the darkness for the target although she already knew who it was. A sob rose in her throat as flickering orange light from a lamp above a wooden doorway revealed a man prostrate on the ground. He wore the trousers and shirt of a westerner and she identified the shining, brown shoes he had put on that morning. Davies had been cleaning them when she left for her secret appointment with the doctor. She ran towards the man. It was definitely Davies and it was her fault he was dead.

The ground beneath her transformed from a path to a muddy swamp, and each step dragged her down, sucking her into its depth. The souk evaporated. The buildings vanished but she could still see Davies lying prone on the ground, a neat round, red hole in his forehead. Her legs became leaden and she couldn't reach him. She was now sinking in the mud that was up to her waist and still she sank. She screamed his name but she knew it was too late. He had gone.

Robyn woke with a start, face and head covered in sweat. It was stuffy in the bedroom. The damn dream had rattled her. She had not been to blame for Davies's death. Then why did she feel so guilty? She opened the window and stared outside. A large white moon cast light over the neighbourhood, illuminating it as if it were daytime. Stars filled the sky. Robyn watched as a fox made its way stealthily under a fence and into the garden bordering hers. It leapt gracefully onto a bin and pulled out the remains of a discarded chicken carcass, and then, dragging its find, headed back the way it had come. Robyn followed its progress as it stole past swings, trampolines and scattered garden furniture, navigating fences and leaping high to reach a garden only a few houses away from her own where it headed to a tumbledown shed in a neglected garden. A small snout appeared from under the building to greet her followed by another and with excited yelps they snuffled around their mother and her find. This maternal act filled Robyn's heart with an inexplicable sadness. Unable to deal with it she made her way into the spare room and putting on her jogging outfit and trainers she headed outside to run away the pain and anguish.

* * *

The next morning she dropped in at Ross's office. She only planned on staying for an hour or so. She was moving to police headquarters to continue the investigation. They possessed far more sophisticated software than Ross. She'd only been on the case two days but already it felt like it was moving too slowly. Ross was engrossed in writing a report, two fingers tapping at the keyboard, eyes glued to the screen as he concentrated on his typing.

Robyn slid into her usual seat and typed 'Farnborough' into the search engine.

Ross looked over. 'What are you up to?'

'You finished that report?'

He beamed at her, the corners of his smile lifting his cheeks. 'You shouldn't answer a question with a question but yes, I've finished the report and I am now off the case. Robert Brannigan is having a relationship with his friend Anthony Potter. His wife was not as surprised as I expected her to be. Anyway, that's sorted and if you need a hand, I'm all yours.' He picked up his e-cigarette and dragged on it. 'Although I'm sure you've got a crack team behind you.'

'Mulholland's got most of them tied up on a drugs operation so I'm flying solo at the moment. Your help would be welcome.'

'Any clues yet?'

'Not many. I'm looking at Farnborough in Hampshire.'

'Isn't that where the airshow is every two years?'

'You got it. I don't think aviation was Lucas's thing. All I have so far is that after many years of not speaking to each other, Paul and Lucas met up at Paul's house – once, that I can be sure of, but possibly more than that. Soon after that first meeting, Paul Matthews, who rarely left his house, decided he was going to visit a friend in Farnborough but before that happened, he fell over in the woods and died. I need more, Ross. I must find Paul's laptop to give me an idea of what they were up to.'

'So what are you going to do next?'

Robyn shut her eyes for a moment. Ross waited while she thought through the possibilities. She drew a deep breath and opened her eyes.

'We haven't got much to go on but if I could find that laptop, it might help. Geraldine is a good housekeeper but I bet she hasn't actually searched for it. As far as she's concerned it was always on the island in the kitchen so if it isn't there, it's gone. I think otherwise. I believe he was working on it before he went for the fateful run and left it somewhere else. I couldn't nose around while she was there but I happen to know the house is up for sale. I don't think I'd get a warrant to search the premises either. Mulholland is pretty snowed under and as far as she is concerned this isn't top priority. And I can't go back there posing as a buyer in case the cleaner is about and sees me. I don't suppose you could arrange an appointment for you and Jeanette to go and view it, could you? While you're there sneak around and see if you can find the laptop. You're very good at tracking stuff. A human bloodhound when it comes to lost items.'

Ross laughed. 'Just because I uncovered your car keys last week when you'd left them on my desk instead of yours.'

Robyn smiled at him. 'Well, that and the fact you are thorough. If anyone can find it, you can. That okay with you?'

'As long as Jeanette doesn't get any fancy ideas and think we're moving to a big house in the country, I'll do it,' he replied, the lazy grin still stretched across his face. 'I'll come up with some subterfuge, get her to distract the estate agent and sneak off.'

'Great. I'm going to find out more about Paul Matthews and Farnborough and then I'm going to the gym.'

Ross threw her a look.

'Don't you dare say anything. I have a marathon to run in a few weeks and I need to train.'

Ross made a sign of zipping his mouth. She sat back with a small sigh. It was true, she had signed up for a ten-kilometre charity run, but the real reason she was going to the gym was different. She wondered how long she was going to be able to keep running from the truth. She shook herself from such gloomy considerations and concentrated on her job.

Ross left her behind the computer where she read through newspaper articles about Paul's death. Geraldine had said Paul ran most days. He was a healthy man who looked after himself. It was most unfortunate he suffered a heart attack while running, but possible. Robyn mused further then dialled the number for Uttoxeter police station and, identifying herself, asked to speak to the officer who had been called to the scene when Paul's body had been discovered.

Sergeant Drayton came to the phone, a rustling of papers indicated he was checking his records from that night. He introduced himself then spoke slowly and clearly.

'Mr Matthews was discovered at nineteen hundred hours on July twenty-fifth by a member of the public,' he said. 'A Julian Crow from Abbots Bromley was walking his dog in the woods by Blithfield Reservoir and came across the body of a man. He immediately rang for assistance and although paramedics arrived quickly, Mr Matthews was declared dead at the scene.'

'The local newspaper said he had a heart attack. Is that correct?'

'No, it was not the case. It was thought he might have had a heart attack but the coroner later ruled that out. Obviously, there was interest in the late Mr Matthews, given his past career, and the local press was a bit too quick off the mark, shall we say? The article went to press before the correct verdict was announced. Mr Matthews actually died in slightly unusual circumstances, or a freak accident, whatever you wish to call it. He tripped and fell badly, hitting his head against a tree which resulted in his death.'

'Did you see the body?' she asked. 'I mean, before it was removed.'

Sergeant Drayton cleared his throat. 'I was on the scene within fifteen minutes. It was obvious Paul Matthews was dead. There was a significant amount of blood down the right-hand side of his head and temple and there were blood deposits on the tree next to where he had fallen. It was later confirmed that the blood on the tree bark matched that of Paul Matthews.' He coughed to clear his throat once more. 'On closer examination, I discovered both palms of his hands were grazed. There was a light powdery residue on both palms which we later discovered came from a birch tree he had grabbed in an attempt to prevent his fall. The coroner declared accidental death. It appeared Mr Matthews had been running over uneven ground and tripped on his own shoelace, falling forward heavily and banging his temple against another birch tree. The temporal artery was ruptured, resulting in immediate death.'

'There was no evidence to point to suspicious circumstances, then?'

Sergeant Drayton's voice became offhand. 'No, ma'am. I checked the area myself and there was nothing suspicious. The blood on the tree was a match for Mr Matthews' blood – type B positive,' he added. 'There was no evidence of a third party present at the time of death, and the head injury itself contained particles of tree bark and powder consistent with a fall against a tree.'

'Thank you, Sergeant Drayton. You've been most helpful.'

'You're welcome,' he replied. 'May I ask if you have reason to believe Mr Matthews died under suspicious circumstances?'

'No. I haven't. I am actually searching for his son, Lucas Matthews, who disappeared from his home just before this unfortunate accident, and I'm trying to establish any connection between the two events. It seemed logical to talk to the person who saw the late Paul Matthews at the scene of his death.'

'I see.'

'If you happen across Lucas Matthews in Uttoxeter please let me know. His wife is concerned about his disappearance. Details on him will be circulated to all stations and I'm in charge of the case, so give me a ring if you have anything.'

Robyn tapped her fingernails against the desk – a staccato rhythm that quickly ended. An Internet search confirmed that three of the major bones forming the skull are joined at the temple. A forceful blow could cave in this junction of the skull causing death. It appeared the late Paul Matthews had suffered an unfortunate accident. Robyn shook her head. Some folk really had no luck at all.

CHAPTER EIGHTEEN

THEN

That toffee-nosed Chloe Planter had it coming. The snidey cow is always surrounded by her adoring fans, laughing at those of us who don't fit in.

'Chloe, I love your hair like that.'

'Chloe, do you want to come over to my place this weekend for a sleepover?'

'Chloe, you played so well on Tuesday.'

'Oh, Chloe…' Until my brain screams at me and wants to shriek at them all and rip Chloe Planter's hair out of her pretty little head and smash my fist into her perfect face. I hate her. Not because she is so perfect but because she's one of those people who stirs things up then stands back with a smug expression, waiting for one of her hangers-on to take up the mission and ruin another kid's life.

I have been one of her prime targets ever since we moved here and I started at this school. I don't think my reputation can have reached the school here or she wouldn't have dared to single me out.

It all began in the changing rooms. I dread doing sports. Not just because I am not one of nature's athletes nor a team player but because the pre- and post-match routine of undressing in front of anyone, even chattering girls, sends me into one of my moods. I can't abide undressing in front of anyone. I can feel their eyes ripping away the layers of clothes as if they're peeling an onion and I know they'll laugh once they see what is hidden under the baggy shirt and loose-fitting skirt.

Then I don't know what I'll do. My mum used to write notes to keep me off sports but in the end, once the drink got hold of her and I had to shake her booze-addled body awake every morning, I began to fake her signature and write them myself. At my last school I had several bad colds, stomach aches, and a host of bizarre illnesses and mysterious rashes almost every week and I had to be excused from games. The teachers must have realised I was not ill but I think they were relieved not to have me on any squad – poor specimen that I am. I would be a hindrance to any team.

This secondary school was one of those modern-thinking places. The headmaster wears jeans and thinks he looks cool. He tries to 'get down' with the kids here but I see him for what he is. He doesn't care about any of us. He only wants his school to gain a good reputation then he'll get a new position at a top school where he'll earn more money.

Mum insisted we changed my name again. I've had three different names in the last four years. She's really fed up with me this time. She didn't want to move again. It wasn't really my fault. If Danny Windsor and his horrible friend hadn't trapped me in the corridor and tried to kiss me, it'd have been fine. Stupid Chris Edding put him up to it. Danny would never have kissed me if he hadn't been dared. Who'd want to kiss someone like me? I've spent the last few years transforming into the world's most unattractive girl. It's a shame because I didn't mind Danny. He'd been one of the only boys not to make any cruel comments about me. That day in the corridor, I had been on my way to English when Chris and Danny approached from the other direction. I didn't think anything of it at first until I saw the sneer on Chris's face. He nudged Danny with his elbow and muttered something. Danny grinned back. I was aware they were up to something because they looked around first to check it was clear and then converged towards me. Before I knew it they had pushed me against the wall and both were blocking me from escape. A panic rose in my chest. I could see the spittle fly from Chris's mouth as he spoke to Danny, a look of triumph on his face.

'Go on,' urged Chris. 'We dared you, remember. You can't back out.'

For a second, I just thought Danny was going to say something to me but he didn't. He licked his lips and hesitated. A range of emotions crossed his face, including disgust. I could see he didn't want to be near me. He disliked me as much as the other boys who called me a 'skank' and a 'minger'. Chris whispered again.

'Go on. You can do it. Kiss the ugly bitch.'

My panic transformed into something else and I felt a familiar anger. Danny lowered his head towards me, his lips ready to lock on mine. The next moment he let out a howl, his head shot back and blood poured down his face, through his fingers and splodged down the front of his white school shirt.

'Oh my God. You headbutted him! You're mental,' Chris shouted, dragging the bleeding Danny away. 'She's fucking mental,' he repeated as a classroom door flew open and Mr Dobbs, the deputy head, hurtled out of his room like a greyhound out of a trap. I've never seen a grown man move so quickly. He grabbed me by the scruff of my neck, not that I intended going anywhere. I was calmly giving Chris the evil eye and enjoying the fear now evident in his eyes. He wouldn't mess with me ever again. All the while I stared at him, poor Danny, covered in crimson blood, was groaning and crying at the same time.

No one believed my version of what had occurred. That came as no surprise. Danny and Chris stuck to their story that they stopped me in the corridor to ask if I knew what the homework had been for English and I had attacked them both for no good reason. I didn't care when I was suspended. My mum did.

'What is it with you?' she screamed for the umpteenth time as she marched me to the bus stop. 'Can't you be nice to anyone? I'm sick of having to move every time you cause trouble.'

I didn't like to remind her that she was the reason we left the last village. Once it had got out about her entertaining men, some offended local daubed our door with the word 'tart' and she was shunned by just *about everyone. In the end, she couldn't stand the icy stares and verbal abuse so we upped and left to another area where she's got work in a casino and where we live in a grotty flat over a kebab shop.*

We sat on the bus in silence. I stared out at the heavy, grey skies and watched the rain crying dirty tears down the filthy windows and wished I didn't ever have to go to school again. I talked to Dad about it. He said it was a bummer and I'd done the right thing headbutting Danny. He's usually sympathetic. He understands me so much better than my mum who was so cross I could almost feel her vibrating with anger. She'd head straight for her not-so-secret supply of vodka when we got back to the flat and would drown herself in an alcoholic haze, letting it numb the pain so she could forget she had bred a monster of a daughter. I, however, had nothing to numb my own pain.

Back at the flat, I threw my schoolbag onto floor and slumped on the settee waiting to be reprimanded. It followed the same pattern as usual. She cried and asked the same questions: 'Why had I ruined her life? Why couldn't I just try for once? What had she done wrong to deserve this life?' I couldn't answer any of the questions. I let her rant. She stopped once the alcohol warmed her veins and took the edge off her anger. Then she began the all-too-familiar trip down memory lane, mumbling about when she was beautiful and desired by good-looking men. She always ended up reminiscing about Paul Matthews and how her life might have been so different if it hadn't been snatched away from her by her own flesh and blood. At that point I usually zoned out. I knew she believed it was my fault that her life was in tatters but I knew differently and one day I would prove it to her.

Her drinking was becoming more frequent and each time she was drunk she would blame me for the mess that was her life. I don't headbutt other people as a rule but she had been forced to move twice before because of my antics. I can't help it. It's who I am. It's who I've had to become to survive.

* * *

Now we were trying a new life in the south, far away from Danny and his parents who had threatened to have charges pressed against me until my mother went round and pleaded with them not to. I don't know what she told them but that night she returned, face pinched and grey, and she marched past me in hostile silence before packing up our possessions. In the morning we were on the road again.

Here at Kelsey School there's a belief that every child can succeed. The staff believes each child should experience every subject and activity and become a 'rounded individual'. We all have to take music and art lessons regardless of our ability and of course we have to participate in sports. The teachers here do not accept requests from parents asking for their child to be let off games lessons.

I have developed a strategy where I undress in the toilets and change into my PE kit. This has worked well for me and I have done the same after games, waiting there while the girls showered and, chattering like parrots, get dressed again. In the mêlée, no one notices I have not showered with them. I slip away unseen. I am good at being a shadow – unnoticed. Or, at least I thought I was.

I'm sitting at the back of the biology lab, head bent over a book, pretending to read a passage about photosynthesis, when Chloe and her clan come in. She slings her backpack onto the front bench but remains standing, her friends giggling and whispering. Sally, her second-in-command, passes something to her and Chloe holds it behind her back. Chloe is one of those girls that everyone has to look at so when she flounces through the laboratory every boy and girl watches her progress.

'Something smells awful in here,' she declares, pushing back her long blonde tresses, wrinkling her nose and sniffing like a dog hunting for truffles. She stops in front of my desk and sniffs even more dramatically.

'It's coming from here,' she says as if I weren't sat there.

Then she whips out a bottle of perfume and sprays it liberally in my direction, making me cough and splutter. The class burst out laughing and someone applauds. I can't see who it was. My eyes are watering badly and I can hardly breathe.

'Dirty, disgusting girl,' she scoffs. 'You really should shower after exercising. You stink of rotten fish.'

Humiliation burns my cheeks and I almost leap up and grab her by the throat but the teacher comes in and after opening the windows to let out the smell of the perfume, the class settles.

I plot my revenge, aware I shall have to do something that will be stealthy and not involve me being expelled again

CHAPTER NINETEEN

The sound of a raised voice woke Abigail. Her mouth felt parched and her eyes gritty. For a while she was discombobulated, then she remembered the events from the day before. She'd been really ill and Izzy… She shot out of the bed and stumbled towards the nursery. Izzy lay fast asleep in her cot, her downy hair stuck up at an angle but her face looking contented.

From downstairs she could hear Jackson's voice. She felt some apprehension as she descended and wondered if the mysterious caller was right about her husband.

Jackson was on his mobile. 'I'm not a mind-reader. But it was only food poisoning. She wasn't at death's door.' There was a pause. 'Okay. I get it. She was really ill. Look, I'm going to go now. I've been up all night. I'm really tired. Yeah. Okay.' Jackson turned at the sound of the door opening, relief spread over his face. 'Angel. How are you? I am so sorry. My phone ran out of battery and I forgot to take my charger.' He strode towards her and enveloped her in his arms, kissing her on her forehead.

She accepted his embrace, unwilling to reveal her true feelings. 'It's okay,' she said. 'Claire came over. I feel better now and Izzy is fine too. I just looked in on her.'

Jackson stepped away. 'Claire's just been filling me in on it all on the phone. Are you sure you feel okay now? Shouldn't we go to the doctor and get you both checked over?'

'What did Claire say?' asked Abigail.

He heaved a sigh. 'Oh, she thinks I'm a terrible husband for not being here when you needed me. And she's right. I should have remembered my phone charger. I was in such a rush when I left. It was all last minute. Claire ripped me off a strip for not phoning you and went off on one about not having another number for me if anything awful had happened.'

'Pity the hotel didn't have a spare charger,' said Abigail lightly.

'I didn't stay in a hotel,' he said. 'I spent the night at the airport on some very hard seats, waiting for my clients to return.'

He gently lifted a strand of hair away from her eye where it had fallen and looked into her eyes. 'I'm sorry I wasn't around for you. Operations phoned as soon as you left for town. I was the only pilot free to take over from James. We had some important clients to fly to Spain. We couldn't afford to lose the contract we have with them. They are good customers. But, if I had known you'd fallen ill, I'd never have gone.'

His eyes were filled with anxiety and sadness. She couldn't believe he was acting. This had to be genuine. The cruel phone call was a hoax. Jackson would not cheat on her. He took her hands in his and spoke again. 'Look, it's been a long night and I have to go back to the airport later. I really am pooped and I need a shower. I'm sure you could do with some more rest and Izzy is asleep. Why don't you come back to bed and wait for me, then we can snuggle up together for a bit?'

She nodded, even though she wasn't sure how she felt about him at the moment.

Jackson gave her a peck on the cheek. He undid the epaulettes on his shirt and slid off the captain's four stripes he usually wore and placed them in the usual spot by his car keys. He looked drained but smiled at her. 'Izzy's definitely okay?' he asked again.

'She's fine.'

'I'll check on her and then grab a shower. See you in a while.'

Abigail boiled the kettle to make tea for them both. As she picked up the mugs, her phone buzzed. Her pulse increased. She reluctantly responded.

'Morning, Abigail. How nice to see you back on your feet and handsome Captain Jackson back home. And where has he been while you have been so poorly?'

Abigail felt her blood warm. 'I have had enough of you,' she hissed. 'Clear off and leave me alone. I don't believe your bullshit about Jackson. So bugger off.'

'Oh, feeling feisty, are we, Abigail? Okay. I'll leave you alone. I suppose that means you don't care about Jackson staying at the luxurious five star Hotel Gran Melia Don Pepe last night, wrapped up in luxurious Egyptian cotton sheets with a "client". Still, you don't want to listen and that's your prerogative. But you can't keep your head buried in the sand forever. I'm afraid this is only the beginning. There's worse to come.'

Once again the phone went dead.

CHAPTER TWENTY

Mary Matthews appeared to have aged since Robyn last saw her. Her eyes were sunken with large blue shadows under them. She ushered Robyn into the sitting room without the confidence she had possessed in the last meeting.

'Any news?' she asked.

Robyn shook her head. 'I'm really sorry but I have had to let my boss know about the "Sugar and Spice" file.'

Mary hung her head. 'I thought you would. I couldn't expect you to ignore something like that. Men don't ordinarily keep files with images of schoolgirls. I think I was in denial. Now, I feel numb. I want this over, Lucas to return and then I can have it all out with him. It's the dishonesty that's hurt me most.' She tugged at a fingernail, its varnish chipped and picked away.

'I don't suppose Lucas mentioned visiting his father recently, did he? Paul Matthews' cleaner saw him talking to his dad a few weeks ago.'

Mary continued to pick at her nails. She let out a noise, a mixture of a sigh and a groan. 'He didn't say a word about it. I thought they had fallen out and didn't speak any more. The more I find out about Lucas, the more I discover how little I knew about him. He wasn't at all the man I fell in love with. He told me he hated his father. Really loathed him for sending him to boarding school after his mother died. Do you know Paul Matthews never even visited him in term time? It was little short of barbaric the way he dumped Lucas. At least, that's what my husband told me. Now, I can't be sure it was the truth. How do I know if anything Lucas told me was true?'

Robyn had no answer to that. In her profession, she had come across expert liars. Lucas was yet another who had managed to live dual lives and fool those close to him.

'Has Lucas mentioned any relatives who live in Farnborough?' asked Robyn when Mary had regained her composure.

She shook her head. 'He had no relatives. Just his father and his hatred of him was deep-rooted. Or so I was led to believe.'

Here was a man who was estranged from his family, who had just ditched a job he apparently loved, had an unhealthy interest in young girls and Thai lady boys, and had kept most of his life secret from the woman he had married. Little wonder he had disappeared. He couldn't keep all that under wraps for too long.

'Is there anything else you have noticed that could help throw some light on his disappearance?' Robyn asked. 'Have there been any strange phone calls for him, or, letters?'

'I can't think of anything else. Wait a moment. A letter came for him today from a building society. I threw it in the pile for him when he returns. Neither of us have accounts with building societies. I assumed it was junk mail. I don't ever open letters addressed to him even if they are spam. Shall I check?'

'Would you, please? It might be useful.'

Mary went to the kitchen and Robyn heard her talking to Archie, her dog. Within minutes, she returned, her face contorted in anger.

'That lying bastard,' she spluttered, brandishing the letter. 'He had an account with thirty thousand pounds in it. He withdrew fifteen thousand a couple of weeks ago and another fifteen the day before he supposedly went to Thailand. He'd been planning this all along. I didn't see it coming. I knew nothing about the account. We have a joint account at Barclays and some other savings together.

But this! It's yet another secret he kept from me. I wonder if there wasn't anything in our relationship that wasn't a sham.'

Mary was trembling with fury. If Robyn actually located Lucas, his marriage to Mary was certainly on shaky ground.

The conversation had left Robyn feeling frustrated and convinced she was missing something. She needed that laptop from Ross. It surely held the key to all of this. She had left Mary Matthews none the wiser about Lucas's visit to his father. He must have had a very important reason to contact the man he had avoided for so long.

* * *

It was half past eight when Robyn entered the gym. She'd walked the thirty minutes it took to reach the fitness centre and was ready for a serious workout. This evening she would concentrate on weight/strength training and on her chest and shoulders. She was satisfied to see only one other person there. She dropped her towel onto the running machine handlebars and limbered up. In front of her on a television screen a newsreader was standing in front of the Houses of Parliament with a serious look on his face. Robyn was out of touch with current affairs. There was a time when she would have been glued to the news and situations at home and abroad. Now, she wanted nothing to do with it. It could all get along without her help.

She warmed up then began work in earnest. She started with chest presses and, grabbing two twenty-kilo dumbbells, she completed three sets of ten repetitions followed by a fourth set using twenty-two kilo weights and just as the muscles were beginning to feel weakened she dropped to the floor and completed fifteen push-ups. This was only the beginning of a rigorous routine that saw her pushing her body to its limits. She completed endless sets of flies, overhead crunches and v-sits before working on her tricep muscles using the rope cable flies. She then attempted to exhaust her muscles and when she could do no more sets dropped to the floor with determination and completed as many tricep dips as she could until she collapsed.

With a grimace she forced herself up on all fours and attempted Spiderman push-ups – a walking push-up incorporating the whole body – until she fell to the floor again. Finally, dripping sweat, she made her way to the pool where, after a cold shower, she swam for half an hour.

Once her body was fatigued, Robyn showered and left the fitness centre to walk back home. The streetlights had come on and cast an orange glow across the pavements. The colours reminded her of the fire-eaters on the Jemaa el-Fnaa who astounded crowds by breathing out huge flames of yellow and orange. The square was where she and Davies had spent their last night together. She was reminded of the sound of the snake charmers bewitching their cobras with flutes and her mind travelled back to the square behind the riad where she had spent her last nights with Davies, breaking all the rules by being together while he was on a mission, yet convincing themselves it was fine…

* * *

'Did you know Jemaa el-Fnaa means "the Assembly of the Dead" and was once where the decapitated heads of criminals were displayed as warnings well into the nineteenth century?' Davies looked up from his guidebook, his dark eyes full of enthusiasm. He loved fact-finding and Marrakesh was an enchanting city full of history and interest.

Robyn stretched on the large double bed and propped herself up on an elbow.

'Yuck, I didn't know that, but I do know that this bed is getting cold without you in it.'

He laughed, tilting his head backwards, and dropped the guidebook. He strode towards the bed and launched on top of her, making her squirm in delight.

'Then, my future lovely wife, we'd better get you warmed back up.'

Their riad – an historic medina town house – was reached by a maze of dark, narrow alleyways leading to an inconspicuous door that opened into a world of tranquillity. The courtyard was built around an impressive lush garden, dominated by a sparrow-filled orange tree that cast its silhouette on the walls, filled with exotic plants and a musky woody scent that seemed to be present wherever they walked. It was the perfect place to rekindle their passion. Robyn had not seen Davies for six weeks and although she had missed him, she had another, more important reason for booking a flight and a room and coming to join him.

At sunset, she and Davies wandered from the hammam, swathed in luxurious, white robes to the riad's rooftop terrace and listened to the mosques' evening calls to prayer that echoed off the tight huddle of rose-tinged medieval houses below and flew towards the tall minaret of the Koutoubia Mosque and the snowy peaks of the Atlas Mountains.

'I love you, you know?' he said eventually.

'I know,' she replied.

'No. I mean I *really* love you,' he said and pulled her towards him. She hadn't sensed any doom then and drunk on happiness, they had dined al fresco under a star-studded sky, breathing in the orange blossom. She wanted to be one hundred per cent sure before she shared her news, and the hotel staff had discreetly given her the name of a doctor to contact. She would visit him while Davies was travelling across the Atlas mountains the following day, a journey that would take him through chocolate-hued landscape, punctuated with olive groves and hillside villages and into the spectacular Atlas mountains, only a two-hour journey away from Marrakesh.

Later that evening, they walked through the square, hand in hand, like any tourist. No one could have known that Davies was on an undercover mission for the Intelligence Corps. They were two lovers, enjoying the 'Red City'. They wandered around the square admiring the carnival of storytellers, acrobats, musicians and entertainers. Davies encouraged her to visit the wizened fortune-teller, sitting under an umbrella with a pack of fortune-telling cards at the ready. The woman turned over palms stained a deep brown with henna; her eyes were the colour of walnuts, with crow's feet etched deeply into her dark skin. She looked Robyn up and down. She beckoned for her to sit beside her and took one of Robyn's hands in her own, rough, worn hands, turning it this way and that and mumbling in an Arabic dialect that Robyn could not understand. Eventually, she pulled out her cards and turning each tarot card over she shook her head and told Robyn big changes were coming. God willing, she would be strong. Robyn, who thought she had an idea of what changes they might be, smiled at the woman and dropped extra dirhams into her hand, thanking her. 'Be strong,' the woman had repeated.

* * *

Try as she might, Robyn couldn't shut out the memories of Marrakesh. She should never have gone there and joined Davies. It had been folly. She had distracted him. She was sure of it. Had he been more focused on his job, he would have spotted the men who ambushed them. He would have known what was going to happen. Of that, Robyn was convinced. She had dulled his natural senses and now she had lost him forever. She had tried to be strong. The fortune teller had been right. What she hadn't told Robyn was how strong she would need to be.

CHAPTER TWENTY-ONE

The doctor had pronounced Abigail and Izzy fit and healthy but had done a blood test on Abigail to check there was nothing untoward left in her system. He agreed it was probably a bug and nothing to worry about.

Abigail texted Jackson. He was at the airport sorting out a problem with one of the aircraft. It had a problem with its fuel tank and he needed his maintenance team to get it resolved quickly. The jet was needed for a flight to Jersey in twenty-four hours. He phoned her back.

'So you're both okay?' he asked.

'We're fine. How's the jet?'

'Got to order some parts but they'll be here in the morning and it should be fixed in time. I'm going to have a chat with the senior engineer then I have a meeting with Howard.'

Howard Pitts was his business partner who had helped finance the aviation company. He was a sleeping partner but now and again he and Jackson got together so Jackson could keep him informed of how the business was doing.

'I shouldn't be too long with him. Fancy a takeaway and a bottle of wine tonight?'

'Sounds great.'

'I'll sort it out on my way home. Go and relax and have a bath or something and I'll arrange the dinner.'

This was most unlike him. Either he wanted to make up for not being at home when she was ill or he really had something to hide. At the moment she preferred to believe the former.

As she pulled into her drive she couldn't help but notice the Ford Fiesta parked there. A figure descended from the purple car as Abigail pulled up, a smile on her face. It was Rachel. Abigail was startled. How on earth had she got her address?

'Hi, Abby,' she shouted as Abigail freed Izzy from the seat and lifted her from the car.

'Hi, Izzy,' continued Rachel in a silly voice. 'How's the little cutie today?' she burbled.

'What are you doing here?' asked Abigail, trying not to sound rude.

'Zoe gave me your address. I hope you don't mind. She told me how ill you'd both been so I came around with these.' She stooped to bend into her car and pulled out a large bouquet of flowers exploding with colour; sunflowers with their vibrant golden petals and radiant, sunshine-shaped flowers, cerise germini, dark pink Oriental lilies, and alstroemeria in a stunning hot pink with green alchemilla mollis, salal and pittosporum, they were wrapped and trimmed with a cerise voile ribbon and presented in gift packaging.

'They're for you,' Rachel explained. 'A sort of get-well-soon. I always think flowers can cheer you up when you're ill or feeling down.' She passed them to Abigail then laughed. 'Sorry, you can't carry flowers and a wriggling child. I'll hold them. I was going to leave them on your doorstep but I'm so glad I caught you.'

Abigail was astounded. 'You shouldn't have. Gosh. Thank you. Come in,' she said, feeling she could hardly leave Rachel outside after such a generous gesture.

'Only if you're sure,' replied Rachel, beaming at her. Izzy gurgled. 'Oh, I have something for you too, little poppet,' she continued, rattling a carrier bag that was in her other hand.

Abigail urged her into the house where they headed for the kitchen. Rachel's eyes widened when she saw it.

'Oh my, what a beautiful house and what a kitchen!'

'Thank you. It took a long time to get it right but we're pleased with it,' she replied, putting Izzy into her high chair then taking the flowers from Rachel. Rachel pulled out a pile of coloured stacking cups and showed them to Abigail.

'I hope you haven't got any of these. I read that babies at this age are starting to use their motor skills and I went onto another website and discovered these are one of the most popular toys for babies Izzy's age.' A smile spread across her face. 'They'll help her develop those skills and keep her occupied for ages.' She passed a yellow cup to Izzy who studied it for a moment and then put it in her mouth.

Abigail laughed. 'Someone had better explain to this madam that she should start using those motor skills soon and remind her she has feet and hands for exploring too, not just her mouth. Coffee? Tea?'

Toffee strolled into the room to greet them.

'Tea please. Oh, isn't she lovely?' said Rachel, stooping to stroke Toffee who appreciating the attention, purred around her ankles. She stroked him one more time then straightened up and dropped onto the seat next to Izzy.

Abigail corrected her. 'This is Toffee. He's a boy actually although he's not very macho. He's a softie at heart and scared of other cats. Aren't you, you big wussie?'

'I'd love an animal. Can't have any in the flat I'm renting. The landlord doesn't want tenants with animals. My ex was allergic to fur so we didn't have any pets.' She jiggled a green cup at Izzy and showed her how to stack it on top of a blue one. Izzy gurgled, dropped the yellow cup and reached for the green cup that ended up in her mouth while she eyed Rachel.

'It's very kind of you to bring me flowers,' said Abigail, feeling a little awkward. Rachel was staring at Izzy intently. There was something out of the ordinary about the woman that she couldn't put her finger on. She continued, 'Zoe phoned me this morning first thing to commiserate. She caught the stomach-bug thing a few weeks ago. I hope no one else has been infected by me.'

'I think we'd have known by now,' replied Rachel, absorbed in watching Izzy shake a blue cup with enthusiasm.

Abigail made a pot of tea and brought it to the table.

'We haven't had much chance to get to know each other,' said Rachel, sipping her tea, 'but I already feel I know you. You have a very good aura,' she added. 'I am usually a good judge of people. Your aura is bright pink. Pink Aura people are by nature loving and giving. They love to be loved too,' she added.

Abigail sat in silence as Rachel spoke passionately about auras.

'Pink Aura people are very romantic and once they have found their soulmate will stay faithful, loving and loyal for life,' she continued, gazing intently at Abigail. 'And, the Pink Aura individual is a natural healer, highly sensitive to the needs of others and has strong psychic abilities. They hate injustice, poverty and conflicts. They strive always to make the world a better place and will make personal sacrifices in the pursuit of this ideal.'

She stopped and sat back calmly. 'It's not hogwash,' she said. 'I can see you're sceptical but I've studied auras for years. They're fascinating. All living things that need oxygen to survive have an aura. They generate a large magnetic energy field that can be sensed, felt and even seen around the physical body. We all can tell when someone doesn't feel good to us, like they are full of anger. You do not need to be psychic to feel or read an aura. Take Claire, for example,' she said. 'I couldn't help but notice Claire's aura yesterday. It was dark brown and that indicates selfishness, fault-finding, and a tendency towards deception. That lady has issues. She is surrounded by darkness. She's also stealing your aura when she is close to you, draining you.' She took another sip and grinned at Izzy. 'And you, you little poppet, are full of energy and light,' she added to Izzy. 'Izzy has a silver aura. It shines brightly. She will be well blessed in looks, personality and talent. Those with silver auras are usually incredibly lucky people. So, Izzy, what do you think?'

Izzy grinned at Rachel and banged her cup on the table.

Abigail had no idea what to say. Rachel was freaking her out with her conversation about auras. 'Wow! That's amazing. I had no idea.'

'There's lots we don't know about. We should try and open our minds. Auras are usually three feet away from the body. You can see them if you open your mind. You need to be aware of them. If a person walks very close to you, they may unintentionally steal some of your energy. Have you never been speaking to someone and thought "They're in my space" and then you backed away? It's because they have intruded into your aura and that can interrupt your personal flow of energy.'

It began to make sense to Abigail but she was still uneasy with the conversation. Silence fell again as Rachel drained her tea and played stacking cups with Izzy. Without warning she stood to leave. 'Have you got to go to work?' asked Abigail, relieved the woman was going.

A frown creased Rachel's brow. 'To be honest I didn't much feel like going in so I called in sick. Awful, I know, and I bet fate will now make me ill but I couldn't face staring into people's mouths.' She looked into the distance. 'I'm a bit fed up with everything,' she continued. 'It's been a tough few weeks. Well, a tough few years, if I am honest. I rather fancy a career change. Become a life coach or similar. There has to be more to life than teeth and staring at the walls of my rented flat. It's time for me to face the demons in my life. I have to resolve a few issues and then move on.'

A silence hung between them. Abigail had no idea what to say to this woman.

'Do you mind if I use your bathroom before I go?'

'No, be my guest. There's a guest toilet down the corridor on the left.'

'Thanks. Back in a jiffy.'

Abigail washed up the cups and talked to Izzy while she waited. It was a while before she heard the sound of running water and Rachel emerged again.

'Thanks for the tea. Glad you're feeling better. I enjoyed our chat. Hope to see you again soon. And remember, look after your aura. Bye, little sweetie,' she added, blowing a kiss to Izzy.

Abigail nodded. 'Thank you for the flowers and for Izzy's present. That was so thoughtful of you.'

'It was nothing. That's what friends do,' she said as she made her way to the front door.

Having shut the front door and heard Rachel's car leave, Abigail felt a sense of relief. Rachel meant well but she was too serious and intense for Abigail.

'Come on, Izzy,' she said. 'Time for a bath. You're having an early night because Mummy and Daddy are going to have some "us" time.'

She lifted the baby, kissed her on the head. Izzy was certainly a happy baby. Maybe there was something in what Rachel said about being light and lucky. She wasn't convinced about Claire though. Rachel had clearly taken a dislike to Claire and that was all there was to it. She climbed the stairs singing 'Twinkle Twinkle' to Izzy then stopped in surprise. The doors to the nursery and their bedroom were open. She knew she had shut them that morning. She always shut them. Rachel must have been upstairs. She looked in the nursery first. It looked the same as usual except the toys in Izzy's cot were now all sitting up in a row at one end. She felt affronted. Rachel had a cheek coming into her child's room and touching her toys. The woman was definitely strange. She would avoid her in the future. She would insist Zoe didn't bring Rachel to any more meet-ups. Abigail moved the toys back before checking her own bedroom to see if anything had been touched.

Above their bed hung a framed naked photograph of her. It was the photo Jackson most loved. In it she sat astride a chair, completely naked apart from heels, her swollen belly on display along with her breasts, her hair cascading down her back, eyes focused on the camera and her lips in a sexy pout. It was certain Rachel would have seen it and that irritated her further. It wasn't a photograph she wanted people to see, especially strange women who snooped around houses.

She played with Izzy, then bathed her and was tucking her into her cot when a noise from downstairs alerted her to the fact Jackson was home.

'Hey!' she shouted as she descended the stairs. A carryout bag and a bottle of wine were on the kitchen table and Jackson was looking at the flowers.

'They're from Rachel,' she said, moving towards the cupboard to retrieve the plates. 'She's just moved into the area. She's sort of joined up with me, Claire and Zoe. She's Zoe's friend really. Zoe introduced us to her. Anyway, Zoe told her I was ill and she came around with flowers. Nice of her, wasn't it?'

Jackson held up a card that had been attached to the outside of the flowers. 'That was generous of her, considering she hasn't known you long,' he replied.

'I thought that too,' said Abigail, opening the drawer and pulling out knives and forks. It went quiet. Jackson turned towards her brandishing a small card. It says, '"To Abby, with love from Rich". Nice flowers. Maybe he is rich. Rich Rich. It has a certain ring to it.'

Abigail dropped a fork. It clattered onto the table then tumbled to the floor. 'I don't know anyone called Rich,' she protested.

Jackson shrugged. 'It definitely says Rich.'

Abigail didn't pick up on the light-hearted tone in his voice. Or the crinkle in his eyes as he tried to keep a straight face. She continued, her face reddening, the tension she had felt earlier surfacing. 'But they aren't from Rich. They are from Rachel. It maybe should read "from Rach". Rachel stayed for a cup of tea and she brought Izzy some stacking cups.' She pointed at the cups lined up on the high chair tray. 'This is absurd. Are you suggesting I'm involved with another man? How bloody dare you.'

Jackson turned his back to her. She felt her heart hammering. She wanted to scream at him. There he was taking the moral high ground over some flowers when she had more reason to suspect his fidelity. She was about to tackle him on the subject when he turned and faced her. His eyes had darkened, his mood now flat.

'I was only teasing you, Abby. Couldn't you tell? I thought it would lift the atmosphere. Apparently, it didn't. I got it wrong.'

'Atmosphere?' She put her hands on her hips and glared at him.

'Well, you haven't been that easy to live with,' he commented. 'And before you go off on one, I know why. Izzy, motherhood and so on. I get it but I miss the old Abby. You weren't so prickly then and wouldn't have jumped down my throat. You were always the first to break down and laugh.'

He fixed his eyes on her. Abigail tried hard to keep her bubbling emotions in check. On the surface his comment was not unreasonable but the horrible robotic voice on her mobile echoed in her ears.

'Well, I've not had much to laugh at recently. And it's not because of Izzy.' She swallowed before continuing in a quiet, serious voice. 'Jackson, are you seeing someone else?'

'What? Where's that come from? Why would you ask me such a thing?' he replied. A vein throbbed in his temple. His eyes narrowed. 'That is the most stupid thing you've ever asked. I'm not even going to answer it. Abby, I don't know what the hell is going on. Maybe your hormones are haywire after having Izzy, or you spend too much time brooding at home, but sort yourself out and don't ask such ridiculous questions again.'

'Don't be so bloody condescending. I haven't made this up. I'm not some hysterical woman who spends all day watching television soap operas! I had an anonymous call. Someone accused you of having a relationship.'

'Who would say such a thing? And who am I supposed to be having a relationship with?'

Abby hung her head. 'They didn't say. I don't know who made the call.'

'You don't know who this troublemaker is and this person doesn't say any more than I'm playing away and you believed them? Listen to yourself, Abby. I'm saying no more. Work it out yourself and when you're feeling more reasonable, you'll understand why you sound ridiculous. I'm going out.'

Jackson slammed the front door.

Abigail slumped forwards, hands holding her head that hurt so much with confusion. What was happening to her? Jackson and she used to laugh and tease each other mercilessly and yet she felt so strangled by concerns over Izzy and this bloody stalker who was hassling her and telling her things about Jackson, and convincing her that there were secrets she didn't know. She was the queen of keeping secrets. She ought to cut Jackson some slack. This was getting ridiculous. Why was she letting some wacko upset her so much?

A crackling from the baby monitor alerted her to Izzy's cries. She had woken. Probably because of their argument. She heaved herself up to attend to her baby and caught a glimpse of movement by the window. She screwed her eyes to see what it was, peered through the glass and shrieked in alarm as she spotted a figure in her garden. Someone had been staring in and watching her. She dropped to her knees and hid out of sight, her breath coming fast as she considered her options. She pulled it out and prepared to dial. Sense told her to check again. Anxiously, she rose and peeped outside again but the figure had gone. In its place stood a small tree, its boughs waving in the light breeze that had blown up. She exhaled. She had mistaken the tree for a person. Her nerves were getting the better of her. However, she still checked the front door was locked then hurried upstairs to comfort Izzy and take her into her own bedroom for the night.

Outside, a shadowy figure slid along the hedgerow in the garden and disappeared out into the street.

CHAPTER TWENTY-TWO

The intercom at Mary Matthews' home buzzed impatiently. She answered it and asked who was calling. The response took her by surprise.

'Hi. It's about Lucas. Can I speak to you?'

Mary shut Archie in the kitchen with a dog chew to keep him quiet and opened the door, lips pressed together in a thin line as she surveyed the young woman holding a cake box. The young woman smiled at her.

'Hi again, I know this will seem odd but Lucas sent me. He's concerned about you. He's really sorry about upsetting you but he's had to keep you in the dark to keep you safe.'

'Lucas? Is he all right?' Mary gasped, relief allowing her shoulders to relax. Up until this moment she had been ready to scream at him for his deceit but now she was only focused on his well-being.

'He's fine but he's in hiding. Someone is after him.'

Mary breathed a huge sigh of relief. 'It's about the photographs. I was right. I couldn't believe he had a warped interest in girls. He has been investigating someone at work. I thought that would be it.'

The girl nodded and put a finger up to her lips. 'Best not to say anything. You never know who is watching or listening.'

Something else crossed Mary's mind. 'But who are you? Why are you involved?' She looked the young woman up and down suspiciously. She wore coloured leggings and a loose jumper in bright green that matched her hair. 'You're not his girlfriend, are you?'

The girl spluttered in delight. 'Gosh no. This is going to come as a surprise but I'm his sister, Natasha. We haven't been in touch for years but he contacted me when he found out he was in trouble and wanted to go to ground. I seemed the best idea, given we haven't been in contact for years. I bet hardly anyone knows I'm his sister. He's going to involve the police as soon as he has enough evidence, and we think they'll offer him some protection but for now he's holed up somewhere safe.'

She gazed at Mary with open brown eyes. 'Hard to take in, isn't it?' she said. 'I had trouble believing it when he landed on my doorstep, I can tell you.'

Mary was torn between learning more and being guarded. She didn't know this woman at all and Lucas had never mentioned a sister. The woman offered a genuine smile, an envelope and the cake box.

'He sent a letter for you to explain everything and strangely a cake. Well, he asked me to buy it. I got it from my local shop. The woman who owns it uses organic fruits from her garden in all her baking. They're usually pretty good. Lucas has tried one and enjoyed it. He said it wasn't as good as your baking. This was his idea. He hopes you and I will sit down over cake and a pot of tea and get to know each other a little. I am your sister-in-law, after all. I was so surprised when he turned up. In the same week I see my brother after a couple of decades and find out I have a new sister-in-law. He didn't stop talking about you.'

Archie, the dog, let out a volley of angry barks.

'That must be Archie,' said the woman. 'I have a gift for him too.' She held up a toy rubber rabbit. 'Lucas said he loves to play.'

Mary opened the door wider. 'You'd better come in,' she said.

* * *

The poison didn't take long to work. The cake sat between them, Mary took a second bite from her slice and wiped the crumbs from her mouth.

'Most unusual,' she said.

'It's the fruits,' said the girl. 'They have more of a flavour, don't they, than non-organic? Quite aromatic. I think she added some wine to it as well.'

Natasha had spent the entire time filling her in on her brother's exploits at home when they were children and going into detail about the glamorous life they had enjoyed with their father, the actor. Tales of Monte Carlo and the Cannes Film Festival, of meeting famous film stars and hanging out on set watching their father film episodes of *Doctor Pippin.*

Mary was astounded. Lucas had never spoken so passionately of his childhood. Natasha told stories of her and her brother learning to sail and ride ponies until the sad accident that took his eye.

'It was silly, really. He was playfighting a friend. They had long sticks and were fencing. They got carried away and his friend misjudged his aim. His stick went into Lucas's eyeball,' Natasha said, sadly. 'It was during the holidays. We only really had time together in the holidays. Then, the following summer, Dad and Lucas had a massive fallout because Lucas drove Dad's car to the village without permission, and without a licence. He was only larking about but Dad got really cross. Lucas sulked because he was banned from going to a music festival. He held a grudge for years and soon afterwards he left for university and never returned. Dad got on his high horse and no matter how often I tried to persuade him to patch things up, he never did, and Lucas has stayed away from us both since.'

Mary was incredulous. She had never known her husband at all. He had enjoyed a quite normal childhood yet turned out so full of woe. She had felt so sorry for him yet he wasn't the sad, misunderstood person she believed him to be. He had kept so many secrets from her. He had claimed he hated his childhood and father and yet here was Natasha telling her about all the fun they had had together. It seemed so incongruous.

Then Mary's sixth sense kicked in. She felt like her brain had slowed down and she struggled to make sense of what it was screaming at her. The woman smiling broadly at her had not touched her own slice of cake. She had deliberately kept talking and sipping the tea but it was an act. She wasn't Lucas's sister. If she was, why had Lucas not kept in touch with her given she wasn't to blame for the fallout with his father? Before she felt her heart beginning to race there was a moment of lucidity as Mary realised she had fallen victim to an evil plot. She couldn't breathe. She opened her mouth to take in oxygen but it made no difference; she couldn't get any air. Her muscles began to twitch and spasm. The pain was dreadful. Mary had no control as her body began to thrash. Pain rose in her chest and she felt life being squeezed out of her. Natasha cocked her head to one side and grinned. It was no longer a friendly smile.

'Oh dear, Mary. It appears you are dying. Not long now. Cyanide should only take about fifteen minutes. You've taken a little longer than I expected. Just for the record, your husband was a lousy brother, a disgusting individual. You were an idiot to love him…'

Mary tried to speak. This was all wrong. She needed to explain but a sudden spasm of pain followed by another ripped through her, causing her body to convulse violently and her head to be thrown about, preventing her from any action. She fell sideways onto the floor, eyes open in fear and understanding.

The woman with green hair rose. Mary felt the scene drift away as gradually her senses shut down and she plunged into the dark.

The woman picked up the toy rabbit that the dog had dropped at her feet, his tongue out, eager to play the game.

'Good boy,' she said as she threw the toy rabbit into the kitchen. The animal scuttled off to retrieve it. She shut the door on it and gazed around the room as she put on her plastic gloves. She sneered at the fans on the wall and the ornaments. Her eye caught the guitar standing in the corner and she felt a surge of rage. No doubt it belonged to Lucas. She strode towards it, put it over her knee and broke the neck in two. She felt an instant relief. Returning to the coffee table, she collected her slice of cake and followed the dog to the kitchen where she tipped the cake into the box, washed her cup and plate thoroughly in hot water while the animal squeaked the toy with pleasure. She dried the cup and replaced it with the others arranged on the fancy dresser. She wiped the tops with disinfectant wipes and left, taking the cake box with her.

The dog watched her departure mournfully, then trotted to his mistress on the floor, dropped his toy by her head and licked her face to wake her.

CHAPTER TWENTY-THREE

THEN

It is easier than I thought to ruin Chloe Planter's life. After the awful perfume episode, we had a chemistry lesson. That's when I got my idea. I couldn't do it that afternoon but I am prepared for today.

I head back to the lab after the lesson and say I've left my book there. Timing is everything. Mr Watts is about to lock up and eager to get to lunch. He is always the first teacher to arrive in the lunch hall and the kids often joke about him never getting fed at home. I give him a sob story about how I need my book for the homework he set, and I have left it in the laboratory. I tell him I want to get started on the work now as I have lots of homework to do tonight. I manage to look concerned and slightly tearful so he lets me back in the laboratory. He's a bit away with the fairies and doesn't even know my name. He is a genius when it comes to chemistry but a total buffoon when it comes to pupils, which bodes well for me.

'Yes, in you go. I'll wait for you…'

'Chloe,' I say. 'Chloe Planter.'

He beams at me as if I've discovered a rare new element. 'Yes, Chloe, of course.' Pleased that he has identified another pupil.

I race into the laboratory. I know what I need. I slipped some of the chemical we'd been using in the lesson into a hidey-hole in the classroom. It's normally locked away and we are only given a little to use but it'll be enough for my purposes. No one noticed me as I poured it into the small travel spray container I brought to class and had hidden in my pocket. No one noticed me when I stole the spray from Superdrug in town either. However, I didn't dare risk being seen putting the spray into my school bag, especially as Mr Watts insists all bags are left to one side of the laboratory so we don't fall over them while we are working with chemicals.

I nip over to the bench where I was sitting, slide my hand into the space above it and extract the spray container, putting it into my bag with care. I pull my book out of my bag and race out again.

'Thank you, Mr Watts,' I say. 'I couldn't have done my homework without it.'

'He smiles, locks the door and leaves, all thoughts of me forgotten as the aroma of sausages and beefburgers fills his nostrils.

Of course, I don't carry out my plan immediately. That would certainly draw attention to me or to someone in our class. I wait. I put up with Chloe's torments for another three days. She and her revolting cronies have now started to put pegs on their noses when they see me. Someone has left anti-dandruff shampoo on my desk. I scowl and ignore them. I can put up with them. It won't happen for much longer.

'She's rank,' I hear as I sidle into the changing rooms for PE. 'Her hair is so greasy. Why doesn't she look after herself? She'd be okay if she made some effort.'

''Cos she's a skank. And, she'll never be okay.'

'It's almost like she wants to look horrible.'

'Maybe she does. She certainly doesn't want to mix with anyone. Maybe she's nuts.'

'She looks crazy some days. And she talks to herself. I heard her muttering in the corridor. She was talking and answering someone but there was no one there. Mad. She's definitely mad.'

They are clearly talking about me. One of them is right. I don't want to be pretty. I don't want to look nice. I know what happens to pretty girls. In fact, I'll be doing Chloe a favour when I carry out my plan. My father lets out a warm chuckle. He's rather proud of what I've come up with. So am I. I decide to give games a miss today and leave the changing rooms to find the perfect spot for my revenge.

* * *

It's not until the weekend that I get the opportunity to carry out my plan. I've been waiting outside her house all morning. Chloe is going to town to meet Jason Moffat. I overheard her bragging to her friends about it. She's wearing a tight top that makes her tits look even bigger than normal and jeans that look like they've been painted on. Jason Moffat is one of the most popular boys in the school. He captains the school football team and is older than us by two years. He's sixteen and will be leaving school this year. There's talk that West Bromwich Albion is interested in having him on their junior squad.

Chloe's face is plastered in make-up and she has a confident swagger as she heads to the bus stop.

She doesn't acknowledge me as I approach her from the opposite direction. My hair is hidden under a baseball cap and I am wearing a man's jacket stolen from a charity shop. I've padded the shoulders so I look much larger than I am. I actually look like a bloke. I've even drawn a slight moustache under my nose with eyebrow pencil and made marks on my face that look like stubble. My father thought I'd done an excellent job. 'You could be an actress or work in film,' he said as I admired my reflection in the mirror. 'Even I hardly recognise you.'

There is no one else in the street. Chloe is so busy staring at her phone she doesn't see me until the last minute. She looks up in surprise as she almost walks into me.

'Stupid girl,' I spit and lift the container and squirt it at her. She turns her head but too late and the hydrochloric acid runs down the left-hand side of her face and dribbles over her wide mouth. She screams dramatically, scrubbing at her cheek and lips and then howls as the pain sets in, dropping to her knees on the pavement.

I run off at speed and when I have cleared the corner, I abandon my jacket together with the cap, stuffing them into a carrier bag that was concealed in the jacket pocket. I wipe the make-up from my face with a wet wipe and saunter away, attracting no more attention than usual. I'll dump the bag outside the charity shop where I nicked the jacket. They'll get it back and a nice cap to boot. You shouldn't really steal from charity, after all.

I allow myself a smirk of satisfaction. Chloe will now understand what it is like to be a misfit and laughed at. She'll never be the same again. Well, that makes two of us, I muse.

CHAPTER TWENTY-FOUR

Izzy was asleep and Jackson was not due back until late evening. There had been no more cruel phone calls. She had digested Jackson's words and his response to her accusations and decided the caller was trying to shake her marriage. If he or she rang again, she was going to let rip. When Jackson returned after their argument, neither had spoken about it. Abigail was confident they'd get over it. Their relationship was strong enough to weather a few petty arguments.

She'd phoned Claire earlier. Claire's voice had announced that she was out of the studio and would get back to her as soon as she could. Zoe had answered on the fifth ring. She was apologetic: 'Sorry, Abby. I'm at a fitness conference in Harrogate for the next two days. It's all about health and safety. Not supposed to have my phone on. Have to go. I'll chat to you when it's over,' she had whispered before ringing off.

Abigail picked up her phone and thumbed through the apps. It had been a while since she'd checked her Facebook account. The app wouldn't open so she went into a search engine and brought up her profile. As she did so her flesh went cold. Her profile picture had been changed and now showed a naked woman sitting on a chair – it was the photo that hung in their bedroom.

Her fingers trembled as she saw the same photograph enlarged on her page. The comments that were left under it ranged from disgusting, lewd responses to outraged ones. Her face burned with humiliation. No one was meant to see this photograph. She had only posed for Jackson. The photograph had been posted only a few hours ago. Someone had known her password and accessed her account, posting as if he or she were her. That same person had changed her profile from 'private' so only friends could see what she wrote, to 'public' so anyone could see it. Her naked body and Facebook wall were on display to everyone who had access to the Internet.

Worse than the revealing picture were the horrible messages she had supposedly written on friend's walls and status updates she had written about herself.

'Feeling so randy just bought myself this bad boy. Can't wait for Jackson to use it on me.' Under it was a picture of a huge vibrator.

'Anyone want a threesome with me and Jackson? We don't care what sex you are.'

Her mouth fell open at the crude messages. She had also accused her work colleagues at the boutique of stealing clothes and written vile comments about others, calling them names. A message on Zoe's wall read, 'Have you told your latest boyfriend about your genital warts?' And another on Claire's wall read, 'Zoe says you're a loser. I think she's right. You're a female Billy-No-Mates. Neither of us really like you.' The thought that someone had not only hacked her account but also posted these awful comments made her feel sick. And, how had they got a copy of the photograph from her bedroom?

With shaking hands she set about getting back into her account but it was impossible. She emailed Facebook to tell them she had been hacked and asked them to shut her account down. She hoped they did it soon. She emailed as many people as possible who were her friends on Facebook to tell them that none of the ghastly messages and photos had actually been posted by her and asked them to spread the word that she was not responsible for them.

Her temple drummed, heralding an impending headache. She let out a moan of despair as she turned off the computer. She was sure not everyone would believe her claim she had been hacked. This had to be the work of the same person who had been calling her. There were only a few explanations as to how they got a copy of the photograph in the bedroom and one of them was by direct entry to her home. The thought chilled her. Tomorrow she would definitely call a locksmith and get the locks changed. She ought to have done it immediately after the note had been removed from her drawer. Jackson wasn't on Facebook and was unlikely to find out about the posts unless someone told him. That was a bridge she would cross when she had to. She'd explain only if she had to. For now, she would do what she could to keep her past from him. She would fight back.

A small rustling and a light cough made her sit up sharply. The rushing of blood filled her ears as her heart began to pound. Someone was in the house. She didn't know how to react. She should call the police. She picked up her mobile and then dropped it as a childish, high-pitched voice whispered, 'Bye, bye, Mummy.'

Stifling a scream, she sat bolt upright, her head turning this way and that. The voice had come from the baby monitor on the television stand. There was an intruder in Izzy's room.

Abigail sprinted faster than she had ever sprinted before, up the stairs and burst into the nursery. The room was completely empty and Izzy lay fast asleep, her toy rag-dog in one hand.

CHAPTER TWENTY-FIVE

Geraldine Marsh rode her bike to the front gate of the Farmhouse and dismounted. She wiped her forehead. It had taken a lot out of her today. Once upon a time she could have ridden the hill without getting puffed, but nowadays she was lucky if she made it to the top without having to get off and push.

It was a bright day and she spent a moment catching her ragged breath and looking over the reservoir. She never tired of the view although she probably would not be able to look at it from this height again for much longer. Once the house sold, she would spend her days back in the village. It was unlikely new owners would want to employ an old lady like her to clean.

It had all been such a shame. Mr Matthews dying like that had shocked her to her core. Life was so fragile. She propped her bike against the wall as usual, and collected the post from the large wooden letter box. It was habit. She always collected the post for him when she cleaned. She'd drop it in the laundry room for him to pick up when he was ready. He didn't get much post. Today, she didn't know what else to do with the letters. Somebody would deal with them in time.

It was not her usual cleaning day. She normally didn't work on a Thursday and instead would go to the leisure centre in town and swim. She wasn't a good swimmer but it was exercise and kept her joints moving. At her age it was important to stay moving and stretched. She might consider going to one of the Pilates classes she had heard about. They took place in the village hall every Tuesday evening. She'd have plenty of spare time once she stopped work for good at the Farmhouse.

She let herself in the back entrance and dropped the post on a table in the laundry room before ambling into the kitchen. The detective had wanted Paul's laptop and Geraldine had decided to come and search for it. She started in the kitchen but she already knew it wasn't in any obvious locations. She thought Mr Matthews might have taken it to his bedroom, put it under his bed and it had been pushed further under by her vacuum cleaner. That was the only thing she could think of: after all, she had cleaned the house meticulously as she always did, and not uncovered it.

She had booked a ticket that morning to see *Chicago*, just as she had said she would. She would go and see the show in London and maybe even have a glass of wine during the interval and raise it to Mr Matthews. She was looking forward to going to London. It would be an adventure.

The house seemed very empty. Geraldine had never really liked the place. It always seemed full of unhappiness. It was dreadfully gloomy, the rooms left as they had always been. Mr Matthews had so much wealth yet he had never made any house improvements. If it had been her house she would have thrown out everything in the children's bedrooms and painted them bright colours, put in new furniture and erased the memories of the past. It was almost as if Mr Matthews wanted to be reminded of them. As if he was punishing himself. She reached his bedroom and got down on her knees, wriggling her body as far as she could under the bed. There was nothing there. She backed out and decided she'd try the other rooms just in case he had gone in one of them and left the laptop there.

It was as she came out of the bedroom she heard a sneeze that appeared to come from upstairs. She froze. There was somebody in the room on the third floor. She might be old but her hearing was sharp. She would tiptoe back downstairs and phone the police. It might be burglars. Mr Matthews did not have many valuables but intruders wouldn't know that. They'd see a huge house and believe there was something worth taking.

Geraldine Marsh scurried along the landing and reached the top of the stairs when she felt rather than heard the person behind her. She turned and caught a glimpse of a face before she felt two hands push roughly on her shoulders, and she tumbled backwards, down and down, the face before her fading as she fell, tumbling over and over until her head smacked against the tiles and she saw no more.

CHAPTER TWENTY-SIX

Ross arranged to meet Robyn at his offices on her way to headquarters. He threw the door open with a trumpeting noise.

'There you go,' he said, sliding an old Toshiba laptop onto her old desk. 'Thought it better to give it to you here than at the station.'

'Really? Is it because you miss me, Ross? That's why you asked me to meet you here?'

'You sussed me. Actually, I didn't want to go to the station. Makes me have these urges to return to the force. I miss the cut and thrust but don't tell Jeanette. She doesn't like me talking that way. It's a quieter life for me these days, like it or not.'

Before she could thank him he began a grumbling tirade, 'What a place! The glossy brochure hides a multitude of sins. It's certainly a big house but it needs lots of work doing to it. I don't think Paul Matthews was one for DIY or employing anyone to fix things. The agent kept telling us to look at the potential of the place. By "potential" I think he really meant the cost of knocking it all down and starting again. The conservatory leaked, for one. It was pouring down and there were several buckets catching drips. They were right old trip hazards but not as lethal as the floor in the entrance. Slide over on that and you'd crack your skull wide open. I'm surprised Paul Matthews didn't die that way, never mind falling over in the woods. The agent said the tiles had all been exported from Italy and were made of expensive marble. What a stupid covering for a floor. They were slippery, hard and cold. Someone should have put some carpet on top of them,' he continued. Ross hated shoddy workmanship or neglect of homes. He was as proud of his house's exterior and workmanship as Jeanette was the interior.

'Several of the original fireplaces had been boarded up, and the bathrooms were tired and dated. Jeanette has a thing about clean, smart shiny taps. Those were so corroded you'd never get them clean again.

'And it was eerie. The reception rooms are like the house equivalent of the *Mary Celeste*. The rooms are filled with enormous settees and huge puffy cushions set out so they face each other. Anyone sitting there would be staring at the person opposite. Bit like being in a doctors' waiting room. There's a piano in one room with music set up on a stand like someone was about to play it and then, *poof*, they vanished. In the dining room there are candelabras set up on a long table and even china side plates laid out! When did you last see a house with candelabras?

'Upstairs was the worst. I was nearly out of breath by the time I reached the top of the first set of stairs. It was like climbing Mount Everest. It had one of those galleried landings that overlooks the entrance hall. Could be very impressive and his bedroom, or "the master suite" as the bloke in the shiny suit called it, was okay. It was large with an en-suite bathroom but the other bedrooms off the landing had been left as if the kids were still there. One was in dark gloomy colours with a couple of posters of bands on the wall and the other was obviously a girl's room. Must have been Natasha's. She left behind books and a few bits and pieces – old games, a radio, some CDs, that sort of thing. There was another room upstairs. The agent said it could be used as a bedroom but it was locked and he couldn't open it. He's had to tell head office so they can contact the cleaner and get it open. So, all in all, a depressing place. It needs a family who'll spend some money on it and give it a new lease of life. Bit secluded for most folk, though.

Who wants to live on a windy hill in the middle of nowhere with woods all around them? The Munster family, maybe?'

'You've not put in an offer on it, then?'

Ross barked a loud laugh. 'Not a chance. Jeanette couldn't wait to get out of the place. She said it had bad vibes. I think she's been reading too many horror stories.'

'So tell me, how did you get your hands on this laptop? I hope you haven't been breaking any laws.'

The corners of Ross's mouth twitched. 'I am zee greatest detective,' he said in a phony French accent.

'You certainly surprised me. And I know how good you are. Come on, stop crowing about it with that smug look on your face and tell me what you did. I know you didn't steal it because you are one of the straightest guys I know. You do everything – well, almost everything – by the book. Can't see you shoving it up your Old Guys Rule T-shirt as you walked around the house.'

'You know me too well. Actually, it was easy. On our way around the place, I noticed a leaflet on the mantelpiece in the snug. I can tell you're annoyed you didn't spot it when you were there.'

It was true. Robyn prided herself on her observational skills. 'Get on with it,' she replied.

'It was a leaflet for Andy's computer repair shop in Rugeley. I put two and two together and after we left the house, we headed into the town. Andy's was one of those hard-to-find places, a shop no bigger than my garage, stuffed round the back of a small business park. Took ages to locate it. Jeanette was about ready to give up when we finally stumbled across it. The place was like a waste-recycling unit, piled high with old computers, gadgets and stuff I couldn't recognise. Andy's one of those computer geeky sorts you see in sitcoms – glasses, little goatee beard thing on his chin, and an expression of perpetual confusion, as if he isn't sure he's in the real world or a virtual one. I asked if the laptop for Mr

Matthews was ready for collection. "It's been ready for a while, Mr Matthews. I got rid of the virus. It's as good as new. I defragged it for you too." The poor guy had no idea who I was. He's obviously better with machines than people. He'd make a terrible witness at a robbery. Can you imagine it? "Describe the thief, Andy?" "Well, uhm, he had an HP fifteen inch, Intel Pentium four gigabyte, one terabyte, with a Pentium n3710 quad-core processor and one point six gigahertz processor speed, under his arm.""

Ross allowed himself a smile. 'Anyway, he attempted to baffle me by talking computer gobbledygook about the laptop and what he'd done to it, then charged me sixty quid and handed it over. Couldn't have been simpler.'

'Fantastic! Now I just need to get into it and we might have some answers.'

'Shall I bill Staffordshire Police for the sixty pounds?' he asked with a grin.

'Tell you what. I'll give you the money and I'll wait until Mulholland is in a cheery mood and claim it back.'

'You'll be waiting a while. Might get it about the time you're due your old-age pension,' he quipped, leaving her to work out how to obtain the information she needed from the laptop.

* * *

She had managed a brief meeting with her small team that morning before leaving for Farnborough. Walking back through the station, Robyn had felt a comforting familiarity. Ross had been correct when he had said it would be as if she hadn't been away. Most of the officers were holed up in the large briefing room, several scribbling on pads as she walked past. She glanced through the large glass door. Sergeant Phil Clarke spotted her and lifted a hand in greeting. She headed for her office at the end of the corridor. It was the same office she had been using before she left. She half expected to see the same calendar on the wall that she had hung up the year Davies was killed. She took a deep breath as she entered. The office had received a makeover and had been recently painted. There were new swivel chairs, and the old filing cabinet with paint peeling from it and drawers that stuck had been replaced with an up-to-date one. Large files marked with cases and dates were on new shelves.

'Morning, ma'am,' Mitz Patel said, a small smile lifting the corners of his mouth. 'Good to be working with you again.'

'Nice to see you again too, Mitz, and you can drop the *ma'am*, as you well know. You know the routine, Carter or Robyn, or if you must, call me boss.'

Patel was an eager 34-year-old who still lived with his parents. Like her other colleagues, she was surprised Mitz had not yet met his ideal partner. He was bright, good-looking and very considerate. He took all the banter about living at home from those at the station in good spirit, often adding to it. Tales of his failed blind dates were frequently a topic of conversation when it was quiet.

'Coffee?' He pointed at the coffee machine in the corner. 'It's brand new. No more boiling a kettle in the canteen.'

'No, thanks. I need to leave in a minute.'

'Shame, it's rather good although I wouldn't bother with the cappuccino, if I were you. It's like drinking soapy water.'

'I'll bear that in mind. You're being ultra considerate today, Mitz. You must be extremely pleased to see me.'

'Just setting a good example, boss,' he replied, pointing towards the stern young woman with her black hair scraped back in a tight ponytail. Her face was free of make-up but she was attractive with large almond-coloured eyes and dark eyebrows, and she stared keenly at Robyn. She stood behind her desk like a schoolgirl waiting permission to sit.

'Morning, you must be Anna Shamash. Nice to meet you. Okay, here's how it works. Don't question anything I ask you to do and we'll get on fine. I work fast and I don't suffer fools. If in doubt, ask Mitz here. He knows how I operate – oh, and I like my coffee black with no sugar.'

The girl nodded. 'Yes, ma'am.'

'And never call me *ma'am*. It makes me feel ancient. I'm just an officer like you, doing a job. We work together on my watch. Okay?'

The girl managed a tight smile. 'Yes, boss,' she said.

Robyn gave her a smile.

'We've got a missing man, Lucas Matthews. I've handed over details to our paedophile unit too as he might be involved in some ring but at the moment we are focused on unearthing him. I have reason to believe he is in Farnborough and I need you two to track down some people who might know him or be associated with him.'

She handed out the list of names compiled from her search of Paul's browsing history. It included Natasha Matthews, Jane and Jack Clifford, Josh Clifford and the elusive Christina Clifford née Forman, the woman who had once been Paul Matthews' fiancée.

'Keep in touch with me and see what you can find out about these people and I want addresses too. DCI Mulholland says you can assist me but I'm to make sure I don't abscond with you halfway around the country. I've got my hands on this laptop which might have more useful information. So far I've succeeded in getting into Paul Matthews' email account and checked on his Internet searches. Have a look. Anna, you any good at this sort of thing?'

'Yes, boss. I'm a dab hand.'

'Okay, I'm impressed. I'll be even more impressed if you find anything else on that laptop. So, I'll leave this with you.' She placed the laptop in front of Anna and grinned at them both. 'Try to behave, children, and I'll talk to you later.'

* * *

Dark grey clouds rolled in from the south as Robyn joined merging traffic on the M25 past Heathrow. Forecasters had promised storms and it seemed that, for once, their predictions would come true.

Traffic was heavy and the journey was taking her longer than she thought. She ran through the events of the last few hours as she snaked down the motorway along with frustrated holidaymakers and commuters. Getting into Paul Matthews' email account had been simpler than she anticipated. Robyn had considered what was important to the man before typing in his wife Linda's name and date of birth. It was surprising how many people used that method to create a password for accounts. Davies had told her that, one day as she logged on to her own emails. Davies had worked in Intelligence for years and knew all about sequences and passwords. He had cracked her own email password in only a few minutes, guessing correctly that she had used her first car's make and number plate.

'You should use a combination of random letters, numbers and symbols,' he said. 'People use familiar names and numbers because they can't remember odd sequences but you can. You've got a great memory.' She had changed her password that day.

Paul Matthews was not one to use his laptop often. His inbox had only a handful of emails and all of them were correspondence between him and Lucas. There was not much to go on but at least she now had a smattering of names and clues. The first email, sent two months earlier, had been terse and proved there was little affection between the two men. Lucas had written to his father:

From: LucasMatthews@BlinkleyManorPrepSchool.com
To: TwitcherPippin@hotmail.com
Subject: News
Date: Fri, June 3, 2016 at 11:18:08 + 0100
Dad,

I understand it has been a number of years since we spoke and we didn't part on the best of terms but something that affects us both has happened and I need to talk to you urgently.

Please can we arrange to talk? I can come to the house if that is convenient. Wednesday mornings are free. I don't work then.

Lucas

From: TwitcherPippin@hotmail.com

To: LucasMatthews@BlinkleyManorPrepSchool.com

Subject: News

Date: Mon, June 6, 2016 at 19:39:00 + 0100

Dear Lucas,

What a surprise to hear from you after all these years. I see you still have little time for small talk and have not even asked how I am. I can't imagine what has spooked you so much you suddenly need to speak to me or indeed how it affects me but I suppose, given I am your father, I ought to hear you out.

Make it ten o'clock this Wednesday if it is urgent.

Dad

The next email was sent over a week later and more intriguing:

From: TwitcherPippin@hotmail.com

To: LucasMatthews@BlinkleyManorPrepSchool.com

Subject: News

Date: Fri, June 17, 2016 at 12:25:00 + 0100

Dear Lucas,

Further to our conversation, I have deposited the amount you requested in your account at the Leek United Building Society. I suggest you do what you have to although as I told you, I am most unhappy you have involved me. You brought this on yourself.

Please do not ask me to help you again. I have done more than my fair share to assist you. I have stuck up for you far too often in the past and I don't wish to be party to any more of your outrageous conduct.

This is not really my problem, however, I feel duty bound to offer you this help, even though it sickens me to do so. I hope this brings an end to it all.

Handing in your resignation to the school will be the only option. You need to cease your tasteless behaviour. Get some professional help. See a psychiatrist and sort out your life. You are a married man with responsibilities now. Live up to them for goodness sake.
Dad

Three emails followed.

From: LucasMatthews@BlinkleyManorPrepSchool.com
To: TwitcherPippin@hotmail.com
Subject: News
Date: Tues, June 21, 2016 at 08:03:00 + 0100
Dad,

I did everything as instructed but I fear it has not been enough. I can't write down what has happened in an email. I desperately need to see you again. I shall come by tomorrow when I finish work, after six o' clock.
Lucas

From: TwitcherPippin@hotmail.com
To: LucasMatthews@BlinkleyManorPrepSchool.com
Subject: News
Date: Fri, July 01, 2016 at 19:39:00 + 0100
Lucas,

I'm sticking to my decision. I'm not giving you any more money.

You ought to report this all to the police, although I appreciate that will only make your life worse.

I don't know what else to suggest. Maybe you should talk to your wife about it.

Dad

The last email was from Paul sent five days before he died:

From: TwitcherPippin@hotmail.com
To: LucasMatthews@BlinkleyManorPrepSchool.com
Subject: News
Date: Wed, July 20th 2016 at 20:12:30
Lucas,
I've stumbled across something and I think I know where we might find her. If we can track her down we can stop this once and for all. Come by tomorrow and I'll explain.
Dad

Paul Matthews had died on 25 July and Lucas Matthews had gone missing the very same day. Robyn trawled through Paul's browsing history and examining only the days between the last email he sent to his son and his death, she unearthed searches for Christina Forman, Jane, Jack Clifford and Josh Clifford as well as for shops, schools, dentists, doctors and businesses in the Farnborough area.

Paul had created a document entitled *Farnborough* in which he had listed addresses and phone numbers for various locations in the town. Many had the word 'no' typed next to them, leading Robyn to assume Paul had contacted them and not come across who or what he wanted. A few remained as possibles, and so her first stop was at the Keep Fit Gym.

Paul had been on various websites, learning about the town. Consequently, Robyn discovered that one of Farnborough's famous citizens was exiled Eugénie, wife of Emperor Napoleon III, and Empress of the French who purchased Farnborough Hill, a large property which was to be her home until her death in 1920. The house had an interesting history and was even a convalescent home during the Great War. It then became a leading independent Catholic day school for girls, and, more interestingly for Robyn, appeared in Paul Matthews' document where he had not only put the name of the school in capital letters but also added a date – 28 July. She would investigate it further.

* * *

The first fat raindrops spilled from the heavens as Robyn pulled into the shopping centre car park at the Meads. She wondered what the French empress would make of the place now. It was difficult to imagine what it might have been like centuries ago although the clock house on the roundabout gave her an idea of a sleepier place, most unlike this modern-day version. Farnborough had seen many changes over the years with the rapid growth of the town. The international airshow brought thousands of people to the town, and it had grown accordingly, with huge redevelopment in the shopping centres. If Empress Eugénie had been alive today she would have been able to shop until she dropped. Robyn pushed open her car door and prepared to run to the fitness centre as heavy rain began to fall.

The gym was much smaller than the one Robyn used. A lean girl with her hair scraped back in a ponytail stood behind a reception desk tapping at her phone. She wore a bright yellow T-shirt emblazoned with the Keep Fit Gym logo and shorts that showed off sculptured, unblemished legs. She looked up as Robyn entered.

'Horrid day, isn't it?' she said. 'Are you my new client?'

'It is and no, I'm not,' replied Robyn, wiping drips from her face with one hand. She pulled out her warrant card and showed it to the woman.

'I wonder if you can help me. I'm looking for a missing man. Would you mind looking at a photograph to see if you recognise him?'

'Go on. I'm not sure I'll be much help, unless he's one of my clients.'

Robyn extracted a copy of the photograph of Lucas that had been in Mary Matthews' lounge. The girl looked at it and immediately shook her head. 'Never seen him. Try asking Martin. He'll be back in a minute. I'm covering the desk while he gets something to eat. He usually mans reception.'

Stacey's client arrived and she ushered her into the office behind the desk and turned back to Robyn. 'He'll only be a minute. Depends on the queue in the supermarket. You can wait here.'

She was correct for within seconds a bedraggled figure appeared through the door, dripping water. The young man shook a soaking wet umbrella that had blown inside out and muttered, 'Useless. I may as well have not had it, or gone out waving a daisy over my head.' His voice was light and his face broke into a cheerful grin as he caught sight of Robyn. 'Won't be a sec,' he said. His trainers squelched as he moved across the room, the noise making him grimace dramatically, and in one fluid movement he bent down and removed his footwear.

'Sorry,' he said. 'I can't bear wet feet.' He dried his feet with a towel hidden behind the desk. 'Okay, that's better. What can I do for you? Are you interested in signing up? We have an excellent spinning class. Although I'm a little biased – it's my class.' He grinned, revealing a gap between shining white teeth. 'I'm Martin,' he added.

Robyn smiled at him. He seemed a nice lad. He leaned towards her as she lowered her voice conspiratorially. 'Actually, I'm after your help. I'm Detective Inspector Robyn Carter and I'm searching for a missing person.' She slid her identification across the desk and he examined it before returning it with lips pressed together and a more serious demeanour. Robyn continued, 'I believe the person was in this area a while ago and maybe even came in here. Stacey told me you were really good with clients and had a great memory and I wondered if you had seen him.'

She pushed forward the photograph. Martin's eyes lit up immediately and he nodded.

'I definitely remember this man. He didn't give a name but I christened him Mr Creepy. It was a week ago today when I saw him. That was Thursday the twenty-eighth of July. I remember it well because I'd just finished taking a body-pump class for Stacey because she'd called in sick, and I was filling my bottle of water up over there.' He pointed at a large water dispenser. 'I was parched. It'd been really hot in the studio. The air con wasn't working, you see. I was dripping sweat and about to grab a shower when he marched in and asked to sign up with a personal trainer. Tonya was supposed to be on the desk, not me, but she'd gone off somewhere, so I dealt with him. Before I opened my mouth, he said it had to be Zoe. He was adamant he wanted Zoe and said his friend was currently training with her and had highly recommended her. Now that seemed strange to me because Zoe hasn't worked here since January. His eyes weren't right either, one of them didn't move. I didn't know which eye to look into and he kept staring at me. Made me feel really uncomfortable and gave me the creeps, hence the nickname. I'm a very good judge of character and people like him don't come here and ask to sign up just like that without checking out what we have to offer or what it costs.

'I told him Zoe had left and he seemed pretty annoyed. You know when you don't quite trust someone? Well, that's how I felt about him. He asked where she'd gone and I told him I didn't know. I didn't like his attitude and I wasn't going to send a strange man after one of my friends. He might have been one of those crazy-boyfriend types.'

He crossed his arms and pursed his lips.

'You did the right thing,' Robyn said, earning another smile from the young man. 'I don't suppose you'd mind telling me where Zoe went, would you?'

'Zoe took a job in London with Super Fit at a really flash gym and now she earns far more money than she ever did here. I wish Super Fit would give me a job. I keep hoping Zoe will put a good word in for me. I've got her phone number if you want it. Sometimes we meet up. I miss her. She was such a laugh and a very good instructor. Her classes were always oversubscribed.'

He scrolled down the contacts on his iPhone, wrote down the number on a leaflet for the gym and handed it over with a flourish. He gave her another smile as she thanked him. 'Any time. And, if you are in the area for a few days, come along to one of my classes.'

Outside, the world was still grey but the rain was easing. No sooner had she got into her car than PC Patel phoned.

'Got some info for you as requested. Jane Clifford is in a nursing home near Derby. I've arranged for you to visit her tomorrow lunchtime. DCI Mulholland needs both Anna and me all day tomorrow or I'd go. Hope that's okay.'

'I'll ask Ross Cunningham to visit her. I'd rather stay here. I've got a few more places to visit. I wasn't planning on hanging around for too long. I'm staying at the Aviator hotel tonight. It backs onto the airport, and since Paul Matthews wrote down TAG Aviation in his file marked *Farnborough*, I thought I'd go and hang around there and see if anyone knows Lucas. I'm going to Farnborough Hill convent tomorrow then I'll head back.'

'I'm still trying to track down Christina and the other names. Anna is working on the laptop. I'll get back to you as soon as I have more news for you.'

He disconnected and Robyn dialled Ross's number to ask him to visit Jane Clifford.

'That's fine,' he said. 'I'll go over on my way to my new job. It's for a nanny-monitoring service. They want a surveillance camera in almost every room. I don't think they can trust their nanny much.'

'You might be missing a couple of the cameras. Jeanette asked me to rig the office so she could check you weren't sneaking in chocolate bars and crisps. She's pretty sure you are bringing in junk food.'

There was a spluttering sound at the other end of the phone. 'Please tell me you are joking.'

Robyn laughed and ended the call, only to have her mobile buzz again.

'Boss, I think you should know. There's been an incident at Paul Matthews' house. The old lady who cleaned – Geraldine Marsh. She's been found dead there.'

CHAPTER TWENTY-SEVEN

THEN

The bus stinks of damp clothing and wet hair. I wrinkle my nose as more passengers climb aboard. A middle-aged woman in leggings and a raincoat, carrying several bags of shopping, gives me an indifferent stare and squeezes beside me, filling the seat with bags spilling into my space. There's no apology. I throw the woman a cursory glance and notice the tired, drawn face and disappointment hidden in her eyes. Her yellowed fingers bear no wedding ring, only the telltale signs of heavy smoking. The woman ignores me and sits with her legs spread, bags of shopping balanced on her lap and a mobile phone pressed under her chin as she continues her conversation in a loud voice, ignorant to all around her.

'No, I told you already. I didn't pick up any scones from M&S. They were way too expensive. I don't know why you insist on wasting your money on such luxuries. Yes, of course I collected your pension. I couldn't have got your shopping if I hadn't, could I? I couldn't get any library books by Georgette Heyer so I got you one by Jackie Collins.' There's a pause. 'I really don't know why I bother helping you out. Well, if you don't like Jackie Collins, I'll read it. Honestly!' She tuts in an exasperated fashion. The conversation continues for some time with the woman getting increasingly frustrated. In the end she stabs at the off button and huffs, then to no one in particular she says, 'Mothers! They never stop treating you like a kid.' She turns towards another passenger in the opposite seat to her and complains.

'She's eighty years old and treats me like I'm ten. "Do this, do that." I wish the old bat were dead some days. I've dragged around town to get her shopping and all she's done is moan. Pity she can't get it herself. If she hadn't broken her hip, she could have. I've got better things to do than go out and get her stuff.'

I ignore the woman and wonder what it would be like to be treated like a kid. I haven't been treated like a child for years. I'm the one who looks after our home, cleans it, cooks and shops for us both these days. If it weren't for me, there would be no home. At the moment, my own mother is probably unconscious in bed after a night entertaining her boss. These days she spends more and more time in bed. The booze and the drugs are doing for her. She's becoming emaciated and has a haunted look on her face all the time. She has retained some of her good looks but the way she's going, it won't be long before the boss loses interest in her, then where will we be?

I have plans to be gone by then. I've been saving, little by little, for the last few months. I'm not going to be like my mother and have sex with men for money or for a house. I have other ways of getting money. That's the bonus of being a ghost. No one notices you. My father thinks I'm a genius at remaining undetected. I've perfected the art over the years and since the episode with Chloe Baker, I've even managed to keep a lid on my temper, although both Dad and me know that inside I'm stewing quietly. Some days the pressure in my head threatens to make me explode and I have to go and stab myself to stop it. I look at what my mother has become and exact my revenge. My father has counselled me to bide my time. I have to learn to live first. I have to create a harmless identity and become that person. I have to convince others that I am that person, then, one day, I'll be able to get even with those who are guilty for my lost childhood and present circumstances.

The woman makes a noise like a deflating balloon and struggles to her feet as the bus lurches to a standstill. She waddles towards the door and clinging to the handrail, clambers down, her packages dangling. The bus pulls away and the woman fades into the distance.

At the next stop I get off, along with several other passengers. I stoop to tie up my bootlace, letting them all move away. Once I'm alone I pull the woman's purse out of my pocket. She didn't notice me slide my hand into her bag and take it. It contains one hundred and eighty pounds; no doubt some of it was the old lady's pension money. I toss the purse into the nearest bin and shove the money into my pocket. I need it more than an old lady. I need it to escape from my miserable life.

CHAPTER TWENTY-EIGHT

Abigail felt trapped like a butterfly caught and imprisoned in a jam jar she had no idea how to fight her way out of. Outside, black clouds hung like heavy drapes and rain tumbled from the sky, bouncing on the patio and spitting large drops against the wooden containers of pansies which flattened in submission, their petals drooping and ripped.

She was as unsettled as the weather. Her nerves ragged with anxiety and tiredness. She had not slept all night. Jackson beside her had been unaware of the turmoil in her head. It had required every ounce of restraint not to burst into tears and tell him what was happening to her and to them. She had sent messages to all her close friends asking them not to tell Jackson about what had been posted on Facebook. She explained that she had been hacked and did not want to worry him as he was snowed under with work obligations, but there was always a possibility that somebody would blab. It was the early hours of the morning before she fell into a dreamless sleep. She had woken to an empty bed. Jackson could be heard downstairs with Izzy.

Abigail picked up her phone from the bedside cupboard and logged onto her Facebook account only to discover more disgusting messages had appeared.

She sent another email to Facebook asking them to close her account, and left another message for Zoe – her third – telling her she had been hacked and to ignore the messages. Then she telephoned Claire who was understanding and sympathetic.

'I'll tell everyone you've definitely been hacked and none of the messages are from you. We share a lot of online friends. Have you spoken to Zoe?'

'She's at a conference so she probably hasn't been on Facebook. I left a message telling her there are some horrible messages but they aren't from me.'

'Zoe will know you didn't post them,' Claire replied. 'Your real friends will know you couldn't have posted any of this rubbish. I'm online now and these messages don't even sound like you. How on earth did anyone get hold of that photograph of you?'

'Have you got any copies on your computer or files?'

'I delete all the files once clients have chosen and downloaded the photographs they want. There are no copies. After a couple of weeks they are removed completely. Is it possible someone Jackson knows has managed to do this? His co-pilots sometimes visit your home, don't they? They might have snapped a shot of the photograph in your bedroom on their phone.'

Abigail thought that unlikely. Overnight she remembered Rachel had been poking about her house. She would have had the opportunity to take a photo of the picture. What puzzled her was why the woman would do such a thing? She seemed to genuinely like Abigail and Izzy. Then she remembered Rachel's mobile was not a smartphone. It had no Wi-Fi and so would not be able to upload photos to the Internet. The other possibility was that it was the creep who kept ringing her and who was trying to wreck her marriage. Now, it seemed he or she was trying to remove her friends and support. Abigail was gradually being branded a liar or slightly crazy. No matter how many times she denied writing the horrible messages online, people were beginning to suspect she was guilty of it.

Claire continued. 'Look, don't worry about it. I'll email Facebook and say you've had your account hacked and it'll soon be resolved.'

'Don't bother,' replied a weary Abigail. 'I've already done it. I'll find out who's behind this eventually.'

Claire agreed and rang off after telling her to stay strong.

Once she felt calmer, Abigail dressed and went downstairs. Jackson had fed Izzy and was sitting with her on his knee, reading her a story about a caterpillar. He looked up and gave Abigail a lopsided smile, last night's row forgotten.

'Look, Izzy, it's Mummy. Isn't she gorgeous? Even when she's just woken up, she's lovely.'

He winked at her and although she smiled back at him, it felt false. She hated hiding anything from her husband, even though she had done exactly that for years. It was time to come clean. She needed to tell him about the phone calls and why she was getting them…

'You looked so peaceful, I left you in bed,' he said. 'You don't get many chances to catch up on sleep. I was thinking maybe we could ask my mum to come down from Sheffield for a few days and look after Izzy and we'll take a break. Have a date night or even a weekend away. It'd do us both good. We haven't had a moment for each other since…' He left it unsaid.

'Since Izzy,' she said. 'That might be a good idea. I need to learn to let go. Izzy needs me but I need you. Your mum will love being with her. She hasn't seen her since she was very tiny. It'll be good for her too.'

Jackson grinned at Izzy and chucked her gently under her chin. 'You'll be a good girl for Granny, won't you?' The baby gurgled. Abigail steeled herself, ready to divulge the secrets she had been carrying for years, then his phone rang. He answered it, Izzy still on his knee trying to reach for his mobile. His face became serious; a frown pulled his eyebrows down. Abigail busied herself in the kitchen until he appeared again. She opened her mouth to speak but he was not in the mood to listen.

'James hasn't shown up again,' he complained. 'I'll have to go and sort out the roster and persuade Dan to come off leave to take the flight to Switzerland. I might need to hire some more staff. We'll lose the business if we can't find pilots to fly the clients. I'll have to cut and run. See you tonight. Come on, Splodge, Mummy's going to look after you now 'cos Daddy has to go to work.'

He passed Izzy to Abigail and planting a kiss on his wife's lips, grabbed his hat and left. She would have to wait for another more appropriate time to tell him.

* * *

By late afternoon, Jackson had still not returned. Izzy was crawling on a gym mat, babbling merrily to herself. She grabbed at the hanging mirror, spotted her own reflection and crowed. The sound lifted Abigail's spirits and she turned towards her child.

'Come on, let's play peekaboo,' she said, sitting Izzy up on her lap. 'Shall Mummy play peekaboo with Izzy?' She covered her own eyes with her hands and asked, 'Where's Izzy? Where's Izzy?' Izzy babbled incoherently. Uncovering them in one quick movement, she said in an upbeat voice, 'There she is.' The child clapped her hands in delight.

Abigail laughed at the response and repeated the game several times before reversing the game and covering Izzy's eyes with her hands. Her heart ached with love for Izzy and she wished she could remember times when her own mother had played games like this with her. She doubted that would have been the case. She had no warm memories of early days or bright toys, songs or story times. She pushed the thoughts away. If she dwelt on them too much, other nastier memories would float to the surface and she couldn't have that. Her past was exactly that – in the past. Even Jackson had no idea of what she had been through. She had fabricated a life that he would understand. She had made up stories about trips abroad and Christmas days filled with laughter and visits to adventure parks. A life where her parents had been proud of their girl until both had passed away in a car accident while she was working abroad in Turkey.

Jackson had enjoyed a happy, wholesome upbringing with parents who had read to him every evening, eaten Sunday roast with him and spent summer holidays at the seaside in a small cottage they owned, scouring beaches for shells and small creatures, or flown kites with him, or treated him to donkey rides and ice cream. Jackson often spoke of his precious childhood filled with glorious memories that Abigail would have cherished had they been her own. His mother had not worked and had welcomed him when he returned each night from school with freshly baked cakes and jam sandwiches for tea. They had been a perfect family unit. How Abigail wished she could have had such normality in her life. She had that now. She had a life with Jackson and Izzy and Toffee.

Toffee leapt onto a kitchen chair and began to groom himself. Abigail collected Izzy and sat her on her knee. 'Story time,' she said. Izzy grabbed at her sock and tried to pull it off while her mother spoke.

'Once upon a time there was a little girl who lived in a nice house with a fluffy cat. Do you know what the cat's name was? Toffee, because he was the colour of cream toffee.' Izzy looked up as if listening. 'She had a mummy who loved her very much and a daddy who also loved her very much.'

* * *

Izzy played contentedly in her playpen, leaving Abigail free to prepare dinner for Jackson and her. She had set the table as she used to before they had had Izzy. Three thick red candles stood in the centre waiting to be lit. Next to them was a bottle of uncorked red wine. It would be a romantic night. She would put effort back into her relationship with Jackson.

She checked the clock on the cooker, saw she had about twenty minutes before Jackson would be home, and scooped up Izzy. Since the shock of hearing the imaginary whispering voice, Abigail was loath to leave her unattended. She wasn't willing to take any chances even if the voices had all been in her head. The locksmith she called that morning had changed all the locks in the house but now she would have to explain to Jackson why she had felt the need to do this. He would think she was being stupid. Still, that was a risk she would have to take.

'Come on, little cherub. You can come with me while I get ready,' she said, carrying the baby upstairs into the bedroom with her. Izzy rolled around the king-sized bed while Abigail zipped through the rails of expensive clothes. A few minutes later, with hair fluffed out, she was dressed in tight jeans and a white top that left little to the imagination. Her deep red glossed lips looked inviting and she practised a sexy pout in front of the mirror. Tonight she would remind him who he had fallen in love with. She would put the terror and upset of the last few days behind her. She would tell the anonymous caller to get lost and threaten to report them to the police. She was going to end it now and go back to her normal life, the life she had worked so hard to create.

'Do you think Daddy will like this outfit?' she asked Izzy who cooed back. 'I think he will. I think Daddy will like it very much. And we'll all be a very happy family, forever.'

Returning downstairs she noticed she had an email alert. It came from an unknown email address with the handle concerned-friend@hotmail.com. The email subject read 'The Truth'. A sense of foreboding took over, almost as if she could feel the contents of the email and knew they were about to alter the course of her life. She placed Izzy in her high chair with a rice cake.

She picked up her mobile to read the contents of the email then hesitated. She could erase it and be none the wiser. She could continue her life as it was and tonight have a wonderful meal with Jackson and then sit beside him on the settee and laugh and drink wine, before falling into each other's arms. Her world went into slow motion as she automatically clicked onto the email that read, 'First she'll take your husband's heart. What will she take next? Your house? Your life? Your child?' Abigail's hand trembled as she downloaded the attachments.

The first photograph was of a woman planting a kiss on Jackson's mouth in a bar. The second and third were more explicit. Although Abigail could not make out the face of the man being ridden by the naked woman whose face was screwed up in ecstasy, she spotted the captain's hat by the bedside. She let out a low moan. These photographs were of Jackson and his lover – a woman she had known for three years. The woman in the photograph was magnificent in her nudity – her breasts firm and round, her midriff a washboard and her strong thighs wrapped around the man. Her hair had fallen forward and concealed some of her face but there was no denying it. The woman with green hair in the photograph was Zoe.

CHAPTER TWENTY-NINE

The Aviator hotel in Farnborough was created for elite travellers moving between London and the world's leading destinations. It overlooked the main runway of what many consider to be Europe's most prestigious executive airport, and boasted unique architecture. Even the lifts followed an aviation theme with aircraft-styled video windows playing back images of the clouds whisking by at thirty-five thousand feet.

Robyn had stayed in many hotels over the years but none as plush as this. Her bedroom interior was contemporary yet rich and comfortable with walnut panelling, leather furniture and a bathroom with black glass walls, granite vanity tops and chrome finishing. Dark wood venetian blinds hung before large windows that looked out onto Farnborough airfield.

The one-time military aerodrome and research station had been transformed into a svelte civil airport. The control tower that vaguely resembled the famous TWA terminal at JFK airport, New York, the deftly engineered and gently undulating aircraft hangar, and the coolly elegant terminal building were stylish and impressive. The three-storey, steel-framed terminal building resembled a giant wing. She had read that TAG Aviation described it as a 'virtual aircraft without a fuselage. It appeared as though the building itself has just touched down on the runway and taxied into position.'

She watched as a small jet prepared for take-off and headed towards the runway. She remained transfixed while the engines rotated and it moved forward, the noise increasing along with its speed until it suddenly rose from the ground with a resonant roar and a grace that Robyn found familiar and comforting. She had watched one like it take off during her 'other life', when a mission had required Davies and two colleagues to be quickly and surreptitiously transported to the south of France, where their fluent knowledge of French and undercover skills had resulted in the capture of a small cell of terrorists.

She dumped her bag in the walk-in wardrobe and grabbed a cold bottle of water from the fridge before phoning Mitz Patel.

'Nothing more to report. The local farmer saw Geraldine's bike parked outside the house when he went to cut the hedge. He thought it unusual because she's not normally there on a Thursday. When the bike was still there later that day, he knocked on the door. The door was unlocked so he opened it and spotted her body at the bottom of the stairs. Sergeant Austin James was called to the scene but there were no suspicious circumstances. It appears she slipped and fell.'

'Seems odd that Paul Matthews tripped and fell in the woods and now his housekeeper has done the same in the house.'

'There was no evidence to suggest otherwise.'

'I'd like you to take another look.'

'What about DCI Mulholland?'

'I'll square it. I want you to make sure. Check for anything at all that might point at this being more than an accident. And call me as soon as you've found something.'

'What if I don't?'

'You will.'

Next, Robyn called Zoe Cooper, identified herself as a police officer and arranged to meet the woman later at the hotel when Zoe returned from work. The rest of the afternoon was slightly more frustrating. She rang DCI Mulholland and explained she wanted PC Patel to check the scene at the Farmhouse. Louisa did not sound best pleased.

'I don't want my officers being sent on wild goose chases, Robyn. I thought I made it clear I needed him at the station. We are ridiculously short-handed at the moment.'

'I appreciate that but I have a hunch that Geraldine Marsh's death is connected somehow to this case.'

'Here we go. You're following your hunches. The report was quite clear. The housekeeper slipped and fell. There was no one else in the house. You are reading too much into it.'

'So you won't let PC Patel check the house?'

Mulholland exhaled noisily. 'He can go. I hope you're right. I don't like wasting my valued officer's time.'

Robyn then had a new problem. She attempted to gain entry to the airfield, but without an actual booking or ID clearance, security was unwilling to let her onto the site. Her warrant card and expert negotiation skills failed her. No one was willing to talk to her or let her have access to the airfield. She phoned BizzyAir and was told that unless she was a passenger on one of their aircraft, she could not be admitted to the terminal regardless of her rank in the police force. It was hopeless. She couldn't request assistance from Louisa Mulholland. She had already annoyed her superior sufficiently for one day and there wasn't time to go through all the protocols or evidence she needed to get behind the gates. A thought crossed her mind. What Louisa didn't know would not hurt. She would try less conventional means to get onto the airfield.

Robyn stepped into one of the lifts, checking herself in the mirrors which reflected several images of an elegant woman with hair expertly styled in a perfect bun, wearing a tailored blue trouser suit and a multicoloured scarf knotted to one side of her neck.

She waited close to the reception desk, hidden from view on one of the many seats hidden in the alcoves. Luck was on her side and she did not have to wait long before a group of businessmen exited the bar area, preparing to take leave of each other. They huddled in a group close to her and she could hear their every word.

'Well, Mr Carlisle, it's been a pleasure to meet you. Have a good trip,' said one, holding out his hand. 'Wish we were going with you. It sounds like quite an event.'

'It's not every day you get to see a power station being blown up.' Robyn eased forward to catch a glimpse of the men. Mr Carlisle appeared to be in his fifties, over six feet tall, with muddy blond hair reaching his collar, dressed in a white shirt and black trousers with scuffed shoes. He had the confident air of a businessman but clearly did not take pride in his appearance. His companion, several inches shorter, was dressed in a grey suit that did nothing for his florid complexion. He continued speaking, 'Thank you for lunch. Richard here will be in touch next week. I'm off to Portugal this weekend. Promised "her indoors" a nice holiday. She's been nagging me all year to take her away. Okay, we'd better get going. The others should be at the airfield by now. Better join them or they'll take off without us.'

'I doubt they'd leave without the boss,' said one of the men with a chuckle.

'I think they'd relish the opportunity to leave me behind,' replied Carlisle.

Robyn stole away down the staircase, past the flickering flames of the open fires and velvet sofas and headed outside into the grey day, where she waited by a Valet Parking sign. Timing was now everything. As the men emerged from the hotel, the taxi pulled up on cue. Robyn advanced and grabbed the door handle.

The taxi driver leaned towards the open window and asked, 'TAG Aviation?'

'Yes, said Robyn, climbing in and buckling up.

'Yes, us too,' replied the short man in the grey suit.

'I'm supposed to collect a Mr Carlisle?' said the taxi driver, looking back at Robyn.

'That's me,' said Carlisle.

'Then I'm for you, not this lady. Sorry, love, you'll have to get out.'

'But I've been waiting fifteen minutes already for a taxi and I need to get to the airfield. I'll be late for the flight if I don't go now,' she replied politely. She leaned out towards the two men outside. 'Are you going to the airfield? Could I share with you? I really am going to be late if I don't.'

Carlisle looked her up and down, his gaze unwavering before he said, 'Since we're all headed for the same destination, why not? No point in hanging around any longer than necessary. We don't mind if you don't.'

'Oh thank you. You are real gentlemen,' she said with a winning smile. Carlisle climbed in, choosing the seat opposite Robyn. His companion, who seemed less delighted by the prospect, gave a curt nod then ignored Robyn and continued his conversation.

'So is Rick meeting us up in Glasgow?'

'Only if he's got rid of his hangover. He sounded well oiled last night. Still, not every day you win a contract to knock down the biggest power station in Scotland.'

'He ought to wait until it's successful. If it all goes wrong, he'll be right up the creek.'

'He's an expert in blowing up buildings. It'll be fine. No doubt we'll all be watching and cheering and watching it over and over again on the news later.'

He glanced at Robyn who was looking out of the window and pretending not to understand.

'We're going to Glasgow. Going to watch the largest power station in Scotland being blown up.'

'Do you own the station?'

'We're in scrap metal. We get to sort through it once it's down, so in a way, yes we do,' he replied proudly. 'Where are you flying to?'

'Back to France. To Nice,' she replied.

'Business flight?'

'I'm crew on a privately owned jet. I'm afraid I can't tell you who it belongs to but he needs to return today which is earlier than we anticipated, so I've been called back. No stopover as planned. Thank you for letting me ride with you.' She smiled apologetically as she pulled out her mobile, pretending it had rung, and launched into a phoney conversation in French, preventing further conversation with the men, who then continued chatting about the power station in lowered voices.

Soon they pulled up at the gates for TAG Aviation Farnborough airport and were met by a man with a clipboard.

'Tail number please,' he asked. Richard dragged out a piece of paper from a calf-leather wallet and squinted at it.

'It's W. I. G. L,' he said, reading out the letters. 'We're part of a group who might already be here.'

The man checked his clipboard. Robyn kept up her imaginary conversation, smiling only once at the guard who assumed she was with the two men. He waved them through.

The taxi dropped them by the executive lounge. Robyn terminated her call and insisted on paying her share of the taxi fare. As they descended, shouts from a small group of men gathered outside the terminal made her travelling companions look up.

'Hi, chaps,' yelled Richard. 'I'm afraid I couldn't get rid of him,' he shouted, pointing at Carlisle who grinned good-naturedly. There were choruses of fake booing and then laughter as the men joined the group and all entered reception together. In the muddle of voices and men slapping down various travel documents on the desk, Robyn was able to slip past the receptionist and into the terminal.

She followed the corridor until she reached the pilot and crew lounge. It was as stylish as the hotel she just left. The room had been designed in greys and reds, with stylish striped cushions on large settees, a snooze area and kitchen, and a line of computers at desks. Behind a computer sat a first officer. Robyn identified his position from the three stripes on his blazer sleeve. He was studying weather maps intently and barely gave her a second glance as she strode to a settee, head high, and nodded in his direction before sitting down and drawing out a sheet of paper from her bag. After a while she tutted loudly, causing the man to look up.

'Sorry, just seen we are collecting a passenger we've flown before. He was such a problem last time. Lucas Matthews. Have you ever had the pleasure?'

'No, can't say I have. Hope he behaves this time. Who are you with? I haven't seen you in here before.'

'A private flight. Whisky India Golf Lima,' she added, recalling the tail number from the flight Carlisle and his cronies were taking and using the phonetic alphabet that she knew the pilot would expect. 'Off to Glasgow.'

The pilot nodded. 'The Lear jet. I saw it land. Nice craft.' The door opened and a lean man about sixty years old, with steely grey hair and bottle-green eyes entered the room. Hat under his arm, he bore the insignia and bearing of a seasoned captain. 'Afternoon, Dan. Looks like a good one,' he said in a clipped voice. 'You all set to go?'

'Just checking the weather. Should be good weather conditions en route and they're expecting twenty-four degrees and a light south-west wind at Schiphol so I don't envisage any difficulties.'

Dan put on his Ray-Bans and hat, completing the uniform of a well-heeled, private pilot. He nodded again at Robyn and spoke, 'Hope your passenger behaves.'

'Who's that then?' asked the captain as they made for the door.

'Lucas Matthews,' Robyn replied.

'Lucas?' said the captain. 'Name rings a bell. I think he's the guy that was hounding Jackson. He kept calling and asking for him. Sally on reception was sick of him phoning. She complained about him and his attitude. He got quite nasty with her at one point. Jackson was going to tear him off a strip and call him back. I don't know if he did or not but it wasn't mentioned again. He was definitely odd. I didn't think he would cause any harm though. As I recall he was intense, that's the word, intense, and a little bit strange. At least he's not hassling Jackson any more. I'm sure he'll behave for you though,' he added and gave Robyn a wink.

They left for their flight. Robyn walked out of the building with confidence, even acknowledging the girl on reception with a goodbye. Sometimes it paid to be obvious rather than skulk in the shadows. You could hide well in plain view. She walked away from the terminal and rang for a taxi to collect her. She now had another name – Jackson. She only needed a surname then she might be able to track him down.

* * *

Zoe was on time. She arrived at the Sky Bar dressed in a cream lace dress and gladiator sandals tied around shapely calves. The combination together with her green hair caused heads to turn. She meandered over to Robyn who was waiting by the bar.

'Hi. I'm Zoe,' she announced, sliding onto the stool next to Robyn and catching the waiter's eye. 'Hi, Christophe,' she said to the handsome barman – a striking dark-haired man with sharp cheekbones and sensual lips, who would not have looked out of place on the catwalk.

'Fancy a drink?' asked Robyn.

'Large sparkling water and lime please? I've got a raging thirst. I've taught four classes this afternoon, back to back, and the train was packed with people. I'm totally dehydrated. I'll look like a giant dried-up prune if I don't get some liquid inside me soon.'

'Make that two.'

The barman poured the drinks and passed them over. Zoe took a long sip and made an appreciative noise.

'That's better. Thank you.' She gave Robyn a perfect white smile. 'A detective, eh? That's got to be interesting. I used to love *Juliet Bravo* on the telly.'

'It's not quite like the television but it has its moments.'

Zoe took another slug of her water and sighed. 'Much better,' she said. 'I love police dramas and those programmes about detectives like *Endeavour* or *Sherlock*. I'd prefer being a private investigator to being in the police. I've always fancied being the bait for one of those "honey trap" jobs.' She grinned widely, crossed her legs and feigned an appropriate wanton pose.

She waved at the barman. 'Christophe? Do you think I could get a job as man bait?'

He laughed. 'I thought you already did that job.'

'Cheeky,' she replied. 'You're only jealous because I pick up more men than you do.'

'True. You're so right. However, I am a changed man now,' he replied, pointing at the wedding band on his finger.

Zoe laughed. 'You still flirt for England. You'll never stop.'

He laughed again and shook his head at her.

Robyn witnessed the camaraderie between the two. 'You must come here a lot.'

'Very good, DI Carter. I drop in now and then but I've known Christophe for two years, since he joined one of my Pilates classes. I've never had such a popular class. Women from far and wide joined it just to watch handsome Christophe here do impossible moves in his ultra-tight shorts. He broke every one of their hearts when they discovered he was going to marry Declan.'

Christophe gave a bright smile. 'You have broken your fair share of hearts too, hun,' he said before moving away to serve another customer. Zoe adopted a serious face.

'So, you're looking for someone?'

'A man named Lucas Matthews. I think he was trying to get in touch with you for some reason. Your name has come up in the investigation.'

'I'm not a suspect or anything, am I?'

'No. There's no crime here. I'm just searching for a missing individual and hoped you had seen him.'

'The name isn't at all familiar. Have you got a picture of him?' She drained her glass.

Robyn slid the photo of Lucas across the bar. Zoe examined it closely and tapped it with a neatly painted nail that matched the colour of her hair. 'I've definitely seen him but I can't think where.' She screwed up her eyes, trying to conjure up the place and time but after a moment opened them again. 'No, can't think where. I've not spoken to him but I've seen him somewhere. I shouldn't be worried, should I?'

'I don't believe so. I think he's trying to contact you and I'm pretty certain he doesn't intend any harm. But if you see him, please call me immediately.'

Robyn scribbled on one of Ross's business cards. 'If you can remember when or where you saw him, give me a call. That's my personal number.'

'Definitely. Okay. I better get going. I haven't eaten since breakfast. Nice talking to you. Bye, Christophe,' she shouted, blowing him a kiss as she left. 'See you on Friday.'

'Nice woman,' said Robyn, engaging the barman in conversation.

'She's such fun. Always so bubbly and a bit mad. It's like she's on something. She races about at ninety miles an hour all the time. Love her to bits though.'

'Does she come in often?'

'Not as much as she'd like to. She loves it here. It's the men, you see,' he said in a quiet voice. 'All these businessmen, and needless to say, the pilots who come here for a drink after a flight. Zoe loves men in uniform.'

'Do you know all the pilots then?'

'Most of them.'

'Do you know Jackson?'

'Jackson Thorne,' he exclaimed. 'Of course I do. He owns BizzyAir Business Aviation. They have a couple of jets parked over at the terminal. Now if I weren't married, I'd throw myself at that man. Actually, you should ask Zoe about Jackson. They're good friends.'

Robyn couldn't ask him any further questions as a group of people came in and he was suddenly occupied. She decided to go back to her room and check out Jackson Thorne and wait to hear from PC Patel. She hoped her gut feeling would pay off or she'd rapidly lose face with her senior officer.

CHAPTER THIRTY

THEN

The bus is almost empty apart from two elderly people this afternoon on what I am calling my liberation day. My mother's working at the bar and won't be home until late. I'll have the rest of the day to celebrate the end of school, exams and everything that has bound me to the life I hate. I can't wait to start afresh. There'll be no one to hold me back now. I'm pretty sure I've done well enough in my exams to gain grades that will help me get a decent job, although at this stage I don't care what that job is as long as it allows me to pay rent on my own flat and get away from this town. I won't have too long to wait and if I'm lucky I'll get some temporary work in a shop or somewhere to tide me over until I get a full-time salary.

I pull out the local newspaper that I bought to search for jobs, and then the postcard of a rainbow-coloured heart, and I stare at it. Once I get my exam results it will be time to send the card to Grandma Jane. It would be lovely to see my grandparents again but they would be horrified by my appearance. I would probably give them both heart attacks. I daren't let them see how much I've changed over the years. They would hate my black spiky hair, gaunt looks and the Doc Martin boots I always wear. They have happy memories of a golden-tressed child with pink cheeks. Best not to spoil that for them. As much I would like to see them, I can't risk it. They would probably insist I live with them and that is not part of the big picture.

Dad suggested sending postcards to my grandparents, and so every time we moved house, I'd steal money from Mum's purse and buy a card and a stamp then send it Grandma Jane. I never wrote a message on it but I thought Grandma Jane would know who had sent it. I always chose a heart for her. She would work it out and know that I was alive and well and thinking of them both.

The bus clatters to a halt and I alight. I am for once in a reasonably good mood. The future is beginning to look brighter. I think about where I might live and what I might do. I have a good idea of what I'd like and it doesn't involve bars, nightclubs or men. I am only a few paces away from our house when I spot the lumbering frame of my mum's boss, Dirk. He's waiting by the gate. He's wearing his usual attire of jeans and shirt with a button-down collar. He thinks he looks fashionable and with it but I think he looks a dick. Dirk the dick. He appears to be particularly pleased with himself and grins like a half-witted fool when he sees me. I am never fooled by his smile. His looks are deceptive. Dirk can be ruthless, one mean son of a bitch. I've heard some pretty frightening tales about him and men who've had fingers chopped off or been kneecapped because they owed him money. He isn't much nicer to the women in his life although my mum has fared better than most. He seems to like her and doesn't rough her up like he did his last girlfriend. He knocked out her front teeth and smashed her face because she stole some of his stash of cocaine. She was in intensive care for weeks and was never able to eat properly again after the event. Dirk stubs out a cigarette on the path and waits for me to approach.

'Mum's not in,' I say.

'I know,' he replies, displaying dirty yellow teeth. Someone ought to tell him about toothpaste.

'What do you want, Dirk?'

He gives me a look and his eyes travel down to my chest. 'What d'ya think I want?'

'In your dreams,' I reply then wish I hadn't.

His features change in an instant and his arm snakes out, grabbing mine and twisting it high behind my back. The pain shoots through me so quickly and sharply it makes me yelp.

'Don't get cocky with me,' he snarls. 'You think you're too good for me, don't ya? Well, you're not. You're a skinny cow with no tits and a face that looks like it's always sucking lemons. You need to be taught a lesson.'

He forces me to the front door. 'Open it,' he commands and yanks on my arm again, sending another bolt of pain through it. I wince this time but don't cry out.

He hustles me into the house, releases my arm and pushes me hard towards the lounge. I stumble forward and only just prevent myself from falling onto the floor. He towers above me, his chest puffed out. The broken veins on his face stand out an angry red.

'If it weren't for me, you'd have nowhere to live. Your old lady couldn't afford a nice place like this. In fact, she couldn't afford anything. You'd be on the streets so you, you snotty bitch, will show me a little respect.' He raises his hand and slaps me hard across the face. I rub at my smarting cheek and glare at him.

'You can take that bloody look off your face. I'm not interested in your body. I doubt anyone is. I've seen you in the bathroom and seen all those marks on your legs. You're a right turn-off. I'd rather shag a sheep. I want you to collect a package for me. You're pretty good at skulking about and not being noticed. I want you to collect from someone and bring it directly to me, get it? If you don't, I might have to show your mum the back of my hand and my belt. I think a few straps across her face with this buckle will finish off her looks for good.' He rubs at the brass buckle in the shape of a serpent on his leather belt. 'So, you'll do it, right? And keep quiet about it.'

I nod dumbly. As much as my mother annoys me, I wouldn't want her harmed by this goon.

'Here's the address. Get going. Bring the package to the back door of the club and up to my office.'

He hands me a scruffy piece of paper accompanied by a steely look. 'Want some advice? You really should try to do something about your appearance. You're a mess. No one is going to want you if you look like that.'

He leaves the house, his comments stinging in my ears. I don't want to make an effort with my appearance. I wouldn't want to end up with someone like him as my boyfriend, besides, I know what happens to pretty girls. I'm perfectly happy the way I am.

I ponder my predicament. No doubt there'll be drugs in the package I am to collect. I curse Dirk. This won't be the last time he uses me either. I just know it. I heard him on the phone last night mumbling about one of his employees getting banged up. I bet that poor sod was the usual courier. Dirk knows how to press my buttons. I won't let anything happen to my mum. I can't leave now. If I do, she'll get beaten up or worse still, end up in a body bag at the local morgue. I'll do what he asks but I have a dreadful feeling he'll use me again and again until I get caught by the police.

Red mist descends. I am trapped again. I kick the wall; my boots make a satisfying noise as they connect with it. I wish it were Dirk's face. A picture – a reproduction of a pale blue butterfly, falls to the floor and the glass covering it smashes. I retrieve it from the floor and gaze at the painting of the delicate creature, with gossamer wings. I once read that in popular culture, the butterfly symbolises transient or short-lived beauty and looking at it I feel a connection to it. Like the butterfly, I have lived through various transformations but unlike it I shall never be beautiful. I feel a pain in my heart and I wish the butterfly in the painting could fly away now the glass is broken and more than anything I wish that I could join it.

CHAPTER THIRTY-ONE

Ross was shown into what the friendly nurse had called, 'The Green Room'. The walls were green but a dreary, miserable green, one that had had all the life sucked out of it, much like the residents who were sat in chairs dotted about the room. He hated places like this. The last time he had visited a care home had been to see his mother, and that had been a horrendous experience with her screaming and crying to be let out and all the while the nurses holding her down. She hadn't lasted much longer. The nurses said it was the cancer that had made her cry and shout and not comprehend where she was. Ross knew better. His mother had dreaded being left there to rot.

He moved towards the hunched figure, dozing in a chair and, bending down, spoke gently. 'Mrs Clifford, can I speak to you?'

She woke instantly. Her wizened face, with skin as thin as aged parchment, pulled into a smile as she searched his face. 'Josh?' she said. 'You've come to see me.'

'I'm sorry. I'm not Josh, I'm Ross, Ross Cunningham. I'm an investigator. I hoped you could help me.'

The light extinguished from her eyes as she searched his face. 'Not Josh,' she whispered more to herself than anyone in particular. 'What do you want?' she asked more lucidly.

Ross had come across this before too. His mother had had moments when she could talk articulately as if nothing was wrong with her then would be overcome by the dreadful cloud of confusion that would send her skidding back into the recesses of her mind, unable to communicate or recognise him.

'I'm a private investigator but I'm working a case with a police detective from the Staffordshire police force. We're searching for a missing person name of Lucas Matthews.'

'I don't know him,' she replied and shook her head.

'We believe your daughter-in-law Christina might have known him.'

The woman sat up in her seat, a new energy about her. 'My ex-daughter-in-law,' she said, a vivid scarlet spot appearing on her cheeks. Her eyes unfocused for a moment as memories rushed back. 'I knew from the start when Josh brought her home, she'd be trouble. He was besotted. She was all legs and fluttering eyelashes. He wouldn't have listened to me even if I told him. He'd have thought I was being a jealous mother. It was the way she wound him round her little finger that upset me most. He was such a bright lad, with friends and prospects and his whole life shining brightly in front of him. Then he married her and was always at her beck and call. He became nothing more than a puppet who jumped at her every whim and caprice. She spent his money faster than he could earn it. My poor boy.' A faraway look replaced her emotional outburst as Mrs Clifford retreated to her world of memories, no longer cognisant of Ross beside her. He waited. He had waited often for his mother to rejoin the real world until, finally, she could no longer find her way back and he lost her forever.

Without warning, Jane Clifford spoke again. 'He worked every hour of the day to keep up with her demands. He bought her new cars almost every year. She'd make those big eyes at him until he caved in. She was what people call "high maintenance", with trips to salons, teeth-whitening, false nails and all that nonsense. No doubt influenced by the pictures in the glossy magazines she read. And, I can't begin to estimate what she spent on make-up and facials and the latest trendy fashions. You'd have thought Josh was on a footballer's salary instead of a brewery manager's, the way she carried on. He didn't stop her. He let her have her way no matter what the cost. His father, God rest his soul, said Josh was a doormat. I could see it was wearing Josh out. He began working longer hours and took on some night shifts to feed her spending habits. She didn't work, of course. Spent all day shopping.' She looked into the distance, her eyes moistening as she spoke. 'I suppose the tiredness and worry played its part in the end. He maybe wasn't concentrating on the driving, the day he had the accident. He drove straight into the back of a parked lorry on the hard shoulder. Couldn't have seen it. The traffic officers said he must have misjudged where he was. He died,' she said simply.

'I'm sorry,' he said.

Jane Clifford eyed him. 'You look a bit like him. How I imagine he would look today. If he were still with us. Your eyes are similar – you have kind eyes,' she added. 'He was killed in a senseless accident that might have been avoided had he looked up in time and seen he was no longer on the carriageway. It shattered our world. Josh was all we had – him and little Alice.'

Ross sat forward. 'Alice, she was your granddaughter.'

'Was or is. I don't know if she's alive or where she is. She was a light in our lives. After Josh died, she was even more important to us. So fragile, so precious.' Jane Clifford's eyes filled with tears. 'Only a few months after Josh died, she – Christina – began hanging around bars, the sailing club, and golf clubs. She was trying to snare another man. It didn't take long before she hitched up with an actor called Paul Matthews. She wanted to start a new life, shutting us off.' She stopped for a second, and tapped the tips of her fingers together. 'Matthews. You asked me about Lucas Matthews. Is there a connection?'

'Lucas is Paul's son.'

'Of course. I did know that. I had forgotten. I forget things these days.'

She stopped again and stared at nothing in particular. Ross didn't push her. He sat back in his chair until Jane Clifford was ready to talk again.

'It didn't last even though they got engaged. Soon after Christina and Alice moved into his house, there were problems with his children and Alice. I don't know the ins and outs of it but the relationship crumbled. Christina visited us soon after she broke up with Paul Matthews. She was all tears and regrets. We were there for her even though we were not happy about her. She really wasn't the sort of daughter-in-law anyone could like or love. She was so hard and distant. I put it down to losing her own parents and I really tried to get closer to her, but even after ten years of being married to my son, I knew next to nothing about her. Alice visited more often after the break-up with Paul Matthews. She had changed too. Something was broken inside her and we were anxious about her. Then we discovered Christina had become an escort – one of those women who gets paid for accompanying men, but it was more than just going out with men to functions.' Her voice lowered again and she whispered, 'She was getting paid for sex.' She tutted quietly. 'Poor Josh. He would have been mortified to know what his wife had turned into. It wasn't long before she fell in with some lowlife sorts. She claimed she was working in a bar but we knew what went on after hours.'

Jane Clifford tugged at the beige cardigan and wrapped it tighter around her. 'And as for Alice, we became even more concerned about her well-being. I was convinced she was being neglected. She always looked so pale and ill. I wanted her to come and live with us but she only stayed when Christina was too busy to look after her. It was obvious to us that Christina wasn't interested in her daughter. I couldn't keep quiet about it. I was horrified. Jack, my husband, told me not to say anything but I couldn't help myself. One day when Christina came to collect Alice, I challenged Christina about it. She went crazy and without warning, took our granddaughter from us. She called us some terrible names and accused us of interfering, then left overnight and we never saw them again. Jack was right. I should have kept silent. I wonder what would have happened if I had or if I had engaged an investigator to search for her after they left. Someone like you. You would have got her back. You look like a man who would understand about family. Have you got any children?'

'No. We haven't been blessed with children but we wanted them. Badly,' he added. 'Now there's only Jeanette and me but we're good. We've accepted our lot.'

'One has to Mr… I'm sorry, I've forgotten your name,' she said, looking concerned.

'Ross. You can call me Ross.'

'And you can call me Jane. It's very nice to talk to you. I don't get any visitors. Since I lost my husband there's only me.'

'Then I shall come and visit you again.'

The corners of her mouth pulled upwards. 'That would be lovely. Thank you.'

'What a shame Alice can't visit."

'She probably has no idea where I am. She didn't get in touch again either although there were some postcards.'

'Postcards?'

'The first card arrived a few years after we had the dreadful fallout with Christine. It was a photograph of a large red heart but it had nothing written on the back of it, only a kiss. I had no idea who sent them but part of me hoped it was Alice and she would come home to us. I kept the card and a few months later another arrived, then there were others. Would you like to see them? I keep them in my room in my special box.'

'I'd like that.'

* * *

Robyn had reached Farnborough Hill School when Ross rang but the urgency in his voice caused her to stay in the car to listen to him. He was recounting his visit to see Mrs Clifford.

'So, Christina got involved with the actor Paul Matthews and stopped going to visit Josh's parents. They never got on that well anyhow but Mrs Clifford was hurt by the fact they were dropped as if they'd never been part of her life. Next thing, it was all over. She was thrown out of Paul's house and was back looking for a man to keep her. She began to get desperate and started looking in other places other than posh clubs, and began hanging around bars. She then picked up the wrong sort, if you know what I mean, and followed a different path – she became an escort and not a high-class one at that. Jane Clifford wasn't willing to say more on that subject. She had a massive row with Christina after which Christina walked out and never spoke to the Cliffords again. Mr Clifford took the whole episode very badly and shortly afterwards he suffered a heart attack. He survived it but was never the same afterwards. She believes he suffered a broken heart, what with losing Josh and then Christina going as she did. Mrs Clifford blames it on Christina. Says she's poisonous.'

'Why would Mr Clifford be so upset that his daughter-in-law had broken contact with him?'

'Aha,' said Ross. Robyn could hear him smacking his lips together ready to give her the information she needed. 'Christina took their only granddaughter with her and they never saw the girl again.'

'What's the girl's name?'

'Alice, and the last Mr and Mrs Clifford heard, both mother and daughter were headed to Derby or Nottingham. I have more information that will interest you. Four years after Christina and her daughter disappeared, Mrs Clifford received an anonymous postcard that she thinks came from Alice. It was postmarked Uttoxeter. She received another card with another heart on it the following year, this time posted from Lichfield. A couple of years later she got another with a Birmingham postmark and approximately five years ago, another with a postmark from—'

'You're going to say Farnborough, aren't you?'

'Oh, how could you tell?'

'You almost got excited. I could hear it in the tone of your voice.'

'I never get excited.'

'That's what Jeanette says,' she teased.

'Did you hear that sound? It was my sides splitting with laughter.'

'Ha! Okay. Tell me.'

'You guessed it. The card came with a Farnborough postmark.'

Robyn felt a rush of adrenalin. 'So if the cards came from Christina or Alice, then both of them could still be in Farnborough. Maybe that's why Paul has Farnborough Hill in his document file. It could be where Alice went to school. I'll see if any Alice Clifford or Alice Forman attended here. Great work, Ross. I'll hug you when I get back.'

Ross grunted. 'Good luck. See you soon. Don't forget dinner this week. Jeanette is looking forward to cooking for you.'

'I won't forget.'

Mitz Patel rang as soon as she ended her call with Ross.

'Nothing. I can't find anything suspicious. I checked the stairs for any object she may have slipped on but there's nothing. Sorry.'

'Okay, Mitz. Thanks anyway.'

Robyn stared at her mobile, the edge taken off her initial excitement and wondered what she was going to say to Louisa Mulholland.

CHAPTER THIRTY-TWO

The sky was a rare blue and clouds of white gulls circled above a field, following the green tractors as they trundled up and down, turning the cut crops back into the soil. That morning had been fresh, and the dampness in the air reminded Abigail that although it was August, autumn would not be too long in coming.

She focused on the night before. It had not gone well. She had wanted to tackle Jackson about the photographs of him and Zoe but instead they had rowed about her changing the locks.

'What in God's name has possessed you to have all the locks changed?' growled Jackson when she opened the door at last. 'I've been fumbling with this key for the last ten minutes. You might have told me or warned me, or even asked me,' he said, throwing his pilot's bag down in the hallway and stalking into the kitchen.

'I meant to call you but I had a lot on my mind.'

He let out a noise of exasperation which annoyed her further.

'I had a scare a couple of nights ago. I thought someone was in the house.'

Jackson stopped scowling. 'An intruder? Why didn't you tell me?'

'Because there wasn't anyone. I was mistaken but at the time I really believed I saw someone in the nursery. I was sure they'd come to kidnap Izzy. It was the night I was sick.'

Jackson's face had changed and now wore the look of pained incredulity. She folded her arms and snapped at him.

'You look like you don't believe me.'

'Abby, how would anyone get in? We have the keys. The door was locked and you were inside. And, why would anyone want to kidnap Izzy? It's not like I'm a wealthy sheikh. They're not going to take her and demand millions of pounds. You're becoming overprotective. You might have discussed this with me before changing all the locks and locking me out of my own house.'

'So it's about you standing outside for ten minutes, is it? Never mind that I was worried sick about our baby.'

'Oh, for crying out loud. I've had a shit day. I don't need this. Give me the new key. No one is going to take Izzy. You need to lighten up. You're becoming paranoid. You don't get out enough. Phone Claire or Zoe and arrange to go out. I'll look after Izzy. You need to let go or you'll smother Izzy by being overprotective.'

She was so outraged by his response that she stormed off to bed. She hadn't the energy or fight to challenge him about the photographs. She collected Izzy and put her in their bed. She wasn't letting anyone take her baby, and if Jackson thought she was being paranoid, then tough. She had reason to be.

Jackson had discovered her in bed with Izzy and become even angrier, telling her to take her child back to the cot but she refused until Jackson, sick of it all, took off to the spare room.

Overnight she reflected on the email. She didn't feel any anger or hurt. She should be furious about the discovery that Jackson and one of her best friends were screwing, but for the time being she felt too numb for any emotional outburst. It all felt too surreal. Izzy, asleep beside her, snuffled quietly. Abigail wondered what she was dreaming about and tucked the duvet around her. Izzy was the most special thing in her life. Nothing mattered as long as she had Izzy.

The morning had brought more problems at BizzyAir and Jackson had departed earlier than usual. Abigail attempted some half-hearted housework and played with Izzy for a while, but she felt disorientated and decided to go to town instead. She was going to ring Claire to arrange to meet-up but at the last minute remembered her friend had left for Scotland to capture some shots of the wildlife for a magazine. She sent a text, telling Claire she missed her and hoped she was enjoying Scotland. She pressed send and wished Claire hadn't gone. Abigail really needed a friend.

Abigail drove to town, parked and ambled aimlessly around the streets. She hovered outside the boutique. She wanted to go in and explain about the photograph and messages she hadn't posted on Facebook but each time she made a move, an invisible hand drew her back. She couldn't bear her former colleagues not believing her or the accusatory looks they might throw at her.

She reversed the pushchair and made for the café where she had last met the girls, then heard her name shouted. It was Rachel. She kissed Abigail on both cheeks, and then taking her by the shoulders looked into her face, an expression of concern furrowing her plucked eyebrows.

'Now, tell me honestly. How are you? You look peaky.'

Abigail wanted to pull away from the woman but at that moment she felt a deep sadness overcome her and tears spilled from her eyes.

'Oh, there, there, Abby. I didn't mean to upset you,' said Rachel. 'Come on; let's get you a nice cup of tea. I'll push Izzy.'

The coffee shop was quiet apart from a couple of youngsters working on laptops. Rachel bustled about, grabbed a high chair and had buckled Izzy in before Abigail had fully registered what was happening.

'Now, wait there and I'll get us tea,' said Rachel, heading purposefully to the counter and returning with two pots and cups. She made a show of breaking a large biscuit into small pieces and handing them to Izzy who, delighted at the attention, pushed them into her mouth and watched Rachel with large eyes.

'What a lovely surprise to see you both,' gushed Rachel. 'I must say though, you look a little run-down, Abby. Have you been taking care of your aura?'

Abigail shook her head. 'I haven't had a chance to think about it.'

'You must. It's important to look after all aspects of your health. I can give your aura a health check, if you like. It'll make you feel much better.'

'That's very kind of you but I don't really have time. I have to go and visit Claire soon.' She winced inside at the lie.

Rachel wrinkled her nose. 'Well that won't help you much. That woman's not good for you.'

'What makes you say that? You don't know her very well.'

'But I have seen her aura and I've heard what Zoe has to say about her.'

'Zoe?'

'Yes. She isn't Claire's biggest fan. She thinks Claire's a killjoy and I tend to agree with her.'

Abigail felt affronted on behalf of her friend. Claire wasn't the greatest conversationalist but she was a good and loyal friend. She had helped Zoe apply for her new job, photographing her for the application. She, Zoe and Claire had been out on several occasions together and Abigail had never noticed any tension between them. Zoe joked about Claire's serious attitude and Claire teased Zoe about her casual approach to life but both got on well. Or at least, Abigail had always thought so. She wondered what Zoe had said about her. As if reading her mind, Rachel added, 'Zoe told me you are much more fun when Claire isn't around. You loosen up more. She told me about your trip to Leeds.'

Abigail recalled that trip. They had all planned to go to Leeds for a girls' weekend to celebrate Zoe dumping her latest boyfriend. At the last minute, Claire had dropped out, but since the room was paid for, she and Zoe had travelled up together. They spent the weekend shopping in the day, and in the evening cajoling bouncers into letting them into nightclubs where they had drunk disgusting cocktails, then danced and laughed themselves senseless.

Abigail wasn't keen to discuss Claire with Rachel. She poured her tea and sipped it.

'This is very kind of you, again. Let me pay for it.'

'I wouldn't dream of it. I always believe kindness is spread. If I do something nice then the universe will repay me somehow, although that isn't a reason for doing a kindness. The universe has a way of dealing with good and bad energy. I try to spread good energy.'

'So, are you still working at the dental surgery?'

'No. I handed in my notice. I decided it was time to move on. I'm training in crystal therapy now. You should have a treatment. It will make you far more relaxed. I can come around to your house and treat you. I'm only training but I'm sure I could help.'

'That'd be lovely,' replied Abigail, hoping Rachel didn't suggest a time soon.

Izzy put out a hand for some more biscuit. Rachel obliged and passed her another piece.

'Is she able to talk much yet?' she asked.

'Nothing sensible. Only gibberish. If she sees her reflection in a mirror she'll chatter to it. I've been trying to teach her real words.'

'Say, "Hello, Auntie Rachel,"' said Rachel in a babyish voice. Abigail cringed.

Rachel passed another piece of biscuit to Izzy. 'Are you feeling better now?' she asked Abigail.

'Yes, thanks. I was thinking about going to visit some of the girls I used to work with.'

'Is that at the boutique?'

'Yes, how did you know?'

'Zoe told me. She said you used to get her a discount there and she got some super outfits. I went in earlier but there wasn't anything my style. In fact, I didn't think much of the staff there. They pretty much ignored me. They were too busy gossiping. Someone they know posted a photograph of herself in the nude on some social networking site. What a silly thing to do. I suppose it was one of those women who likes to shock or is an attention-seeker. I can't understand people like that. I avoid social media. It's full of people who are self-important and constantly bleating on about their woes or bragging about what they have or where they're going on their next holiday.

'I read a study that said sites like that are likely to cause depression. You log on, see photographs of other people's apparent perfect lives and feel even worse about your own rubbish one. I've got enough misery without adding to it, thank you very much. Who cares if you've been to the Seychelles or if you are drinking a cappuccino or if you went to yoga and ate tofu for lunch?

'I felt sorry for the woman they were discussing though. They were pretty nasty about her. Poor thing. I bet she's regretting ever doing it. Anyway, while they were gossiping, I looked around the rails, thought their stuff was overpriced and left without them even acknowledging me. I may as well have been invisible,' she said with a huff.

Heat rose up Abigail's neck and into her face. She was sure she had gone scarlet and lowered her gaze, pretending to fiddle with her teapot. Rachel seemed oblivious to her discomfort and continued babbling about clothes. Abigail was glad when her mobile bleeped. It was a text from Claire telling her about the miserable weather which was making photographing difficult, but it gave Abigail a chance to make her excuses and leave.

'Sorry, I have to go. I'd completely forgotten Jackson's dry cleaning. He's reminded me I need to pick up his uniform and drop it off at the airport. He needs it for tonight.'

Even to her ears it sounded like a blatant lie. Rachel's eyes searched her own. Abigail knew she did not believe her.

'What a shame. Pity he couldn't get it himself on his way to work. Is he flying anywhere interesting?'

'I don't know. He doesn't tell me about every job. It's just a day's work to him wherever he goes. He doesn't often get to visit the destination. He's usually in the crew lounge at whichever airport, preparing for the return journey. Now and again he stays over or goes into the nearest town. He was in Corsica last week. He brought me back some wine biscuits that are a specialty of the region and a little donkey for Izzy.'

She was babbling and she knew it. She wanted to get away from this woman who stared intently at her and could probably read her thoughts.

'Better get going. Come on, Izzy.' She picked up the child who allowed herself to be placed into the buggy without fuss and watched the world around her as the women said their goodbyes.

'I hope you'll let me practise crystal therapy on you another time,' said Rachel, standing up. Abigail found herself wrapped in sinewy arms and a pungent scent of patchouli oil.

'That'd be super. Another time.'

'I look forward to it. Bye, Izzy. Say, "Bye, bye, Auntie Rachel."'

Izzy looked up through large blue eyes and smiled.

Abigail wheeled Izzy outside and took a deep breath.

She would take Izzy for a drive and get away from town in case she ran into Rachel again. Her heart was heavy as she walked past the shop where she had worked for a few happy years. People could be so fickle. She would not have believed her old work colleagues would have spoken badly of her but they had. She flipped open her mobile, checked her Facebook page and gave a sigh of relief. Her account had been suspended and was no longer accessible. At least no one else would be able to judge her.

Her fingers hovered over the keys, tempting her to examine the contents of the email once more. As she stared at the mobile, torn between looking at and obliterating the email, the phone rang with a withheld number and the familiar robotic voice greeted her.

'Afternoon, Abigail. I hope you liked my present to you. Nice shots of your husband and his new love, weren't they? Little did they realise I was watching them.'

'It's not a present and you're insane.'

'Oh, it is a gift, Abigail. It's a gift of the truth. Lies harm. Lies hurt. The truth liberates. You should try it sometime. In fact, you should try it now before it's too late. Go on, Abigail, this is your last chance, try and tell the truth.'

CHAPTER THIRTY-THREE

Farnborough Hill School, once a grand Victorian house, was set in sixty-five picturesque acres of land, including secluded gardens and woodland. Situated on the highest point in Hampshire, it had magnificent views over the surrounding countryside. Robyn could not fail to be impressed by the school and its range of facilities but she was not here on a tour. She needed answers.

The headmistress, Josephine Blakemore, was new to the school. A small woman, who barely filled her large leather chair, she was formidable in spite of her slight frame and quiet manner. She spoke with a gentle Scottish burr.

'Well, Detective Inspector Carter, after we spoke on the phone, I asked my secretary to go through the records for you. As I told you, I have only recently been appointed here. Surprisingly, she only came across one Alice who attended the school in the early 1980s, so she would be in her forties now.'

'And that means she is too old. I'm searching for someone in her early twenties. I don't suppose you took on any staff by the name of Forman in the last seven years?'

'To my knowledge, we haven't. Let me check for you.'

Josephine Blakemore left Robyn staring out of the window across vast playing fields. They were currently deserted but would soon be filled with shouts and cheers as teams played each other. Robyn idly wondered if Amélie enjoyed hockey or netball. The headmistress returned, a pair of glasses perched on her head. She stood beside the desk, back straight, arms behind her back.

'We've hired twenty-four people in that time – mostly male grounds staff and of course teachers. I'm afraid there is no one by the name of Forman.'

'I have one more question. Has anyone by the name of Paul Matthews been to visit you?'

Josephine Blakemore slid her glasses down and peered at her smartphone. 'I keep all appointments on this,' she explained. 'I'd be lost without it. There it is. I thought the name was familiar. Paul Matthews made an appointment to see me on the twenty-eighth of July but he didn't show up.'

Robyn chewed on her lip. Paul had not shown up because he was dead by then. The woman put her phone on the table.

'I'm sorry I couldn't have been of more assistance.'

Robyn took it as her cue to leave and thanking the woman, left feeling frustrated.

* * *

Now sheets of A4 paper lay strewn over the floor in the Sky Suite. Robyn sat cross-legged on the settee, trying to work out what Lucas and his father had discovered that had led them to Farnborough. Who were they looking for? Paul had mentioned *her* in his email to Lucas, and how they could *put an end to* something if they could find her.

Robyn looked over her findings again. First, Lucas had got in contact with his father after years of not speaking to him and asked him for money. After that, he emailed his father saying something had gone wrong and he needed to see him. Robyn tapped her teeth with her pencil. She read through what she had written about Paul. Paul, who had no time for his son, still gave him thirty thousand pounds when he asked for it. It smacked of blackmail. Why else would Lucas need so much money?

Paul had been looking into Farnborough and written down various places to check out, including Farnborough Hill School,

TAG Aviation and the gym where Zoe had worked. And finally, Paul's housekeeper had also said Paul planned on 'looking up someone'. It all led to Farnborough.

The muscles in her neck were bunching up. She stretched her head from side to side, holding the stretch until she felt the tension ease. Her mind churned over the facts again. If Paul and Lucas were looking for Alice or Christina Forman, why had Lucas tried to track down Zoe Cooper at the gym?

She picked at a club sandwich and ruminated. The internal phone rang, breaking her concentration. It was Christophe, the barman from the Sky Bar.

'I'm sorry to disturb you, Detective Inspector Carter,' he said. 'You were asking about Jackson Thorne last evening. I wanted to let you know if you would like to chat to him, he's in the bar. He walked in about ten minutes ago.'

'Great. Thanks, Christophe,' said Robyn. 'I'll be there in a jiffy.'

She grabbed her bag and headed to the first floor. There was a lot of noise in the bar. Several men in evening dress were standing in groups and it took her a while to spot Jackson, who was at the far end with another man, both in uniform. Jackson Thorne was undoubtedly a striking man – over six foot tall with broad shoulders and a muscular physique. He stood with quiet confidence.

Robyn passed through the crowd and stood before the two pilots. She extended a hand and introduced herself. Jackson raised an eyebrow when she announced she was Detective Inspector Carter. She explained the situation briefly.

'I'm trying to locate a man. I have reason to believe he might have tried to contact you. His name is Lucas Matthews. I have a photograph of him, if you wouldn't mind looking at it?'

Jackson levelled his gaze at her. 'I know who he is. He was trying to get hold of me about a week ago. He wouldn't leave a message but kept calling the BizzyAir switchboard. My receptionist took his number even though he was rude to her. I rang him back and left a message asking him not to call BizzyAir again unless he could be civil. He didn't reply. That was six days ago.'

'So you wouldn't know him, if I showed you a photograph?'

'I haven't met him but let me see it anyway.'

She gave him the picture. Jackson studied it and passed it back. 'Sorry, I don't know him.'

'Hang on a second,' said his companion, who up until now had been silent. 'I might have seen him.'

The man, shorter and slimmer than his colleague, took the photograph, pursed his lips and nodded. 'I have seen him. He was here when we came back from taking that group of engineers to Scotland. You remember, Jackson. We popped in here for a quick drink. Travis, the guy who organised the trip invited us – insisted on it. That was the night Gavin…'

His sentence remained unfinished. A dark cloud skittered across Jackson's features. 'No. I don't recall seeing him at all,' he replied. 'Sorry, Detective, but I haven't seen him or spoken to him.'

'I might have been mistaken but I thought he was here at the hotel,' muttered Jackson's colleague, now returning the photograph to Robyn and finishing his drink. 'You could try reception. He might have been a guest here.'

Something had happened. An unspoken command had passed between the men and neither wanted to speak to her. She scrawled her contact details on two of Ross's business cards before passing them over.

'Should you see him again, please let me know. It is important I find him. His wife is beside herself with worry,' she added by way of an explanation.

She left them to their conversation, aware that they were now talking in angry whispers. She picked up the name 'Gavin' and the words 'Keep quiet'. She waited outside the bar and soon both men left. Jackson had acted strangely. Had he met Lucas and lied to her? His eyes had been completely focused on her when he had told her about the phone calls. There had been no discerning flicker of the eyeball to the right as often happened when someone was lying. However, he was keeping something from her.

She nipped back into the bar and beckoned Christophe. 'Thanks for the heads-up about Jackson. The chap he was with…' she said.

'Stu?'

'Yes, Stu. He mentioned someone named Gavin?'

'That'd be Gavin Singer. Early forties, I think, married, two children. Chief pilot for BizzyAir Business Aviation. Known Jackson for years. Jackson was his best man at his wedding.'

Robyn handed over the photograph of Lucas. 'I don't suppose you've seen this man, have you?'

'Peroni in a bottle. I never forget an order. That's the sign of a good barman, isn't it?'

'He's been here.'

'Once that I can recall. He stood at the corner of the bar, over there.' He pointed to the far end of the bar. 'He refused a glass. Mumbled something about bottles being safer. I didn't pay him much attention because we had a large group from a conference in before dinner. That was the night Zoe was drunk. I've never seen her like that before. She's normally teetotal and only has the odd glass of wine to celebrate. She must have had an entire crate. Jackson was here too. He was with Stu and Gavin. They all got together at one point but I lost track of what happened. I do remember seeing this guy,' he tapped the photograph, 'staring at her but Zoe attracts attention wherever she goes. I was really busy so I didn't see him go. He paid cash so I guess he wasn't a hotel guest.'

Christophe couldn't give her any more information but now she knew that Zoe, Jackson, Stu and Gavin had all been in the bar at the same time as Lucas. Christophe was pretty certain it had been seven days earlier.

'If ever you need a sidekick, I'd love to join you,' he said with a grin. 'I'm very observant.'

Robyn tried the restaurants in the hotel and reception but no one else had seen Lucas. Before she went back upstairs, she showed the photograph to the concierge and struck lucky.

'I remember him,' said the sandy-haired man, dressed in an immaculately pressed maroon uniform. 'He came staggering down the stairs with a woman. He was so drunk she was supporting him, her arm under his. I asked them if they wanted a taxi but they didn't even answer me. They just walked out. There's no need for rudeness,' he complained. 'I'm only doing my job. Some people treat us as if we're nobodies.'

Robyn sympathised with him.

'One more thing,' he said after some thought. 'I couldn't help but notice that the woman had green hair.'

Robyn headed outside and called Mitz Patel. 'I need you to find out everything you can about Zoe Cooper. I think she might have met up with our missing man Lucas Matthews.'

There was a pause before Mitz spoke. 'He isn't missing any more. Mulholland's just told me to call you. He's turned up at Blinkley Manor School. There's one problem. He's dead. Mulholland wants to talk to you.'

* * *

Chief Inspector Louisa Mulholland spoke in her usual, efficient manner. 'DI Carter, your missing person has been discovered. Derbyshire police have notified us that the body of Lucas Matthews was found this afternoon in bushes adjacent to the playing fields of Blinkley Preparatory School. It looks as if he's been murdered. Too early to say more at the moment.'

Robyn cursed silently. Louisa Mulholland continued, 'I've spoken to their DCI and we're putting you in charge of the investigation since you already have information and leads on him. DI Tom Shearer is the SOCO on this so you'll need to liaise with him.'

Robyn grimaced. Tom Shearer usually managed to rub her up the wrong way. His cocky, devil-may-care attitude irritated her.

I'll leave you to get in touch with DI Shearer. He'll meet you at the scene. I told him you were in the south-east. He's expecting you. I guess it's a baptism of fire for you. Not even back five minutes and already looking into a murder. Welcome back to the real world, Robyn. Shall I leave you to inform the next of kin?'

'Yes, I'll arrange to see Mary Matthews or send someone over. Can't help but feel sorry for her. She's only just coming to terms with the fact that her husband has kept secrets from her and now he's dead.'

'There's not time for too much sentiment in our jobs, Robyn, as you know.'

Traffic was light but it still took just over two hours before she pulled into the drive of Blinkley Manor Preparatory School. There were several vehicles gathered on the large drive. Shearer's black Porsche was at the front of a line of cars, abandoned haphazardly as if he had jumped out of it before it had come to a complete stop. Yellow police tape in the distance indicated the area where the body was. She left her car behind a squad car.

The ground was damp from the early evening dew as she approached the bright yellow tapes that cordoned off the crime scene.

PC Patel had spotted her arrival and acknowledged her with a nod of his head. 'I've spoken to Nick Pearson-Firth who discovered the body and got a statement. I haven't had a chance yet to interview anyone else who might be on site. Mr Pearson-Firth said that most of the staff were still away for the summer. He was here because he had interviews lined up today and tomorrow for Mr Matthews' replacement. I'll go bang on some doors and see if anyone noticed anything suspicious the last few days.'

'That's what I like about you, you always anticipate my instructions,' Robyn replied. 'Okay, off you go. I'll meet up with you here when you're done. Oh, and please ask Nick Pearson-Firth if his wife and daughter are around and if he heard from Lucas Matthews before today.'

Mitz Patel departed in the direction of the building. As Robyn moved closer, a figure emerged from the bushes and approached her. She recognised it immediately as Sam Gooch, a forensic photographer. Sam was in his early sixties but still sprightly.

'Hi, Sam. All done?'

'Detective Inspector Carter. I heard you were returning. God knows why. If I had a chance to give this up, I'd leave it all behind, move to a desert island and live in a hut away from all this madness.'

Sam always complained about the country and his job yet it was unlikely he would ever move away. He had five grandchildren who he adored.

'I've got everything I need. I'm off. Good luck with this one.'

Robyn watched him as he strode towards his car and shivered in the cooling air. She had been ill prepared for this and cursed the fact. Ordinarily, she would have had flat boots and a coat ready in the boot of her car. As it was, she was inadequately attired in a skirt and blouse ensemble with leather shoes whose heels were sinking in the soft ground. They had seemed appropriate attire for visiting school headmistresses and for the hotel but she wished she had taken time to change. She ducked under the tape and moved towards the stench.

A tall figure broke out from the shadows of the vegetation, taking in Robyn's appearance with an amused expression. Shearer's powder-blue eyes rested for a while on her bare legs. A grin twitched at the corner of his mouth. 'So, Robyn, I hear you couldn't stay away from proper detective work. The private-eye thing was too tame for you. Still, it's probably ideal for old Ross. He can't take too much excitement these days, eh? Pottering about, chasing fraud claims or dealing with old ladies who have lost their cats. That's about all he's capable of.'

Robyn drew herself up to her full height. 'Evening, Tom. Ross is very well and it was extremely interesting working with him,' she replied, irritated by Shearer's snarky voice. 'I'll be sure to pass on your regards when I see him next.' She knew she shouldn't rise to his taunts. He was rude to everyone but a thorough and brilliant crime-scene officer.

'Please do. Although he's probably forgotten us all now given the exciting new career he has chosen. He'll be far too busy to think about us poor sods.' He maintained a steady look, urging her to retort but she bit her tongue and got on with business.

'What do we have?' she asked as she moved closer. The smell was stronger here; a cloying sweetness that indicated Lucas Matthews was decaying nicely. It was chilly by the trees and for the second time that evening she wished she had brought a coat with her.

Shearer held her gaze a little longer then tired of the game and focused instead on the man lying on the ground some distance behind him. He pointed at the body with his torch. 'Lucas Matthews. Discovered at three-thirty this afternoon by Nick Pearson-Firth who was out walking his dog. He rang the police.'

Robyn approached the body. She was no stranger to death but the foul, sickly-sweet odour of methane and hydrogen sulfide emanating from the bloated corpse turned her stomach. The club sandwich she had consumed at the hotel rose uncomfortably in her throat. She swallowed and breathed through her mouth slowly.

The body of the man lying on the floor was barely recognisable from the photographs she had seen at his home. His face was puffy and blood-coloured foam was leaking from his nostrils and mouth. His glass eye stared at her, the surface incongruously shiny, while his other eye-socket contained only ragged bits of flesh, its contents eaten away by insects. She took shallow breaths, tried to obliterate the nausea that threatened to take over, and studied the corpse more closely. What she had first believed to be flesh was wriggling. A plump maggot lifted raised its head from the masses in the socket and swayed like a snake being charmed. She resisted the urge to shudder. Shearer would exploit any signs of weakness.

Lucas Matthews' face was tinged with green, not unusual in body decomposition when tissues begin to release gas and green substances that transform the colour of skin. His mouth was agape, tongue protruding. A piece of blubbery flesh hung from his lips as if he were eating a final meal.

Shearer continued in a more sober tone. 'Judging by the state of him, I would suggest he has been dead a while. Decomposition happens faster above ground as you know and not only has he been in an area filled with insects and creatures, it's been warm this week. As you can see, there is bloating of the abdomen and fluid leakage from the lungs apparent around the nose and mouth, and his tongue is protruding from his mouth in line with tissue decomposition of a body that has been dead for about eight days.'

Robyn bent towards the corpse's head, preparing herself for more maggots. 'There's something else here in his mouth,' she said. 'Tissue of another type.'

'Ah, I'll get to that in a moment,' continued Shearer. 'There are no obvious injuries that might have caused death. I can't see any defence wounds, cuts or blows to his body, nor anything under his nails. Blood flow is consistent with falling backwards. Clothing has been ripped apart and I noticed small, red spots like burn marks on his skin near his heart, although the flesh is beginning to discolour and I can't work out what they are. We'll have to wait for the coroner's report.'

He aimed his torch beam at Lucas's chest where his shirt fell away, his top buttons undone, revealing his hairless chest. The marks Shearer mentioned were slightly larger than a pea. Shearer shone his torch down the corpse. Lucas's trousers were bunched around his ankles along with his underpants. His legs were a pale green colour and smooth. 'There are more marks around the groin area. First impression is some form of stun gun might have caused them.'

He paused while Robyn studied the prone figure on the ground. Lucas's genitals had been removed.

She took a shallow breath. The smell was all pervading. She would have to move away from the corpse soon. Shearer looked repulsed by the sight of the mutilation. She spoke, 'The attacker focused on damaging his genital region.'

Shearer nodded in agreement. 'His assailant took a sharp implement to his nether regions and hacked off his penis and testicles. Poor chap. I can't imagine what it would feel like to have your crown jewels chopped off. The killer removed his manhood, and as the pièce de résistance,' Shearer indicated with his torch, 'stuffed it all into the victim's mouth.'

The light from the torch flickered across the body, making the scene even more macabre. He turned to observe her reaction. She shook her head at the gruesome sight.

'Sounds like the sort of thing an ex-lover might do, or an angry wife or someone who was furious with Lucas Matthews. Reminds me of that Wayne Bobbitt case years ago,' said Robyn.

Shearer nodded. 'Except Mrs Bobbitt didn't ram his John Thomas back into Wayne Bobbitt's mouth, and he lived to tell the tale. Lucas is as dead as a post.'

'Would mutilation of this type be likely to kill him?'

'Possibly the shock of it all. I don't know.'

'There doesn't seem to have been a struggle. He appears to have come here, dropped his trousers and then been murdered.'

'Correct. There's no evidence of a body being dragged here. No weapon, stun gun, cattle prod or otherwise at the scene, although it might come to light when we search again in the morning. There are no fingerprints or even glove prints on his body.' He shook his head as he spoke.

Robyn thought. 'The maiming was deliberate, not an after-thought. The murderer brought him to this spot for a reason, or invited him here, and again that must be important.'

'That's for you to find out, Robyn. I can only assist with my humble findings.'

'Somebody really hated him,' she said, standing up again.

'It's a violent but calculated act. This wasn't a spur of the moment attack. It had been planned. Dig into his past and you'll no doubt uncover who has done this.' Shearer bent to cover Lucas's body with the sheet. 'Nasty,' he said. 'Very nasty.' He stood and faced Robyn. 'Do you want to walk the area with me?'

It was a challenge rather than a request. DI Shearer was unlikely to have missed anything at all. Robyn shook her head.

'No. I'll wait for the coroner's report and see if I can find out more about Lucas Matthews. I've been tracking him all week. I'll ask Patel to tell his wife that he's dead. He's good with people.'

Ah, Constable Mitz Patel,' he replied. 'Very gentle and polite. Lives with Mummy and Daddy and is barely out of nappies. Where do they get these kids from?'

Robyn bristled again. Shearer's mood fluctuated from good to bad without warning.

'The youth today haven't got what it takes,' mumbled Shearer. 'They play all these violent video games but put them in front of a real murder victim and they go green and vomit.'

His tone riled her again. 'PC Patel does not play violent video games to my knowledge, nor would he vomit.'

Shearer sneered. 'Ha! That's where you are wrong, Robyn. He threw up earlier in the bushes before you arrived.'

She opened her mouth to speak and his face changed again. 'Only joking,' he said. 'Just pulling at your tight strings, Carter. You need to loosen up a little. Mind, it must be difficult to loosen anything in those clothes.' Involuntarily, she tugged at the skirt. He rewarded her with a beaming smile that changed his face. 'Glad to see you didn't flinch at all.' He nodded back at Lucas.

'I've seen worse than this,' she replied, ignoring his steady gaze. He contemplated her for a moment longer before speaking again. 'Okay, here's another weird thing. Not only did Lucas Matthews have his penis and testicles stuffed in his mouth but, more bizarrely, he had a furry toy rabbit tucked under his arm.' He held up a transparent bag containing the toy. It was streaked with brown stains, no doubt from blood. She took it from him and examined it.

'It looks new.'

'I thought so too. It hasn't any identifiers on it but there can't be many shops that sell toy rabbits like that.'

'I'll set Patel onto it. He can check out toyshops and department stores.'

'Yes, that's a far more suitable occupation for him. He'll be all right looking for furry toys. At least it won't make him sick.'

'You really should watch that sledgehammer wit of yours, Tom. It'll get you into trouble one day.'

'My dear, it already has. On many an occasion,' he said. 'Now, if you'll excuse me, I must get tidied up here and let Lucas head off to the morgue. I don't want to hold you up any longer. You have a murderer to find.' With that he dismissed her and wandered in the direction of the ambulance further down the drive, whistling as he went.

CHAPTER THIRTY-FOUR

THEN

Two years of being a drug courier and I am sick to death of it. If it weren't for the threatening looks Dirk the dick gives me every time I ask if I can pack it in, I'd tell him where he could shove his lousy drugs. The bonus of me traipsing about with packages is that my mother hasn't had any nasty bruises or mysterious injuries, and I receive fifty quid for every package.

I've used the money wisely. It's seen me through college and an evening course I took, so when I can finally escape Dirk's clutches I can have a career or at least a semi-normal life. This underworld life is poisonous and ageing. I'm only eighteen and already I have the world-weary look of someone much older.

The people I deal with are normally best avoided. I keep out of trouble and under the radar by dressing more like a man than a woman. Everyone thinks I'm gay because I ignore all the innuendos and suggestions from the guys I pick up from. Dirk's men all think so too. I let them. I mostly wear combat trousers and button-down jackets with boots and keep my hair very short. My lean shape doesn't attract attention from them either.

It's not that I don't like men. I do. I just don't want anything to do with the sort of men who hang around clubs doling out drugs to kids who may die, or get hooked on them. Besides, for a while I had Liam and didn't need anyone else.

Liam Waters enrolled in the same evening class as me. He was shy and gentle with ginger hair and blue eyes the colour of cornflowers. One evening after class, he left at the same time as me and I'm not sure how it happened but we ended up in a coffee shop, chatting about life. Of course, I lied about mine. I invented an entire family, three brothers and a dog named Billy. He told me all about his mother and father who ran a farm in southern Ireland. It sounded idyllic and the closer we became, the more I fantasised about moving to Ireland with him and helping raise new-born lambs or taking one of the three sheepdogs out into the fields.

I slept with him on our third date. He was loving and kind and generous. He didn't pressure me into going to bed with him. I wanted to. I wanted to know what it was like to make love to someone you loved. It was beautiful.

Like everything in my life, it came to a bitter end. Dirk found out about Liam and in a drunken fury told me to end my relationship with him in case I blabbed about the drug business. I told him I would never talk but he gave me an ultimatum: finish with Liam or he'd have his goons kneecap him.

I can't even talk about it now without a lump forming in my throat and my heart dropping to the base of my stomach like a boulder. I told Liam it was over and I was going out with someone else. He believed me. Well, he would. I am an expert liar. He gave up the evening course and went back home to lick his wounds. It seemed he was as crazy in love with me as I had been with him.

My heart has no more room for love now and I only have one emotion that drives me – hatred. It is that emotion that has helped me conjure up a plan to resolve my current predicament. I need to dispose of Dirk and I think I know how.

I've been researching poisons on my smartphone. You can purchase just about anything you need online so I look at procuring some tablets that might do the job called Tetramisole. Drug dealers have been known to cut cocaine with what is, initially, a white powder supposed to be used for worming animals. Large doses can poison humans, leading to fever and difficulty breathing caused by the swelling of lips and throat. Victims are at risk of losing consciousness, numbness and seizures. I like the sound of the last part. Tetramisole also weakens the immune system – making cocaine users more susceptible to infections. I don't want Dirk to get an infection. I want him to die. I soon figure it would be difficult for me to get hold of Tetramisole without drawing attention to myself so I slip out of my room, my dark grey hoodie pulled up so no one can work out if I am male or female. I head to the local store that sells everything you could want from bath salts to kitchen equipment and writing paper to car polish. They have an extensive section on home and garden and it doesn't take long to locate the poisons.

A couple in their sixties come and stand beside me and argue over which type of grass seed to purchase. I try to make myself invisible and stare at the flower seeds. There are various boxes of multicoloured wild flowers or boxes of huge orange blooms I've never seen before, mixed with bright blue cornflowers and poppies. We have a scrappy backyard at the moment. It's mostly weeds and patio. Mum has never bothered with it other than to plonk a chair out there and sunbathe. Sometimes Dirk and his cronies go outside and smoke. Judging by the smell, they aren't puffing on cigarettes. I often wonder what it would like if it was grassed over with borders of plants and flowers. It'd be like living in the countryside. As it is, it's like living in a war zone.

One day, I'll have a garden and I'll purchase some seeds like these or real flowers already grown in pots. It would be wonderful to sit among them and take in their scent, listen to bumble bees collecting nectar or watch their colourful heads bobbing in the breeze, like they're agreeing with my every thought and word. I'd be able to forget all my worries then.

The couple next to me looks drab in beige and faded blue outfits. Their faces are washed out too, like life has sucked the energy out of them.

The husband has a beer belly. No doubt he escapes to the local pub to get away most evenings. The wife is small and chubby. She doesn't look like she ever does any gardening. Her voice is whiny and high-pitched and her lips thin. They are moaning about a mole that's churned up their grass. She wants her husband to put down proper turf but he doesn't see the point given the mole will probably churn it up again.

So engrossed are they in their discussion, they do not notice me slip the box into my plastic carrier bag and leave without being challenged. Rat poison for Dirk. It seems so appropriate.

When I get home, he's fast asleep in front of the television. He's been living at our house for the last seven months. I think even my mother is fed up of his disgusting habits and challenging ways. She is in their bedroom, no doubt knocked out on booze. They got in very late last night after being at the club. I worry that she'll also develop a taste for more serious drugs given she is around them so much. All Dirk's friends take something and spend far too much time at our house. For the moment the booze and the odd spliff is enough for her to escape from the reality that has become her life. I listen by the bedroom door. She is snoring softly. She'll be asleep for ages. It's time to put my plan into action.

First, I rummage in the toilet cistern. Dirk keeps his personal secret supply there. It's in a convenient place in case we ever get raided and he has to flush it down the toilet. I heard him tell my mother to keep away from it or he'd kill her. Now and again he disappears in here for a fix. He has no idea I know that's what he's doing or that I have uncovered his stash. He doesn't have much idea about anything. I take the candy to my room and tip out the contents onto a magazine laid on my dressing table. It's grade-A stuff. I don plastic gloves I took from a petrol station in town. They are supposed to stop people getting diesel on their hands but they are equally useful to those of us attempting to poison someone we detest with rat poison without harming ourselves. I put on an extra two pairs on each hand for assured protection and shake out the amount of poison I think I'll require then add some more 'for luck'.

When I am satisfied I have enough to ensure he will be ingesting a fatal dose, I tip the powder back into his baggie, seal it and then replace it as I found it, in a ziplock bag inside the toilet cistern. If I am right, he'll probably use it tonight. It's Friday and he'll undoubtedly toot some at the nightclub where he hangs out on a weekend.

If all goes to plan, he won't come home in the early hours and I shall finally be free to start a new life. My father is delighted. He loathes Dirk as much as me and he and I have been planning this for a while. He says I should take Mum with me when I go but I explain I can't. It's time for me to morph into someone else or I'll never be able to carry out the endgame plan. He agrees and Mr Big Ears propped up on my bed applauds silently with furry paws.

CHAPTER THIRTY-FIVE

Abigail pulled into Sycamore Road, close to the children's playground at King George V playing fields. The park was very popular and offered a good mix of sporting activities, family fun and recreational use, with many organised events and music festivals, especially over summer.

In spite of the late afternoon sunshine and the noises of carefree children, Abigail could not settle. She had to face up to the truth. She didn't want her secrets. She carried a lifetime of them. She hadn't got the energy to deal with any more of them.

She stopped at the nearest bench and sat down. Izzy was occupied watching some children racing about playing tag. Abigail stared into space, numb and oblivious to all around her. Time passed and still she sat. A cool breeze began to blow and the shadows lengthened. She tucked a blanket around Izzy who had fallen asleep. Abigail looked at her child's peaceful face but felt nothing other than a heavy sadness that seemed to weigh her heart down. The wonderful life she had created for herself was coming to an end.

Without much thought to what she was doing, she rolled the buggy back to the car and clipped Izzy back into her car seat. A sigh escaped her lips and with it a resignation. The evidence spoke for itself and she needed to hear the truth from his own lips. She would talk to Jackson.

* * *

Abigail drove for over an hour. Dusk was falling and evening stars were now visible in a pink and orange sky as she drove past the duck pond. Izzy continued to sleep. She pulled up by the stone owl. Jackson's Maserati was not yet back. This time she knew it wouldn't be. He had sent a text message explaining he had missed his departure slot due to a late passenger and would now be home at ten.

Her phone buzzed with another text from a withheld number. She squinted to read the new message as she opened the car door. This is what happens to people who hide the truth.'

It had to be from her stalker. She hesitated for a moment before dragging the carrycot out of the back of the Range Rover and turning towards the front door, stopping suddenly in her tracks. Something was attached to her door. At first, she thought it was a large plastic carrier bag, but the puddle on the doorstep below it indicated it was something more sinister. She replaced the carrycot on the seat and approached the door. Her eyes identified the red stain on the doorstep and travelled upwards. The blood in her veins turned to ice. A strangled sob came from her throat. Hanging from the wooden door was Toffee, his sightless eyes staring at her, a six-inch nail through his throat.

CHAPTER THIRTY-SIX

The warmth of the day had gone and Jeanette wrapped a cardigan around her shoulders as she, Ross and Robyn sat outside on their patio, which was illuminated by a string of star-shaped fairy lights that surrounded the wooden structure. Several candles gave off a faint lemon scent.

Robyn stretched her legs under the table and listened to the sounds of frogs beginning to chorus in a nearby pond. At Blinkley Manor she had remembered she had been due at Ross and Jeanette's for dinner. She had phoned and explained the situation, then, after liaising with PC Patel, had left the crime scene to belt around to their house, full of excuses and remorse. She had been persuaded to join them for a coffee.

'What next then, Robyn?' said Jeanette, adding a small spoon of sugar to her coffee and stirring carefully. They'd been discussing the Lucas Matthews case.

'I'll have to interview Zoe Cooper again and find out what happened on the night that she and Lucas left the Aviator hotel together. I think I'll try and get Stu Grant on his own. Jackson was definitely keeping something from me.'

'It's quite exciting, isn't it?' said Jeanette, sitting next to Ross and placing a delicate hand on his knee. 'Much more interesting than some of your recent private investigator cases, although I did chuckle when Ross told me about Bob. Fancy Ross not working out what was going on there.'

Ross shrugged. 'I certainly didn't see that one coming. It's this sheltered life I lead, my dear,' he added, smiling at his wife. 'I'm not worldly enough.'

Jeanette scoffed, 'You missed the signs, that's all. Anyway, that was yet another successful result. Your case is trickier, Robyn. It's like one of those murder-mystery cases.'

'It's a conundrum, that's for sure,' said Robyn.

'How are you getting on back at the station?' asked Ross.

'It's not as bad as I thought. Some things have changed but Mitz Patel is the same. There's a new officer, Anna Shamash. Bit quiet but has potential. Mulholland is spinning plates and the rest of the station is occupied with a big drugs operation. It's all hush-hush. I feel a bit weird though. It's like I don't quite belong yet.'

'You'll be fine. It's only like you've been on secondment. You know that lot. Some of them won't have noticed you've been off at all. David Marker, for one. He's always got his head in the clouds.'

Robyn smiled. 'You're probably right. It'll be okay.'

They sat in companionable silence for a while.

'Robyn, have you visited Brigitte recently?' Jeanette asked.

Robyn had guessed the question would come up. Jeanette knew all about Brigitte and the fact it was Amélie's birthday. Robyn had been prepared for the gentle questioning.

'I saw them before I nipped down to Farnborough. Amélie loves her Fitbit. They're off to France to stay with Brigitte's mother.'

Jeanette sipped at her coffee. 'Lovely woman. Is Amélie okay?'

'She's getting better. Brigitte says she doesn't cry so much.'

'Good. She took it badly, didn't she?'

Jeanette was referring to Davies's sudden death. Davies had almost finished his assignment and they had spoken to Amélie on Skype only two days before it happened. They had promised to take her on holiday with them as soon as they got back. Amélie, all smiles, full of excitement, asking questions about camels and deserts; her father, eyes shining as he chatted to his daughter. Robyn could still see them all, her and Davies huddled in front of the laptop, waving, blowing kisses. Amélie was beyond shocked when Robyn returned without her father. It had required some time for her to accept the reality of what had occurred, but for Robyn the nightmares continued.

'And you, Robyn?' said Jeanette softly. 'Are you okay?'

'I'm getting there.'

'Please don't think I'm interfering but you look drawn. I'm concerned about you and I think you might need to talk to someone professional about it all.'

Robyn's words came out in a rush to match the sudden anger rising in her, an anger she normally kept under tight control. 'I don't want to talk to anyone. I'm fine. I don't need any help and certainly not from some shrink who'll get me to talk about my childhood memories and play stupid word association games that'll only serve to prove I am full of remorse and anger and denial and other shit caused by Davies' dying.'

Jeanette lowered her gaze. Ross squeezed her hand.

'Don't take it out on Jeanette,' he said in a low, even voice. 'She only means well.'

Robyn sighed. 'I'm so sorry, Jeanette. I shouldn't have snapped at you. I was out of order. I can't get it out of my head. I should never have insisted on joining him in Morocco. I was a distraction. I knew better but I went anyway.'

'We've been through this before,' said Ross. 'It wasn't your fault. Davies was a careful, cautious and professional man. His mind would have been on the job and the ambush was something he hadn't suspected. You're going to have to let go of that guilt. It's eating you away – literally,' he continued, nodding at her thin frame. 'We're your friends. We know how tough it's been but it is time to move on and put this all behind you.'

'Brigitte said pretty much the same and even asked if I was seeing anyone yet. Not in so many words but she was telling me the same thing. It's time to move on. I just wish I were able to. I am sorry, Jeanette.'

'I know. It's fine,' replied Jeanette. 'But listen to your friends. We have your best interests at heart.'

The conversation was interrupted by Robyn's mobile. She raised her eyebrows in apology as she took the call, moving towards the house while Jeanette and Ross chatted.

'There's been another murder, Boss,' said Mitz Patel. 'It's Mary Matthews.'

'Lucas's wife. Where?'

'Her house. I went around to break the news about her husband and found her.'

'I'm on my way. Ask PC Marker to join us and to bring Anna with him.'

She returned to her friends.

'So sorry, I have to cut and run. Another murder. It's Mary Matthews. This is becoming crazy.'

Ross nodded gravely. 'It's turning into a right bloodbath. It's times like this I'm glad I'm out of it all.'

'Me too,' said Jeanette, holding his hand. 'Take care, Robyn, and don't get too bogged down. The job can suck the life out of you if you don't watch it.'

With that warning ringing in her ears, she headed off to Mulwood Avenue, wondering how many more people were going to be murdered before she uncovered the killer.

CHAPTER THIRTY-SEVEN

THEN

It was only a matter of time before I caught him. I've been biding my time forever since I found out where he was working. It's taken me over two years to track him down but it's all been worth it.

From my vantage point I can see him. I watch his bare backside as he performs an indecent act upon a girl who is little more than twelve. She is one of his pupils. I watched them leave her house. She's dressed in school uniform and carrying a flute case. I followed them here to the woods. This is not her first time with him. She came freely. She is infatuated with him. She would be. He's her music tutor and makes her feel important and grown up while she is a naive young girl who believes the lies her teacher tells her.

I take several photographs of him, his mouth open as he climaxes and of the girl – dark hair in plaits, large hazel eyes – who has no idea that this man is a monster.

I fight back the loathing and urge to drag him out of his car and smash his head against the pavement. I have to play it clever. 'Think of the endgame,' says my father.

'I always do,' I reply.

Ten minutes later and he is on the move. He takes the girl to McDonald's and then back to her house. She waves as she goes back inside to the safety of her family, who have no idea that she has not been to a music practice.

He heads off to his own home where he has a wife waiting for him. I am as sickened by him now as I was all those years ago. A leopard does not change his spots and Lucas Matthews is as depraved now as he was then.

I watch as he pulls up to his large house and the gates close behind him. He may think he is safe and secure but he is not. I send one of the photographs to his email address and a message:

I want fifteen thousand pounds or I shall ruin your life.

I offer him a temporary email address for his reply. I shall ditch it once I receive an answer. It is live for up to twenty-four hours. I'm sure he'll reply before then.

Of course, I don't really care about the money. I'm going to give it to my mother to help her buy a new place to live. Ever since Dirk passed away having snorted a fatal mixture of cocaine laced with rat poison, she's been at a loose end and I worry she'll go back on the game to make ends meet. At the moment, she's working in a casino and can just about afford the rent on the house each month, but I can never tell with her. She sometimes wastes her earnings on going to a beauty salon or tanning shop, or on really expensive shoes. She's been putting it about in an attempt to get another boyfriend, but after being with Dirk, not many men are keen to go out with her.

To be honest, she looks a bit ropy these days. She tries too hard. She's bleached her hair white blonde and her tops are always too low, displaying her wares that aren't as attractive as they once were. I was at her house last night when a taxi driver brought her home drunk. She tried to pay him with sex but he was a decent man and helped carry her to our door.

'I've got a wife and a kid,' he said. 'I wouldn't want my wife to throw herself at someone 'cos she was drunk.'

I felt a rush of gratitude and paid him out of the tea caddy that houses our food money.

If she gets enough money she'll move away. She says she wants to go to the seaside – Devon or Cornwall. She's had enough of city and town *life. She wants to breathe in fresh air, buy a little dog and walk along the beach each morning. I hope she takes the money and rents there. I would visit her often if she moved by the sea. If this works out, I'll ask Lucas for a larger amount of money. It's the least he can do for her. I don't need his money. What I really want is Lucas's head on a plate and I shall get that in time.*

CHAPTER THIRTY-EIGHT

Jackson ran his hand through his hair, turned and paced the room for the fifth time. Abigail was sniffling on the settee, her eyes red-rimmed, and her face gaunt.

'We must contact the police,' he said. 'This should be reported.'

She raised her face to his. 'No,' she said, so quietly he almost didn't hear it. 'It's my fault this has happened.'

He dropped down beside her. 'How? How can you be blamed for our cat being murdered.'

'We're being targeted by someone.'

'What?'

'Some creep is trying to destroy our lives. It started a couple of weeks ago. A threatening note was posted through the letter box. It was made up from words cut out of a newspaper. It was about keeping secrets,' she added, not wishing to tell him the exact wording. 'This has all been about keeping secrets. Just before I found Toffee, I got a text saying, "This is what happens to people who keep secrets."'

Jackson's eyes grew large. 'Secrets? This is mad. Someone who thinks you're keeping secrets killed Toffee. Show me the text.'

Her hand trembled. 'I can't. The text has vanished.'

'What do you mean "vanished"?'

'It disappeared almost as soon as I read it.'

'You deleted it?'

'No. It just went.'

Jackson frowned. 'That's not possible. Did you press a button by mistake? You could easily have deleted it by mistake.'

'It's not the only text to disappear,' she continued. 'The text saying you were keeping secrets from me vanished too.'

Jackson rubbed his forehead as if it ached, his eyes were pained and eyebrows furrowed. 'You have had texts from a stalker that have disappeared,' he repeated slowly, assimilating the information.

Abigail began to get irked. Jackson was not buying into her version of events. She continued more, her voice more urgent. 'And, I received a phone call from someone who said they were going to destroy me and everyone I care about.'

'Abby, this is really serious.'

She ignored him and continued, 'Then things began to happen. My Facebook account was hacked. I'm sure it was hacked by the stalker. The bastard wrote dreadful comments to my friends and posted a picture of the photograph that's in our bedroom. Only someone who got into our house could have had access to that picture.'

She let her words sink in.

'Then, there were more telephone calls. The creep uses a voice-altering device so I don't know who it is. It's really unnerving.'

She took a breath but could not look Jackson in the face. She would have to tell him she knew about his affair and soon she would have to divulge her own secrets and she was fearful of his reaction. This could be the very end of their relationship. She began to become less coherent, eager to explain what had been happening, her words falling from her lips without thought.

'And then what about the noises I heard over the baby monitor? Somebody was in the house. I'm sure of it now. I wasn't at the time. I thought it might be my imagination but now I'm positive someone was in Izzy's room. This lunatic is spying on us and knows everything we do. That's why I had to have the locks changed. I know you didn't believe me at the time. I didn't make it clear enough.'

Jackson took a while to register what she was saying. 'This could be dangerous. Look what the nutcase has done to our cat. This is the work of somebody malicious, cruel and depraved. He could do the same to us. Fetch the note he sent you. It's evidence. We'll phone the police and tell them what's been happening and move out for a few days until they can find out who it is.'

'It's gone,' she said. 'The stalker broke in and took it.'

Jackson shook his head in disbelief. 'How? We've got a burglar alarm. It hasn't gone off and there's only you and me know the code. Hang on; you changed the codes the other day just before you changed all the locks. You said it was because you'd read somewhere they should be changed every few years. Why didn't you tell me then?'

'I thought I could handle it myself. I figured once the locks were changed that would be the end of it. I'd get rid of the son-of-a-bitch. I was going to threaten them with the police.'

'You should have said something at the time, Abby. Why didn't you? *We* could have alerted the police. You shouldn't have kept this to yourself.'

'I was frightened and I thought it was a horrible joke. I wanted it to end but the person kept phoning me and telling me things.'

'What things?'

'Things about you. They told me you were keeping secrets, Jackson. Then they sent me proof that you were.'

Jackson pinched the bridge of his nose then let out a long sigh. In her heightened state of anxiety, she mistook it for disbelief.

'Someone did break in. Some crazy has been spying on me. They watch what I'm doing.' She looked at Jackson, his face unreadable. 'You don't believe me, do you?'

He slumped down next to her on the settee and put a warm hand on her knee. She pushed it away, a rush of anger replacing the feeling of self-doubt and anxiety.

'I believe you but what evidence have you got, Abby?' he asked, quietly. 'We have to have something to show the police. I can't go to them and tell them my wife is terrified because someone has sent her messages we no longer have, and has had her Facebook account hacked. Facebook will deal with that anyway. I can't tell the police you received a threatening note that was then stolen from a house with top-of-the-range security alarms fitted. They'd find it hard to believe any of it, including you thinking you see people in our baby's nursery. You can understand that, can't you? They'll maybe even assume you are making it up. This person hasn't attacked you or threatened to kill you or harm you. They've just messed with your head. And we can't even be sure this madman killed Toffee. The text that disappeared might be unconnected to his death. I'm trying to look at this logically, Abby. I want to believe you but we can't waste police time with this. The worst crime is that Toffee has been killed but I'm not even sure they'll be able to help with that. We simply don't have concrete proof that some psycho is menacing us.'

She hesitated a moment, now infuriated that Jackson was making her sound like a crazy woman. Toffee was dead. Someone was to blame and Jackson was treating her like an idiot. She crossed her arms. 'I've got evidence. I have an email with attachments,' she said, her voice rising as the upset finally bubbled up inside her. 'This crackpot who keeps ringing, told me you were having an affair and I didn't believe them but now I have proof.' Her voice was no longer quiet. She allowed the pent-up frustration and anger flood her body. All pretence at normality was gone. She could no longer hold back the fury that spilled out of every pore in her body. 'And don't try and deny it. I know you are, you lying, cheating bastard.'

Jackson's eyes widened. 'We talked about this before. Whatever makes you think I'm having an affair?' he replied vehemently.

She spat, 'Someone *knows* you are. They've been spying on you too so you can drop the innocent pretence!' Her eyes blazed as words like weapons were hurled at him. 'They witnessed your sordid display, Jackson. They watched and waited for you to do it again and photographed you having sex and then they sent me the evidence. I could barely look at those photographs. They made me want to be sick. How could you? How could you have sex with one of my friends? It all fits because when you were supposedly flying to Spain instead of James, Zoe was also away at some made-up conference. I hate her for this. I hate you both.' She suddenly raised both hands in a gesture of comprehension. 'That's it. That's what the text message meant. "This is what happens to people who hide the truth." This is about you. The text was referring to you keeping secrets. It's all been about you and your damn affair. It's your fault Toffee is dead.'

Jackson gave her a long look. 'This is some huge mistake. Someone is messing with you. This is ludicrous. I would never do such a thing, angel,' he pleaded. 'I can't believe you'd think I would. Show me these photographs. There must be some logical explanation.'

'Don't you call me "angel", you cheat.'

She scrabbled frantically inside her handbag on the floor beside the settee, and lifted out her mobile. She stabbed at some buttons. Then stabbed again. A look of bewilderment fell across her face. 'I can't find the email. It's vanished and so have all the downloaded photographs. They were there earlier.'

She moved across the room to the computer and powered it up, her fingers hovering over the keyboard, her hands beginning to shake. She typed her password and gained access to her emails, scrolling through them all and checking deleted boxes. 'It's not here,' she said again. 'It's been deleted. How can that have happened? This bloody psycho's gained access to my emails now and deleted them. There *were* photographs.' Her voice trailed off. She hardly dared to glance in his direction.

Jackson stood to face her and scowled. 'Listen to yourself, Abigail. This all sounds ridiculous. It's like some bad plot on a television soap.'

'Don't be so ruddy patronising,' she howled. 'Shut up and listen to me instead of being so defensive.'

Jackson glared at her. 'I'll listen when you start making sense and when this email turns up you can show the photographs to me. That is, if they really exist. Or maybe they're like the magical disappearing person in the house and the texts that have vanished and the threatening note that can't be found.'

'Of course they exist.'

'Have you proof of any of this, Abigail? Have you anything at all? Because from where I'm standing, I can only see a highly strung woman who is making preposterous accusations that she can't substantiate. I accept that you are upset because of what has happened to Toffee but the rest of this is little short of lunacy.'

'Wait a minute. I am not backing down. I have got proof I'm not making all of this up. I won't have you look at me like I'm barmy.' As she scrolled through her phone call log, Abigail felt ill. The call log had been erased. She now had no proof that she had ever received or made any calls to the unknown number. She threw the phone onto the floor in one angry gesture.

'The call log has vanished too. And before you say anything, I am not making this up. Everything I've told you happened. I know some wacko came into our home, which is why I had the locks changed, and I have been getting calls from that person. All the time I thought it was my fault this was happening and it turns out it's yours. I know about your sleazy affair with Zoe. Those photographs were of you both.' She choked on her words.

Jackson rounded on her. 'For the last time, I am not having, nor have ever had an affair with anyone and certainly not with Zoe. I thought you knew me better than that. Ring her. Ask her. Ask her or accuse her and see what her reaction is. This is descending into farce. I thought it was about Toffee and you being stalked. I thought it was about being menaced and getting threatening calls but you've turned it all around into some quarrel about me shagging women. What's going on? Have you been making some of this stuff up to get more attention from me, or are you so insecure about our relationship that you have to throw all this nonsense about? For crying out loud, Abigail.' He stopped, turned on his heel and marched towards the door.

'Jackson, where are you going?' she screamed.

'To bury our cat and then I'm going out before I say something I'll regret. When you're less hysterical we'll talk again. You're not making sense. I don't know what's going on any more, Abby. Ever since we had Izzy you've pushed me away and now all this. I don't know which malevolent person killed Toffee but I do know you're not yourself. I'm beginning to wonder if you shouldn't see a doctor. You're stressed.'

'I'm not stressed,' she shrieked. 'I've been getting calls about your affair for the last few days. I didn't believe them at first but I've seen the evidence with my own eyes. You and Zoe Cooper. I am not bloody well stressed. What about the night you were in Spain? How could anyone know about that unless they were watching you? They told me you spent the night at the Hotel Gran Melia Don Pepe with your girlfriend. I wouldn't know that unless I had been told.'

'Unbelievable. I didn't spend the night at any hotel. I was at the airport just like I told you. Remember? If you want corroboration on that story, phone Gavin. You've got a mobile,' he said, pointing to it. 'Call him and ask. He'll tell you we were both at the airport.

I've never even heard of the damn hotel. Check it out. It probably doesn't even exist. Maybe you should have done exactly that earlier. Then you'd have believed me. And while you're at it, call Zoe. Get your head straightened out. I'm sick of listening to this shit.'

Abigail buried her head in her hands. 'I don't understand.'

His voice was cold. 'I don't either. When you find these mysterious, incriminating photographs, then bring them to me. I'd like the opportunity to verify my innocence.'

He shut the door quietly, leaving Abigail curled up on the settee, her hands wrapped in a tight ball, her arms hugging her knees. Her heart was racing. She had almost blurted out other things – secrets she had kept hidden for too long. She had messed this up. She shouldn't have got so mad about the photographs. She had been blinded by anger and consequently had not been able to argue reasonably, and now she'd lost her opportunity to explain why all of this was truly her fault. The events of the last few days became jumbled up like tangled clothing in a washing machine and she could no longer think clearly. The note had been removed. The text and call log had been erased from her mobile and the photographs of Jackson and Zoe had gone. And, worst of all, sweet, gentle Toffee was dead. Her brain could not cope with it all.

She curled up on the settee, the sound of her own sobs drowning all noises until a sound she recognised penetrated her moans and she heard a whisper of noise.

'Bye, bye, Mummy.'

She cried out and hurtled up the stairs, falling onto her knees in the nursery in front of Izzy's cot. Her baby lay fast asleep, rag dog by her side. Above the bed, the mobile of gaily coloured aeroplanes rotated, music playing as they flew in never-ending circles. Someone had been in the nursery. Abigail sat propped against the cot, snuffling back tears, and wondering if she wasn't losing her mind.

CHAPTER THIRTY-NINE

THEN

It's been quite easy to exact money from Lucas. He went running to his daddy who then gave him what he needed. I set the whole thing up beautifully. My destination for the exchange is Blithfield Reservoir, which happens to be adjacent to where Paul Matthews lives.

I leave my car in Abbots Bromley parked down a side street, well away from the reservoir car park. I'm not going to get caught out. I shoulder my backpack and take a route that walkers favour, heading north towards Uttoxeter. I don't take the road that goes over Blithfield Reservoir but choose the second turning that after three quarters of a mile leads me into a drive signposted Blithfield Walks and Education Centre. I take the second longest of the three walks around the reservoir. This is the route Lucas will also have to take. I grin at that fact. I fancy making Lucas sweat a bit.

The reservoir is recognised as a premier trout fishery and is home to Blithfield Anglers as well as Blithfield Sailing Club. This time of the year lots of people visit but the place doesn't officially open until eight o'clock in the morning, so I can put my plan into action without being spotted by anyone.

The instructions in my emails were explicit. One of the conditions was that he jacked in his job – I don't think someone like him should be anywhere near children. He's lucky I haven't reported him to the police. I would but then that would ruin my other plans for him.

I have arranged for Lucas to go to the second of two bird hides on what they call the red route in Broompit Plantation, where there are also the remains of the old marl pits used in building the reservoir dam. I've walked the route myself several times to ensure I have chosen wisely. Lucas has to drop an envelope filled with used fifty-pound notes under the bench in the hide and leave. It is simple.

I hide in the woods an hour before he is due. I want to make sure he or that father of his doesn't set me up. The woods are calm apart from the occasional tapping of a nuthatch or a greater-spotted woodpecker. I sit under a tree, camouflaged against it, and watch the bird feeder station as various tits alight on the nuts and fly off again. A sight of a roe deer oblivious to my presence rewards me. Somehow this makes me feel important and accepted at the same time. I feel I belong here in this wood. The peace seeps into my soul and warms my heart. I could live here. Forever. The thought appeals hugely and I fantasise about having a small wooden house hidden away from everyone.

No one else is in the woods and at seven-thirty on the dot, I spot the figure of Lucas as he checks his map, looks about furtively and enters the hide. I leave it a good twenty minutes before I stroll into the hide, slide onto the bench and pull out the envelope marked 'Zoe'. I give a smile, tuck it into my backpack and disappear into the woods again.

CHAPTER FORTY

Robyn drew up outside the house at Mulwood Avenue. The gate was open and the BMW cabriolet was parked outside, as it had been the first time she had visited Mary Matthews. Her officers were waiting for her beside Mitz's car. Anna Shamash was deathly pale, her face an unreadable mask.

'You up for this?' she asked the girl. Anna nodded. 'Chew this,' Robyn went on, throwing Anna a piece of gum. 'Concentrate on your breathing and remember it is just a body. No more than that. Pretend it is made of rubber or some other material. Best not to focus on it being a human. If you feel sick at any time, come outside. Remember, we've all been there. The first body is the worst. It gets easier.'

She rapped on the open door to alert her colleague inside and entered.

'In here,' said PC David Marker. He stood next to the sitting room door where Robyn had interviewed the woman only a few days earlier. She followed him into the room, pursued by her officers.

She glanced around the fussy room with its Spanish fans on the wall and its surfaces cluttered with ornaments. The settee was empty, one cushion plumped up, the other on the floor. On the coffee table stood a cup, teapot and plate, and lying between the settee and the table was the body of Mary Matthews, eyes wide open, her face a twisted mask of fear. Robyn heard a noise behind her. Anna had rushed outside.

'What do we have?'

'Not much. Looks like a heart attack or convulsion of some sort, stroke maybe. Time of death approximately twenty-four hours ago. She's still showing signs of rigor mortis. No evidence of a third party. There are remnants of cold tea in her cup and crumbs on the plate. Nothing suspicious, although her face is unusually pink.'

'It is, isn't it? Only one plate and cup?'

'She appears to have been alone.'

'That's a large pot of tea for one. Surely, if you're alone, you tend to make a cup or a mug and this is expensive china she's using.' Robyn picked up the cup with gloved fingers and examined the base. It was like the one she had drunk from. 'It's Villeroy & Boch. You don't ordinarily use your best plates and cups for a mid-morning cuppa. Something doesn't add up here. This is the sort of crockery you get out when you have a guest – a special guest, or someone you want to impress. And cake? Do you cut yourself a piece of cake and sit and eat it alone, using your best china set?'

Mitz shook his head. 'I only have mugs. They came from Argos. My gran has a best set of china. She used to use it when she had visitors. Mum doesn't. She uses whatever cup comes to hand. It's an old person's thing, isn't it? Or someone posh. They'd have posh crockery.'

Robyn agreed with him. 'Can we check to see if there's any more of the cake she was eating? See if there's empty packaging or a cake tin out? If she baked it herself, there'll be a cake tin somewhere. Mitz, check the pantry.'

Anna came back into the room, a little colour in her cheeks. Robyn gave her a nod of approval. 'Help Mitz look for a cake tin or Tupperware tub or anything that contains cake. Check the wastebin for packaging or a cake box. Something isn't right here.'

Robyn swept the room with her eyes. The guitar that had been in the corner of the room now lay on the floor, its fretted neck broken in two. She couldn't imagine Mary Matthews destroying it, no matter how angry she was with Lucas. It meant too much to her.

'Take that guitar in for fingerprinting, David,' she said. 'Where's the dog? There should be a Scotty-type dog.'

'It's a decent guitar – an Alhambra Classical. My lad is learning the guitar. His isn't as nice as this one.'

'Where's the dog, David?' repeated Robyn.

'Oh, it's with the neighbour,' replied PC Marker.

Robyn resisted tutting. David Marker could be quite frustrating at times. She pulled at her ear. On the surface, it appeared Mary Matthews had suffered a heart attack or similar, her face was contorted as if in agony. She would have to wait for an autopsy. This might be a horrible coincidence but Robyn did not believe in coincidences.

Anna Shamash appeared in the doorway. 'I don't know if this is significant,' she said, 'but I found this on the floor.'

She held up a toy rubber rabbit.

'I understand why you picked up on it but the rabbit we found at Blinkley Manor School was large and fluffy. That's just a dog toy.'

'I've got a dog and I'd never buy a hideous thing like this for him,' Anna replied. She brandished the toy that had a painted face and large blue eyes and eyebrows that gave it a surprised look. It's the sort of toy you'd give a baby not a dog. Well, you'd have given it to a baby in the 1950s. It's so kitsch,' she said, wrinkling her nose at it. 'I think you should look at the base.'

She passed the rubber rabbit to Robyn. It let out a squeak as Robyn took it. She grimaced at the sound and squinted at the base between the rabbit's feet. Scratched onto it in capital letters were the words 'RIP Mary'. Robyn felt an electric jolt. They were onto something at last. She pointed to the plate on the table. 'Get those crumbs checked out. Find out what she was eating. Get the tea checked too. Mitz, go talk to the neighbours. See who visited yesterday morning. Get car number plates of any vehicles in the vicinity, anything you can. David, ask the boys in to clear up here. We need an autopsy on this as soon as possible. Anna, good job. You can come back to the station with me. I want you to find out what you can about this rabbit and where it might have been purchased. I need to talk to Mulholland.'

* * *

It had seemed like only a few days since Robyn had stumbled in to DCI Mulholland's office to hand in her notice. Detective Chief Inspector Louisa Mulholland hadn't changed much. She had a few more pronounced frown lines but apart from that she had the same dyed dark-blonde hair cut in a severe bob, the same dark-blue round-framed glasses that hid keen olive-green eyes, and the same warm smile.

'If there is anything you need, don't hesitate to ask. As I told you on the phone, we're thin on resources at the moment but I still have no objection to outside help from Ross Cunningham for your investigation as well as officers Patel and Shamash. We should be through with Operation Goofy in the next few days and then you can have more manpower if you require it.'

DCI Mulholland rested her chin on her steepled fingers. 'I'd rather like to wrap this one up quickly. Two murders on my patch are two too many. You've been tracking Lucas Matthews. Have you come across any suspects yet?'

Robyn gathered her thoughts. Mulholland preferred officers to be open and clear.

'We're checking out his work colleagues and people who have employed him as a tutor, but I believe his murder and quite possibly that of his wife's are linked to someone in Farnborough. I have reason to believe he was hunting for a person there who could end up being our perp. I'd like permission to return to Hampshire to investigate it further rather than waste time here. I want to leave officers Patel and Shamash to do the follow-ups here and take my investigation to Farnborough.'

'If you think it will lead to the discovery of his killer, then yes. I'll talk to Hampshire police and let them know you are working on their turf. I don't need to remind you that you have to play this one by the book. We both know you can be headstrong. It would be advisable to behave in a more conventional fashion, no dashing off on one of your famous hunches. Do we understand each other? You wasted one of my officer's time, sending him out on a wild goose chase because you suspected Geraldine Marsh was murdered. You're a very good detective but not all of your premonitions come to fruition.'

'But can I say my hunches have helped solve many cases?'

'I'm not questioning your ability, Robyn, I am merely requesting you keep your sudden urges to race off on a tangent to a minimum. I don't like rattling cages and DCI Corrance at Hampshire Constabulary is a highly respected officer who likes to work by the book.'

'Understood.'

'Keep me informed then.'

Mulholland picked up a report and began sifting through it. It was a sign that Robyn was dismissed. Mulholland didn't look up as Robyn left. It was her nature. Her mind would now be on something else. Robyn wondered if she would turn into a Mulholland, focused full time on cases simply to stop the hurt getting to her.

Robyn marched into the office. Anna was hunched over a desk, staring at a computer screen.

'How are you getting on?'

'The remains of Mary Matthews' tea and cake has been sent to the lab. Still waiting for the coroner's report for both victims. I've requested they fast track them for us. PC Patel has written up the statements from Blinkley Manor School. They're on your desk. No one saw anything strange. Waiting to hear if anyone was spotted at or near Mary Matthews' house yesterday. I've been running through sites, looking for the squeaky, rubber toy rabbit. Most dog toys are balls or in the shapes of bones, not rabbits, besides, it looks old with its painted face.' She navigated the sites expertly with her mouse and suddenly exclaimed. 'Got it! I thought it was unusual. It's a vintage rabbit from the 1960s, originally made in Italy. Not sure how much that tells us for the moment.'

'I don't think we'll be able to narrow down where it came from,' said Robyn. 'It could have been recently purchased or in a family for years.' She flicked through the Lucas Matthews file that was on Patel's desk. It was open at the photograph of Lucas lying on his back, a toy rabbit under his arm. The rabbit was the sort you would give a baby or a small child. It was a cuddly soft-furred toy with very long droopy ears. It was folded into Lucas's body and looking up at him. She put the file down and surveyed the plastic evidence bag containing the rabbit.

'I've also begun looking at local toy shops in search of a toy rabbit similar to that one,' said Anna Shamash. 'There are rabbits at Toys R Us but they're patchwork and not furry. There are plenty of toy rabbits online,' she added, scrolling down the list to show her superior who moved across to join her. 'That one's nice,' Anna said, pointing at a long-eared soft toy with a bashful look on its face and twinkling ears. 'I might buy that for my niece's birthday.'

'This isn't the shopping channel, PC Shamash,' replied Robyn, a small smile playing on her lips. 'I'm returning to Farnborough to see if I can pick up where I left off. I want to interview Zoe Cooper. Not only does her name keep cropping up but also she was spotted leaving the Aviator hotel a few nights ago with Lucas Matthews. The timing corresponds to when he was murdered. She's denied knowing him but something isn't right there. If you need me, I'll be on my mobile. Do we know Nick Pearson-Firth's movements for the week?'

'Spent most of the week with his family at their cottage in Devon but came back two days ago as he had interviews lined up all day yesterday. After interviewing three people for Lucas Matthews' old position, he took his dog for a walk. The dog ran off into the wooded area and didn't return when he shouted, so Mr Pearson-Firth followed it. The dog was snuffling around the body. He pulled the dog away and rang the police. He said he'd seen enough television dramas to know not to disturb the scene.'

Robyn nodded. 'When Mitz returns, ask him to check up on all of Lucas Matthews' work colleagues. See if anyone had a grudge against him. Lucas gave private music lessons too so check out those families. And let me know when you've uncovered where the rabbits were purchased. There was no mobile phone on Lucas Matthews' body. The killer might have appropriated it. See if it has been used or if we can track it down. And, find out where Lucas Matthews was staying in Farnborough. It wasn't the Aviator hotel.'

'Anything else, boss?'

'Find out what you can about Natasha Matthews, including an address for her. She ought to be told that her brother and father are dead. I can't think of anything else for the moment. That lot should keep you out of mischief for a while.'

Robyn left the young woman bent back over the computer, scrolling through pages. Her gut told her the answer to this was in Farnborough.

CHAPTER FORTY-ONE

THEN

I had enough. It was time to kill Paul. After I obtained another fifteen thousand pounds from Lucas, Dad pointed out that the Matthews family owed me far more than money. He was furious that they thought they could pay me off so easily and expect me to drift away into the background without causing them any more grief.

'People like them get away with everything,' he grumbled.

He was right. I'd spent the night at Mum's house. It needed a good clean and she'd forgotten to put the rubbish out again. The bin stank and when I tipped the waste out into the large recycling bin in the yard bluebottles flew out of it, buzzing angrily around my head.

Mum's beginning to worry me. She's spending more time at the local pub and there's a new bloke on the scene – Frank. Frank is a weedy, slimy, weaselly-looking man who works in a betting shop. I don't know what Mum sees in him other than he drives an old Jaguar X8 sports car. She is always swayed by what she thinks are posh cars. He opens the door to Mum's house in shorts and a vest that reveal puny arms and legs, and sneers at me when I ask who he is.

'I'm your mum's new beau,' he says, trying to sound clever.

Mum shouts for me to come through and I try to ignore Frank, who smells of some disgusting, pungent aftershave that makes me want to gag. Mum's pleased to see me but I can't hand over the money to her, not with Frank in the room, so after a cup of tea I make my excuses and leave.

Frank has wound me up. I'm supposed to be looking after my mother, not him. I've gone to a lot of trouble to make sure she has money and we can set up somewhere else that will be her home forever. Frank isn't supposed to be part of that picture. It'll be a place where she won't have to prostitute herself any more. Dad is even more unhappy about Frank than me and together we chunter about him all the way up the motorway.

I drove non-stop to Abbots Bromley. I needed to feel that peace and calm I enjoyed while I waited for Lucas to deposit the money in the hides, so after two and a half hours, I pull into the reservoir car park and breathe a sigh.

It's mid-afternoon and many of the ramblers have left. There are only three cars in the car park. I take the path that leads through the wood and will join the meadow. I want to walk beside the water for a while before I murder Paul, and try to spot the swans, terns, waders and geese that frequent the reservoir, and then stroll into the woods to observe the birds on the feeders. It'll be what I need to take my mind off Frank.

No sooner have I got into the woods than I spot a figure jogging up the slope. My heart lurches. It's Paul Matthews. He's earlier than I expected. I act speedily. I have some washing line in my pocket. Dad reminds me I was going to mend Mum's broken rotary line with it. I whip it out and tie it around a tree and attach the other end to a tree stump. I have time to put on plastic gloves that I always carry in my pocket. I never know when I might need a pair. Paul is still jogging. I'm sure he hasn't seen me. Everything is in place. I take a step backwards away from the path and look around. I spot a branch that has conveniently fallen from a tree in recent winds. I collect it and wait in the gloom of the trees.

As Paul Matthews, lost in his own world, races past me, his shoe catches on the washing line. He loses his footing, his arms reach out and try to grab a tree trunk but he bangs his head against the tree, falling *into it and grazing his hands as he attempts to save himself. He tumbles to the floor in a heap. His ankle is twisted, and, stunned, he struggles to stand. He calls out for assistance and eventually I come forward.*

He doesn't spot the branch behind my back. Ever the actor he pretends he cares about me. He calls me by my name and says he wants to talk, but it is too late for talking. That particular ship sailed a long time ago. The fury that has been burning in my stomach for sixteen years is unleashed and I swing the branch as hard as I can and hit him on the side of the head.

He drops. I kick him gently with a boot. He doesn't moan. His body is lifeless. I have killed him. I move him into position and clear up behind me, whistling a ditty as I do. Funny how murdering someone you hate lifts your spirits for a while.

I check to see if anyone has witnessed my actions but there is no one in sight. I lose the branch among the leaves and head back to the car park, empty of vehicles.

Suddenly I feel renewed, as if I have a purpose again. Dad whispers in my ear and I agree. Next on my kill list will be Lucas.

CHAPTER FORTY-TWO

'Welcome back to the Aviator hotel, Detective Inspector Carter. I understand you are not staying with us this time.'

'I'm not sure at the moment. It depends,' replied Robyn, smiling politely. 'I've arranged to meet someone. I booked a conference room so I could work while I wait.'

'Yes, it's been set up for you. Fourth floor,' continued the well-groomed girl behind the desk.

Robyn took the lift to the conference room where she threw all her paperwork onto the desk area and ran through it. There was a link between this town and Lucas's death. She was sure of it. On the journey, she had called to mind the places Paul Matthews had written down in the *Farnborough* file on his laptop. The trip to Farnborough Hill School had confused her but, as she left the M3, it struck her that she had asked the headmistress the wrong question. She phoned the school and spoke to the registrar who confirmed her suspicion. Zoe Cooper had attended the school for one year. She rang her cousin.

'We were barking up the wrong tree,' she told Ross. 'We were asking about Alice when we should have been asking about Zoe Cooper. Zoe joined the school in her last year, took and passed all her GCSE exams but didn't stay on for sixth form.'

'That's interesting.'

'And what's more interesting is that Lucas Matthews had been asking the school about Zoe. He visited it on the twenty-eighth of

July. That was the day Paul had arranged to meet the headmistress. However, Lucas didn't see the headmistress. He spoke to the registrar directly.'

'Zoe is involved in this then?'

'Looks that way.'

'Want me to try and find out more about her?'

'You're okay. I've got Anna and Mitz working flat out on it.'

'That's good. Mitz Patel's got nothing better to do with his time, unless he's suddenly discovered love.'

'Still young, single and available. I think he's trying to work his way up the ranks before he gets involved with anyone.'

'Wise chap.'

'I just rang to talk to Zoe but it's gone to answerphone. I spoke to the fitness studio where she works and they told me she is taking classes for the rest of the afternoon. I'll ask her later why she was spotted walking out of the hotel with Lucas Matthews just before he was murdered. I'd rather not call her into the station just yet, even though she appears to be our only suspect. By all accounts the DCI here is a tough nut and he'll want this all done by the book. I don't want to drag her in for formal questioning at this stage. I only have one witness who claimed to see a woman with green hair leave the building. I need more than that before I can pull her in or charge her.'

'Go with what you're comfortable with. The DCI at Hampshire Constabulary doesn't need to know your policing methods and neither does Louisa Mulholland.'

'I'll do it my way then. I'm also going to talk to Stu Grant at lunchtime. I phoned BizzyAir Business Aviation and he's meeting me at the hotel on his way to work. Again, I didn't want to call him into the station. Thought he'd be more relaxed at the hotel. He might have something useful for me, but I need to get him alone.'

'You're not using the thumbscrews on him, are you?'

Robyn chuckled. 'I thought I might.'

'I'm en route to Jane Clifford. Just stopping off to get her some flowers to cheer her up. Her room looked so gloomy the last time I visited her.'

That was Ross, he had a big heart. He came across as a grouch but he cared about people. He had cared too much when he was on the force, and there were too many distressed victims to care about. It had taken its toll and added to his already skyrocketing stress levels. At least in his new line of work he could pick and choose his cases and hopefully get satisfaction from his job without so much stress.

* * *

Two hours later Robyn's eyes felt full of grit. Comments in neat cursive writing linked by arrows and red lines revealed the extent of her research. She stretched her arms above her head and yawned, then stood up, rolling her shoulders to iron out the tension in them.

She'd written that Paul Matthews had been discovered dead near his home on 25 July, five days after he sent his last email to Lucas – a verdict of accidental death had been declared. Lucas had waited until the end of the school year then coincidentally disappeared that same day. Lucas had either killed Paul Matthews then gone on a hunt in Farnborough for an unnamed female, or he had not known his father was dead, having gone undercover to find the woman. He had not divulged anything to his wife and pretended he was going to Thailand. As far as Mary Matthews was concerned he had gone completely off the radar. That was strange. No matter what secrets he kept from his wife he could easily have rung her, even if it were to keep up the pretence of being away. Lucas had visited Farnborough Hill School, the Keep Fit Gym, and the Aviator hotel on 28 July and over the three days before that he had tried to get hold of Jackson Thorne as part of his search for Zoe Cooper, becoming abusive when he couldn't get a response.

It all smacked of a desperate man. Yet, when he finally noticed Zoe on 28 July at the Aviator Sky Bar, he had not approached her. That part bugged Robyn. Even if the group of men had put him off, surely his desire to talk to her would have outweighed that. He'd come a long way, searched for her and then not spoken to her. It made no sense. And then, there was the fact Zoe was seen leaving the hotel with him later that same evening. Had no one else seen them together?

Someone had wanted Lucas dead – was it to stop him following Zoe? Had Zoe murdered him? The act of cutting off his genitals and leaving them in his mouth suggested someone was disgusted with him. It had to be someone with strength to overpower the man and then commit such an act. The toy rabbit by his body bothered Robyn too. Since discovering the rubber toy rabbit at the Matthews' house, she felt more than ever that it meant something important, but it was a clue that she could not work out. She was not making sufficient progress uncovering his and probably Mary's murderer.

She screwed up her eyes in concentration but none of it fitted together or gave her a single clue as to where she should look next. There were too many question marks and pieces that made no sense, like the fact that Paul had worked out he and Lucas needed to find Zoe Cooper and that she lived in Farnborough. How on earth had he come to that conclusion? How had he conjured up that name? Was it linked to Alice or Christina Forman?

Farnborough was miles away from Staffordshire and completely unconnected to his life there, so why had he chosen that town? A flicker of something flitted across her mind and evaporated. There it was again, that niggle, that suggestion she was onto something.

She was about to leave the room for some dinner when her phone buzzed. It was Mitz.

'I've located Christina Forman.'

'You superstar. Where is she?'

'In a garden of remembrance near Oxford, place called Bicester.'

'Dead? That's a problem. I was hoping she was living in Farnborough or nearby.'

'She died on the sixteenth of June.'

'That's just over eight weeks ago.'

'That's correct. Strangled by her lover. I've got the details here. Want me to send them to you?'

'Yes, do that. Thanks, Mitz.'

She rang her cousin and explained about Christina.

'You want to join me at the remembrance garden later today? I'm still fumbling about here. I know I'm close to working it all out but a distraction might help me get things into place. I'll email you directions and address. Should only take me just over an hour. I'll ring when I leave.'

'Sure. See you there.'

'Ross.'

'Yes.'

'Thank you. You're a great guy.'

'I know. I'm just one big, lovable hunk.'

* * *

Stu Grant knocked at the door and came in. He dropped his hat onto the table and slipped onto one of the chairs opposite her.

'Thanks for seeing me. I'm really hoping you can help me further,' said Robyn. 'I'm struggling to work out Lucas Matthews' movements during the week he was here. And I wondered if you happened to notice Zoe Cooper talking to him at any stage of the evening when you were all at the bar together.'

She waited to gauge Stu's reaction but he did not display any signs other than mild surprise.

'Zoe? No. She was with us the whole time. Has something happened to the chap? You wouldn't be questioning me unless there'd been a development.'

'I'm not at liberty to discuss any such matters, sir. I'm just trying to work out his movements.'

Stu's mouth turned downwards and he nodded gravely. 'Well, I can't really tell you any more than I already did. I thought I spotted him in the Sky Bar. He was standing in a corner. He was drinking from a bottle. That's it.'

'I'd like to know a little more about Zoe Cooper. I need to know what happened that night to help get a series of events in order.'

Stu shook his head. 'I can't see how that'll help.'

'It's important. I believe Lucas Matthews was hunting Zoe and might have tracked her to the Sky Bar on the night you, Gavin and Jackson were there together with her.'

'Look, I'm not sure I should. It's all a bit personal.' He chewed at his lips for a moment, struggling with his conscience. 'Okay. We were having a quick drink with a client. Zoe arrived soon after us. She's a nice girl, very bubbly but she was a little worse for wear that night. She was… how should I put it – uninhibited, friendly. All of the guys at BizzyAir know Zoe. She did a boot camp for us last year. Put us through our paces, I can tell you. She had us working so hard I thought I was going to have a heart attack. She's very dedicated to her fitness. She used to pop into the Sky Bar after work when she was at the Keep Fit Gym. She knows quite a few members of staff here. She comes in less often now she's working in London. As I said, she's a really nice woman and I can't imagine she's involved in any wrong doings. I don't know what else to tell you. She's a close friend of Jackson's wife. Maybe you should talk to her. Be careful what you say. What happened the other night, well, it's delicate.'

He looked away.

'Are you saying Zoe was indiscreet that night? That she made out with one of your colleagues?'

Stu nodded. 'It was a surprise to see her like that. She was all over him. It was most unlike her. He's a married man. He loves his wife. If it gets back to her she'll string him by his balls, I can tell you. She's not the understanding sort. It's not for me to say any more. Other people will get hurt if I do. I don't think Zoe will have anything to do with your enquiries and you will gain nothing by pursuing this line of enquiry other than upset people I know and care about.'

'Don't worry. I am discreet too. I'm not here to be judgemental. I'm trying to uncover what Lucas Matthews was up to. The problem I have is that your story doesn't tally with what else I have been told. I understand Zoe left the hotel with Lucas Matthews. She was seen. According to my sources, she was leading him out because he was drunk.'

Stu let out a snort of derision. 'Your source is completely inaccurate. To start with, she was so inebriated she could barely stand up herself, and secondly, she left with one of my colleagues. Please don't interview him. It really could destroy his relationship if his wife finds out. It was a one-off. No one else needs to know about it.'

'I understand. Thank you.'

Stu looked relieved. 'I'm afraid that's all I can tell you.' He checked his watch. 'I'm sorry. I have to leave now. Good luck with your investigations. Please bear in mind what I said. I would hate my friends to suffer thanks to you probing into matters.'

'As I said, I'm discreet. I won't ruin Jackson Thorne's marriage.'

He hesitated for a second, before saying, 'Not Jackson, DI Carter. That would never happen. Zoe had a one-night stand with Gavin Singer, and given his wife is a top lawyer it would be best to keep schtum about it.'

As Robyn watched Stu Grant disappear down the stairs, her mobile buzzed. She didn't recognise the number.

'Detective Inspector Carter?'

'Yes.'

'It's Jackson Thorne. Are you still in the area? I need to talk to you, urgently.'

CHAPTER FORTY-THREE

THEN

How can this have happened? I only saw her last week when that awful Frank was at her house.

I've come back with my bag of money to give it to her and tell her it is time to start a whole new life. She has thirty thousand pounds to use as a deposit on a house or flat by the sea. With what I earn, I'll be able to pay mortgage repayments on it and she won't have to worry about being beaten up, used, abused or ill-treated ever again. I'm making up for all the bad times. I'm turning her life around for her. I'm saying sorry the only way I know how and now it's too late.

I punch my fist against the wall of the bedroom. It hurts like hell but I don't care. Hot, angry tears fill my eyes. I never cry, I won't cry now, but in spite of my efforts tears drop anyway and anger and sadness mix together, and the small girl hidden deep inside me wants nothing more than to run to her motionless form and be held by her.

She's lying on the bed, eyes wide open, handcuffed to the bedpost, wearing a garish red, faux-leather bondage outfit that makes me want to gag. How could she stoop to this level? Surely, she had some dignity left?

My father can't speak either. He is as shocked as me and eventually I hear a small stifled sob that can only be him. His heart is breaking. He has loved her through everything that has happened and now it is too late for our plan to give her what she has only ever wanted – security and love.

I can't look at her any more and although I want to release her from the handcuffs and hold her so tightly I bring her back to life, I know I can't. I have to leave her for the police to find. They'll work out what has happened and track down Frank, for it is surely him who is to blame for this. From where I stand I can see dark marks on her neck. He has strangled her. I ought to go after him and bash his skull in but my father tells me this time I should leave and let Frank get what he deserves.

I refrain from kissing her. I'll try hard to wipe this image from my mind. I want to remember the lady in the tulle princess gown, whose golden hair hung in glossy curls and who was my world, not this woman, bone thin and world worn. I experience tightness in my chest like an invisible python is squeezing the life out of me and a horrible, howling, wild noise fills the room. I think it is coming from my father but it is not. It is coming from me.

I have failed her. This part of my perfect plan has not worked out but I shall make sure the second part does. Someone will pay heavily for this and that someone will be Abigail.

CHAPTER FORTY-FOUR

Jackson Thorne sat opposite her, fingers tapping lightly on the table, his body infused with nervous energy.

'Thanks for seeing me.'

'It's no problem. I was surprised you phoned.' Robyn sat back in the leather Rocket chair and observed his actions.

'I don't know who else to talk to. I didn't want to rush off to the local police. My wife Abigail believes someone is targeting us. Our cat was killed and nailed to our door last night. Abigail insists someone has been phoning her and is watching our movements, but the calls and texts have all been deleted from her mobile. She's making all sorts of wild claims and can't prove any of them. I'm worried about Abby but I'm also worried that someone killed our cat because of me.'

'Go on,' said Robyn. 'Tell me what you think and I'll see how I can help.'

'This chap Lucas who you've been looking for. He was after me for a whole week, pestering and pestering and I didn't get back to him. What if he did this because I didn't contact him?'

'Pestering you about what?'

'He wanted to meet up. I ignored his calls. I thought he was a salesman. Sometimes they don't say they're from a company and you speak to them thinking they're a client, and they try to flog you all sorts of stuff. I was overworked and I didn't want to talk to any salesman. I was out every day on flights and had no time for him.'

He stopped and placed his hands flat on the table and looked at Robyn.

'Okay, here's what really happened. After the fifth or sixth message, I rang Lucas Matthews back just to get rid of him. He answered his phone and I spoke to him,' he said and exhaled heavily. 'He wanted me to give Abigail a message. He wouldn't tell me what that message was over the phone only that it was very important and I needed to pass it to her, as she would never listen to him. I asked him why not but he repeated that he needed to speak to me in person. I took him for some weirdo. I told him I wouldn't pass on anything and to quit calling me. I was pretty rude to him. I thought the bloke was trying to wind me up. I really didn't consider it to be any more than a lousy prank call from some oddbod. He didn't ring again after that.'

'He wanted you to pass a message to Abigail?'

'That's right. I didn't think much more about it after the telephone conversation. I figured he was unbalanced and I didn't bring it up with Abby in case I worried her unduly. She doesn't know him. If she did, the name would have cropped up in conversation at some stage during our married life. We don't hide stuff from each other. I know about her life before me and there has been no mention of a Lucas Matthews.' He heaved a sigh again. 'After I went to bed last night and had calmed down, I worried he had been hounding Abby because I wouldn't answer his calls and that he actually killed Toffee. I know. It sounds a ludicrous idea now I've spoken it out loud to you but I'm clutching at straws.'

Robyn observed his face as he spoke, searching for telltale signs he was lying but he seemed sincere, his eyes never leaving her own, lines etched on his forehead as he tried to work out why anyone could commit such a callous act. She wondered if Abigail would seem so truthful if she were interviewed. She would keep quiet about Lucas being dead. She wanted to see what Abigail had to say first.

'I can't think what he'd achieve by murdering your cat. Let's run through other possibilities.'

'I can't think of any others, Detective. I've been awake most of the night trying to fathom out who would do this. The only clue I have is that Abigail received a text before she found Toffee. It said something like "This is what happens to people who keep secrets" and I have been keeping a secret, DI Carter, keeping it even from my wife.'

'Go on.'

'Gavin Singer, a colleague had a fling, an affair, or one-night stand, whatever you want to call it, with Abigail's friend Zoe. Gavin really does not want word of it to spread to his wife and the best way was for us to promise to keep quiet. I couldn't say anything to Abby, especially as she's friends with Zoe. She's got such a high moral code when it comes to fidelity and marriage and would be incredibly disapproving of Zoe shagging a married man. You know how women get chatting. She'd definitely say something or tell her other friend Claire, who'd tell another friend, and before you knew it, Gavin's wife would find out, and that would be awful. I hope to goodness it isn't because I've kept quiet that Abigail is now a victim of some nutcase.'

'It would have to be someone who knew of the affair and was aware you'd made that pact. If they were harassing you and your wife, they'd also be doing the same to Stu and almost certainly to Gavin and Zoe. Why would you be the one to suffer? I expect the others have had no stalkers or mysterious phone calls, or they'd surely have mentioned them to you. You're good friends. It's most likely unrelated to Gavin and Zoe, and to Lucas Matthews. Have you made any enemies that you know of? Neighbours? People whose business you've acquired, or disgruntled clients, or anyone who might feel let down by you?'

'I can't come up with anyone. The business is sound and to my knowledge all our clients are satisfied with what we offer. We haven't had any complaints lodged against us. Same with the staff. We all get along well. I've known most of the guys who work at BizzyAir for a long time.'

'So, maybe it is someone who Abigail knows. Did you discuss her concerns? She thinks she's been watched, you said?'

'I didn't discuss her *concerns*, as you call them. They were more like bizarre rants at the time. It all happened late last night after we discovered Toffee. It was Abigail who found him. She phoned me in a complete panic. Fortunately, I'd just touched down and was at the airfield. We had a tail wind and got back sooner than I expected. I left Stu to deal with the clients and offloading, ensuring the aircraft was hangared and so on and charged home. It was pretty gruesome seeing him nailed to the door. Then we had an almighty row and I slept in the spare room. She wasn't up when I left this morning. I had your number from when you spoke to us before, so I wondered if you could help. I'm not sure if this is the sort of thing detectives look into.'

His eyebrows rose, creasing his forehead further as he looked at Robyn. His pallor and bruised circles under his eyes indicated a sleepless night.

'I didn't handle the situation very well. I thought she was being hysterical. It's been a tough few months since Izzy was born. Abby hasn't been herself. Don't get me wrong, she's a great mum, but it's been a huge change for her and she's been withdrawn and reclusive. Especially the last couple of months.'

He scrubbed at the stubble on his chin. 'I'm not criticising Abby but some days she's too cocooned in her own world with Izzy to see there's another world turning around and around without her.'

'Well, I think we should look into her allegations. How about I drop back with you and have a chat to Abigail?'

'I can drive you there now if that's okay.'

'I'd prefer to follow you. I have to head off to an interview afterwards.'

As Robyn walked to her car, she thought about how she'd deal with Abigail. It was a great shame about her cat, but not only did Robyn want to know why Lucas was trying to contact Abigail, she had another reason to question the woman – Abigail knew Zoe.

CHAPTER FORTY-FIVE

NOW

Stupid damn cat. It was supposed to get into the bag I've brought around and then hide out at my house until Abigail was frantic with worry. She loves it to bits and I was looking forward to seeing her worried sick about losing it. Instead, the stupid animal tried to escape and when I cornered it, it hissed and struck out at me. So much for being a tame cat. Cats have sixth senses. Maybe it could see the evil in me.

I smooth antiseptic cream on the deep scratches on my wrist. I don't want to get the wound infected. It stings like mad but pain doesn't bother me. It's nothing compared to some of the cuts I've given myself over the years. I'm not into animal cruelty, but once that thing drew its claws and attacked me, I acted in self-defence and bashed it on the head to quieten it. I didn't know it would take such little effort to kill it. All that working out in my makeshift gym has given me a strength I didn't know I possessed. It'll be useful for the next part of my plan – getting rid of Lucas.

I mentally go over what I'm calling my 'Abigail Torment List' to cheer myself up.

Have I made her anxious? Yes.

Have I begun to alienate her from her friends? Yes.

Have I caused fractures in her relationship? Yes.

Have I gradually removed those she loves from her life? Yes.

Have I left her unhinged and alone and wishing she was dead? Not yet but I soon shall.

Looking at the limp body of what had once been Abigail's pet, I decide to leave it for her to find. That'll make her see I'm not playing about. So far she hasn't quite understood that I'm someone who will cause bedlam. Besides, I'm sick of her droning on about Izzy and Jackson and her bloody perfect life. I've listened to her for long enough. It makes my head hurt. Abby has it all. Well, not at the moment. Nothing like discovering your pet cat nailed to your door to spoil your day.

My father thinks that comment is hilarious and laughs so loudly I can hear the sound reverberate around my room.

CHAPTER FORTY-SIX

Abigail stared at her phone, her brow creased in bewilderment. The clinic had phoned. The doctor wished to talk to her about the blood tests he had administered when she was sick, and she was to attend the clinic later that same day.

She hadn't spoken to Jackson since their conversation the night before. She had deliberately stayed in bed, Izzy by her side, until he got the message and went to work. She couldn't deal with the whole Jackson and Zoe thing. She had spent most of the night awake, wondering if Zoe would be capable of killing Toffee, and had come to the conclusion that jealousy did strange things to people. She had seen the film *Fatal Attraction*. It was possible that Zoe, let down by Jackson, had killed Toffee in a fit of pique. The rational part of her mind reasoned that Zoe would not harm a living creature, until she remembered a conversation she had had with the woman. They had been at a nightclub and Zoe was tired, yawning most of the evening and unwilling to dance. She'd been kept awake by the neighbour's dog barking all night for three nights in a row and it was getting to her.

'Bloody animal,' she had said. 'I was this close to going down-stairs and banging it on the head with a shovel.'

While Izzy was playing contentedly in her playpen, Abigail rang the only person who would understand.

'What's happened?' asked Claire. Between sobs, Abigail explained about Toffee. Claire was enraged and upset in equal measures.

'How could they?' she said. 'Not Toffee. He's such a gentle, sweet cat.'

Abigail felt hot tears run down her face once more.

'Oh, Abby, I'm so sorry. Are you okay? Have you spoken to the police? Scotland is so far away from you but I can come down. I can get in my car and come back to you. I could be there by tomorrow. You need some support.'

'I'll be all right. Don't return on my count. You can't give up on this job. You'll lose your contract with the magazine. You wanted it so badly. You can't back out of it over this. And, I don't want to call the police. I think I know who's behind it.'

Claire was silent at the other end of the phone.

'I think it was Zoe,' said Abigail. 'I think it was a bunny-boiler moment of jealousy.' She couldn't hold back any more and told her best friend all about the photographs and Jackson's denial.

Claire let out a growl of rage. 'That cow. She's destroying your life. What's possessed her? Just because she normally throws herself at every available man, she assumes she can ruin her friend's marriage and then, when she doesn't get her own way, she does this! It's outrageous. I'm going to go around to her house as soon as I return and tell her what I think of her, and then I'm going to report her for doing this to Toffee. She can't get away with it.'

'Claire, leave it. It's my problem. I'm going to fix it. Leave it, please. First, I need to talk to Jackson. I have to uncover the real details of what's been going on with him and Zoe. It's only fair.'

'I think you're being far too generous. I'd probably have shredded all his uniforms by now and then started on him with the scissors when he returned home. I guess that's why I live alone. I'd make a terrible girlfriend. You do what you have to and remember I am here if you need me.'

'I'll tackle Jackson about it again when he comes home. Wait a minute. I can hear his car now. I'll phone you later.'

* * *

Jackson's Maserati roared into the driveway as she ended the call. He came into the house with a tall, athletic woman in her early thirties.

'Abby, this is Detective Inspector Robyn Carter. I contacted her. I thought about what you told me and we need to find out who did that terrible thing last night.' He couldn't bring himself to be blunt. Izzy squealed in delight at seeing her father and held up her hands to be picked up, wriggling to the end of the playpen to reach him.

'Hey, Splodge,' he said, leaning in to collect her. The baby stared at Robyn with large eyes then gave her a huge grin.

'She's such a show off,' said Jackson as Izzy tried to attract Robyn's attention by leaning across in her direction and beaming at her. Robyn grinned back.

'Come on, Izzy, let's get Rover.' Jackson reached into the playpen and brought out her toy dog, handing it to Izzy and settling her down on his knee.

Abigail observed the scene with a detached air. 'Sorry to have troubled you, Detective but we don't require your help,' she said, tersely. 'I'm pretty certain I know who is responsible for it.'

'You do?' said Jackson, his mouth opening in surprise.

'So do you. It's Zoe Cooper.'

'Zoe? That's impossible.'

'I think a woman scorned is capable of many things,' retorted Abigail.

'What are you on about?' he replied, his voice rising.

'You and Zoe. It's quite simple. You are shagging Zoe. Zoe decides she wants to spend more time with you so she attempts to make my life miserable and drive me crazy with anxiety, phoning me to let me know you are being unfaithful, making me doubt our relationship, then tries to scare me by killing our cat.'

'This is completely crazy. For one thing, I am not having an affair with Zoe. I told you all this, last night. When did you dream up this latest ridiculous scenario? And for the record, I'm getting thoroughly sick of you constantly accusing me of having sex with various people. Can we get back to the real concerns instead of this nonsense?'

Abigail directed her attention to Robyn and spoke with an icy calm she did not feel. 'An anonymous person sent me photographs of him with Zoe,' she explained to Robyn who had been quietly observing the couple's behaviour. 'They were attached to an email. There were three photographs. In the first she's kissing Jackson and then there were some of him—'

'Someone is messing with your head, Abigail. I haven't touched Zoe. Talk to her. She'll tell you the truth. It isn't me in the photographs. It can't be. I don't want to discuss it any longer. I brought DI Carter here to try and assist. I was concerned that there was some truth to what you told me about being hounded and watched.'

'Then if it isn't you, who is in the photographs?'

'Will you drop it? It could be anyone but it isn't me. Be reasonable. Zoe's had lots of relationships. You know that. She's always got a new bloke on the go.'

Robyn spoke up, 'I think you need to trust your husband, Abigail. Is it okay if I call you Abigail? The mind can play tricks on you and sees what has been suggested even though it isn't real. Without the photographs it's difficult to say who is in them. Who are you going to believe? Someone who hasn't even got the courage to reveal who they are, and is obviously trying to cause trouble, or your husband who you know well? Listen to him and talk to your friend Zoe before this all gets out of hand.'

The fight went whooshing out of Abigail. Robyn was right. She dropped onto a chair. 'Okay,' she mumbled.

Jackson rose. 'Izzy needs changing. I'll sort her. You talk to DI Carter. Tell her what you told me about the person who's been calling you.'

After he left the room, Abigail rubbed her eyes. 'I'm sorry you've been dragged into this.'

'It's not a problem. I wanted to help. I'm terribly sorry about your cat.'

'Thanks.'

Abigail fell silent. Robyn needed to gain her trust. 'Is that your sister?' Robyn asked, spotting a photograph of Abigail with a woman about the same age as Abigail. The woman sported a nose ring and dark cropped spiky hair. She was sitting on a bed, with an arm around Abigail and posing with a very small baby in her arms. The picture was next to a wedding photograph of Abigail and Jackson.

'That's Claire, my friend. That was just after Izzy was born. Claire was almost as excited about Izzy as we were. She still is. Loves her to bits. Jackson took the picture. It's a nice photo of Claire. She doesn't smile often.'

'It's good to have friends.'

'Yeah, she's a really good friend. I haven't seen enough of her recently. She's been so busy. Her photography business has done well. We talk a lot on the phone or message each other. I wish she were here now. She'd help me work out what is going on. She's away on an assignment. I spoke to her earlier and she wanted to travel all the way back from Scotland to be with me. I'm lucky to have her. She's my only real friend. Well, her and Jackson.'

'I often wish I had a best friend. Doing this job makes it difficult to have any friends. It's long hours and when you do get home it's bath, bed or straight to the fridge for a tub of ice cream and then watch a chick flick. I spend my free time in the gym. It helps me forget I'm alone. You forget a lot of things when your muscles hurt so much you can barely walk.'

Abigail thawed a little and managed a weak smile.

Robyn waited for a moment then added, 'Your husband's genuinely concerned about you. You know that?'

Abigail nodded.

'I'm sure it isn't as bad as you believe it is.'

'I don't know who to trust. Who is doing this to me?'

'You can start by trusting me. This isn't my territory though. You need to call it into the nearest station. Jackson explained that you have reason to believe someone is watching you and has been telephoning you. Has the person who's been calling threatened you?'

'Only to say they are going to destroy my life. They try to scare me by using some voice-altering device. They seem to know what I'm doing at certain times so I know they're watching me. They could even be watching me now.'

She looked around the room with wild eyes.

'It all began when I was sent an anonymous note about keeping secrets. After that, I got a text saying Jackson was keeping secrets from me. Up until the first call, I thought it was a silly prank, then I got a phone call from someone who knew what I was wearing at the café in town, followed by another call when I reached home. They knew I was being sick at the time. They couldn't know that unless they were spying on me. My Facebook account got hacked and my friends were sent horrid messages from me. I changed the house alarm code after that episode, and the locks. I ought to have confessed everything to Jackson then but I thought I could handle it all. I didn't imagine it was serious. I had more calls then telling me Jackson was shagging women, and finally the email with the photographs attached. Now, I don't know how to trust Jackson and he thinks I'm completely neurotic. I daren't tell him I've been hearing voices too or he'll really believe I'm crazy.'

'Voices?'

'Oh, it's nothing. My mind's been playing tricks on me. I keep imagining someone is in Izzy's room and when I get there, there's no one. I've been reading too much into day-to-day noises, I've been so tired. I've never felt so worn out. Whoever is doing this is destroying my life.' She corrected herself, 'Zoe could be the person destroying my life.'

Abigail was distraught and in need of some assurances, while Robyn wanted to find out more about Zoe. She spoke calmly. 'If you want my opinion, I think your husband is telling the truth. I don't think he is having a relationship with your friend Zoe.'

'How can you be certain of that? You don't know him?'

'I've come across accomplished liars in my profession. I don't think your husband is one of them. Photographs can be photoshopped or altered. Are the photographs clear shots of him? Is it really him? Can you see his face or his body or any identifying marks that prove beyond doubt it is your man? In this day and age you can transfer anyone's face onto a different body and produce convincing pictures. Don't jump to conclusions. Jackson told me you've been worn out the last few weeks and tiredness affects how you think and function. This mysterious caller knows that. They are using your weaknesses to manipulate you. They have gone to extraordinary lengths to send you photographs and also to erase them before you can show them to Jackson and tackle him on the subject. If they were genuine photographs, surely they wouldn't have deleted them?' Robyn remained sceptical about the mystery phone calls and photographs but for the time being she was more interested in gaining the woman's trust.

Abigail covered her face with her hands and let out a long, painful groan. 'You're right. Of course you're right. I've been so wound up and tormented by that damn person that I believed them. It didn't cross my mind that those photographs were anything other than real.' She rocked on her chair. 'I'm making such a mess of everything,' she moaned. 'And poor, poor Toffee.'

'Your cat's death could be unconnected. It could just have been a random act of violence. Someone who hates cats.' Robyn smiled at her. 'I expect the calls are cruel prank calls from someone who is jealous of you but given the fact your cat is dead, I would definitely get someone to look into it. You can't be too careful. I recommend you try the Hampshire Constabulary and report what has happened and let them take it from there. I wouldn't worry unnecessarily but if someone has deliberately killed Toffee then you need to take precautions to keep yourselves safe.'

'I'll sound like I'm making the whole thing up. The call log and texts have gone from my mobile. I can't prove anything. Jackson said as much last night before I got so mad with him I stopped listening.'

'You'd be surprised what technicians can do with mobiles. They can find lost data and trace your texts or call logs. Contact Hampshire Constabulary online or call the station for your area. Explain I have spoken to you and arrange an appointment to visit them, or for an officer to come and see you. You really ought to let the police investigate this. I don't want to scare you but from what you've told me, there is cause enough for concern and they should look into it for you.'

Abigail thought for a moment. 'You're not from the area then? How come Jackson asked you to help?'

'I was on a case down here in Farnborough and interviewed Jackson. He couldn't assist but I gave him one of my business cards. When this happened to you, he got in touch.'

'You're still here in Farnborough. Does that mean you haven't solved your case?'

'Not yet, no. I was hunting for a missing man.'

Jackson returned with an ebullient Izzy who crawled towards Robyn and sat by her feet, happily chewing on a rusk.

Robyn chose that moment to ask. 'Maybe you can help me. Do you know or have you ever heard of a man who goes by the name of Lucas Matthews?'

Jackson threw Robyn a quick look but she ignored him, concentrating only on Abigail who blew her nose on a tissue before shaking her head and answering, 'No. I've never heard of him.'

'Would you look at a photograph of him for me, please? He was very interested in Zoe for some reason and you might have spotted him in the area.'

Abigail paled as Robyn pulled out the picture and handed it over. Abigail glanced at it and handed it back. 'No, sorry. I haven't seen him before.'

'Look again. He might have been in a café when you were with Zoe or in the street while you were shopping. Is there nothing familiar about him? Zoe thought she had seen him somewhere but couldn't remember where. Are you certain you haven't spotted him?'

'No. I definitely haven't seen him.' Abigail returned the photograph and wiped her nose again.

Robyn slipped the photograph back into a folder in her bag. 'Oh well, it was worth asking. Okay, if you have no more questions about what to do, I'll get going.'

Abigail bent to collect Izzy and cuddled her tightly. 'Thank you for your help,' she said, turning away quickly as Jackson showed Robyn out.

The door shut behind Robyn and she meandered to her car, processing the information she had just gleaned. Whilst Jackson was telling the truth about not having an affair, his wife was lying about the photograph she had just looked at. Robyn had observed the widening of her eyes when the name Lucas Matthews was mentioned and had seen her stalling for time by blowing her nose.

Abigail had unconsciously twisted the tissue tightly while looking at the photo. Robyn was convinced Abigail Thorne knew Lucas Matthews.

Abigail stood at the lounge window and watched Robyn pull away. Jackson returned and waited for her to turn around. She stood for a while before speaking. 'I don't want to discuss this any more at the moment.'

He knew by her tone that it was pointless to push her on the subject.

'Okay. But we need to sort it out. I'm going to contact the police as DI Carter suggested. I think it's important we do.'

'I guess so. But let's talk first.' She headed for the door, Izzy in her arms. 'I have to go out. We'll talk this evening. Leave it until I can collect my thoughts.'

Jackson called out, 'It'll be all right.'

'I know,' she replied and, gathering up her bag with her free hand, took Izzy upstairs.

CHAPTER FORTY-SEVEN

Robyn pulled up beside Ross's car. He was leaning against it, dressed in jeans and a grey T-shirt. She stared at the entrance of the garden of remembrance. Inside lay Christina Forman: wife to Josh Clifford, fiancée to Paul Matthews and mother to Alice.

'I just got off the phone with Mitz,' said Robyn. 'He's been talking to the SOCO on the Christina Forman case again to get all the facts. Poor cow was strangled during an S&M session with her boyfriend, Frank Parsons. Parsons went missing for a couple of days but was tracked down to one of his favourite haunts – a pub in Bicester. He confessed as soon as they arrested him and said it was an accident. The local police thought otherwise. There was an anonymous phone call from a concerned citizen who claimed to have heard the couple rowing and then seen Frank strike her, then drag her inside the house. He denied it, of course, but given the state of her, there was fair reason to believe he had murdered her. However, Mitz says there is insufficient evidence and Frank will probably only get sentenced for death by misadventure. Case is not for another month.'

'What a rotten end to her life,' said Ross.

'Lousy. She hadn't had the best of times beforehand. Parsons told the police she'd been on the game for years. She'd used a load of aliases but she'd gone back to using Christina Forman when he met her. She told him she missed being Christina.'

Robyn stared off into the distance. 'I wonder if Alice knows that her mother is dead.'

'Maybe. Maybe not. I hope Alice's life improved. Maybe she married a rich bloke and lived happily ever after.'

'That only happens in fairy tales, Ross. Anyway, we have a massive clue.'

'I thought you were looking perkier than usual.'

'Mitz said officers at the scene uncovered S&M bondage kit strewn about the place and that Christina was in the full leather outfit, attached to the bed by handcuffs. They also discovered a fluffy toy rabbit propped up on the bed beside her. Their initial thoughts were that this was part of the game they were playing until Parsons lost his temper and strangled her, or it was a gift she had been given. He's going to text photographs of the crime scene when they have been sent over.'

Robyn smiled at Ross. 'First, Lucas was holding a rabbit at his death scene, then we found a rubber toy rabbit at Mary's house, and now Christina has one on her bed. It has to be related.'

'Great. You deserve a lucky break. I hope it is and not just a coincidence. Want to see Christina's resting place now?'

'I suppose so. I feel I ought to.'

They trundled into the garden of remembrance and past all the tributes to loved ones. Neither spoke. Both had lost people they were close to and this only brought back unhappy memories. They stopped in front of a small plaque.

IN LOVING MEMORY OF CHRISTINA JUSTINE FORMAN – A BEAUTIFUL BUTTERFLY WHO NOW FLAPS HER GOSSAMER WINGS IN ETERNALLY BRIGHT SKIES

Robyn wondered if Alice had arranged the words on the stone. 'Tragic isn't it?' Ross said.

'Death is,' she replied. 'Any death is tragic, especially for those left behind.'

Ross put an arm around her shoulders and for a moment she leaned into him. She savoured the kind gesture.

'Okay, kiddo,' he said in a poor American accent. 'Go find this Alice or whoever you are looking for and get this case sorted.'

'I think I'm getting there, Ross. I can feel it. I have the jigsaw pieces. I just have to fit them together.'

'Well, if anyone can crack it, it's you. Let me know if you need me. Jeanette will be glad I'm going home early. She wants me to go dancing with her.'

'Line, ballroom or tap?' asked Robyn, delighted at the thought of Ross attempting to dance.

'Salsa,' he replied, wrinkling his nose. 'I wish you'd asked me to help you. Now look what you've forced me into.'

Robyn chuckled. 'Make sure you send me a selfie of you in your outfit,' she shouted, as he wandered back to his car. He raised a finger and carried on walking.

CHAPTER FORTY-EIGHT

'Are you accusing me of taking a drug that made me sick – so sick I could hardly function – and which I think poisoned my baby as well?'

The doctor looked up from the computer screen, removed his glasses and sat back in his chair.

'Abby, I am suggesting nothing of the sort. I am merely telling you we discovered traces of ipecac in your blood. Let me explain what that is and how serious it might have been had you ingested any more than you did.

'Ipecac is a small, perennial tropical plant native to the forests of Bolivia and Brazil and has been widely used in syrup form as a potent and effective emetic. In layman terms, an emetic is a substance that induces vomiting and diarrhoea when administered orally or by injection.'

Abigail was not fully taking in the doctor's words. Somebody had poisoned her and now she had a good idea who that was – bloody Lucas Matthews. Why hadn't she thought of him before? It was only after the policewoman mentioned him that it became apparent who was responsible for the calls and everything else. Lucas Matthews was a total bastard. He, of all people, would know how important Izzy was to her. He was deliberately scaring her and now she'd just found out he could have actually killed her baby. She thought back to the day in the café. Rachel had bought the drinks and had ordered syrup with her coffee. At the time she wondered why Rachel had felt the need to put it in her drink yet had not questioned it. The syrup had been so strong Abigail had not been able to taste the coffee. What better way to disguise the ipecac? Her mind whirred with possibilities. Rachel and Lucas must have secretly planned the whole thing together.

'So, have you taken any ipecac at all, Mrs Thorne?'

The doctor was clearly anxious that she was doing harm to herself. He suspected she had swallowed the stuff deliberately to make herself sick. If she admitted to having taken it he would chastise her, but if she told him someone had tried to poison her, what would his reaction be? Would he tell the police?'

A knot formed in her stomach. She wanted to get out of the surgery and search for Lucas. He had promised he would leave her be and yet now he was back to torment her. Well, he wasn't going to succeed this time around.

'No,' she said.

He spoke kindly. 'It is not uncommon for women who wish to lose weight to use it. It is accessible on the Internet. You have lost quite a lot of weight in the last few months,' he continued. 'Over a stone, to be exact.'

'I'm not bulimic,' she answered. 'I know what you're suggesting but I would never take something like that. It's been a stressful few months. That's all.' She felt tears springing to her eyes again. 'Please don't tell anyone but I think someone deliberately put ipecac into a coffee I had that day. You can't tell anyone though. Besides, there is the matter of patient confidentiality.'

Dr Toman shook his head. 'Abigail, I'm sorry but if you're telling me a person or persons have deliberately spiked a drink with ipecac then I have a duty of care to let the authorities know. And, if you suspect Izzy was also tainted by it, then that sets off all sorts of alarms.'

She wished she hadn't mentioned it now. She needed to buy some time because she was going to track down Lucas Matthews and rectify all this mess. She pleaded with the doctor.

'I don't know who could have dropped it into my coffee. I was out with three friends at the coffee house in town and when I came home I suddenly became really sick. It must have happened at the café. I didn't go anywhere else and no one other than Izzy and me was sick. None of my friends fell ill. I hardly think an employee would tamper with a drink so I suspect it has to be one of the women who were with me that day. What shall I do?'

'Leave it with me. I'm afraid the police will want to speak to you. Tell them what you know. It'll be fine. You and Izzy are okay now, aren't you?'

Her head bobbed in acknowledgement.

'Go home, Abby,' he said. 'Tell Jackson what you told me and leave it to the authorities.'

She left the surgery in a fury. Lucas Matthews had gone one step too far. If Rachel knew Lucas, and was involved in his plans to upset her life, then Abigail was going to speak to her too. The police might do their job but Abigail wanted to confront Rachel herself. Everything was swimming into focus. Rachel passing the rainbow teddy to Izzy in the café with possible traces of ipecac on her fingers from dropping it in Abigail's coffee, or she might have deliberately wiped the teddy bear with ipecac. Izzy had put the teddy in her mouth, as she did with most objects. No wonder the poor little mite had been so sick. Abigail shuddered at the thought of how much more serious it might have been. The thought of what might have happened awakened a fierce maternal instinct in her. How dare Rachel jeopardise her child's life and at the same time pretend she cared about Izzy, showering her with gifts? What a twisted, warped mind she must have.

The more Abigail thought about it, the more obvious it all became. How could she have missed the signs? Rachel bringing around flowers but snooping around the house and taking snaps of the photograph in the bedroom. She must have had a smartphone with her, after all.

Rachel conveniently waylaying her at the café while Toffee was being caught and killed. Abigail bet that Rachel had also fabricated the story about everyone at the boutique talking about her to unnerve her. She had to be part of Lucas's scheme to mess up her life.

How did Rachel fit into the picture? Why was she keen to rake up the past or destroy Abby's life? Was she in love with Lucas?

Abigail felt heat rising through her body as she became increasingly furious with the woman and with Lucas. Why couldn't he have left her alone? She deserved that, at least. Yet here he was messing up her present life much like he'd messed up her past life. The bastard. She was going to find out where he was and she'd start by visiting Rachel Croft.

Abigail strapped her daughter into the back of the car once more. She slammed her handbag onto the passenger seat and punched out a text to Rachel on her phone. She kept it brief, saying she wanted to meet her at the George V playing fields at four o'clock. Within seconds she had a reply. Rachel was looking forward to it but she was giving a client a crystal treatment and couldn't make it until after she had finished. She would meet Abigail at five if that were convenient. Abigail replied it was, threw the car into gear and left the surgery car park. She couldn't wait to confront Rachel.

* * *

Her phone rang before she had driven half a mile.

'Well, well, well,' said a familiar computerised voice. 'Going somewhere nice?'

'Lucas, you total arse, why are you doing this? You and Paul promised you would let me live my life and not contact me, and now you're being a bloody nuisance. You've been scaring me half to death. I'm not putting up with it any longer.'

There was a burst of laughter.

'Poor Paul. He's dead, you know? Aren't you upset about that?'

'I didn't know. How would I know? I haven't had any contact with him for years. Am I supposed to say I feel sorry? Because I don't. He died a long time ago as far as I'm concerned. Why are you harassing me, Lucas?'

'Why do think, Abigail?'

'This is ridiculous. And you can turn off that voice-altering device you've been using. It isn't frightening me. Tell me what you want and stop this stupid game.'

There was a silence at the end of the phone and then a snigger.

'And I know Rachel is involved. How else could you have got ipecac into my drink and that photo of me you put on Facebook? I'm not stupid.'

'Gosh! You worked that out all by yourself. How clever of you.'

'Don't be such a supercilious pig. I was going to confront Rachel but now I think I'll drive straight to the police station and tell them all about you stalking me. The doctor will be reporting the whole ipecac incident too, so you are sure to receive some form of punishment. I hope it's jail for a very long time. You can't poison babies and get away with it.'

There was a silence during which time Abigail wondered if Lucas had hung up, then a crackle and he spoke again, 'Okay. You win. I'll stop all the nonsense and leave you and your family alone but we need to talk first. It's really important.'

'I don't believe you. What could be so important you need to talk to me?'

'Meet me. I promise I'll go away afterwards. Carry on down the main road and pull over at the Meads car park and we'll meet. Go to the area in front of Keep Fit Gym. There are fewer cars there.'

'How do you know where I am? Are you tracking my car? You bloody are, aren't you? Lucas, I hate you! You've gone too far. I'm still going to report you to the police. Afterwards, I am going to make you wish you hadn't come back into my life.'

'I understand. The Meads. Ten minutes.'

The call ended and Abigail, torn between going to the police and meeting with Lucas, thumped her steering wheel in frustration. She would see what explanation he offered and then report him and his sidekick, Rachel.

* * *

Abigail pulled into a space near to a blue people-carrier and waited. The car park was emptier here away from the big supermarket that dominated the far end. A Mini pulled up and a couple got out. A woman in a scruffy coat carrying several carrier bags shuffled towards the bus stop at the far end of the car park. Abigail was beginning to wonder if this was another of Lucas's games when she spotted a dark-haired man in a loose grey jacket and blue trousers. He halted by the parade of shops and appeared to search the car park, his head turning this way and that. She couldn't decide if it was him. He was certainly about the right age. Before she could call out to him, he ambled in her direction. It was Lucas. She felt her anger bubbling again. The lousy son-of-a-bitch had a casual air about him that made her want to scream at him.

He approached the passenger window and tapped on it, indicating she should open the door. There was no way she intended letting him into her car. Instead, she rolled down the window and leaned across to speak to him then stopped in horror. It wasn't Lucas. How could she have believed he was? This man was older and his face was unshaven. His eyes were green, not ebony black. Before she could react, he reached into the car, grabbed her handbag and raced away. She let out a howl of annoyance and without even thinking about what she was doing, she threw open her door and shot off after the man. Her money, credit cards and mobile were in the bag. She wasn't going to let some degenerate run off with them.

She ran quickly, made ground and was in reach of catching him when he dived into an alleyway that led to the shopping centre and tossed her bag into the air. It fell to the floor, spilling its contents. She drew to a sharp halt and knelt down, grabbing at her purse and lipstick and mobile which seemed unscathed. When she looked up, the man had vanished and she was alone in the alleyway. Her phone rang and an icy hand gripped her heart as she answered it. She held the phone to her ear and heard a faint whisper, 'Bye, bye, Mummy.'

She turned on her heel and ran as fast as she could back to her car. As she raced, she already knew what to expect, even though a desperate hope kept her legs moving, pumping with all the energy she could muster to get back. The rear door was wide open. Her breath rose and fell in fearful gasps but it was too late. She could already see what she dreaded most. The back seat was empty. Izzy had gone.

CHAPTER FORTY-NINE

It was almost midnight when Robyn telephoned Ross. He wasn't too pleased to be woken up.

'It's silly o'clock,' he grunted. 'I hope this is important.'

'It's about the rabbits. The one on Christina's bed and the others – the one at the scene of Lucas's murder and the dog toy.'

'Great. You've woken me up from a dream in which I was eating my way through a giant beefburger to talk about toy rabbits.'

Robyn ignored him. 'I think there might be a fourth rabbit. What if Paul Matthews' death wasn't an accident? What if someone killed him and left a toy rabbit hidden at the scene? What do you think?'

'You are asking me if Paul Matthews was murdered and didn't accidentally trip up and hit his head, even though that verdict was reached by professionals. And, that an experienced crime scene officer might have missed something as obvious as a toy rabbit? I say it's most unlikely and good night.'

'No, listen. Don't hang up. It's possible. A killer could have set up a trap for Paul. It's possible it was made to look like an accident. Think about it, Ross. Paul, Lucas and Mary all dead within a few weeks of each other. It's odd. What if the killer left a clue at the scene that was missed?'

'It's a long shot, Robyn. I think you are sleep-deprived and if I had been the officer at that particular scene and you made a suggestion like that, I would be most put out. I might even report you.'

'Yes, you are right. I couldn't accuse a fellow officer of not doing a good job. Thanks, Ross. Sleep well.'

'What, that's it?'

'Yes, go back to bed. I couldn't go down official lines over this.'

'No. You'd upset lots of people.'

'Yes. I agree with you. You're absolutely right. Thank you. Night.'

There was a pause during which neither hung up then Ross said, 'I get it.'

'Get what?'

'You want me to comb the area to see if there's a stupid, stuffed toy rabbit, don't you?'

'No. I couldn't ask you to do that. That would be presuming too much: after all, this is my case. I'll have to figure out another way. Or, I could do it myself. If I leave now, I could get there in a couple of hours and be back in time to interview Zoe Cooper. Mulholland needn't know. She's already warned me not to go off on a tangent. It's not a problem. I'll figure a way of looking for it myself.'

Ross sighed. 'I give up. I'll do it.'

'Do what?'

'I'll go back through the route that Paul Matthews took that day and see if I can spot a toy rabbit but I'd like you to know that I think it's a dumb idea and I am most unhappy about it. It's a long route, isn't it? I'll have to take my walking shoes. Is this some ploy to get me to exercise and lose more weight? Did you and Jeanette come up with this idea?'

'No. But some fresh air will put you in a good mood.'

He muttered some inaudible response.

'So you'll check for me?'

'Yes, I will. Now can I get some beauty sleep before my big adventure?'

'Night, Ross and… thanks. You're the best.'

'I know I am. Now go to bed and stop annoying folk.'

* * *

Robyn sat back in her chair. It was unlikely she would sleep. The case was beginning to get to her. Zoe's name cropped up too often for her to be ignored. And, Zoe was quite possibly the last person to see Lucas Matthews alive, if the concierge who spotted them leaving the hotel was to be believed. Yet Zoe had claimed she didn't know the man and couldn't place when or where she had seen him. She was either an expert liar or telling the truth. Robyn would find out soon. She had arranged to talk to Zoe Cooper first thing in the morning.

CHAPTER FIFTY

NOW

Learn to track one phone and you can track them all. It's a piece of cake when you know how to do it. All I needed to do this was to find out the phone's IMEI number. I discovered that by opening up Abigail's mobile and typing '*#06#'. It let me install spyware which can track her movements and allow me to monitor every text or email she sends and receives.

It was easy to get hold of Abigail's phone. She always keeps it in her handbag or on the table in the kitchen or wherever she happens to be. I've had numerous opportunities to slip away with it for a few seconds to get the IMEI and add the hacker code and spyware. Now I can see who she phones and I can read all text messages and even better I can delete them and call logs. Moreover, I've even fitted a tracker on Abigail's posh Range Rover which I purchased from a detective agency's website. I know where she is at any time.

At the moment, she is driving away from the doctor's surgery in town. Oh dear, I expect the doctor has uncovered the ipecac I slipped into her drink. It was only a matter of time. I had hoped she would blame Zoe, after all, I have been setting Zoe up for all of this, but it appears dear, confused Abigail has misread the clues I have given her and is now going to meet Rachel. I hope she isn't going to involve that new-age hippy and blab about everything that's been happening. I wouldn't put it past that woman to work everything out.

Abigail now knows what it's like to be branded a liar and to lose her friends. The whole Facebook hacking scandal worked rather better than I expected. It seems not many people like show-offs, especially rude ones.

I've succeeded in rocking her world and she is showing the signs of strain. It's been enjoyable watching her crumble little by little. I had a head start as she was already exhausted from looking after her baby so it hasn't taken much to push her towards the edge – a few calls suggesting her husband was playing away shook her enough to make the rest of the plan work. However, I have not quite succeeded.

I've tried hard to destroy her relationship with Jackson but I can't seem to quite crack that particular nut. I can't understand why not. The photographs I sent Abby of Zoe having a mad, drug-induced sex session with that old fogey Gavin were very convincing. Much better than photoshopped pictures. I had considered photoshopping but you can't beat real photographs. That's one of the problems with the photographic industry these days. Anyone can produce a fabulous photograph using software. It takes the skill away from real photographers.

I had to watch the entire sick-making video to get the stills I needed. Old Gavin had the time of his life but poor Zoe seemed to be doing all the hard work. Never mind, she'll have enjoyed the practice.

I managed to create two pictures from the video that were ambiguous enough to convince Abigail that Zoe was having sex with Jackson although I had to crop some of Gavin's head. Of course, I also had the money shot with Zoe snogging Jackson. I was sure that they would be sufficient to convince Abigail her husband was being unfaithful, yet she is still with Jackson. Neither has moved out of the house. I deleted the email and the call log. I figured I could cause plenty of distrust if there was no evidence. Jackson must have thick skin or really be blinkered by love. I don't know why it hasn't worked. Anyway, I'm moving on now. I've had enough of playing about and tormenting Abby. It is time for the endgame.

CHAPTER FIFTY-ONE

Zoe was standing outside the station by the café, a cardboard cup of coffee in her hand. She was dressed in patterned Lycra leggings and a crop top. She spotted Robyn getting out of her car and waved.

'We've got twenty minutes,' she said. 'The next train after that will make me late for my first class.'

'I won't keep you. Thanks for seeing me.'

Robyn took in the high cheekbones, large grey eyes and elfin features. She got the feeling again she was missing something vital but she couldn't put her finger on it. She'd thought hard about how best to question Zoe and decided on a friendly approach instead of bombarding her with questions.

'It's about the night you went to the Sky Bar at the Aviator hotel and met up with Jackson and his friends.'

Zoe's face dropped. 'How much do you know about that?'

'Maybe you should tell me. I have one reported sighting of you leaving the hotel with Lucas Matthews and another version of what happened.'

'Lucas Matthews. That's the man who was asking about me at Keep Fit Gym, isn't it? I told you before, I have never heard of the man. I genuinely do not know him and I definitely did not leave the Aviator hotel with him. I may have been drunk but I would have known if that had happened.'

Robyn nodded. 'I thought that would be the case. Your where-abouts have been confirmed for that night.'

'So you know I spent the night with a married man,' Zoe said, looking down at her cup.

'You don't need to be worried about that. I think everyone concerned will keep quiet.'

Zoe breathed a sigh of relief. 'It's troubled me ever since it happened. I never, ever mess about with friend's husbands, or any husband for that matter. I usually stick to single guys. I've only recently begun seeing a guy at work – Adam – and I wouldn't want him to find out I'd been putting it about. I'm hoping this relationship will work. That night was a dreadful one. I'm an absolute lightweight when it comes to alcohol and I'm normally teetotal. I only drink when there's a celebration and then I usually stick to one glass of wine or a spritzer. I'm careful about how much alcohol I consume. Obviously, I need to be in a fit state to do the job I do. Besides, I don't much like it. I think the cocktail I drank had far more alcohol in it than I thought. It went straight to my head and I lost all my inhibitions.'

'Why were you drinking that night?'

'Oh, a friend invited me to join her at the Propaganda. She'd got a new contract and wanted to celebrate. It's one of the liveliest bars in Fleet and has a DJ at weekends. It has nice leather sofas too. We tried a cocktail each. I had an espresso martini and she had a pornstar martini. No idea what was in them. She chose them and they tasted really good. We decided to move on because it was a Tuesday evening and they hold salsa lessons on Tuesdays at the bar. We didn't fancy that and the place was becoming noisy, so she suggested we went off to the Aviator and the Sky Bar where they make some of the best cocktails. We phoned for a taxi and by the time it arrived, I was starting to feel quite squiffy. I got worse on the journey there. I remember giggling a lot but I can't remember at what. I laughed so much I nearly peed myself. I think the taxi driver was glad when we got out.'

She shrugged helplessly.

'By the time we got to the Sky Bar, things were getting hazy. I remember saying hello to the guys – Jackson, Stu and Gavin. I've known them all for ages. I love them to bits. I've trained them all at some stage. Pilots have to maintain their fitness so, around about the time they have medicals due, they usually do a crash course in fitness with me. Then, after that it gets very muddled. I can't really tell you how I ended up with Gavin. I don't think either of us intended it to happen. He was about to escort me downstairs and take me home, and he was so kind and gentle. I think I pushed him against a wall and kissed him and before I knew what happened, he responded and, well, you know the rest.'

Robyn nodded.

'Wish I hadn't. I've ruined a good friendship there. It'll be so difficult to behave normally around him if I get invited to one of their barbecues or bump into them. It's a good thing I work in London now. I might consider selling up here and rent closer to work, especially if things work out with Adam. The commute is a fag most days.'

'What happened to your friend? What was her name? Did she not hang out with you at the Sky Bar?'

'Claire. Claire Lewis. She lives locally. She's a photographer. She was celebrating because she won a contract with a big magazine to do some wildlife shots in Scotland. She was so excited. She's up there now. I got a text from her yesterday. Claire cried off almost as soon as we got into the hotel. She received a call from a neighbour to say her house alarm was going off and she needed to go home and sort it. She panicked in case an intruder had set it off. I volunteered to go with her but she refused to let me. Since I was at the hotel, I thought I might as well go to the bar and say hello to Christophe, so I stayed. I don't think I managed to say hello to Christophe,' she added. 'Claire rang the next day to say it was a false alarm. She was well cheesed off. She'd fancied a proper night out with me. I didn't tell her about Gavin.'

'Stu told me he saw Lucas Matthews at the bar that night.'

Zoe cocked her head to one side, then a smile spread across her face. 'That's it. That's where I spotted him. I thought his face was familiar. He was at the bar with a bottle of beer in his hand. I noticed him because he looked so serious and he was alone. No one stands alone at a bar for so long. They are usually waiting for somebody to join them but he didn't look like he was. He was staring at us all, like he was the odd one out. Now I remember.'

'Did he talk to you?'

'No. I stayed with the guys. I wasn't in a fit state to walk across a room alone and I was getting it on with Gavin.'

'Did you see Lucas in any other part of the hotel? Maybe when you went to the toilet?'

'No. I didn't leave the bar until I went home with Gavin. They'll all vouch for me.'

'And you definitely didn't accompany him downstairs or bump into him downstairs at the entrance?'

'Absolutely not. I left the hotel with Gavin. He came back to my place. If you check with Gavin, he'll confirm that, but please, don't say anything in front of his wife. She's a ballsy lawyer. She'll take him for everything he's got and prevent him seeing his kids ever again. He's so worried she'll find out. We really shouldn't have shagged. We both regret it. Gavin asked Jackson and Stu to keep quiet about it too. He says he can trust them.'

'Can you account for your movements the next day?'

'Am I a suspect?'

'No. Just ensuring I know where everyone was who saw Lucas Matthews that night.'

'I was with Gavin until mid-morning the following day. I had a terrible hangover so I dropped by Keep Fit Gym to work it out of my system. It's the best way for me to deal with that sort of thing. I trained for a couple of hours and then stood in for Stacey on the desk while she took Toni's classes for her, so she could go and visit her gran who wasn't well. I had hoped to meet Martin but he was off that day. After Stacey finished her shift at about six, we grabbed a bite to eat at Wetherspoons around the corner from the gym, and I went home after that and Skyped Adam. I was in work early the next morning, and stayed in London all week with Adam until last night when I came back here to get some fresh clothes and sort through my post. I thought it was best to stay away. I didn't want to bump into Gavin or his wife. Farnborough can be a small place at times.'

'I'm going to ask one last time, even though you've answered this question. Have you ever met Lucas Matthews before or seen him anywhere other than the Aviator hotel?'

'Hand on heart; I have never heard of this man before you mentioned him. I have never spoken to him or met with him or anything with him. I have no idea who he is.'

'What about Mary Matthews?'

'No,' replied Zoe with a frown. 'Not heard of her either. Is she related?'

'She's his wife.'

'Poor thing. I bet she's worried senseless about him.'

'Okay, thank you again, Zoe. I appreciate your help.'

'Is that it?'

'For the moment.' A crackled announcement interrupted them. 'That's my train. Call me if you have any other questions.'

'I shall.'

Robyn watched as Zoe dashed through the station entrance and over the bridge, arriving on the other side just as her train to London pulled in. She piled onto the train with the other commuters, her green hair standing out in the crowd of greys, browns and blondes who shuffled into the carriages. A whistle blew and the train pulled away again. Robyn closed her eyes. That nagging feeling was back again. It was the same feeling she had every time she looked at Zoe Cooper's face. What was it? What was she missing?

She sat for a while in her car. She was so close to the solution she could almost touch it. She ran through what she had one more time: Lucas Matthews had been tracking Zoe Cooper but that night in the bar he did not approach her.

Her phone lit up. Detective Inspector Shearer was after her. He was terse.

'Coroner's report is through. I'll send over a copy to your email but I thought you'd want to know that Lucas Matthews was attacked with a stun gun. The murderer not only used it to torture him in the genitals but also held it close to his heart and probably caused a heart attack. Details are in the report. The report also states that due to the maggot activity in his body he was likely to have been dead for five days prior to being discovered, which coincides with the last sighting of him at the Aviator hotel in Farnborough.'

'Thanks. So our murderer stunned him then he had a heart attack?'

'It appears that way. I hate to blow my own trumpet, being a modest sort of chap, but I was spot on with those red marks. They were burns from a stun gun.'

'Okay, thanks, Tom. Appreciate you calling me direct.'

'I figured you'd have PC Softy doing all the desk work so it was easier to tell you myself.'

'I am too busy to think of a suitable retort to that comment. He's a good officer, you know?'

'Course he is. Needs to toughen up though. It's a big bad world, DI Carter, as we both know. Any closer to your murderer?'

'I'm so close I can almost tell you what deodorant they wear.'

Shearer chuckled. 'Report is on its way. Catch you around, Robyn.'

She dialled Mitz to get an update and was pleased to hear him sounding enthusiastic.

'Finally located your rabbit. It's a Jellycat Really Big Bashful Bunny Soft Toy in cream. Can be purchased online or in large retail stores.'

'On that subject, did you receive the Christina Forman photographs?'

'I did and I examined the toy rabbit in the photograph but it's nothing like the one at Blinkley. It is a much older toy. You can see where it has lost some of its fur. I can't find a match for it so it must be a toy that is no longer sold.'

There was a voice in the background. Anna was talking.

'I'll put Anna on,' said Mitz.

'Hi, boss. The autopsy on Mary Matthews has been emailed across. She died of cyanide poisoning. I won't read out the entire report but it states that the hypostasis was brick-red, due to excess oxyhaemoglobin and to the presence of cyanmethemoglobin.'

Robyn's eyebrows raised in surprise. She knew cyanide interfered with the red cells' abilities to extract oxygen, causing 'internal asphyxia'. Mary Matthews had literally suffocated to death as she breathed in oxygen she couldn't use.

'That's helpful,' said Robyn. 'So, we are now definitely looking for a killer who has murdered Lucas and Mary Matthews. You still not turned up any unusual vehicle activity at Mary's house, Mitz?'

'Nothing. The neighbours keep themselves to themselves and don't seem to notice what goes on. And she had those gates that hid her property.'

'That's a nuisance. We could do with a break.' Robyn gathered her thoughts before she spoke again. 'I'm fairly convinced Paul Matthews' and Geraldine Marsh's deaths are related to this case, and

I want to look into them again if possible. I'm banging my head against a wall here for a suspect. I've interviewed Zoe Cooper and it's highly unlikely she is involved in any of the murders. She not only denies being with Lucas the night he left the hotel – which was the last sighting of him and most likely the last night he was alive – but she has an airtight alibi for that night, no motive and an alibi for the rest of the week so that rules her out. Did you dig any dirt at all on her?'

'Nothing that helps us. Zoe Charlotte Cooper, unmarried, aged twenty-five, lives in rented accommodation in Farnborough. Attended Farnborough Hill where she was a keen gymnast. Trained at college to become a fitness instructor. Has several fitness qualifications, no convictions and has glowing references from ex-employers. Her bank accounts are solvent and her credit rating's good so no financial problems. Nothing else has been flagged up. I've got more information but none of it points to anything other than a hard-working individual who has not had so much as a parking ticket. Her parents are both alive and now live in Cardiff, and she has an older sister who has emigrated to Australia.'

'She's such an improbable suspect. And, I can't fathom why Paul Matthews and Lucas wanted to find her?'

Mitz joined the conversation now on speakerphone.

'Not sure how much this helps but I've had difficulty finding information on both Natasha Matthews and Abigail Thorne. I'm concentrating on Abigail Thorne at the moment. There is little on her before she came to Farnborough, no family members, no school records, nothing.'

Robyn sat up. 'Go on. This sounds interesting.'

'It's a bit peculiar, that's for sure. It's like she didn't exist as a child or young adult. I have passport details for an Abigail Susannah Bridges; born in Leeds, date of birth twenty-fifth November 1986. I have nothing else on her until May 2010 when she worked in hospitality at the 2010 Farnborough Air Show. She then took up employment at the boutique in Farnborough, selling upmarket designer evening clothes and brideswear and stayed there until 2015 when she took maternity leave but did not return to work after the birth of Isobel Willow Thorne. She married Jackson Scott Thorne in May 2011. It was a small private affair in Farnborough. I couldn't unearth much more information about it other than we already have. I think that's about it for Abigail Thorne.'

'Keep digging and chase up the tech boys. I want to know what else was on Paul Matthews' laptop. I'm going back to his house now. I'm sure I missed something there. When you've done all that, meet me there.'

She ended the call. It was a blow that the rabbit at Christina's death scene had not been the same as the one at Lucas's. She might just be barking up the wrong tree with this line of thought. Robyn needed to solve this case. It was not beyond her skills. She had lost so much in the last year; she needed to prove to herself she hadn't lost everything.

CHAPTER FIFTY-TWO

THEN

The plan is going well. I've managed to cajole Zoe into joining me at Propaganda. It's busy as usual when we arrive and I pretend to be mega-excited about a new contract I am supposed to have with a magazine. Zoe kisses me on both cheeks and squeals in delight. We dance about like excited schoolgirls and I say the treat is on me. I order her a huge espresso martini and slip some Rohypnol into it. I ordered the pills from an online site that didn't even ask for a prescription for them. It'll make her get drunk very quickly, and feel all warm and loving, which is pretty much what I need. Zoe is quite reckless when she's drunk and I am banking on that fact tonight.

I've been tracking Jackson's phone as well as Abigail's. He's as bad as her for leaving stuff lying about. If they had less money they might pay more attention to their belongings. When I was visiting them I spotted it on the dashboard in his flash car with the door unlocked. He really should be more security-conscious. If I'd wanted to, I could have hot-wired his car and driven off with it. Okay, that's maybe a bit beyond my skills, but swiping his mobile and hiding around the corner of the house while I opened it up and installed the spyware was simple enough. I was a little concerned he would come out to his car but I had a story lined up if I had been spotted and I am pretty good at stealing things so I would have been able to slide it back into one of his pockets if I'd needed to. I returned the phone and left. Neither were any the wiser.

I bought the spyware online legally; so no worries there. Apparently wives who think their husbands are cheating on them often use this method. Thanks to my spyware I happen to know that Jackson is going to be at the Sky Bar in half an hour which gives me time to get Zoe ready for her performance. She's going to be an important pawn in my private game of chess.

We're about to enter the hotel when I pretend my neighbour is calling.

'Oh no. I'll be right there. No. Don't call the police,' I bleat. 'Not after last time. They'll think I'm a time waster.'

Zoe is anxious for me. I am almost tearful.

'Oh, Zoe, my house alarm has gone off. I need to get back. The neighbours think they saw someone running away from the house. They want to call the police.'

'Oh no, I'll come with you,' she slurs. 'You can't face burglars alone.'

'They'll be long gone. No. You stay here and celebrate without me. I'll call you.'

She looks confused, as well she may, given the amount of alcohol and drugs in her system. 'Christophe, Jackson and the others are here,' I say to encourage her.

'Are they?' she replies cheerfully and giving me a peck on the cheek and a hug, she tells me to take care and totters off into the lobby. I wait only a moment and follow her up the stairs where voices indicate the Sky Bar is fairly full. I stand by the open door. I have my phone set to camera in preparation. I'm counting on her. She's so easy to spot with her ridiculous green hair and my instincts are proved correct as she lurches towards the group of pilots, throwing her arms around them and kissing them all on the lips, much as I have seen her do before on the rare occasions she has been drunk. I aim my phone and take as many photographs as I can. One or two of them will be ideal.

Poor old scapegoat Zoe. I have used her identity often. I like aliases and Zoe makes an excellent one. I have two fake email accounts in her name and several other accounts, including one with Amazon. It makes sense to use them when I shop for certain items. I also have a box at the post office in her name where I take delivery of my parcels. I get so used to using her name that I sometimes use it by accident. A while ago I used it for a photograph competition. It was tricky as I won the competition but since they sent my prize – a top-of-the-range Nikon camera – to "Zoe's" post-office address, I came out of it okay.

I'm about to leave when out of the corner of my eye I spot him – Lucas Matthews. My heart quickens. What's brought him here to the Aviator hotel? Has he discovered where I live? I try to control my heartbeat, taking slow breaths as I often do when I'm stressed. I notice he is looking at Zoe, a puzzled expression on his face. Dad is chuckling. 'Now here's the opportunity you've been waiting for,' he says.

He's right. I've brought my bag of tricks in case I needed to disguise myself as Zoe, but they'll be put to better use now. I study Lucas. He is watching Zoe who has just stumbled drunkenly into Gavin. Gavin holds her up, his face grinning at her in a friendly but lustful way. Zoe has that effect on men. They all want to look after her and care for her. She doesn't need that though. She's a modern-day woman. She enjoys her life exactly as it is. I suppose that's what I like about her and even though I intend messing up her life, it is with a modicum of regret. However, needs must. Lucas can't tear his eyes away from her. It seems he has worked out who has been blackmailing him and it won't be long before he says something to Zoe. I need to act now before he spoils everything.

I sit on a chair, hiding behind a crowd of men in evening suits, though I can see Lucas glance in my direction occasionally. I have an idea. I need to be bold to carry it out. Dad whispers words of encouragement. I head towards where Lucas is standing, lean over the bar to ask the barman for a gin and tonic and accidentally sweep his bottle of beer off the bar. Before he can react, I wave my hands in despair and apologise loudly in an accent that manages to sound authentically Eastern European, and then insist on buying him another.

'Please. So sorry. I get you more beer,' I say, swiping at the spillage with a large tissue. 'Sorry, barman. I make big mess.' Lucas loses interest in me, shrugs and accepts the offer, turning back to Zoe who is now hanging on to Gavin's arm for dear life and leaning into his shoulder. It wouldn't surprise me if the pair end up in bed together and I smile. I set up a hidden spy camera in Zoe's bedroom two weeks ago. It records onto an SD card whenever it senses motion and has a capacity of up to 64 GB, giving weeks of recording time. Zoe has no idea of its true purpose. It's very similar to the one in Abigail's mansion. The cameras are quite popular for watching over vulnerable people such as the elderly or children and are sometimes known as nanny cams or granny cams. If I'm fortunate, it'll record something X-rated that I can use to aid my plan.

The barman passes me another Peroni and with one swift movement no one sees I tip in some of the Rohypnol I used to spike Zoe's drink. I offer apologies again and put the drink on the bar for Lucas to pick up and when I am sure he has drunk from the bottle, I steal away to the toilets where I change into my disguise.

My waiting pays off and Lucas leaves the bar. He has not challenged Zoe. No doubt the men surrounding her scared him off. His eyes are unfocused and he is wavering a little. I wait until he has navigated his way to the stairs then I appear beside him.

'Mr Matthews,' I say. 'I believe you've been looking for me.'

'Zoe Cooper?' he asks, eyes blinking in surprise. One eye moves to stare at me.

'That's right, and we need to talk.'

'You look different.'

'It's just this dim light here,' I say as I accompany him down the stairs and out of the building. A concierge hidden behind a desk asks if we require a taxi but I daren't let him see my face so I walk on through the door without replying. I grab Lucas's arm and guide him to my car.

Outside, it is quiet. The building, in the shape of a propeller, was clearly built with aviation in mind. I am impressed by it as I stand in the car park waiting to see if we have been spotted. There is the drone of the occasional car as it drives past and I savour the freshening air that has replaced the sultry heat of the day. I am certain no one can see us. I have parked away from the hotel and no rooms overlook the car park. He is feeling the effects of the drugs now and like an obedient child, allows me to push him into the boot of my car. I shut the lid with haste and drive. I know exactly what I am going to do to him.

CHAPTER FIFTY-THREE

'I understand this is incredibly stressful, Mrs Thorne, but I need you to try and recall as much as possible. Can you describe the man who stole your handbag?'

Abigail looked up at the police sergeant, her face swollen with crying. He had a caring face with warm brown eyes. He had accompanied her into the room at the back of the station and made her a cup of tea with lots of sugar while she had sat and sobbed. Everything was a fog now. This all felt unreal. Any minute now she would wake up. Izzy would be in her cot, waiting for her. This wasn't happening.

She could remember screaming when she discovered Izzy missing, and running around the car park, blood turned to ice, hunting for her, screaming her name, pleading for her to be returned. People had stopped and stared, none of them helping her, none of them comprehending her terrifying misery. She must have looked like a wild woman. Then there had been a mature woman, wearing a brown uniform like those worn by staff in the supermarket. She had approached Abigail, whose head was turning back and forth as if on a coiled spring, trying to spot Izzy. The woman had managed to get Abigail to explain.

'My baby. She's been snatched,' Abigail had gasped, pulling away again to run towards a young woman pushing a buggy. The baby snuggled under a yellow blanket wasn't Izzy and Abigail had fallen to her knees, simultaneously screaming and crying, her heart shattered into a million pieces.

The police had been called to the scene. One had stayed behind to question people and look for her baby girl. They had wanted to take her to the station but she didn't want to leave the car park in case it had all been a horrible mistake and Izzy was returned. But of course it wasn't a mistake. At last, a female officer, the one sat next to her now, had driven her to the station not far from the shopping centre, and tried to contact Jackson. Jackson was in the Channel Islands but was now headed home. Abigail could no longer think clearly. She wanted Jackson. More than that, she wanted her baby back.

'He was about six foot, dark brown or black hair.' She stopped as tears filled her eyes again and cascaded down her face. The female PC next to her patted her hand gently. 'I can't remember what he looked like. He had blue trousers and a grey bomber jacket and heavy eyebrows and green eyes. That's when I realised he wasn't Lucas.'

'Were you expecting to meet Lucas?'

She nodded. 'He'd phoned me. We arranged to meet at the Meads.'

'Is Lucas a friend?'

'No,' said Abigail. 'He's my brother.'

CHAPTER FIFTY-FOUR

NOW

People are so gullible and Abigail is no exception. She provided me with the perfect opportunity to grab Izzy. She actually believed I was Lucas. How wrong could she be?

I am so quick thinking. I only had ten minutes to organise everything. Fortunately, I was already at the Meads when I phoned her. The homeless man didn't question me when I offered him fifty pounds to approach a white Range Rover Evoque in the car park and grab the occupant's handbag from the passenger seat. Abigail ought to know better. We are constantly warned about leaving handbags on front seats of cars, and as for winding down a window to a stranger – tsk, tsk, Abigail. I told the man he wasn't to keep the handbag or contents, or I'd report him to the police. He was to drop it in the alleyway and then hide in the supermarket. I explained it was all a prank. He didn't care what I told him, fifty quid was fifty quid and I think he'd have done almost anything for it.

I didn't have long to disguise myself but an old coat out of the charity shop and a headscarf did the trick. I rammed a couple of plastic bags full of stuff from the recycling bins at the back of the car park, so it looked like I had shopping in them, and shuffled past her car. She barely looked in my direction. Hiding in full view always works.

I had anticipated her moves. I banked on the fact she would be so steamed up about Lucas that she wouldn't think clearly and would act on instinct when the man stole her bag. I know her well enough. After all, we've been best mates for a few years. I bargained on her leaving Izzy for a few moments. If she hadn't chased after him I'd have come up with something else. I stationed myself behind an estate car out of view and she didn't spot me watching as she belted after the man.

It only took a few seconds to unclip Izzy's car seat and lug it out. I sauntered in the opposite direction to Abigail. My car was parked at the other side of the supermarket. It's best not to draw attention to yourself when you are kidnapping a child, so I behaved as if she were my own. I popped her into one of the supermarket trolleys along with the bags. People take no notice of a woman and baby if the mother is murmuring to her offspring and ignoring everything else. It's just another mother and child going shopping.

Oh, Abigail, what emotions will you experience now? Disbelief? Horror? Anxiety? True unhappiness? Good. You deserve to feel them all.

CHAPTER FIFTY-FIVE

The drive back to Paul Matthews' house seemed to take forever and Robyn, stiff from sitting for so long without a break, flung her car door open and breathed in the fresh air with relief. Ross's car was parked on the drive. He was no doubt hunting for a toy rabbit in the woods.

She got out of the car and stretched her arms high above her head. Her back creaked. An indication that time was ticking and she was getting older. She stretched her neck from side to side, taking in the vista below. A herd of young black and white cows grazed in the field and in the distance, a red tractor trundled down a field, towing a trailer laden with bales of hay.

'You owe me a meal out and a chocolate bar,' said Ross, appearing up the slope, his face red. He carried a jacket over his arm. Sweat stains had spread under the arms of his T-shirt.

'I'll treat you to a delicious quinoa and mung-bean salad at the health bar in town. How about that?'

Ross made disgusting noises. She waited until he stopped.

'Was I right?'

He shook his head. 'Couldn't find it. I looked up in trees and places a detective might not have looked but there was no rabbit. Sorry.'

Robyn cursed. She was convinced the rabbit would be in the woods. She was losing her touch. Maybe she should retire from the force once and for all and join Ross full-time. She stared at the woods and chewed on her lip before speaking again.

'I'm going to check Paul's house again.'

'You got a warrant or do I have to pretend to buy the place again?'

'It's all legal this time. Mitz Patel is at the estate agent getting the key. Got a warrant and everything. Mulholland is brassed off with me though. She wants a murderer dragged through the station doors and I haven't found anyone I can bring in. I honestly thought I had a pattern going on with the rabbits and that I could prove Paul's murder wasn't an accident – that we have a serial killer on our hands.'

'We all make mistakes,' said Ross, seeing the look on her face.

'I know, but I was so sure about it. I was positive there was a link between the deaths of Christina, Lucas, Mary and Paul. I still am. I can't let it go.'

Ross leant against the car. 'Look, I'm pooped. I'm going to leave you to it. I need a shower.'

'Really sorry this was a waste of time, Ross. I'll treat you to that meal.'

'You're okay. I enjoyed the walk. It's very relaxing in there. Jeanette will be happy with me. And it did me good. Call me if you want anything else. But,' he added, 'not another long hike in the woods again too soon.'

He clambered into his car and drove off with a wave, passing PC Patel as he went.

PC Patel beamed as he and Anna approached the house. 'Got the key. Apparently, the house is off the market though. There's some dispute over the will.'

He passed the key to Robyn who opened the door to the impressive hallway.

Anna drew a breath as she took in the grand entrance hall. 'What a huge pad.'

'Yeah, my mum and dad would love this.' He pointed at the staircase at the end of the hallway. 'Those stairs would be a nightmare though for my gran. They're really steep. She can't manage stairs.'

'Your gran lives with you too?' asked Anna.

'Yeah, she's in the annexe. It used to be a garage but my dad converted it when my granddad died, so my gran could live with us. She has her own bathroom and toilet and sitting room. She stays there a lot but sometimes she comes and watches television with us. She's lovely, is my gran. Makes the best onion bhajis in the world.'

Robyn smiled at him. 'You're a proper family man, aren't you?'

'Yeah. I love my parents. They've been really good to me. I'd like to buy a house on the same street as them then I could still see them regularly. I wouldn't have to do that if we all lived in a house like this. It'd be wicked.'

'I'm not sure what I'm looking for, so if you two want to have a poke around, I'm going into the kitchen. I keep getting a feeling I missed something when I was there last.'

She left Anna staring at the conservatory and went back into the kitchen where she had stood with Geraldine Marsh.

The place looked exactly the same as the last time she had visited. The DVDs were still on the floor next to the DVD player and the magazines were piled on the island. She walked towards the snug area and looked around it, taking in the black leather chair and mismatched furniture. It felt lonely here. It was large but empty, devoid of any warmth, laughter or love that should exist in a house like this. If PC Patel and his family lived here it would be a different place, she mused. She eyed the collection of DVDs. There was a series of programmes about animals in the Arctic, several on animals in Africa and various documentaries on birds – but nothing to help her.

PC Patel wandered into the kitchen. 'Anna is upstairs. Found anything?

'I'm stumped. What do you see, Mitz? I'm searching for something that might help explain why Paul Matthews was interested in going to Farnborough.'

'Are there any letters, cards or correspondence from someone who lives there? We usually leave our letters in a letter rack on the kitchen top if they need dealing with. You know, bills, that sort of thing. Maybe he got a letter from someone who lives there.'

'There's nothing visible,' replied Robyn, looking about the room. 'No letter rack.'

'He seemed obsessed with nature. I've never seen so many DVDs on the subject. Penguins, elephants, underwater creatures, birds. He liked birds,' continued Mitz Patel, eyeing the collection of DVDs. 'No films at all. That's unusual. He was a serious man, unless he had a subscription to a movie channel.'

Robyn moved towards the island. 'Keep looking and keep talking. What else do you see, Mitz?'

'He's also got loads of magazines. Are they all to do with animals and birds too? He obviously reads a lot. And, he doesn't throw his magazines away. Once I've read one, I dump it. These are all laid out in regular piles too. Considering the rest of the place looks a bit of a mess, he's super tidy when it comes to his magazines. There must be some bills or letters somewhere in the house. Nobody has no mail at all,' he continued, moving towards the laundry room.

Robyn stared at the top magazine thoughtfully. 'You're right. His magazines are tidy. So why is there one magazine open and bent back at this page?' she shouted.

'He was reading it before he went out?'

'Possible.' Robyn picked up the magazine and stared at the page open to reveal the winning photographs in a photography competition. The shot of the beautiful creamy brown marsh eagle was a worthy winner. Robyn suddenly felt the hairs on her neck rise. This was the clue she had been searching for. Underneath the photograph was a headshot of the winner. The name read Miss Zoe Cooper, Farnborough. The name might read Zoe Cooper but Robyn recognised the picture of the unsmiling woman in the headshot. It was not Zoe. She had seen that face before in one of Abigail's photographs. It was Claire Lewis.

She tapped the photograph. 'Bingo! Paul Matthews saw this picture and recognised the woman in it. This is the connection we've been searching for. Paul Matthews knew her face but not her name and from this article he assumed her name was Zoe Cooper. We have a suspect at last,' she said, triumphantly.

'So who's that in the photograph?' asked Mitz, returning with a handful of letters.

'She's not who Paul Matthews thought she was. The woman in the picture is Claire Lewis. She's one of Zoe's friends and is also best friends with Abigail Thorne. I saw a photograph of her at Abigail's house, that's how I know it's her.'

Mitz handed her the mail in his hands. 'Being a big posh house, there's no letter box opening in the door,' he said, 'but there is a large wooden letter box outside on the wall. I think someone collected the post and placed it in the laundry room unopened. Maybe Paul Matthews did it himself before he went for a run. There isn't much mail but there's one letter you might want to look at. It's postmarked Farnborough the day before Paul Matthews died.'

Robyn put down the magazine. Adrenalin began to course through her veins. 'Have you got any gloves?'

He pulled out some plastic gloves from his pocket and passed her a pair.

'Always prepared. I think you'll go far, PC Patel.'

'Hope so, ma'am. Have to earn enough to get my own place.'

Robyn pulled on the gloves and took the letter from Mitz. She slit it open with a finger and pulled out the card inside. The face of it bore a photograph of a rabbit chewing grass. Inside was a message written in capital letters.

Robyn read,
Run rabbit run, today is going to be your last race.
The tortoise always wins.
RIP Paul Matthews.
Alice.

She passed the card to Mitz and called Anna who bounded down the stairs to join them.

'It's well spooky up there. The rooms are all so miserable and dated. Those stairs are lethal too. I slipped and nearly landed on my bum. Hardly surprising Geraldine Matthews lost her footing. What have you got?'

'A whopping clue and lead thanks to Mitz. Have this card checked for prints. We need to get hold of Claire Lewis for questioning as soon as possible. Phone Hampshire Constabulary and alert them. She's apparently in Scotland but might be due home soon. Try to locate her whereabouts using her mobile and service provider and once you've an idea, target guest houses, hotels and rented accommodation in the vicinity to see if she checked in or out of anywhere. I'm returning to Farnborough to talk to them both. I want Abigail Thorne and Claire Lewis pulled in as soon as possible.'

Robyn threw herself back into her car with renewed enthusiasm. It all revolved around Alice. Alice had come back into the Matthews' lives. And, if Paul Matthews had been correct, then Alice Forman and Claire Lewis were one and the same person. Now Robyn needed to know what had driven the woman to murder Paul Matthews, and if she had also killed Lucas.

The toy rabbit found on Lucas Matthews, the one at Mulwood Avenue and the card they had just lighted upon at Paul's house were significant, and linked the murders. It now seemed likely that Paul Matthews had also been killed. The card was possible proof of this but Robyn needed more than a sinister message to convince her superiors. The tingling sensation that ran up her spine told Robyn she was right with her assumptions. Alice had killed Paul, Lucas and Mary. However, assumptions didn't stand up in court or in front of DCI Mulholland. Robyn had to be one hundred per cent sure and have concrete evidence. She ran through what she had so far.

Paul Matthews believed the photograph in the magazine was of Alice Forman, now masquerading as someone by the name of Zoe Cooper. She was curious how he had recognised the photograph given he had not, presumably, seen Alice for years. That question would have to wait. The photograph was of Claire Lewis, not Zoe Cooper, therefore Claire must have used Zoe's name as an alias, yet this raised the question of why Claire would use her own photo and Zoe's name? Finally, there was the question of why Paul Matthews was hunting down the woman in the photograph. Robyn could only think of one reason and that was because he thought the person in the photograph was blackmailing Lucas.

Robyn drummed her fingers impatiently. She mulled over the information she had. Then her sixth sense kicked in and she thought she knew the reason. What if Claire Lewis had blackmailed Lucas Matthews but used Zoe's name instead of her own?

Robyn could feel the answers tumbling in front of her like blocks, each containing a letter that made no sense until all the blocks were in the correct order. She thought of Davies. He was an expert in conundrums and codes. He would have worked this out far quicker than her. Suddenly, it fell into place. Claire Lewis was Alice, but for some reason she had used Zoe's name for the photography competition. Paul had recognised her in the photo-graph and assumed she was using the alias Zoe Cooper. He had arranged to track her down and shown Lucas the photograph of Claire. Both men had searched for Alice who they supposed was now calling herself Zoe Cooper. When Lucas finally tracked down

Zoe, she hadn't resembled the woman in the photograph. That was why he hadn't approached her at the Sky Bar.

This was a likely explanation. Now she had to prove it. A call came through from PC Patel.

'Got an address for Claire Lewis. Hampshire Constabulary is on it but she hasn't returned home. They tried her studio and her phone but no response from either.'

Robyn groaned. 'I hope she hasn't gone to ground. Get a warrant for her place. Check out all her friends and usual haunts. Let's see if we can flush her out. Also, check the organisers of the photographic contest in the magazine. I want to know where they sent the prize that Zoe Cooper won. Maybe she has an alternative address and is hiding out there.' She read out the information from the magazine she had brought away with her.

'Roger that,' replied PC Patel. 'Also, bad news on Abigail Thorne. She was with Hampshire Constabulary all afternoon. She's just been taken home. It appears her baby has been kidnapped.'

Robyn felt the puzzle pieces shift again.

CHAPTER FIFTY-SIX

Abigail breathed in the warm breeze, carrying the smell of sea salt. Waves tumbled against the shore, their white foamy heads breaking gently before racing up the sandy beach. The sun beat on her face and trickles of moisture ran down the back of her neck. Jackson sat on the sand, Izzy between his legs, building a sandcastle. She was too young to appreciate what he was doing but her eyes, the same colour as the azure sea, sparkled with pleasure. She banged a plastic spade on the freshly upturned pile of sand and chuckled. Abigail felt the warmth of the sun penetrate her body and fill her heart with a heat she had never before experienced. She adored her child. Izzy made her life complete. She shut her eyes and enjoyed the perfect moment.

Then, Jackson shouted her name, his voice full of anxiety and disquiet. She looked for him on the sand but that image was evaporating and now Jackson's face hovered over hers, concern etched on his features, lines where there had never been lines, his eyes sunken and red.

She felt woozy as she tried to pull herself up from the bed. The sedative the doctor had given her had confused her mind and made her limbs sluggish. Why had he come? She couldn't remember. Then it hit her. Izzy had gone. Izzy had gone and Abigail had broken down.

'Are you okay?' Jackson asked, holding her hand in his own.

'Izzy?' she asked, hoping beyond hope that this was all a terrible dream.

Jackson shook his head. 'No news yet. The police are going through CCTV footage to see if anything was captured.'

His face was ashen and he had aged ten years.

'I'm so sorry. I only left her for a few moments. I didn't think...' Her voice trailed off. It didn't matter how often she apologised, this was all her fault. She should never have left Izzy alone in the car. She should have told the truth sooner and none of this would have happened.

'There was a policewoman here to look after you but when I got in I told her to leave. They're sending someone around later to let us know what they're doing and to advise us.' He paused, swallowing back a lump in his throat. 'They might ask more questions. Are you up to it?'

She nodded. 'I don't know what more I can tell them. I told them who's got her. It was Lucas Matthews. He phoned me and arranged to meet me then set me up. Him and his devious friend, Rachel. He lured me to the car park and then got someone to steal my handbag. I didn't think, Jackson. I ran after the man and when I got back, Lucas had snatched her. I should never have agreed to meet him.'

Jackson pressed her hand again. 'No, Abigail. It wasn't Lucas Matthews.'

'It was. He phoned me just after I left the doctor's surgery. You don't know him. He's evil. He's the one who's been stalking me, phoning me, emailing me. He set it all up. He's been planning it carefully so he could take Izzy. He's working with Rachel Croft. I told the police all of this. I told them about the note and the phone calls and being hacked, and how it was all down to Lucas and his accomplice. Rachel was in on it, that's how they slipped ipecac into my drink at the café. That's how the photograph that is hanging over our bed appeared on Facebook.' She shook her head in dismay as she spoke, her words tumbling from her lips, faster and faster until tears formed again and she drew in shuddering breaths.

'Abby,' Jackson insisted. 'It wasn't Lucas Matthews. It couldn't have been. Lucas is dead. The police told me at the station. They tried to contact him and discovered he died almost a week ago. It wasn't him.'

Abigail felt her chest tightening. She couldn't breathe. She gasped and struggled, her breath now coming in short pants. Jackson held her tightly until she calmed. 'Rachel?' she managed to say.

'The police are looking into your claim. They sent a team to her house. They couldn't tell me any more than they were doing everything they could to find Izzy. I came home as soon as I could.'

Her mind went blank. The hurt, pain and fear became physical and she hugged her knees to her chest and rocked forwards and backwards. At last, she stopped, sniffed and turned her face to Jackson's. 'But if Lucas is dead, then who has stolen our baby?'

He shrugged helplessly. 'I wish I knew, Abby. I wish I knew.'

CHAPTER FIFTY-SEVEN

The call came as Robyn was nearing Hartley Witney.

'We have located Lucas Matthews's mobile,' said a triumphant PC Patel. 'He stayed at a Premier Inn in Farnborough. I rang all the local hotels and asked if anyone had left suddenly without checking out. Turns out Lucas Matthews didn't check out as expected and left a holdall and clothes in his room. The hotel charged his credit card for his stay, gathered up his possessions and put them in lost property. Do you want to collect them or should I get someone from Hampshire Constabulary to fetch them?'

'I'll go as soon as I've interviewed Abigail Thorne.'

'Righto. His phone company released his call log too. Nothing on it since last Monday and before that he made calls to several Farnborough numbers. I'll check them all out.'

'Great stuff! We're getting close now, Mitz. I'm positive we're almost in sight of his killer. Any news on Claire Lewis?'

'None yet. Still working on that. It seems like her phone is off and not traceable. I've done background checks and got some information on her. According to her Facebook profile she was born 1990. Birthday down as the twelfth of September, but that needn't be the case. You can pretty much put in what you like on the profile. She hasn't listed any schools, but on her LinkedIn account she states she has HNC qualifications in photography. Her website contains samples of her work and a contact email address. She uses the social media accounts to advertise her photography and her Facebook friends appear to be mostly old clients or local business people in Farnborough. She doesn't post much personal stuff and her only real friends seem to be Zoe Cooper and Abigail Thorne. There are a few photographs of them out together. I haven't stumbled on anything that would help us at this stage but am looking into it further.'

'Blast! Okay, Mitz, let me know as soon as you locate her.'

'Anna has unearthed a deleted file on Paul Matthews' laptop. It is entitled *Abigail*. Not much in it though. There's her home address, details about the house from Zoopla, and the photographs from their wedding which appeared in the online version of the local newspaper. He's got some photographs of BizzyAir Business Aviation jets and a photograph of Jackson with his business partner. There's a photograph of Abigail at some hospitality event that got into the paper too. He's also downloaded an announcement from the *Farnborough News* regarding the birth of Isobel Willow Thorne.'

Robyn chewed on her lip. Mitz continued. 'At school, I had to make a collage of my family using photos and write about each person. This is a bit like that. Is this an electronic scrapbook?'

'I'm about to find out, Mitz.' A thought hit her. 'You had passport details for Abigail. What maiden name did she have?'

'Bridges,' replied Mitz.

'Of course,' said Robyn. 'Bridges. It makes sense.'

'I'm still in the dark.'

'Paul Matthews' first wife, Mitz. She was called Linda Bridges.'

'Ah! Got it. I suppose that's why I'm a PC and you're a DI, ma'am.'

'Keep digging on Claire Lewis and for heaven's sake drop the *ma'am*. I'm sure you've impressed Anna sufficiently by now.'

Robyn pulled into the drive. Jackson opened the front door to the house before she stepped out of her car. He strode up to her. 'Any news? Abigail's going out of her mind with anxiety.'

Robyn ignored his question, looking into his eyes and speaking with sincerity. 'I am really sorry about this. I have to interview her. I know my timing is bad but this can't wait.'

Jackson cocked his head to one side as he suddenly comprehended the situation. 'So your visit isn't about Izzy. You're not here to find our daughter?'

'I'm here to conduct an interview with your wife regarding the death of Lucas Matthews. I believe she might be withholding evidence. I understand this is a difficult time but I have to do my job.'

Robyn tried to be reasonable. The man was obviously distraught.

'But she's in no fit state to talk about Lucas Matthews. She's talking nonsense at times. She was in such a bad way; she even thought that man had stolen Izzy. The detective who interviewed me told me Lucas Matthews was dead. Abigail is too upset to talk about him. She can't help you.'

Jackson folded his arms, refusing to move out of Robyn's way.

A resigned voice behind him made him spin around.

'Jackson, let her in. It's time to tell the truth.' Abigail was standing by the door, her shoulders sagging as if her spirit had been drained.

She turned back into the house and Jackson and Robyn followed her in. Abigail was in the lounge, back on the settee, knees drawn into her chest, clutching the toy dog that Robyn had seen last in Izzy's hands. She looked exhausted, her skin the colour of dough and her eyes red-rimmed and swollen. Part of Robyn wanted to reach out and hold the woman to ease the pain; the same part that knew exactly what it felt like to lose a child.

'I'm so sorry,' she began. 'We are trained for these situations. The team involved will do everything to find her.'

Abigail choked back a sob. 'I don't know who would do this to us. First, I thought it was Zoe. Then I believed it was Lucas along with Rachel Croft. That all seemed to add up, and now, now I don't know anything any more. The police say it was a random snatching, maybe someone who took a chance when I left her. I don't understand how they could do such a thing. I hope she's okay. I couldn't live if anything happened to her.'

Jackson walked to the window and stared outside, a silent sentinel waiting for someone to bring news.

'I am truly sorry to have to question you about this at such a difficult time but I have to know,' said Robyn. 'Lucas Matthews was found dead in Staffordshire.' She waited to give Abigail a chance to understand the importance of what she was about to ask. 'When I questioned you about him, you denied knowing him. You said you had never heard of him. Do you wish to change your statement now?'

Abigail sniffed back tears. 'I didn't want my life to change,' she said. 'I was so happy. I had Jackson, Izzy, friends, everything I ever wanted. Lucas destroyed my life when I was younger and I didn't ever want to hear his name, or see him again. He isn't—' She corrected herself, 'He *wasn't* normal. He was cruel and hateful in ways you wouldn't comprehend: a person you wouldn't want to know. It was because of him I left home. I had to get away. I couldn't stand his superior attitude and his creepy ways any longer. I wiped him from my mind. Until recently, it was fine. I didn't ever think of him and now…' She paused again. 'I'm sorry. I should have told you. I wish I had. Maybe if I had, Izzy would be here still. Lucas Matthews was my brother.'

'I see,' replied Robyn. 'What happened to make you leave home? It must have been serious.'

'It's a long story and I doubt it has any bearing on your investigation. Also, I need to tell Jackson the complete story before I speak to you about it. I owe him that much. I'll tell you what I have already told him. I left home when I was sixteen. I had a major fallout with my father over Lucas and walked out. My father gave me money to start a new life and I did. I went abroad and began again. I changed my surname from Matthews to Bridges, my mother's maiden name, and became Abigail Bridges – a new name, a new person and a new life. Both Lucas and Paul owed me that much and as far as I was concerned they no longer existed. I worked abroad for a long while. The company eventually let me go and I returned to the UK. I was offered a job in hospitality at the Farnborough Air Show. It was good money but a temporary position. I hadn't intended staying after the show. I had planned on going back abroad but I met Jackson.'

Jackson continued to look out of the window as if at any time his daughter would turn up. Robyn wasn't sure if he was listening to the conversation and doubted he was.

'I hadn't seen or heard from either of them until you asked me about Lucas and said he had been searching for Zoe. That same day, I discovered I had been deliberately poisoned with ipecac, put two and two together and decided it must have been Lucas behind all of it, along with an accomplice. That could only be Rachel. I had arranged to meet her, and then I was going to report all of it to the police, when I got a call from the same person that has been phoning me the last few days. I thought it was Lucas. We arranged to meet at the Meads car park and that's where I did something stupid. I raced after a thief, leaving my baby in the car for a few moments and when I got back she'd disappeared.' Abigail spluttered the last few words. Her resolve weakened and she began to cry. Robyn ached for her and what she was going through but, somehow, all of it was connected. She had to fit the pieces together. Abigail wiped her eyes once more and tightened her grip on the rag dog.

'I understand this is hard for you, but please go through the conversation again for me.'

Through gulps and sobs, Abigail repeated the exchange she had had with the caller and the events that led to Izzy disappearing.

'This person told you your father, Paul, was dead?'

Abigail held the toy dog to her face and nodded. 'I didn't care. I was so angry with Lucas for tormenting me. I didn't care about anything and now Lucas is dead too and I still don't care. I just want Izzy back.'

'We'll get her back,' said Robyn, hoping her words did not sound hollow. They needed to get some footage from the CCTV cameras, ask possible witnesses and track down the person responsible.

'One last question. Did Claire know your father or Lucas?'

Abigail tilted her head to one side. 'Claire? No. She's never met either of them. Why are you asking about Claire?'

'I'm trying to understand how someone might have learned you and Lucas were related. Best friends often share secrets and those can unintentionally be leaked to partners or close friends or be overheard.'

'No one knew about Lucas, or my father. I didn't discuss it with anyone, not Claire and not even Jackson. Once I became Abigail Bridges, I put everything behind me.'

'Claire has never asked you about your childhood or chatted about stuff you both liked when you were younger?'

Abigail thought for a moment. 'I can't say we have discussed much, only bands we used to like and schooldays when we hated certain teachers. She went to a few schools. Her parents were in the army and she had to change school a lot. Her parents got divorced when she was still young and she lived with her mother. She hardly saw her dad after the divorce, what with him doing tours and living in other parts of the country. She was bitter about that. Her mum didn't like her visiting him either and made it difficult. By the time she was old enough to make her own choices, her dad had passed away. He got killed in Afghanistan.' She squeezed the toy. The action brought her back to the present and to Izzy. 'I don't see how this is helping you and it isn't helping to get my baby back. Shouldn't you be involved in that rather than asking about my friends?'

Robyn observed the woman who was gradually unravelling in front of her. 'I can assure you that everyone concerned will be searching for Izzy,' she replied. 'It may not seem relevant but sometimes these things lead to other unconnected people and we find perpetrators. You've been really helpful, thank you.'

Abigail sniffed again. 'I've never spoken about the events that made me leave my family,' she reiterated, eyes on the dog in her hands. 'They were too horrible to talk about. I buried them deep inside and now I have to unearth them and speak about the disgusting violation. Jackson will never be able to look at me the same way. My life has been ruined, Detective Carter, and if Izzy is not found, what's left of my shattered life won't be worth living.'

Jackson shifted uncomfortably and turned towards the settee. Abigail pressed her lips tightly together to prevent herself from sobbing again.

'Do you have anyone you can contact about this? Family, friends? Does Claire know that Izzy is missing? She ought to be here for you.'

Robyn was uncomfortable using Abigail's fragile emotions to learn more about Claire but she needed answers and she couldn't shake the notion that Claire was somehow involved in this latest tragedy.

'She's on a photo shoot for a magazine – *Nature World* – in Scotland. I tried calling her earlier but I went through to her answerphone. I left a message.'

Robyn stood up. 'Thank you, Abigail. The police will do everything to get her back. You know that, don't you?'

Robyn felt dispirited as she left the Thornes. She now knew why Paul Matthews had a file on Abigail. Whatever had happened, he had wanted to somehow keep in touch. Even if it was from afar. It was a shame he never got to actually meet his granddaughter. This wasn't her case but she wanted to help look for baby Izzy. She would visit the station and see how proceedings were going.

DCI Corrance might not like her turning up but that was tough. Robyn wasn't going to worry about offending anyone. A baby was missing and she wanted to help find her. First, though, she would collect Lucas's belongings.

CHAPTER FIFTY-EIGHT

The brown holdall weighed very little. Lucas hadn't been planning on being away long. Robyn placed it on the front seat of the Polo and unzipped it. It contained a pile of unwashed, sour-smelling clothes. Putting on a pair of plastic gloves she dug through and unearthed a mobile phone and charger. She was about to call PC Patel with the good news when a flash of white caught her eye. At the bottom of the bag, under some dirty underwear, were two envelopes. She pulled them out. The first was addressed to Mary Matthews and the second to Abigail Thorne.

Robyn felt the familiar buzz of adrenalin as she ripped open the one addressed to Abigail and read:

Dear Abigail

I have not revealed my identity or said anything to your husband that may jeopardise yours. I merely asked him to pass you this letter in the hope that if you get it from him you might not rip it up. Obviously, I can't give it to you personally as I promised many years ago to stay away from you. It is important you read it.

I need to warn you about Alice. She appears to be exacting some sort of revenge and has been blackmailing me. Not satisfied with two payments she has been threatening to extract more and ruin my marriage and my life.

I went to Paul for help. He wasn't thrilled but has done what he can. He has been following your life from afar and knows your address. He advised me to get in contact with your husband at his work rather than surprise you with a visit. Paul discovered Alice's whereabouts by chance, spotting a photograph of her in a nature magazine, and given she now lives in your area, we chose to break our promises in order to alert you, in case she attempts to blackmail you, or worse. She goes by the alias of Zoe Cooper.

I am endeavouring to track her down to prevent whatever game she is playing but you need to be aware in case she uncovers your true identity and decides to approach you.

I hope you are enjoying a better life. I promise not to blight this one for you.

Good luck

Lucas

The envelope addressed to Mary Matthews contained a letter and a second piece of paper. Robyn read the letter:

Dearest Mary,

If you are reading this then something has happened to me and you might have learned some truths that will upset you greatly.

I have a terrible sickness that I have never been able to cure. My penchant for young girls has got me into trouble in the past and has probably resulted in my demise.

Recently, I have been blackmailed following an incident with a young girl. I was forced to give my resignation to the school and had to hand over money.

You must believe me when I say that I fully intended to deal with my addiction. I genuinely wanted to stop. I wanted to be a normal husband. You are the best thing that has happened to me and for that reason I have kept you in the dark about this whole business.

The person who is blackmailing me is from my past. I attacked her and forced myself on her when she was a child. I was drunk and had been taking drugs at a friend's house. She retaliated and stabbed me. That is how I lost my eye.

I thought it was all over but it appears not and she has been threatening not only to exact large amounts of money but, more recently, to harm you.

I have not been in Thailand, as you believe. I didn't want you to get involved in this. I have been attempting to find her before she carries out her threats.

If you are reading this letter, please give the enclosed to the police immediately and ask for protection until they find a woman who goes by the name of Zoe Cooper. Her true identity is Alice Forman. Do not let her near you.

Mary, I am truly sorry for any upset I have caused you. Please know I love you.

Lucas x

The second piece of paper contained letters cut from a paper and said:

NO MONEY IS ENOUGH.
YOU SHALL PAY WITH YOUR LIFE.
I MIGHT VISIT YOUR WIFE AND KILL HER TOO.

SEE LUCAS. THIS IS WHAT FEAR FEELS LIKE.
ALICE

Robyn punched in Ross's number.

'Could you pay Mrs Clifford another visit?' she asked, when he picked up.

'And hello to you, too,' he replied.

'Don't mess about, Ross. This is urgent.' She read out the letters. 'I expect Mrs Clifford has photos of Alice. Can you email me copies of them? I need to study them. Paul and Lucas were after Zoe Cooper but she isn't Alice. My big problem is that I can't work out why Paul recognised the photograph of Claire, while Abigail, who has seen her regularly, didn't. If Claire was really Alice Forman, surely Abigail would have sussed her. I want to see if I can spot any similarities or anything that can prove beyond question that Claire Lewis is Alice Forman. Mulholland will blow her top if I come up with half-baked ideas. Although I kept it from Mulholland, I already messed up on the rabbit thing. I don't want to get this wrong as well.'

'I promised I'd visit Jane again, so I'll ring the care home and go over later.'

'Thanks, Ross. You're one in a million.'

'No need to flatter me, I said I'd go.'

Her phone vibrated. 'Got an incoming call. Thanks again.'

She took the new call and raised her eyebrows in surprise.

'Hello, Detective Inspector Carter? This is Claire Lewis. You left a message to call you. What is it about?'

'Thank you for calling me back, Miss Lewis. I need to talk to you in connection with a Lucas Matthews.'

'I can't say I know him.'

'I would still like to chat to you. It's rather important.'

Robyn heard the hesitation in her voice, 'I'm on an assignment in Scotland at the minute but I'm due to return on Saturday. Can we arrange a meeting then? I still have a few places to visit. I'm working on a feature about the beauty of Scotland. I've been all over the north of the country and into the Trossachs National Park. I'm currently near Inverness at Cromarty. It's a good area for dolphin watching. The Moray Firth bottlenose dolphins are quite renowned here. I've set up my camera equipment and hope to capture them today. It's a good day for photographing them – good visibility.'

Robyn wanted to speak to her sooner than that. She decided to try another tack.

'Have you heard from Abigail Thorne?'

'I haven't but there are some missed calls from her. I was going to ring her after I had spoken to you. I figured you were more important given you are the police.'

'I'm sorry to inform you that her daughter has been abducted.'

There was a sharp intake of breath. 'No,' she said after a moment. 'No, not Izzy. Oh my gosh. Oh poor Abby. No. She'll be distraught. Izzy's been kidnapped. When? Where?'

'Earlier today. She was snatched from her vehicle at the Meads car park.'

'What? That's not possible. How can that have happened? Abigail never lets Izzy out of her sight. Have you any leads? Is anyone searching for her?' She let out a long moan before continuing. 'I must come back and help look for her. I'm sorry, Detective Inspector Carter, but I'll have to ring off. I want to talk to Abby and then I need to return to Farnborough as soon as possible.'

'Miss Lewis, when you get back, please give me a call. I would like to talk to you in a more formal capacity.'

'Of course, although I don't know how much help I'll be. I'll telephone you as soon as I am near Farnborough. Or should I go directly to the police station?'

'Ring me and we'll arrange where to meet.'

'Certainly.' She sounded flustered. 'There's no news on Izzy?'

'Not yet. Sorry.'

'Okay. Bit early, I suppose. I'll call you.'

Robyn stared out of her car window, lips pressed together in concentration. It was difficult to tell if someone was lying over the phone and Claire's reaction had been as expected when learning her best friend's daughter had been abducted. Robyn could feel the frustration eating away at her. She was now no further with this case. She had been certain Claire was actually Alice but if Claire really was in Scotland, then who had abducted Izzy? She phoned PC Patel to confirm Claire Lewis's whereabouts. Claire had said she was in Cromarty but Robyn wanted more proof of that fact. They would start by using Claire's mobile number and check with the service provider. Then they should be able to find her location from the nearest cell tower. Robyn felt that Claire phoning her was all too convenient. She hoped she was right with her feelings. She couldn't afford to get it wrong. She was now searching for a murderer and a kidnapper, and a child's life was at stake.

CHAPTER FIFTY-NINE

NOW

Izzy is looking at me, unperturbed by the events as if being kidnapped is just another interesting experience. I'm not going to dope the poor kid with whisky or anything to keep her quiet. I already made her ill once and that was totally unintentional. I must have had some traces of ipecac on my fingers when I handled her food that day in the café. I was mortified when I heard she had become ill too. That hadn't been my intention. Luckily, she wasn't too harmed by it. No, I don't want to hurt the child. Not yet. I'll have to kill her, of course. There's no other way. How else can I totally annihilate Abigail's life?

Abigail. The name suits her better than Natasha. Natasha was all white face and heavy black eyeliner and moping about the house, mumbling at people and hiding in her room. Abigail is a lighter, more cheerful name. Although Abigail won't be feeling light or cheerful at the moment.

From the boot of my car I pull out a box of toys I have been collecting for Izzy. I read that babies need stimulation and get bored which is why they cry. I hope the toys will keep her occupied for a while until she gets tired and dozes off. I shove the box in the passenger footwell and put on a CD for babies. It's all sorts of strange music but it's supposed to calm their brainwaves. If all else fails, I have a comforter for her and earplugs for me so I don't have to put up with her screaming.

I strap Izzy's carrycot into the passenger seat so she is facing the back of the seat but can see me. She smiles at me, a big cheerful grin. She isn't even missing Abby. I blow a raspberry at her and tickle her feet and smile back.

'We're going on a journey, Izzy. Now, you be a good girl for me while I drive. Then, I have a few things I need to sort out with your mum.'

I drive out of the far exit of the Meads car park and head towards the motorway before I am struck by an idea. Abigail is somehow convinced Rachel Croft is involved with Lucas. I shall exploit that. It'll give me a chance to get clear away. Izzy burbles senseless noises and I beam at her.

'I'm going to take you to where I once lived,' I say. I'll deal with Rachel first and then head to the Farmhouse. I'm really looking forward to seeing the place again. This time it will be different.

CHAPTER SIXTY

'I'm sending the photos now,' said Ross. 'I can't see how they'll help. They're mostly of a little girl. It's impossible to see what she'd look like as an adult.'

'Send them anyway. I might uncover something.'

'There's a few of her with her mother. Do you want those too?'

'Yes, I'll look at those. I've got a job here for you where your skills will be really handy. I need someone to do a sweep of Abigail's house. If she's right about being watched and getting calls and someone knowing what she's up to, I bet she's been bugged. Can you get down here and check for me? I could ask the station for someone but I know you are the best when it comes to hidden cameras and what's on the market. Apparently, I'm supposed to tiptoe around the force down here and not be too demanding.'

'Sounds like Mulholland has put you on a restraining lead this time.'

'That's exactly how it feels.'

'No probs, I'm on my way.'

Robyn entered the police station in Wellington Street, Aldershot, and introduced herself. The sergeant on duty took her into a room where a man in his fifties, dressed in casual attire, gaunt-faced with a touch of grey stubble on his chin, was hovering over a uniformed officer, watching a television screen. The man looked up and extended a slim hand.

'Good afternoon, you must be DCI Corrance,' said Robyn. 'I'm DI Carter. You've been expecting me.'

'Ah yes. You're from Staffordshire. I hear it's all fields and villages with decent pubs and places to go walking up there. Not like down here. Took me over an hour to get into work this morning.'

'It's a little less congested, sir,' she said.

He nodded approvingly. 'I understand you have a case that might be linked to one of ours?'

'Yes, sir. Missing man, now deceased, called Lucas Matthews. It transpires he was Abigail Thorne's brother and her child, Isobel Thorne, was snatched at the Meads car park, Farnborough, earlier today.'

'Yes, Mrs Thorne believed he was behind the abduction but obviously he wasn't. We've got all our officers out on this one,' he said, his grey eyes narrowing. 'We'll catch the culprit.'

'I'm trying to see if there is any relevant connection between the two cases. I won't stomp over your turf.'

'We work as a team here. No room for mavericks.' He gave her a hard look. 'I've heard rumours you're a bit of a loner, Carter. Make sure you share your information. We're working flat out to solve this and get baby Thorne home safe and sound.'

She waited for a second before saying, 'Understood. Is there any chance I could go through the footage from the car park?'

The man tapped the uniformed policeman on the shoulder. 'PC Brendan Warrington is your man. He's been looking at this screen for over an hour and can't spot anyone suspicious near the white Range Rover Evoque. There's footage of the vehicle pulling up then the guy who nicks the handbag comes into view at' – he checked with the PC – 'thirteen-forty hours. He's spotted walking across the car park and then we lose him. Mrs Thorne is seen running towards the shops soon afterwards. We have checked all the cameras in the Meads and there is no one carrying a baby or toddler around that time. I doubt you'll spot anything we've missed but go ahead.'

His sarcastic tone was not lost on Robyn but she ignored it.

'Have you looked at camera footage from earlier than thirteen-forty hours?' Robyn asked.

'Yes, ma'am,' PC Warrington replied.

DCI Corrance made a noise of disgust and departed. 'I'll leave you with Warrington here.'

PC Warrington flicked through his jottings before speaking.

'Ignore the guv. He's in a bad mood. He was brought in from his day off. Yeah, we went back an hour in case there was anyone suspicious lurking about that area. It's a section of the car park that doesn't get used much. Most people park near the supermarket. A couple left a black Nissan Micra ten minutes before Abigail Thorne drew into a space next to a blue people-carrier. We ran footage to see what time the occupants of the people carrier arrived. It was seventy minutes beforehand and a woman vacated it with two children aged approximately between ten and twelve years old. Two middle-aged women crossed towards the Keep Fit Gym minutes before the arrival of the Range Rover. Apart from that and an elderly lady carrying shopping, seen crossing the park at thirteen-thirty-five hours, there's nothing of value and nobody else on the footage.'

'Can you wind it back to let me see the people you mention?'

'Sure. Hope you brought popcorn and drinks with you. It's a pretty dull film,' he joked.

Robyn smiled. He might seem to have an easy manner but the frown lines on his forehead and the nicotine stains on his fingers told a different story.

The footage was rewound and fast-forwarded. There was nothing extraordinary about the people she observed coming and going.

'We're still searching for the thief who stole Mrs Thorne's handbag, but so far, no luck. Our officers have been asking passers-by. He's vanished into thin air. We tracked down the owners of the cars stationed in the car park at the time of the kidnapping, and asked if they had witnessed the scene, but again, we drew a blank. Couldn't ask the elderly lady. She headed in the direction of the bus stop.'

Robyn watched the woman walk across the screen, heavy bags weighing her shoulders down. She wore a coat that was slightly too large for her and a brightly coloured headscarf. Robyn chewed on her lip. She studied the woman who walked by, unaware of the car and the drama playing out inside it, intent on reaching the bus stop.

'Could you rewind that bit and pause it?' she asked. PC Warrington obliged. Robyn squinted at the screen. The picture was too grainy to make out anything. She shook her head.

'I can't spot anything untoward. Is it okay if I set up here for a while?' she asked

'Sure, help yourself.'

'Thanks. It's lousy when you can't make progress in a case like this. You feel like time is pressing on you.'

'It's tough. What's worse, it's a little kid. A mere baby. I hate cases like this. I have two daughters of my own. I can't imagine what it would be like to go through this hell. The parents must be going spare. I have to go to front desk for a while. Shout out if you need anything.'

With a sad shake of his head, he left her to it. Robyn pulled out her laptop and downloaded all the photographs of Alice that Ross had emailed her. They were, as he had said, mostly pictures of a young girl with blonde hair and blue eyes. In some, she stood shyly with her hands behind her back, in others she sat on a large chair grinning happily. Robyn identified her father, Josh, a good-looking man with fair hair and a wide grin. She studied the first photo in which he was making a jigsaw puzzle with his daughter, both hunched over, the same concentration on their faces; the next showed the pair at a zoo by the monkey enclosure where they posed and made funny faces. There was one of Alice sitting on his knee, arm around his neck. It was clear from the pictures that they were close. There was Alice on her first bike, Josh proudly watching as she rode away. There were some of Alice with older people – Jane Clifford and her husband – eating sticks of rock by the seaside. There weren't many of Christina. Given Jane Clifford had not liked her daughter-in-law, this was not a surprise.

Robyn paced around the office. Alice had seemed so content. What reason could she have for exacting revenge on the Matthews? She would have to ask Abigail. She returned to the photographs and scrolled through some more, stopping at a picture of Josh with his arms around a blonde woman – Christina – wearing tight white jeans and pouting at the camera like a professional model on a catwalk, Alice in front of them, wearing ribbons in her long plaited hair and a pretty yellow dress with a wide skirt, clutching a doll. Suddenly time stood still. It wasn't a doll. Robyn zoomed into the picture. It was a toy rabbit – one that looked identical to the rabbit beside Christina's body. The rabbit had belonged to Alice. The deceased were all linked by these rabbits.

Robyn examined all the pictures with care, but try as she might, she could not see any connection to the pretty child in the photographs and the photograph she had of Claire Lewis. The eyes were a different colour and so was the hair. Robyn examined the noses of both of them but again could not see any similarity. The child's snub nose could easily have transformed into Claire's adult nose with the stud in the side, or not. She gave a sigh of frustration and turned off the laptop before reading through what she'd written. It was an hour later when the door opened and the friendly face of Ross appeared.

'I made good time. Gagging for tea and biscuits though. I missed lunch thanks to searching for photographs and driving miles for a demanding DI who keeps getting these hunches.'

'Am I glad to see you. I keep going around in circles. I feel Claire is somehow involved and then I learn she's been in Scotland all week and is unlikely to have murdered Lucas Matthews. I also thought she might be involved in the kidnapping of Isobel Thorne but, again, she isn't here so she can't have snatched her. And, to cap it all, I can't see any similarities between her and Alice. Yet something doesn't seem right. I've got the team trying to locate her whereabouts in Scotland and until they do, I'm going to keep an open mind.'

She fired up the laptop and pointed at the photos set up on it. 'I think I've hit upon Christina's rabbit. Looks like it might have belonged to Alice at one stage, not that this helps in any way.' She tilted back on her chair, hands behind her head.

'I wonder if I'm still up to this, Ross. What if I've lost my instinct? I'm not certain I should stick at this career. I used to be able to follow my gut and be correct. Maybe losing Davies has changed me.'

Ross stood behind her and stared at the pictures on her screen. He took a while to reply.

'You have great instincts. Don't ever give up on yourself. Those of us who know you best haven't, so don't you.'

She swivelled around to meet his eye and sat up. 'Thanks. Come on. Let me take you to the Thorne's house. You can see if you can turn up any tracking devices or cameras. What you don't know about the latest surveillance equipment isn't worth knowing.'

CHAPTER SIXTY-ONE

NOW

Izzy was amazing. I didn't need many toys for her. She spent most of the time pulling at her salmon-pink socks and babbling merrily. I passed her a large plastic highchair toy in the shape of a bee with little rattles and beads and things on it. She was fascinated and played with it for ages. Every time I looked over at her and spoke to her, she looked at me with adoring eyes, like she was my baby, and grinned a happy smile back at me.

Eventually, she dozed off. Her long dark eyelashes curled away from her pale skin and she slept contentedly, holding onto the brand new Mr Big Ears rabbit I had given her. Mr Big Ears the Third looked happy too.

'Nearly at the end,' says my father. I looked at Mr Big Ears, his large soft ears falling over his knowing eyes.

'It's been such a long time but I did what you told me to, Dad. I changed my appearance. I evolved into another person and I concealed my hate and cunning.' He nods in approval. 'And, I waited just as you advised me to,' I tell him. 'I was patient and very clever.'

'Oh yes,' he replies. 'You've been very clever, my dear daughter. I'm so proud of you.'

CHAPTER SIXTY-TWO

'Hi, boss. Can't talk for long. Mulholland is breathing down my neck but I learned something about Natasha Matthews that might be of interest to you. I was searching one of the databases on the PNC and I turned up a Natasha Matthews in 1999. Her name appeared on a clinic register in the south of the UK.' Anna Shamash spoke in hushed tones.

'Why is that interesting?'

'It was an abortion clinic.'

'She'd have only been about twelve years old. She'd barely have started puberty,' replied a shocked Robyn. 'Are you certain it's her?'

'I am. I couldn't find any other information on the PNC databases,' Anna's voice dropped even lower. 'Got to go. The station's all worked up and ready for tonight's sting. It's pretty tense here. I'm sending you the link.'

'Hope it goes well. Thanks for that information.' Robyn mulled over what she had just learned. It seemed implausible that Natasha, now known as Abigail, would have fallen pregnant at such an early age. Robyn sensed the familiar prickling she got when she was close to solving a case. Her phone buzzed.

'You've got that look on your face,' said Ross, sat in the Polo's passenger seat with a chocolate bar in his hand.

'What look?'

'The one that says you are inches away from sussing out what's going on.'

'No. Not quite got it. I keep thinking I'm almost there and then it escapes me again. This case is testing my instinct and I have been wrong over a couple of things.'

They pulled up beside the stone owl. Robyn quickly read the email before getting out of the car. The front door opened. Jackson Thorne looked even more haggard than when she had left him.

'I brought an associate to check out your home. I think there might be something in what Abigail has been saying. Ross here is an expert in surveillance equipment. If your house has been bugged in any way, he'll find out.'

'Do whatever you need to.'

He turned and climbed the stairs.

'He's terribly upset,' said Abigail from the lounge. 'He's had to deal with more than he should ever have had to. He's not only lost Izzy but he's learned he never really knew his wife.'

Abigail was still clutching the rag dog but her tears had stopped. She seemed calmer. 'I should have told him years ago. Keeping it a secret caused more damage. We'd have worked through it if only I had been brave enough to tell him.' Her attitude suddenly changed as she became aware of Ross. 'Why are you here? Have you heard anything about Izzy?'

'Ross is here to search for hidden cameras and the like, and to confirm your suspicions – that you were being watched. We may be able to trace them back to the person who has Izzy.'

'How can you find them?'

'There are quite a few ways,' said Ross, unpacking a bag he carried in with him. 'One low-tech method of finding hidden cameras is to listen. Some motion-sensitive cameras make a soft click or buzz as they turn on when someone walks by. In a noisy, everyday environment, you definitely won't be able to hear them, but if you can turn off lights, radios, televisions and other sources of sound, you may be able to hear a camera activate.' He dropped to his knees, still talking. 'You can find a hidden lens using a torch. You turn off the lights and go slowly, and examine suspicious places from multiple angles. If you see glints of light where there shouldn't be – areas where there are no mirrors, glass or other reflective surfaces – you may have come across a camera. However, I am going to use this,' he announced, extracting a small black device. 'It's a professional-quality hidden-camera detector. This one uses a method much like a torch or the light on a smartphone to find glints from a lens.'

He began searching the room, lifting the device to his eye and sweeping the room, slowly and methodically.

'Nothing here. I'll move to the kitchen.'

Once he had left the room, Abigail slumped onto a chair.

'I can't believe I've allowed this to happen. I had the power to prevent it. I only had to tell Jackson what happened and none of this would have taken place.'

'Abigail, are you talking about what happened to Alice? I know Lucas attacked her and she stabbed him in the eye.'

'Alice? You're asking about Alice. He isn't upset about Alice.'

Her face puckered angrily, then, just as suddenly, changed. She shook her head sadly.

'I also know about the abortion you had, Abigail.'

Abigail appeared to shrink in front of her. She chewed on her bottom lip. Finally she spoke. 'No one believed me. It wasn't what you may think. However, I was to blame for what happened that night to Alice. Sit down and I'll tell you everything.'

* * *

An hour later, Ross laid out his findings on the kitchen table in front of Abigail and Jackson. He had uncovered a camera in the heat alarm in the kitchen. He pointed at the white box.

'These are quite common. You can pick them up easily online. This one is a sophisticated model and has a hidden HD Wi-Fi camera that can transmit and record video to allow the person to watch using an application on their smartphone or computer from anywhere in the world.'

Abigail stared at the innocuous heat alarm. 'It's identical to the smoke alarms we have throughout the house.'

'They are very convincing. Lots of people buy them so they can keep an eye on their property when they are abroad and make sure it is safe, but, like many things these days, there are people who purchase them for darker purposes. I have no idea how long the person has been watching you but it was unlikely you'd have discovered it unless you'd tried to test it out. I haven't located any other fake ones in the house and I've done a complete sweep of the property. I haven't uncovered any other surveillance equipment. However, the baby monitors are another story.' He picked up the audio unit and unscrewed the base and tipped out a small device that he held between his finger and thumb.

'It's a transmitting device.'

Abigail gasped. 'The muffled whispers. It was coming from the baby monitor itself. I thought I was going crazy hearing voices. I assumed they were in my head.'

'More likely from this. Somebody has been playing mind games with you, Mrs Thorne.'

'See, Jackson, I wasn't fabricating any of this,' she said, despairingly. 'I should have been more forceful and had someone check out the place before now. If only…' The words hung in the air.

Robyn spoke before the silence became too heavy to bear. 'We'll take them with us and see if we can trace the purchaser. It's a long shot but any shot is worth taking at the moment. The team back at the station is working on every possible lead. What happened to the support officer that they sent here?'

Jackson looked up, his brow creased. 'We sent her away. We had things we needed to talk about, and besides, I don't want any more strangers hanging about. We're managing on our own. We've been asked to do an appeal on television if they can't find her soon,' he added. 'Makes it seem so real. We have to beg a nutcase to bring our baby back. I don't know if I can. I want to kill the person who has her, not plead with them.'

'I'll do it,' said Abigail. 'I should do it.'

'You have time to consider the TV option. You need to stay strong and stick together,' said Robyn, wondering if the couple – who stood apart from each other at either end of the table and could hardly look each other in the eye – would make it after this ordeal.

CHAPTER SIXTY-THREE

The police station was quiet but a small team was still in place. Robyn and Ross had spent some time trying to work out where the cameras they had uncovered had been purchased. There were many websites that dealt with these devices and, by midnight, Robyn had given up.

'It's another dead end.'

'At least we know Abigail was right. Someone was spying on her – most likely the same person who has Izzy.' Ross turned over the fake heat alarm he had discovered.

'You can find this stuff almost anywhere online these days. Can you believe there is so much of it available? And some of it is pretty convincing. I might have to update my own supply.'

'You get anywhere with the tracker from her car?'

'It's one of the smallest devices on the market and one of the simplest to set up and use. It has a magnetic base so it can be attached simply to a vehicle within seconds without tools. It's a GPS tracker so the punter can find the vehicle using a smartphone, PC or tablet. The bad news is you can buy these on any number of sites, including eBay and Amazon, and it comes with a pre-paid sim card so it will be impossible to identify the purchaser.'

'This is proving fruitless,' said Robyn. 'I don't know what I hoped for but I expected more than this. So basically, the perp can be using an app or device to watch Abigail and track her movements, but unless we get hold of his or her phone or computer, we won't be able to find that out.'

'Pretty much,' Ross replied.

Just when she was ready to call it a day, her phone rang. Mitz Patel sounded sleepy.

'I've just got back from the sting operation so I couldn't call you earlier. Anna and I have been trying to locate Claire Lewis. No joy with getting a fix on her mobile but we've still had a result. We phoned around all the accommodation in that area to see if she had checked in. PC Fowler has left a message to say Mr Jack Bond has called from Cromarty to confirm that Claire Lewis booked one of his cottages – Squirrel Lodge – and arrived Tuesday evening. The owner saw her car outside the cottage yesterday afternoon.'

Robyn could barely keep the disappointment out of her voice. 'That's not what I wanted to hear. Have you got Bond's number? I'll follow it up to make sure it is her.'

PC Patel read out the number.

'Thanks for this, Mitz.'

'No problem. I was too wired to go home anyway.'

They ended the call. Robyn looked across at her cousin, still studying the devices.

'Go grab some sleep. Hand these in at the front office on your way out and see if the people here have more joy.' Robyn yawned.

Ross gave her a look. He knew she would keep gnawing at the problem all night. 'Don't overdo it. Get some sleep too. You've still got Claire Lewis to interview. That might throw up something. What time is she due back?'

'When she spoke to me, she was near Inverness, watching for the Moray Firth dolphins. It would take her at least nine and half hours to get here from Inverness, so hopefully she'll be back sometime tomorrow. That is, if she doesn't stop for any sleep. I'll call her first thing and find out where she is. She's close to Abigail and Zoe so she might know something that will help us.' She rubbed her eyes and mused, 'Abigail doesn't have many friends, does she? She only really knows Zoe and Claire. You'd think she'd know more people, new mums, for example. There are loads of mums and toddlers groups. She seems a bit of a lone wolf.'

Ross threw her a thoughtful look. 'Dolphins. Nice. Has Claire been photographing them all week?'

'She's been all over the north of Scotland and the Trossachs National Park. I expect she's photographing all sorts of wildlife.'

'I might take Jeanette to Scotland for a holiday. She likes dolphins. She'd love to see them in the wild. Maybe we could all go. You could invite Amélie.'

Robyn gave a small smile. 'That's a lovely idea but I think she has a family to do all that sort of thing with.'

'You can never have too large a family,' replied Ross. 'I'm done now. Tomorrow is another day.'

After he left, Robyn reflected on his words. Tomorrow was another day. Probably another angst-riddled day for the Thornes. She had to find out who was responsible for killing Lucas and Paul Matthews, because no matter how many dead ends she came up against, she still believed the murders and the disappearance of Izzy were connected.

From what Abigail had told her earlier, Alice had reason to hate the Matthews. But so did Abigail. In fact, Abigail had more reason. Yet Robyn was convinced Alice had to be behind the murders. But if Alice was not Zoe Cooper and she was not Claire Lewis then who on earth was she?

* * *

On the following morning the station in Aldershot was buzzing with activity. There had been a sighting of the man who attempted to steal Abigail's handbag and officers had been sent to arrest him.

'It's hopeful,' said PC Warrington as he pushed past her, a pile of leaflets about the missing baby in his hand. 'We're distributing these and the local news is doing a reconstruction. We're inviting the Thornes to do an appeal too and plead for Isobel's return.'

Robyn could imagine the trauma of sitting in front of a camera crew, begging for her child to be returned. Poor Abigail. It would be a horrendous ordeal. There was a slim chance someone who had Izzy would see the appeal and return her, but more likely Jackson and Abigail Thorne would bare their heartache and misery in front of thousands of people on national television, only to be met with suspicion and more hoax calls.

Robyn dropped into a chair and closed her eyes. Davies would have worked out what was going on. He was one of the brightest men she had ever met. His mind was sharp and permanently active. If ever she was stuck on a crossword clue, she would ask him and he would answer immediately. He was brilliant at cryptic clues. Since his death she hadn't picked up a crossword.

She allowed her mind to trawl through the recent conversations she'd had, trying to find one fragment that would help her. Izzy's disappearance was part of some game plan. Alice was trying to destroy Abigail's life and so far had destabilised her marriage, successfully alienated some of her friends and caused her extreme stress. Izzy being snatched was part of this. Alice had allowed her grudge against the Matthews to grow and grow and now was out of control. There was no telling what she would do next.

Robyn's mind churned around the facts. Someone was Alice. It wasn't Zoe because she had an alibi for the night Lucas was spotted leaving the hotel, having been in London all week. She couldn't have murdered Lucas Matthews.

To her knowledge, Claire didn't have an alibi for the night Lucas was last seen alive. She had gone home to check on a burglar alarm and gone to bed. She might have returned to the hotel and left with Lucas. Yet Claire couldn't possibly have abducted Izzy from the car park in Farnborough if she was trundling around Scotland, photographing animals. She couldn't be in two places at once. Robyn picked up her mobile and called Jack Bond, the owner of Squirrel Lodge. He answered immediately and his voice boomed in reply to her question.

'Aye, she booked last month. Luckily Squirrel Lodge was vacant. All our cottages are full next week, so it was a good job she didn't call then.'

'Have you met Miss Lewis?'

'I handed her the keys to the house when she arrived. I offered to show her how everything worked, but she was tired after the drive and wanted to get some sleep. I've not seen anything of her since. Her car was there yesterday, as I told the police officer.'

'Is her car at the lodge now?'

'I'm not sure. I'd have to drive over. I live twenty minutes away.'

'Could you please check for me?'

He hesitated before answering. She could imagine the puzzlement on his face. 'Okay. I suppose so.'

'I'd be very grateful, Mr Bond.'

Robyn hung up and juggled with the problem, turning it this way and that in her mind until she came up with a possible solution. She had to face up to the fact that when Izzy was abducted, Claire was in Scotland. She could not have taken the baby. She closed her eyes again. Perhaps there was one possibility. If Claire had someone assisting her then that would make it feasible. She needn't be in two places at once. She could have had someone take Izzy while she was hundreds of miles away. Robyn sat back, satisfied with her deduction. She could imagine Davies silently applauding her.

Abigail had believed that Lucas and Rachel Croft were partners in some way. Rachel wasn't working with Lucas but she might be with someone else, maybe even Claire, now miles away, offering Claire the perfect alibi. Robyn made for the front office where PC Warrington was talking to someone on the phone. He looked up and covered the mouthpiece with a hand. 'Can I help?' he said.

'You spoke to Rachel Croft about Isobel Thorne. Abigail was certain Rachel had something to do with the kidnapping.'

'Officers were sent to her home as soon as Abigail Thorne told us she believed the woman to be working in conjunction with Lucas Matthews. She was out. Once we heard Matthews was dead, we didn't pursue that line of enquiry. Seemed little point.'

'I'd like to interview her. She might know something.'

Brendan Warrington shrugged. 'Okay. Want me to tell the guv?'

'It's okay, I'll let him know.' She located the DCI's office and rapped on the door.

Corrance was staring at his computer, his lip curled.

'Some days I hate my job,' he grumbled. 'Ever since we asked around the shopping centre we've been getting hoax calls from people claiming to have spotted the child. Even had one from Spain and someone who sent a photo of a kid who's about three years old. It's impossible to look into all the claims. It'll be worse if the Thornes make a plea on television. We get some right crazies phoning in. Now someone has posted about it online and #Little-GirlLost is trending on Twitter with hundreds of people posting photographs of babies and children, none of them relevant to this case.' He pointed to the latest tweet thread that claimed Abigail was a lousy mother and had deliberately left her baby. 'Why do people do that sort of thing? This isn't some sort of game we're playing.'

'Beyond me, sir. Social media has its place but it's sometimes abused. I'd like to interview Rachel Croft. Her name came up earlier and I want to see if she knows anything.'

'Knock yourself out,' he replied. 'I don't think it'll be productive but go ahead anyway.'

Robyn thanked him. He grunted something and continued looking at his computer screen. Robyn decided she had outstayed her welcome and left him to it.

CHAPTER SIXTY-FOUR

Rachel's home was a first floor, two-bedroomed maisonette off Reading Road in the heart of Farnborough. It was situated in a bland brick building with communal gardens. Robyn pulled into the space reserved for the property and, bounding up the stairs, hammered on Rachel's door. There was no reply, much as there had been no response to the phone call Robyn had made to her mobile while driving. Like Claire Lewis, Rachel Croft was out of contact.

Robyn knocked again, more loudly. Nothing.

'She must be out. Her car isn't here. According to records it's a dark red Toyota Yaris hybrid,' said Ross.

Robyn kicked the door in frustration and turned to join Ross who was descending the stairs. Then she paused. She could hear a muffled thud coming from inside. It happened again and again.

'Ross, there's someone in there.' She knocked once more and was rewarded with another faint noise in response. There was definitely someone in the place.

'Not a radio?' asked Ross.

'I don't think so. We need to gain entry.'

'We don't have a warrant to enter and I needn't remind you it is illegal to enter a property without the owner's permission, do I?'

'No, but we have reasonable grounds to believe someone has been placed in danger.' She shouted at the door. 'We're coming in, is that okay?' There was yet another noise in response.

'I'll take that as a yes, then,' she said, and adopting a kickboxing stance she kicked out with her right leg, the heel of her boot catching the door accurately near the doorframe. It cracked and gave way.

'Remind me never to get into a fight with you,' said Ross. 'Want me to finish it off?'

'Be my guest,' she replied and moved away, allowing Ross to bull charge the weakened door and smash it open.

They entered the kitchen and hastened to the sound of the thumping, opening the door to a bedroom. Rachel was lying on the floor on the other side of the door, her hands and feet bound by cable ties, her mouth covered by duct tape. She was exhausted and semi-conscious, blood trickling from her head. Grabbing a knife from the kitchen, Robyn sawed at the ties and released Rachel's hands.

'This is going to be sore but only for a minute,' she advised as she prepared to rip the tape from Rachel's face. 'You okay?'

The woman nodded and let out a noise – half howl and half squeal like a frightened pig – as Robyn tugged and pulled it away in one swift movement. Rachel's lips were dry and cracked.

She let out a croaky groan and rubbed her tender wrists. Her hands shook with shock. She rasped, 'Thank you.'

Ross poured her a glass of water and offered it to her. She drank greedily. They lifted her onto the bed and cut her feet free. Ross checked her head wound. It was still bleeding and required attention.

'I'll call an ambulance,' he whispered. Robyn nodded an affirmation then explained to Rachel who they were. 'Take your time. When you feel ready, tell me what happened.' Rachel tried to rub some feeling back into her wrists and ankles before attempting to stand. Robyn held onto her.

'I need to move,' croaked Rachel. Robyn led the trembling woman into the kitchen and sat her down at a modern round oak table with metal legs that had been crafted to look artistic but instead looked cheap. The kitchen had little on show other than basic necessities. It was pretty barren and Robyn suspected Rachel lacked the finances to make it more homely. She filled the kettle with water and prepared a mug from the mug tree with tea from gaudy canisters purchased at a supermarket. Ross checked out the bedroom, allowing Robyn time with Rachel. It was obvious from the upturned stool and bedside table, and from the state of the bedcovers on the floor, that Rachel had struggled to manoeuvre herself from the bed and onto the floor, then shuffled her body close enough to the door to kick it with her feet to attract attention. She must have been exhausted by her efforts.

With Robyn in the kitchen and a cup of tea in her hands, Rachel regained control of her emotions and spoke. 'I had just finished giving a neighbour a treatment. I'm learning how to do crystal therapy and healing. She is one of my guinea pigs. I'd packed up my crystals and was getting ready to meet Abigail Thorne. She's a friend. I was meeting her at five o'clock at the playing fields and I was running late. I have a gift for her – a tiger's-eye crystal.' She pointed at a necklace consisting of a cheap metal chain and a beautiful crystal with bands of yellow-gold running through it.

'It's a powerful stone that aids harmony and balance, and helps release fear and anxiety.' Rachel was rambling. Robyn suspected it was to distract her from facing up to what had happened to her. She listened patiently.

'Traditionally it was carried as an amulet against curses or ill wishing, and is known to give courage, self-confidence and strength of will,' she continued. 'I thought it would help Abby. I can tell people and dark forces are draining her. She needs assistance.' Rachel put a hand against her head and pulled it away quickly, examining the sticky mess of drying blood.

'It's okay. I don't think it's too serious but you'll have to get checked out. Ross has already phoned for an ambulance.'

Rachel gave her a dazed look. 'No thanks. I think I'm okay. I must have hit it when I fell. I'll go and see the doctor later.'

'You've had a terrible shock and you need to be looked over. Your wrists and feet are in need of treatment too.'

Rachel looked down at her raw ankles, impervious for the moment to the discomfort.

Robyn asked again, 'Tell me what happened, Rachel. We need to find out who did this to you.'

'I was getting ready to go out to meet Abby, when I heard someone knocking at my front door. I opened it and a lunatic wearing a mask launched at me. I didn't have time to scream. They pushed me into this room and punched me in the stomach. It winded me completely. I doubled up with pain. I remember wondering why they were doing this, then I got hit again and I fell on the floor. The person laughed. They actually laughed at me. I was so frightened. I thought they were going to kill me. I kept still and tried not to anger them and thought I'd got away with it while they stomped about the kitchen muttering really quietly. I couldn't hear what they were saying but it was a woman's voice. That surprised me. I heard her speak to someone. I'm sure she said "dad" at one point. I strained to hear if there was another person but there didn't seem to be anyone. Then it dawned on me who the person was. I was about to speak to her but she hit me on my head with something very heavy and I blacked out. When I came to, I was on the bed. I couldn't move for those ties. They really cut into me when I moved. She had slapped tape all over my mouth as you saw. I didn't know what to do so I performed my calming exercises and then when I had some energy, I tried kicking the bedside table and door with my feet but no one heard me.' She licked her lips, her brow creased in concentration.

'I think someone came to the door, maybe yesterday afternoon. I heard a rapping and I tried to call out but it was hopeless. I kicked the table again and it fell over but the person left. I fell on the floor and kicked the dressing table but nothing happened. No one returned. I got tired and felt so sick. I kept hoping my neighbours downstairs would hear the noise and come and investigate. I tried to stay calm and kept saying my mantra over and over. I got so weak and tired, I dozed off a couple of times and when I woke it was pitch dark so I tried again but nothing. I was beginning to think no one would ever find me. I wished Abigail would wonder why I hadn't met her and come and see if I was all right.' She began shaking again. Shock of what had happened was setting in. Robyn hoped the ambulance would turn up soon. The woman looked grey and ill. Being trussed up all evening and night had weakened her. She took a sip of tea, her cracked sore lips making her wince.

When you knocked on the door I tried to get you to hear me. I kicked and kicked at the door. Thank you for rescuing me. I don't know how long I'd have been left here alone.'

She shivered at the thought.

'I know you haven't had a chance to look but do you think they've stolen anything?' said Robyn.

Rachel barked a laugh. 'There's nothing of value to take inside. I rent the place and it came with the furniture, such as it is. It's certainly seen better days. I only own some clothes, books, my iPod, which is in there on the table, and some personal stuff that wouldn't interest anyone. There's nothing to steal. I haven't even got a decent television.' She looked about the kitchen and shook her head. 'Can't see that anything is out of place. I only have five pounds in my purse. I doubt they robbed me for that. I'm still waiting for my divorce settlement and then I'm getting out of here. It's miserable. It's like being a student in digs all over again.'

She stood on shaky legs and, clinging to the table, made tentative steps to the kitchen window. She looked outside and breathed deeply, eyes closed. 'My car has gone. She stole my car. The utter bitch.' She turned slowly.

'I'm certain I know who attacked me. There were several giveaways but it was the shoes. I recognised the shoes. I'd seen them before quite recently. They were Ted Baker purple floral-print trainers. Unusual and expensive. The last time I saw a pair like that was in the café in town. Claire Lewis owns a pair. My attacker was a so-called friend. She is responsible for this.'

'We believe Claire Lewis is in Scotland. It can't have been her.'

Rachel shook her head vehemently. 'It was definitely Claire Lewis. I know it was. Her mask slipped when she kicked me with those shoes. I caught a glimpse of her face. Without doubt it was Claire Lewis.'

Robyn threw a look at Ross who stood propped against the kitchen counter.

Rachel was an observant woman. She might have seen or heard more than she realised.

'Can I ask you to try and think if there is anything you might have missed? Did she say anything to you while you were half conscious? Were there any other unusual noises?'

There was a silence during which Rachel shook her head from side to side in anxiety then suddenly opened her eyes wide. 'This might not be relevant,' she said, 'but I think I heard a baby crying when I was on the floor. I was incredibly scared and dazed, but the more I think about it, the more I'm sure I heard a child crying outside. There are no children here in the flats. It's only couples and elderly folk.'

Ross spotted an ambulance arriving and excused himself.

Rachel looked at Robyn with earnest eyes. 'Believe me, please. I am certain Claire Lewis attacked me and for some reason had a child with her.'

'I'll run a check on your car and see if we can locate it. I'll make sure to let you know. Now, the ambulance crew is going to look after you. If you think of anything else at all, call me.'

Rachel reached into a pot of crystals and handed one to Robyn. 'Thank you for saving me. Take this. It's a chrysoprase crystal, an empowering crystal that helps to soothe emotional wounds and strengthen the heart. This crystal will not only help you to combat heartbreak, but it is also great for breaking up any negativity, and bringing hope into difficult situations. Chrysoprase is described as a good friend helping you through experiences of loss.'

Robyn didn't know how to respond. How could the woman have any idea she had lost someone close? Rachel answered her unspoken question.

'I see auras. Your astral aura is misshapen and scarred. It is green, the colour linked to the heart, so I know you are suffering a loss, a bereavement or a break-up. Take the crystal. It will help you.'

Dumbfounded, Robyn took the crystal.

'Her aura is a murky yellow, blended with murky green, and it indicates resentment and jealousy. Claire Lewis is not a nice person. I hope you find her before she does something really dreadful.'

CHAPTER SIXTY-FIVE

NOW

Old hippy Rachel looked like she was going to have a heart attack when she opened her door and saw me waiting with my mask on. Her face went a funny colour of puce and she looked like she was going to scream so I walloped her hard in the solar plexus and she went down like a sack of potatoes.

I dragged her into the kitchen to start with, thinking I might handcuff her to a radiator or somewhere but it was virtually empty of furniture or anything suitable to keep her restrained. I wonder if she's into that feng shui. There was only a weird table with metal legs and a few stools around it. I picked a stool up but it was feather light, so no good for my purpose.

I tried the rest of the place but it was equally unsuitable so in the end I settled for rope, cable ties and duct tape.

Rachel began to groan so I tied her up and plastered enough tape on her mouth to keep her quiet. It gave me particular pleasure to tape up her mouth. She's a most irritating creature and I detest the way she looks at me sometimes as if she sees something distasteful in me. When we last met at the coffee house I spent some of the time fantasising about pouring boiling coffee down her throat so I wouldn't have to listen to her whiny voice. At least now I get to shut her up for a while. Long enough for me to get away.

I laugh at the fact that Abby thinks Rachel is involved with Lucas in this. She's let her imagination really run away with her this time.

Rachel is far too goody-goody for that sort of behaviour. Her bedroom stinks of that oil new age people love so much and she's got crystals hanging from a mirror propped up on a dressing table. There's some strange thing over her bed. I think it's a dreamcatcher. I've heard about them. Now that's one thing I would hate to have. I wouldn't want to catch any of my dreams – they are far too horrible.

I leave Rachel none the wiser as to why she's been attacked. I thought about making it look like a robbery but there is nothing I can break, steal or rob, so I leave empty-handed apart from the key to her car. Izzy is sobbing in my car when I return. I cheer her up by jangling Rachel's car keys at her. She's delighted we are going to change vehicle.

A fizzing sensation has begun in the pit of my stomach. I am getting so close to completing my mission. My father is equally excited. He whispers a quiet 'bravo' as we leave Reading Road and we both hum along to the radio as we prepare to meet Natasha Matthews for the last time.

* * *

The house is still as imposing as it was the day Mum and I arrived. I hated it before I set foot in the place. Mum was all giggly and happy and full of excitement. 'It's a new beginning,' she said as she unloaded the suitcases from the taxi. Paul came rushing out to greet us, happiness bubbling from every pore in his skin.

'You're earlier than I expected,' he said, kissing Mum on the lips and holding her to him. He then noticed me. 'Hello, Alice, welcome to your new home. I'm sure you'll love it here.'

I glowered at him and I could hear Mr Big Ears sneer from under my arm. I was never going to call this place home. It would never be my home.

I use the key I have had for many years. I stole Geraldine Marsh's key. I literally bumped into her in the village and removed it from her coat pocket as I brushed past her. She never suspected a thing and

I'm sure Paul Matthews never doubted it was lost by accident. There will be no cleaner or visitors viewing the house. I have thought of everything. I phoned the estate agent last week and claimed I was a lawyer, Miss Susannah Harrison, representing Natasha Matthews, who was challenging Paul Matthews' will, and I requested they withdrew the property until the estate was settled.

I didn't need to phone Geraldine and tell her her services were no longer required. I dealt with her when she almost discovered me at the house. One steep staircase, one frightened old lady and one hefty push. That solved that issue. She might have recognised me from the village in her dying moments but I'll never know.

There is no challenge to the will, of course. I'm going to destroy the house and its memories. I shall burn it down along with Natasha when she arrives. I transported some cans of petrol out here two days ago and I shall soak the place after I've had a chat to the woman who was going to be my stepsister.

I use the downstairs cloakroom to take off my glasses with their clear lenses that have been part of my disguise the last few years, and remove my contact lenses. The brown eyes and spectacles and all the piercings seem to have fooled Natasha. It's good to dispose of them at last. She has never once suspected who I really am. She'll know soon enough.

I check over the stun gun I brought from the car and consider employing it on her. I used it on Lucas. I zapped him quite a few times until he begged me to stop. I didn't though. I held the stun gun against his chest and held it there while he jigged about like a dancing marionette, his face contorted in agony until he dropped, like someone had cut his strings. His heart gave out. Pity. I had hoped to cut his balls off while he was alive. Still, I put them where they belonged. I had to kill your depraved brother, Natasha. It was inevitable. He persisted in ruining young girl's lives. He abused those he taught too. He was an evil man who should have been stopped years ago. I was too young then to stand up for myself, but now, now I have taken charge. He deserved to die. I wish it had been a more horrible death.

I'm not sorry about your father's 'accident' either. He deserved it. He shouldn't have booted my mum and me out. He was so concerned that the demonic girl he had brought under his roof was going to harm his precious boy, he didn't think about what he was doing. He should have been more caring.

I walk through the hall, looking in at each reception room. Paul has changed nothing in the house. It is almost as I remember it. It even smells the same. I amble up the stairs to Natasha's old bedroom. It looks the same as it did all those years ago. I don't go into Lucas's room but I am sure it has been left too. A shrine to two ungrateful, cruel children. You should have let me stay, Paul. You turfed out the wrong person. I refrain from spitting at Lucas's door.

Paul was off the wall too. Fancy not redecorating or getting in new furniture in all these years. The only thing he seems to have done is put locks on the doors. If only he'd done that beforehand.

I return downstairs to fetch Izzy. I fed her earlier and she gurgles when she sees me coming back. It's odd but it feels like she's my daughter at the moment. I pick her up and she crows in delight. She might like to see my old room, and Mr Big Ears wants to read her a story. There's plenty of time left before I raze the place to the ground.

CHAPTER SIXTY-SIX

Robyn dialled Claire's number. Claire picked up after three rings.

'Hello, Detective Inspector Carter,' she said politely.

'Claire, where are you?'

'I'm on my way back from Scotland, as I told you,' she replied.

'I know you're not. We've spoken to the owner of Squirrel Lodge. He has confirmed that a woman called Janet Foxton is staying there. She said you offered her a free holiday in the cottage. And then there's Rachel Croft. She saw you. She told us you attacked her and she heard Izzy crying. The game's up, Claire.'

There was a silence during which Robyn felt her heart palpitate.

'Have you got Izzy with you at the moment?' she asked evenly.

'Don't be ridiculous. Of course I haven't. I'm just north of Newcastle. I should be with you by teatime. I'll make sure I come and visit you before I go and see Abby.'

'Claire, you can stop pretending now. We know the licence plate number of the car you are driving and we can track you using automatic number-plate recognition. You haven't passed any of the ANPR points along the A9 or A1 to Newcastle upon Tyne so you are not where you say you are. I have officers hunting you down. We are aware you're driving Rachel's car and I can assure you that we will not be long in discovering your actual whereabouts and deploying a team to apprehend you. Please return here before that happens. Bring the child with you. You don't want to make her stressed and upset. She's only a baby. Hand her back, Claire. She needs her mother.'

Claire spluttered. 'I don't have Izzy. Go ahead. Track my car. I have nothing to hide. I'm not the guilty party here, Detective. Maybe you should find out exactly what Abigail is hiding.'

'What do you mean, Claire?'

The connection was severed. Robyn redialled but the line was now dead. Claire had turned off her mobile and probably removed the battery.

'Did you get a location?' she asked PC Warrington.

He shook his head. 'She cut off before we pinpointed it. Sorry.'

Robyn thumped the desk with the palm of her hand. Ross stood back against the door, arms folded, his face impassive. The other three occupants of the room kept their heads down. DCI Corrance was getting increasingly frustrated by the slow progress. He suddenly stood up and started pacing around the room, barking instructions at them all. The tension between him and Robyn was palpable.

Robyn balled her fist and banged it against her head lightly. She was running out of time.

'So what now? Any more bright ideas, Carter?' asked DCI Corrance.

'I'm thinking, sir,' she said, trying to maintain a professional attitude in spite of wanting to yell at him.

There was a knock on the door. The desk sergeant appeared. 'Excuse me, guv. We pulled Thomas Keeper of no fixed abode. He was apparently paid fifty quid to steal a handbag, run away with it and drop it. We showed him the photograph of Claire Lewis and he identified her as the woman who had paid him the money.'

'Great, so now we are all completely convinced that Claire Lewis has abducted Isobel Thorne but we have no idea where she is. Terrific.'

In the corner of the room, a woman in her thirties came off the phone and coughed quietly. 'We've hit another snag,' said the woman, looking at Robyn apologetically. 'Just received a report that the vehicle passed an ANPR point on the M40 fifty minutes ago. It's now parked at Beaconsfield Service station.'

'What? How come we didn't get this information earlier?' said Corrance, a rich flush rising up his neck. 'Is she still at the service station?'

'Officers were immediately dispatched and have searched the station but there's no sign of her, or the child. We believe she's left the area.'

'So how has she escaped from the service station? Hitched a lift? Jumped in a friend's car? Get hold of the CCTV footage. She must be on it somewhere. She can't hide from all the cameras. See if she has the baby with her too. Carter, take over.'

There was an inaudible collective sigh as Corrance stormed out of the room.

Robyn shook her head in disbelief. This was going horribly wrong.

Ross crossed the room. 'Robyn, take it easy. You're taking it personally,' he said quietly.

'She's playing with me. She's messing me about and I hate that. How dare she? What worries me is what she might have done to Izzy. I can't let her get away with this.' She glared into space. Davies would know how to fathom out where the wretched woman was going. How she wished he were here to ask his advice.

Her mobile buzzed. She snatched it from the desk and barked into it, 'Carter.'

'Detective Carter? It's Jackson Thorne. I'm at my wits' end. Abigail has gone. She took off while I was out and I can't get hold of her. I think she might be out looking for Izzy or have had contact from the kidnapper. I can't get hold of her.'

'We'll be right there.'

She picked up her bag and signalled to Ross. 'Come on. We're needed. It's urgent. I just hope we're not too late.'

CHAPTER SIXTY-SEVEN

NOW

'Oh dear, Izzy. I think I've upset Detective Inspector Carter. Never mind. She'll get over it.'

What a shame she worked out that I am not in Scotland. I had set that up so well, too. I booked and paid for the cottage under my name and gave the week's rent away. There are lots of closed groups on Facebook looking for freebies or prizes. I offered the holiday to the members of one group, saying I couldn't go due to illness. Janet Foxton was elated. You would have thought she'd won the lottery when I told her she could have a few days in a pretty lodge in Scotland for free. The only proviso was she told the owner she was Claire Lewis, so as not to negate the booking.

I am a genius. Who else would have thought to dispose of Rachel's car at a service station and swap into another vehicle? I arranged to collect the four-year-old Kia I bought online from Beaconsfield service station. The bloke selling it was only too happy to drive it there and hand it over; after all, I'd already paid him over the odds for it. I left Rachel's car parked neatly out of the way and met up with Darryl Bolt at the café as arranged. Within ten minutes I had the papers and keys to the Kia. I know all about number-plate-recognition cameras and CCTV. We are a nation watched all the time. My disguise as a redhead hippy should fool CCTV cameras for a while. I got the idea from looking at Rachel. I dressed in a long faded skirt and a peasant blouse I swiped from Rachel's wardrobe while she was out cold, and wrapped a small flowered headscarf around Izzy's head. She looked super cute. Anyway, the police won't be able to work out which car I'm in now and that gives me the upper hand.

Detective Inspector Carter sounds decidedly miffed with me. She knows damn fine I have Natasha's daughter but I'm not going to make life easy for her. I watched the clock to ensure I wasn't on my phone for longer than a minute, and then chopped the signal. I was sure they'd be trying to trace my call. Who hasn't seen that happen on a detective drama?

Izzy and I have been watching the birds on the reservoir. She got very excited when she saw them feeding by the hide. I think she likes nature too. What a shame she won't live long enough to enjoy it.

It's time to trap Natasha. I can't access the camera in her house any longer so I suppose it's been unearthed. I can't see if she's at home or with Jackson. I have to hope I have caught her alone and call her. I use my voice-altering device to speak to her. I don't need to use it any longer but I quite enjoy it. It adds a sinister air to proceedings. Natasha picks up immediately.

'Izzy lives or dies depending on you. Tell no one and meet me in three hours. Alone.'

She sobs, 'Please don't hurt her. She's so little. It's not her fault. Please don't.'

'Three hours, Natasha. Time is ticking.'

'Where?'

'Where do you think? Where it all began, Natasha. Where it all began.'

She sobs some more and I cut her off, even though I would love to hear her blub and beg.

I look at Izzy. She's sitting next to Mr Big Ears the Third and playing with a large yellow plastic ring. She's so sweet and innocent. Best to keep her that way.

'Mummy's coming. Isn't that lovely? You, me and Mummy.'

She looks up at me and grins.

CHAPTER SIXTY-EIGHT

'I don't know when she left or where she's going. I've tried her mobile three times and left messages.'

'When did you last have contact with her?'

'After you left, we had another row. She said if I had checked the smoke alarms to make sure they functioned properly then we would have known one was fake. I got mad. I work every hour I can. When I get home, I'm tired and I don't get much chance to switch off from it. It's not like I can come home and sit in front of the football and forget the lousy day I had in the office. I have flight plans to file and the business is nearly always on my mind. I don't have time for household chores or things like pressing smoke alarm buttons.' He spat out the last few words. The stress of the situation was taking its toll badly on him. 'I shouted at her and went off for a walk. I only went to the duck pond and sat for a while until I had calmed down. I hadn't intended being a long time but there's been a lot said today and I had to digest it all.' He scrubbed at his chin. 'I figured I was being unreasonable and returned to try and smooth things out. We need to work as a unit. We have always been a team. I don't want it all to be shattered because of tension and angry words.'

He looked about the room as if Abigail and Izzy would magically reappear.

'It's a nightmare,' he said, eventually. 'A nightmare.'

'Abigail left at about the time you were at the duck pond and you didn't see her car pass you?'

'I didn't see a soul.'

'Ross, call the station and ask for ANPR on Abigail's car. Jackson, stay here in case she returns. She might have gone out because she was angry.'

Jackson shook his head. 'She wouldn't have left the house. She was determined to stay here in case somebody brought back Izzy.'

'Then she has either been taken against her will or she heard from the kidnapper. Come on, Ross. Time is of the essence.'

'Her car's been spotted on the M3 headed northbound to the M25,' said Ross, mobile in his hand as he got into the car.

Robyn pressed her lips together as she drove at speed in the direction of the motorway. Ross waited for her to speak.

'I'm going off piste with this idea,' she said after a moment. 'You in or out?'

'In. Hit me.'

'Abigail could be driving to Paul Matthews' old house.'

'That's a possibility but she could also be going anywhere in the country at the moment.'

'I agree, but Alice Forman is behind this. And she harbours huge resentment about what happened in that house. I think she's there or somewhere near the house and she has told Abigail to join her.'

'Okay. That's logical. Why not call Mitz Patel and get him to check it out? Or, Mulholland? You don't need to charge up there yourself.'

Robyn shook her head. 'Mulholland wasn't keen for me to upset the local police in Farnborough and will ask me to call it in and check with their DCI. He's not going to agree. You've seen him. He makes a T-Rex look friendly and I don't think he'll agree with my thoughts. Besides, he'll want to send his officers and that wouldn't be a good idea. Alice is cunning but volatile. Seeing police arrive could trigger something inside her. Similarly, I could ask Mitz to visit the house; after all, he's not far away; but if Alice spots him, she might kill Izzy, that is, if she hasn't already done so. I don't want to frighten her off or anger her. She obviously wants Abigail to join her as part of her plan and that gives us a chance to intervene if we get a move on. We also need to reach Alice before Abigail gets there. Heaven knows what will happen to her if we don't.'

'What about getting Jackson to fly us up there? He's a pilot.'

'It'll take just as long to drive to an airport, get a plane fuelled and ready and file a flight plan, then find somewhere to land near the destination. Quicker to drive.'

'You thought about it, didn't you?'

'I considered it,' Robyn replied, pressing the accelerator flat to the floor. 'Hang on; this could be a swift journey. I'll call Mulholland en route and let her know I might be breaking a few speed regulations.'

CHAPTER SIXTY-NINE

NOW

'Look, Izzy, there's Mummy, coming up the drive in her sparkling white car. She thinks she can save you but she can't. I'll let her think she can but I'm afraid I am a no-good liar and once I have tricked her into coming upstairs, I am going to set fire to the house. Look at all the petrol cans I have lined up against the wall. They'll smell horrible when I empty them but don't worry because I'm going to smother you with a pillow first so you won't have to choke.'

I lift Izzy high so she can see out of the tiny skylight window but she doesn't spot the car pulling onto the drive. So, Natasha, you made it. Time for a nice sisterly chat.

I leave Izzy in her new makeshift playpen. She'll be quite safe in there. I tell Mr Big Ears the Third he is in charge and head downstairs. I forgot how isolated the bedroom was. They really didn't want me to be part of their family. I was shut away in the attic.

Abigail is hammering on the door when I eventually get downstairs. I stand in the porch and stare at her. Her face is a picture. Her mascara has run and she looks like a badly made-up goth. Ironic really. I feel like laughing but maintain my usual icy regard as she pleads with me to unlock the door and let her in.

Eventually I let her in but not before I make sure she sees the large knife in my hand. That quietens her down. She gulps and blubs a bit but waits at the entrance while I speak.

'Hello, Natasha,' I say. Hardly the wittiest opening line but appropriate. 'I've been expecting you for a long time.'

'Claire,' she says. 'You look different.'

'As you well know, I'm not really Claire. Claire was a nobody who led you to think she cared about you and was your friend while you waltzed about having a great life, phoning her when you could be bothered, or wanted to boast about something, so wrapped up in your textbook life with handsome, debonair, wealthy Jackson Thorne that you really didn't care about weird Claire. If you had, you'd have realised she didn't work much at all and that she didn't have a life, and that she spent all her time on her own. She may have told you she was working for this magazine or on that photo shoot but really Claire was sitting at home working out ways to make Abigail Thorne's world crumble. If you had cared about Claire, you would have known. You'd have bought the magazines and admired Claire's photographs and gone round more often to visit her. If you had cared about Claire you would have gone out with her regularly. Claire had no boyfriends or friends at all, only man-crazy Zoe who would rather be bouncing around an exercise studio, and spoilt Abigail Thorne who didn't care about anyone but herself. So, as you know, I'm not Claire. I'm Alice. Someone else you didn't care about.'

'That's not true. Claire, I love you. You're my best friend. I do call you. I do go out with you.'

'You only rang me when it suited you.'

'No. That's simply not the case. I honestly thought you were busy with your photography, I didn't want to get in your way.'

'Rubbish. You only telephoned when you wanted to brag about something or were bored.'

'That's so unfair.'

'Unfair? You don't get to tell me what is or is not unfair. It was unfair that your family threw us out. It was unfair that our lives became unbearable afterwards and lack of money drove my mum to *prostitute herself. It was unfair that I was forced to commit crimes to stay alive and it was unfair that my mum was murdered by some disgusting lowlife.'*

I reach out and grab Natasha by her arm and press the blade into the nape of her neck. 'I'd be very happy to use this so don't give me reason to,' I hiss as I walk her towards the staircase and up the stairs.

'Alice,' she whispers. 'I'm so sorry. I wanted so much for you to be my sister. I'm so sorry. I was frightened and I've been as lonely as you all my life.'

Her words make me pause. She sounds sincere. For a moment I am disorientated. I decide to leave her in her old bedroom until I get my appetite to murder her back and go and talk to Dad. He'll fire me up again.

I lock Natasha in and, ignoring her cries, mount the stairs to my room. As I enter, Izzy fixes her bright gaze on me and lifts her pudgy arms to be picked up. She trusts me. A flicker of warmth fills my chest. It's an alien feeling and it takes me a while to recognise what it is. I hear my father whisper. 'It's love,' he says.

I play with Izzy and feed her some more pureed vegetable. She gurgles and babbles and makes me laugh when she blows spit bubbles. Did my mother sit and play with me this way before everything went wrong? I'm sure she did.

My thoughts are interrupted for some reason and I can't work out what is different. Then I realise that Natasha, who has been screaming for ages, has shut up at last. What has made her quiet? I glue my ear to my door and strain to listen. There are faint voices and the fifth stair on the staircase to the top floor lets out a tiny groan. Someone is coming upstairs. I lift Izzy onto the bed and wait. I shan't go without a fight and I have yet to ruin Natasha's world. Sorry, Izzy. You are going to have to pay for your mother's sins.

CHAPTER SEVENTY

'I'm leaving the car here. You'd better stay as a lookout. If you see anyone resembling Claire Lewis or spot Abigail, let me know. I'll have my phone on vibrate. Call Mitz and get him to meet you here. I might need backup. Don't let him come up until you hear from me. Understood?'

'Yes, boss,' said Ross with a grin. 'Seriously, I hope you're right with your hunch. Fingers crossed.'

'Thanks.'

Robyn sprinted the last few hundred metres towards the Farmhouse, her limbs a blur as she raced along the hedge-lined lane and up the track to the house. She was banking on her instincts being correct. If she'd got it wrong this time, then there would probably be no saving Natasha.

The hedges had been clipped since she had last been here and now tall fields of leafy maize rose from the field adjacent to Paul's house. The sudden beating of wings as a large flock of sparrows rose and darted for cover in the hedges startled her. She slowed her pace in case she alerted any occupants of Paul's house.

Shadowing the hedge, she approached the house that loomed in front of her. She avoided treading on the gravelled drive and, sticking to the grassier edges, she hugged the brick wall and leaned forward to observe the driveway. Abigail's car was on the drive and a silver grey Kia was parked in an open garage next to the house. She texted the registration of the Kia to Ross with a message to say

Abigail was at the house then slid past the front door and settled in the alleyway at the rear of the property to ascertain if anyone was in the house.

Robyn squatted on her haunches, hidden between the large plastic rubbish bins and a makeshift log store housing various lengths of drying wood. She scanned the building, working out how best to gain entry to the property, then noticed the window in the laundry room was slightly ajar. Robyn gauged she would have just enough room to get through but it would be a very tight squeeze. She hugged the wall and checked inside the house for activity. Seeing no one in the kitchen or the laundry room, she hauled herself up onto the window ledge and balanced on her toes, released the laundry window from its latch and poked her head through. She had to turn this way and that to get her shoulders and upper body through the narrow aperture but persistence paid off. She was deciding how best to land without falling on the floor when the sound of screaming galvanised her into action and she dropped onto the washing machine, somersaulted and landed upright on the floor. The washing machine stood with its front door open, under scrubbed tops that smelt vaguely of bleach. The screams were coming from upstairs. Robyn steered her way through the kitchen and rushed up the stairs, two at a time, halting in front of a bedroom door. Someone was banging on it and screaming. It was Abigail.

Robyn tapped lightly on the door and, pressing her mouth against the side, spoke softly, 'Abigail, it's Robyn Carter. I'm going to get you out.'

The banging stopped. 'Detective Carter?'

'It's me.'

'She has Izzy. Get Izzy.'

'I shall, just wait a second while I get the door open.'

Robyn examined the lock. Claire had removed the key.

'Wait a minute,' she whispered through the door. 'I have to fetch something to open the door.'

There was a muffled reply but Robyn didn't wait to hear it. Time was running out but she had a good idea where Claire was and so she descended the stairs as lightly and quietly as she could and dived into the kitchen. Geraldine Marsh was meticulous in her cleaning and keeping things in order. Hopefully, what Robyn wanted was still in the same place. The small blue Phillips screwdriver was lying in a small Wedgwood dish on a shelf over the sink. She hunted through the drawers for a suitable knife.

Screwdriver in hand, she returned to the door and sliding the knife under the collar where the doorknob met the door, she popped the collar loose to get to the screws holding the doorknob together. She removed them deftly. The doorknob came apart and she slid back the mechanism holding the door closed.

A white-faced Abigail emerged, hands shaking. She looked stunned, her face sore and red but a fury burned in her eyes. She pushed past Robyn and began to ascend the stairs. 'Where is she? She's in her old room, isn't she?'

Robyn gripped her arm. 'Wait a second. We don't want her to harm Izzy. Leave this to me. Let me talk her out of the room.'

They stared at each other; a small vein pulsing in Abigail's neck as she wrestled with this new idea. In the end she acquiesced.

'Don't worry. She won't hurt Izzy unless she feels threatened.'

'How can you be sure?' said Abigail.

'You have to trust me on that. I've thought a lot about what is making Alice tick. I feel she's only used Izzy to draw you here. Izzy wasn't part of what happened here that night all those years ago. She's brought you back for a reason. It's you she wanted all along. She's wanted revenge for a very long time, even before she ran into you again in Farnborough. You told me some of the story before. When I asked you. Tell me again. Tell me exactly what happened that night.'

Abigail choked back her tears. 'It was such a long time ago but I still have nightmares about it. I was babysitting her. She was only eight years old. She was so sweet, big blue eyes and gorgeous, golden hair. She was like a beautiful doll. I was a bit jealous of her. There was me, ugly, hiding behind my goth make-up, wishing I could escape from the place, and then Alice arrived with her mum, Christina. They breezed into our lives and for a while I thought it would be okay. I was in charge that night. Lucas was out with his awful friends. Dad took Christina out to an awards ceremony. It was a big deal. He was hoping to win one. Christina was the new love of his life and even prettier than Alice. He was crazy about her. I hadn't seen him so happy since Mum…' She stopped and wiped away tears. 'I was watching television and didn't hear Lucas come back in through the back door and sneak upstairs. It was only the horrible screams that made me realise something was wrong and when I got into her room, Lucas was on the floor, writhing. He had a pencil stuck in his eye. I didn't know what to do. I blamed myself. I should have known it was going to happen. I knew Lucas. I could have prevented it.

'Alice told my dad and her mum that Lucas had attacked her but he flatly denied it. He made up a story about hearing her crying and they believed him. I knew the truth; I had seen him half-undressed, rolling about the floor. I wanted to tell Dad the reality of the situation so badly but I knew he wouldn't believe me. I'd been in a situation so much like it before. That time, Mum hadn't believed me when I told her that Lucas—' Her eyes pleaded with Robyn. She couldn't continue for a moment, then, swallowing hard went on. 'Lucas blamed me for our mother's illness and death. He said I had upset her so much with my lies that she had got ill. I believed him. After all, I was young and she went crazy when I accused him of—'

Again she could not finish her sentence. Robyn squeezed her hand.

'I know,' she said. 'I know what he did. You don't have to put yourself through that memory again. Let's end this.' She stood, beckoning Abigail to join her. 'You're going to have to have faith in me. Come with me but I'll do the talking. You must remain silent, no matter what.' Robyn hoped she had read the situation right this time. Lives were at stake and she could not afford to get it wrong. Everything hinged on her instincts. She offered a silent prayer.

They both took the stairs to the small room at the top of the house. Robyn spoke loudly. 'Alice, we have to talk. I've got something very important to tell you about Natasha.'

There was no noise from the room.'

'Alice. I know you're in there. Open the door. This is significant. I know you've gone to a lot of trouble to get her here but you need to know this before you go any further.'

'I'm not coming out. You'll arrest me and that'll be that. If you try to come in I'm going to strangle the child, so go away.'

For a moment all was quiet and then Izzy let out a cry. Abigail pushed forward. Robyn shook her head, raised a finger to her lips.

'Alice, for goodness sake. Open the door. Izzy's only a little baby. You're not a child murderer. Let me in. Let me take Izzy to her mother so she can look after her and you and I can have a proper talk. I understand. I know what you've been through. I visited the cemetery and read the beautiful words you left for your mother. She was as beautiful as a butterfly, wasn't she? It must have been so hard for you when she shut you out. You loved her so much.'

There was still no response. Robyn bit her lip and questioned whether her instincts had been right about the rabbit.

'You saw her, didn't you? You discovered your poor mother strangled in her bedroom. You telephoned the police and you left behind something that was important to you as a token of your love. You left your toy rabbit.'

Robyn held her breath. She hoped she hadn't read the situation wrong or this time it would cost a child's life.

At last she heard Alice. 'Izzy doesn't need Natasha. I've been looking after her really well. She likes me a lot.' Izzy's wails increased.

Robyn tried again. 'Alice, you can't hurt Izzy. You're not heartless. And listen. She's crying because she misses her mother. She's only a little girl who craves her mother's love. She needs to be with Natasha. Natasha's her mum. Natasha wants to protect her and look after her and love her.'

There was a howl of rage from inside.

'What does Natasha know about protecting anyone? Ask her. Ask her what happened when she was supposed to be protecting me?'

'There's something you don't know about that and it will change how you feel. Please, let me in. I promise not to move from the doorway. Honestly. If you don't believe me afterwards, then I'll go away and you can do whatever it is you plan on doing. Hear me out, Alice. You owe yourself that much. After everything you have gone through, you deserve to know the truth. Don't you want to hear the truth, Alice?'

She waited. Izzy continued to cry. After what felt like a lifetime to Robyn, there was a click as the door unlocked.

Robyn slipped into the room. The bedroom was painted in pinks, an animal duvet was thrown on the bed and animal figures stared at her from the dressing room table. The room was fusty and dank; dust bunnies lurked under the bed. This was one room that Geraldine Marsh had never entered.

Izzy was sitting on the bed with red cheeks from crying, but stopped her noise when she saw a new person enter the room. She stared at Robyn. In one hand she held onto the foot of a furry toy rabbit.

Alice stood in front of Robyn and brandished a knife. 'Go on,' she hissed. 'This had better be good.'

Robyn relaxed into her role. 'Hi, Alice. I'm Robyn. I'm not here as a detective or a police officer. I'm merely a friend. I won't touch or harm you,' she said, raising her hands in an unthreatening manner.

'I know who you are.'

Robyn continued. 'Izzy seems content. I see she has a new friend.' Izzy jiggled the rabbit from side to side, her tears forgotten. Robyn smiled at the child. 'She seems to love it. Is it a present from you?'

Alice lowered the knife and turned to Izzy. 'Yes, it's Mr Big Ears the Third.'

'He looks like a good listener,' said Robyn lightly. 'I have a teddy bear called Growly. I told him all my secrets when I was younger. I still have him. He lives on my bed now. He's a bit worse for wear. His fur has gone thin and he's lost an ear but I won't ever part with him. He was my friend when I needed someone to listen to me.'

'That's like Mr Big Ears. He's one of the best listeners,' said Alice, her voice softening. The knife now rested by her side.

'Do you want to sit by Izzy in case she falls off the bed?'

'No, she's okay. I'll stand,' replied Alice, regaining her former defensive composure. Robyn lifted her face to Alice's and looked into her spectacle-free eyes. She looked different. Her eyes were the colour of blue ice and just as cold.

'It all happened here in this room, didn't it?'

Alice drew herself up to her full height. She was a couple of inches taller than Robyn. Her arms were muscular, the arms of someone who trained regularly. She heaved a sigh in irritation. 'Get on with it. I know what you're doing. You're trying to be my friend. I don't have any friends. I've never had any friends thanks to the Matthews.' She spat the last name.

'Abigail is your friend.'

Alice laughed. 'No. She definitely is not my friend. You know that. You're not dumb. She was part of it all. She didn't tell her father or my mother that her disgusting, mental nutcase of a brother tried to rape me. I was eight years old!' she screamed. 'I was a child. No one, but *no one*, listened to me. They listened to that lying scumbag and she didn't tell them the facts. My mother hated me all my life for destroying her relationship with Paul. She believed I made up the story because I was jealous she had found love again after my father's death. Can you imagine what that does to a little girl? I only ever wanted to be loved and my mother suddenly shunned me. Can you imagine the hurt?'

'No, I can't but Natasha can. You weren't the only victim, Alice. I can call you Alice, can't I? Natasha understands exactly what you were going through. You weren't the first little girl Lucas had tried to rape. He had already had practice.' She let the message sink in before continuing, 'Alice, Lucas raped his sister. Only, unlike you, Natasha didn't manage to stop him. He didn't just do it once, either. He did it several times, threatening her if she spoke about it. She was terrified, just like you were.'

Alice's mouth dropped. 'No. That can't be,' she mumbled.

'Worse still, Natasha fell pregnant. She became pregnant at twelve years old by her own brother and no one believed he was responsible. Natasha tried to convince her mother of the truth but she refused to listen. Both her parents were convinced their daughter was lying to cover up her promiscuity and Natasha was sent away for an abortion. Her mother became ill soon afterwards. Lucas tormented Natasha with mind games and cruelly blamed her until she actually imagined she was responsible for her own mother's death. And then, her father became withdrawn and she had no one to talk to. Natasha was so lonely she even considered taking her own life.'

Alice shook her head from side to side, trying to understand the enormity of what she had just learned. The knife fell on the floor, forgotten in the midst of heavy sorrow. Emotions escaped that had been held at bay for years. She stumbled backwards and sat on the edge of the bed.

Robyn moved closer to the knife, subtly moving it away from Alice with one light kick. She spotted the cans of petrol lined against the wall and, placing one hand in her pocket for a moment, sent a pre-prepared text to Ross. She kept talking, her voice light and kind.

'Abigail knew what happened the night Lucas attacked you, and she has lived with that knowledge, along with the horror of what she herself went through. She has suffered as much as you have. Her life was destroyed. She left home as soon as she could and she, like you, has been trying to escape her past.'

'Poor Natasha,' Alice whispered.

'So, please don't make her life any worse. She's already suffered the loss of a child and the emotional anguish that went with it. And she lost her mother. She's like you in so many ways, Alice. She really is like your sister. She was so alone for years until she met Jackson and then you. Don't harm Izzy. Natasha will look after her and love her and protect her, all her life. She won't let any harm come to her. She's already suffered more than she deserves. You can understand that, can't you, Alice?'

'I wasn't going to harm Izzy. She's perfect. She laughs at me and is so happy. I wanted to kill her to make Natasha suffer but I can't. I love Izzy.'

'Why don't you hand her over to me and we'll go downstairs and talk to Natasha? She really wants to make it up to you and you mustn't forget, she cares about you. She really was your friend when you were Claire and she was Abigail.'

Robyn edged towards the bed and the child. Izzy gurgled merrily, shook her new toy rabbit several times and threw it on the floor. It landed face down, one leg askew. Alice snapped. 'No. That's naughty, Izzy. You mustn't throw Mr Big Ears,' she said, her eyes suddenly wild. She leaned down to retrieve the rabbit and Robyn moved closer to get her into a headlock or similar but the woman was too quick and standing again, she moved out of reach, the rabbit in her hand.

She wagged a finger at Robyn and in a mocking tone said, 'No you don't. You're not taking me anywhere. I'm staying here and I'm going to kill the child.'

Without warning, Abigail rushed into the room, arms flailing and hurtled towards the bed. Izzy babbled joyfully at seeing her mother. Abigail reached for her and cradled her, rocking her and murmuring, her attention completely on her child. Izzy smiled and wriggled in delight.

'It's over, Alice,' said Robyn. 'The police will be here very soon. My colleague has alerted them. You'll be charged for abduction and for the murders of Paul, Lucas and Mary Matthews.'

Alice looked up. 'She was an idiot to love him.'

'And you wanted to pay Paul and Lucas back for all the hurt they had caused. But why did you kill Geraldine?'

Alice gazed at the rabbit and stroked one of its ears tenderly. She shrugged. 'I was in my room preparing for Izzy coming. The old lady came in. I wasn't expecting her. She was snooping about in Paul's room and I thought she was going to come upstairs, then she heard me sneeze and I knew she was going to call the police. I couldn't have her ruin my plans. It seemed like the only way.'

'We have sufficient evidence to convict you, Alice. You have no other option. Someone will listen to you. Someone will try to help, but you will be sent away. Come with me and leave Natasha and Izzy here.'

'I had to kill them. You understand that. I was a child. No one believed me. No one helped me then. Paul could have but he didn't. He promised he'd look after me and he didn't. He turned his back on me too.'

'Alice,' said Abigail in a very quiet voice, 'I'm so sorry. I did tell my dad the truth about that night. I was scared to death that he wouldn't believe me and I was terrified of what Lucas would do to me if he worked out I'd spoken to my father, but I still told Paul exactly what happened. He took it badly. Instead of turning on Lucas, he threw you and Christina out. But it wasn't because he hated you. He was *protecting* you. He couldn't control Lucas. He had to get you away from Lucas in case worse happened. Dad wouldn't talk to me about it afterwards. He shut himself away and sent us back to school. He couldn't take any more upset. I didn't let you down, Alice. It just didn't work out as I hoped.'

Alice stared at her for a moment. A guttural noise formed in her throat and her eyes became dewy. She held the rabbit to her face. There was a painful silence while she allowed tears to fall onto the fur, then she nodded.

'Yes,' she whispered to an unheard command. 'You're right, Daddy. I need to come and stay with you.'

All of a sudden, she strode to the door, pushing past Robyn and, still clutching the toy rabbit in one hand, she pounded down the stairs to the galleried landing. Without a word she hurled herself over the banister, landing on the marbled floor below with a sickening thud.

Robyn raced to the ground floor. It was too late. Alice's head was turned at an impossible angle, her eyes staring sightlessly at the rabbit that she still held tightly in her hand.

CHAPTER SEVENTY-ONE

The men driving the Audi turned into the lay-by and switched off their engine. They waited for a third man to exit his black Mercedes and stand in front of it, arms open wide to show he was unarmed. The men got out, the second one surveying the area all the while, his face menacing, his shoulders and stance that of a man accustomed to fighting. The first man tucked a large brown packet under his arm and casually sauntered towards the Mercedes.

Robyn had been trailing the car and knew exactly where the Audi was stationed. Her own car was parked further away, next to a field. Robyn climbed the gate into the farmer's field, with its neatly rolled haystacks. She signalled PC Anna Shamash to follow closely behind. Brambles reached out trying to snag her jeans and her bare arms but she navigated her way past them until she reached a spot where the hedge was thinner, opposite the lay-by. The men might think they'd be undetected in this rural area but they were wrong. Robyn was in time to witness the exchange. As the packet was handed over to the owner of the Mercedes, she heard a voice in her earpiece.

'Go, go, go!'

She and Anna rose as one. Opposite them, several heads appeared from behind bushes and officers raced in the direction of the men making the exchange. There was a flurry of activity and shouting. The first thug took a slug at the man receiving the parcel, before swinging at an officer and landing an uppercut blow to the nose, dropping the officer to his knees. The Mercedes owner, an undercover detective, grabbed the arm of the first man and a scuffle ensued. Two officers assisted and the offender was soon lying on the floor cuffed and awaiting a caution. The second goon lashed out, floored PC David Marker, and thundered across the road in Robyn's direction, pursued by a young policeman. She leapt towards him but Anna overtook her, eyes focused on the target. He made it as far as the kerb before the policeman leapt at his legs and rugby-tackled him to the ground. Anna joined him and held the man down while he yelled abuse at them both, bucking like a bronco bull but unable to dislodge either of them. Eventually, with the assistance of others, the man was hauled to his feet and dragged away.

Robyn applauded. 'Nice one,' she shouted loudly to Mitz Patel who was receiving slaps on the back from his colleagues for felling the drug dealer. 'Great job, Anna.'

Anna held up a hand in thanks and joined the team who were now herding the men into cars that had pulled up, ready to take them back to the station.

Robyn's phone vibrated in her pocket and, moving away from the hedgerow, she answered it.

'I've just opened my lunch box and discovered I've been given tofu salad for lunch. Want to join me?' he grumbled.

'What an offer but I couldn't take away any lunch from a hungry man. Jeanette really is spoiling you. Got any dessert?'

'A fruit thing with seeds in it. If she feeds me any more seeds I'll start chirping in the mornings.'

'I could make a joke about tweeting but no doubt that wouldn't amuse you.'

'Too right. I'm starving to death here.'

'Get on with you. You look much better. The diet is paying off. Now stop moaning. Why have you rung?'

'Alice Forman is being laid to rest beside her father's grave tomorrow at three o' clock. Thought you might like to know. I spoke to her grandmother, Jane. She's obviously distraught about the events that occurred and regrets not searching for Alice herself, or insisting on seeing her when Christina took off with her. I told her she had no way of telling that Alice would turn out to be such a mixed-up woman. Jeanette and I are going to have Jane over for lunch on Sunday. I feel sorry for her sitting alone in that home. We'll try and convince her none of this is her fault. There's always an "if only", isn't there? Persuading Christina to allow Alice to visit might have changed the course of events but we'll never know for sure. Families, eh?'

'It's a sad state but at least Abigail is okay and she and Jackson will work through their difficulties. They seem a solid couple.'

'One thing keeps puzzling me,' he continued. 'I get the whole Abigail and Claire thing but how come Paul Matthews recognised the photograph of Claire in the magazine? Even Abigail didn't work out that Claire was Alice so how did Paul Matthews?'

'That particular mystery bugged me too. It was only after I enlarged the photograph in the magazine and studied it carefully that I saw what he saw. Claire is wearing an expensive bracelet with crystals. It seemed incongruous with the rest of Claire's outfit of jeans and baggy jacket, so I checked it out and discovered it's a unique piece made by a jeweller in London. It was commissioned back in 1996 for a Mr Paul Matthews who gave it to his fiancée Christina Forman. You can see the same bracelet in the photograph of the pair of them at the awards ceremony. I expect Claire took it from her mother, or was given it. Either way, it was a vital clue. Paul recognised it and worked out it was Alice in the photograph.'

'I'm so impressed I'm going to donate my entire tofu salad to you. Seriously, well done. That's impressive. Back to normal duty again now. No more juicy cases unless you need any outside help in the future. I have a request to check out a new guy who has applied for a job in a care home and there are quite a few more insurance claims to check out.'

'You're too generous but I'll pass on the salad. I'm on a high carbohydrate diet at the moment. Got to get ready for the race in a couple of weeks. I'll catch you later.'

'Bring me some proper food when you come by next. I'm starting to look like a piece of tofu.'

'No chance. I don't want to anger the lovely Jeanette. You get your own grub. And remember I have got my secret cameras trained on you.'

Ross huffed and disconnected.

Robyn smiled to herself and returned to her Polo. She patted the small parcel beside her on the passenger seat, containing a copy of the brand new Harry Potter book, *Harry Potter and the Cursed Child*. Brigitte and Amélie were flying to France the next day and she wanted to give Amélie her gift before they left.

Robyn may have lost Davies but she was still part of a family, albeit a small one. Although she was not a blood relative she had an important role to play. She would stand in for Davies and be there for his daughter. One day the girl might need her and Robyn would be ready for that time. She would look out for her. After all, that's what family did.

A LETTER FROM CAROL

Dear Reader,

I hope you have enjoyed reading *Little Girl Lost*. It has been so exciting to write about DI Robyn Carter, who has become a huge part of my life this year.

Ever since I published a series of short stories that focused on the darker side of love, I have been itching to write thrillers. It comes from a childhood being brought up on a literary diet of Agatha Christie and Dennis Wheatley novels (I know, what a peculiar mixture). Whenever I get the opportunity to read now, I always reach for a thriller.

Having written many comedies, most with twists and plots that will surprise the reader, I thought it was time to scratch that itch and work on the Detective Inspector Robyn Carter series.

I have always been fascinated by psychology and what makes people tick. Many years ago, I was friends with someone who turned out to have fabricated her entire life. Even when she was found out thanks to an eagle-eyed friend, she denied it all and upped and left. We never saw her again.

Alice is a character who I have taken to heart. Life, circumstances and a lack of love have transformed her into a confused, hurt woman. I think, in the end, she reveals what she might have been had she lived a different life.

Robyn is another damaged soul but she buries herself in work and has her friends. Life will not be the same for her now she has lost

Davies but there will be many cases for her to solve and a network of allies to see her through. I hope very much you've enjoyed *Little Girl Lost* and will join DI Robyn Carter again on her next case.

Can I ask one favour? If you have loved this book, would you please leave a review for me? It doesn't have to be very long but it would mean a lot to me. Thank you so much.

Carol

ACKNOWLEDGMENTS

Little Girl Lost has been incredibly exciting to write but it would not have been possible without my wonderful editor Lydia Vassar-Smith who has held my hand throughout the process.

I must thank Danny Tynen and Kim Nash who rushed to my rescue and helped me understand some of the life of a detective inspector in the police force; they clarified many points and put up with a flurry of manic messages on Facebook when I was unsure of protocols.

Thanks go to Pauline Yong, an amazing lady who looks incredible for fifty, and who is, in part, the inspiration for Robyn Carter. She provided me with all her gruelling training routines.

And finally, I want to thank Angie Marsons, Robert Bryndza and Caroline Mitchell for encouraging me to leave the world of sparkles and puppy dogs and join them on the 'dark side'.

Seriously, the Bookouture authors are an amazingly supportive bunch. Thank you, guys, for keeping me sane this year.